A MOST INTRIGUING LADY

A MOST INTRIGUING LADY

A NOVEL

Sarah Ferguson, Duchess of York

WITH MARGUERITE KAYE

AVON

An Imprint of HarperCollins*Publishers*

A MOST INTRIGUING LADY. Copyright © 2023 by Sarah Ferguson, Duchess of York. All rights reserved. Printed in the United States of America. No part of this book may be used or reproduced in any manner whatsoever without written permission except in the case of brief quotations embodied in critical articles and reviews. For information, address HarperCollins Publishers, 195 Broadway, New York, NY 10007.

HarperCollins books may be purchased for educational, business, or sales promotional use. For information, please email the Special Markets Department at SPsales@harpercollins.com.

FIRST EDITION

Designed by Kyle O'Brien

Library of Congress Cataloging-in-Publication Data
Names: Ferguson, Sarah, Duchess of York, 1959– author.
Title: A most intriguing lady: a novel / Sarah Ferguson, Duchess of York.
Description: First edition. | New York, NY: William Morrow
Identifiers: LCCN 2022009722 | ISBN 9780063216822 (hardcover)
  | ISBN 9780063216846 (ebook) | ISBN 9780063252219 (international edition)
Subjects: LCGFT: Romance fiction. | Novels.
Classification: LCC PR6106.E7655 M67 2022 | DDC 823/.92—dc23/eng/20220413
LC record available at https://lccn.loc.gov/2022009722

ISBN 978-0-06-321682-2
ISBN 978-0-06-325221-9 (international edition)

23 24 25 26 27 LBC 6 5 4 3 2

Because no-one knows you like a sister, or misunderstands you like a sister, and yet loves you like a sister, this book is dedicated to my own dear sister, Jane.

Dear Reader,

A Most Intriguing Lady is my second collaboration with Marguerite Kaye, and my second novel set in the Victorian period. Lady Mary, my heroine, may be familiar to readers of *Her Heart for a Compass* as the youngest daughter of the Duke and Duchess of Buccleuch, but the journey she undertakes is very different from the one her elder sister travels in the previous book. Lady Mary is not a heroine who relishes the limelight—quite the opposite. She's a quiet observer, the kind of person who picks up on every tiny personal detail and foible and who has a real talent for piecing them together to form an accurate picture of the person concerned. Lady Mary is a wallflower, easy to ignore, and very easy to under-estimate. In fact, though she doesn't know it at the beginning of this book, she has all the qualities that would make her an excellent sleuth.

This isn't a detective story, however. It is, like *Her Heart for a Compass*, a story about a woman trying to find her niche in the world, and refusing to fit the mould her lineage demands. Lady Mary has to battle duty and heritage, convention and custom, to live her life in her own manner. Based very loosely on the real life Lady Mary Montagu Douglas Scott, *A Most Intriguing Lady* mingles historical fact and real characters with fiction. From Drumlanrig Castle in the Scottish Borders, to Yorkshire, the spa town of Carlsbad in Bohemia, and on to London, Lady Mary's journey is one of self-discovery and—eventually—finding love.

This is a work of fiction, but in writing it I have drawn some deliberate parallels with my own life and used some of my own experiences to give authenticity to Lady Mary's character. My parents' separation when I was fifteen left me motherless and lonely. Discovering, as an adult, that my parents had lost a little girl, Sophie, helped me understand, sadly too late, at least some of the reasons for their unhappy marriage. Like Lady Mary, I have always instinctively been a people pleaser (sometimes to my own detriment), and I have always wished to be useful. And also like Lady Mary, I have in the past found it easier to play a part, rather than to be my real self. There is a great deal of me in this book, but it is not a book about me. It is a book about another of history's "invisible women," and the next step (of many, I hope!) in my quest to put as many of them as I can on the page. I hope you enjoy *A Most Intriguing Lady* as much as Marguerite and I enjoyed writing it.

A heartfelt thank you to Marguerite for being such a superb co-author and mentor. Our collaboration and friendship goes from strength to strength and I'm already looking forward to our next literary adventure together.

Once again, I'd like to say a huge thank you to Rachal Kahan and all the team at William Morrow for the faith they have shown in me, and all the support they have given both Marguerite and myself throughout the writing process. Deepest gratitude to Lacy Lalene Lynch and Jan Miller for their hard work and dedicated commitment to my life, and my world of books, TV, and media. Huge thanks also to Lisa Milton and Becky Slorach at Mills & Boon, and a special thank you to Flo Nicoll, who gave us such insightful early feedback. Finally, thank you to Susan Lovejoy and Camilla Gordon Lennox, researchers extraordinaire, whose enthusiasm is boundless and whose eye for historical minutiae kept us right. Any mistakes are all our own.

A MOST INTRIGUING LADY

PART I

Drumlanrig Castle,
Scottish Borders

1872

CHAPTER ONE

An Intriguing Encounter

Drumlanrig Castle, Scottish Borders,
Saturday, 24 August 1872

T HE HEADACHE, WHICH HAD ANNOUNCED itself several hours earlier as a dull, insistent throb, was rapidly becoming unbearable, the vise-like band of tension making it difficult to concentrate. He had already been brusque, verging on rude, toward the woman sitting on his right during the fish course, and there were God knows how many more dinner courses to endure. She was a friend of his hostess, the Duchess of Buccleuch. He had feigned interest as she lauded one of the duchess's many projects. Something to do with her renowned kitchen gardens, wasn't it? Yes, that was it: the duke and duchess had taken on so many apprentice gardeners that they were having to build new dormitories to house them all.

The effort to distract himself made his brain ache. He could feel the pain building relentlessly inside him, what he knew was referred to behind his back in the officers' mess as *one of his turns*, making it sound as if he suffered from dizzy spells instead of a debilitating affliction. His muscles ached from the effort required to stop his limbs from trembling. His vision was becoming blurred. His temper, always an accurate barometer of his condition, rose steadily each time he had to cover his wine-glass to prevent one of the footmen from topping it up. Bitter experience had taught him that alcohol made him much worse.

It must have been the grouse shoot this morning that had triggered it. He couldn't think what else it might have been. The crack of the shotguns, the smell of gunpowder were bound to evoke vivid echoes of the past. So it could only have been that, since he'd felt perfectly well otherwise. He should have made his excuses, but then he'd have drawn attention to himself by disrupting the duke's carefully planned assignment of the privileged spots at the shooting positions on his grouse-moor. There would be at least another two shoots later this week; but while the rest of the guests were looking forward to the sport, for him it was simply an endurance test, the means to an end. If he made a favourable impression, it would go a long way towards ensuring a sympathetic audience with the duke; and the duke was in a prime position to influence the one person in the kingdom who could put the necessary wheels in motion. The War Office needed this new department. He desperately wanted this new role. There was even the possibility that another of the duke's guests, expected tomorrow or the next day, might prove to be his first recruit. If things worked out. If!

He would do his best to make sure they did. This was his chance to prove himself and do something worthwhile. If he failed—no, it didn't bear thinking of. Another year of festering away at that desk in Whitehall would see his brain turn to something akin to the porridge they served here for breakfast, or permanently enveloped in the fog that was closing in on him now. This could well be his best and only opportunity to make something of himself and of the department. They were relying on him to make his case. He *could* do it. He *would* do it. He'd find a way to achieve what he'd come here for without letting anyone, especially not the eagle-eyed duke, see what it was costing him.

It was costing him dearly at the moment. The voice in his head screamed at him to retreat to his bedroom and suffer in silence. He could not afford to heed it. He had to ride it out, he had to. Tomorrow was another day. But even if he made it through the remaining courses, there were the toasts to come, and he'd have no option but to drink them, or appear to do so, else offence would be taken, a black mark earned. Whisky, which he loathed anyway, under these circumstances would be like lighting a touchpaper to his combustible mood. After the toasts there would be another hundred guests arriving for the ceilidh. He'd be expected to take part in the various reels. There would be the skirl and screech of bagpipes. Sir Walter Scott's poem, *The Lady of the Lake*, had for some inexplicable reason been translated into Gaelic and was to be recited by an actor in full Highland regalia during supper. The Duke and Duchess of Buccleuch had promised their illustrious guests a *traditional Scotch evening*, and it was bound to go on until the early hours.

Panic gripped him. He never knew precisely how he would react, whether he would become mute or whether he would scream or shout or simply collapse, but he did know he would disgrace himself. If he could get a breath of fresh air, if he could be alone for a few moments, there was a chance he might just make it go away. It was highly unconventional to leave the table in the middle of a banquet, but fate had been kind enough to have him seated on the window side of the dining room.

He pushed back his chair, checked that his host was not looking his way, mumbled an excuse, and made his escape. The tall window directly behind him led to a small terrace on the south side of the castle. A bronze sundial propped up by cupids sat proudly at its centre, but it was the view that caught his attention. The castle stood on the highest point of the sweeping vista spread out before him, its natural boundary formed by the line of trees which stretched along the bank of the tumbling Marr Burn. The parterres which the duchess had restored as part of her epic renovation project were pleasingly symmetrical, laid out like the panes of a large stained glass window set flat into the landscape.

But it couldn't be flat. Drumlanrig sat on an escarpment. Intrigued, he made his way down the stone steps to the gravelled terrace directly below him and discovered the secret of the optical illusion, for the terrace shelved steeply down a grassy bank to the first of several levels. Continuing down the steep path he reached the first terrace which was bordered by a long narrow balustrade he hadn't noticed from the balcony. Vast quantities of earth had been dug and moved in order to tame nature. Whose had been the original vision? How many gardeners were employed in its upkeep? And how many more worked in the renowned kitchen gardens with the succession houses that he now recalled his fellow guest waxing lyrical about?

"Forget the blasted kitchen gardens," he muttered to himself, "focus on this view." Never mind how it had been created or how it was maintained, it was beautiful and it was calming. The sun had set, giving way to a soft twilight. All he required were a few more moments alone to breathe in this lovely air, disperse the fog in his brain, get himself back under control. Perching on the balustrade, he admired the castle. Known locally as the Pink Palace, the Renaissance-style building, with its corner towers with their pepperpot turrets and myriad of chimneys, looked less forbidding and farther away than it actually was, thanks to the tricks the terracing played with perspective.

With a weary sigh, he hauled himself back to his feet. He couldn't stay out here any longer; it was time to get back to the fray before his absence was noted and questions were asked, his history recalled, the opportunity withdrawn. He was holding his hand out in front of him, noting with relief that there was barely a tremor, when out of the corner of his eye, he saw something moving on the narrow stone parapet which ran above the roof between the two towers of the south frontage. Astounded, he watched as the figure unfurled to its full height and took a tentative step forward. The castle was four stories high. A fall would almost certainly result in death.

Forgetting all about his own state of mind, he began to run as fast as he could up the steep path. By the time he reached the terrace, the figure was almost half-way across the narrow balustrade. It was remarkably but unmistakably female, a tall young woman, built on statuesque lines and scantily clad in a short tunic, giving him an excellent view of her long shapely legs. His first thought was that she must be another performer hired to make the evening memorable, practising her art while her audience were at dinner. But as he got close enough to distinguish her features, he realized that only a few moments ago she had been sitting on the opposite side of the dinner table from him, wearing a brown dress. There was no mistaking her, despite the fact that the striking grey eyes had been lowered demurely and the generous mouth set into a bland smile.

What on earth was she doing, and why the devil was she risking her neck? Terrified of distracting her, he stood in the shadow of the steps. She was gaining confidence with every step, her arms outstretched for balance like a tightrope artist in a circus; and as he craned his neck, watching in both admiration and trepidation, she gave a balletic leap forward, landing lightly on her slipper-clad feet, and he could have sworn that she laughed. Then, having completed her death-defying traverse, she abruptly disappeared from view.

"Is that you, Colonel?" Startled, he looked up to see a fellow guest peering over the balcony. "Everything all right?"

"Fine," he answered, astounded by the fact that it was the truth.

"I just popped out for a quick smoke." The lie came easily, his mind perfectly clear as he ran up the stairs.

"Thought it was probably that," the man said, nodding. "I had the same notion myself. Best get back in now, though; they're piping in the haggis. It would be bad form to miss it."

THE WAIL OF THE BAGPIPES greeted Lady Mary Montagu Douglas Scott, the youngest daughter of the Duke and Duchess of Buccleuch, as she raced down the servants' spiral staircase, re-fastening the last few buttons on the bodice of her evening gown. She had worn the tobacco silk despite Mama's request that she don her new lemon gown, which was much more tightly fitted and difficult for her to fasten without the help of her maid. Her trusty brown gown was looser, and far easier to get in and out of without fuss.

Pausing breathless at the door which opened out onto the small service room, she smiled triumphantly. That was definitely the most terrifying and foolish thing she'd ever done in her life, but she had done it. And in the middle of dinner, too! She was giddy, both awed and astonished at her temerity, but she was also bursting with excitement.

It wasn't over yet, however. She had only truly succeeded if her escapade went undetected, which meant she had better wipe the smile off her face. Imagining her mother's reaction should she discover that her youngest daughter had been dancing on the parapet did the trick. Mary straightened her tartan sash and shook out her skirts, noting with dismay that she had forgotten to change out of her special pink slippers. Too late now. Besides, she couldn't imagine that anyone would notice.

Her father's piper, sweating in full Highland regalia, raised an eyebrow at her as she sidled into the dining room behind Jamie, the footman bearing the enormous silver salver of haggis. Her mother threw her a significant look as she sat back down, and Mary signalled an apology, waving discreetly at her tummy. She was fortunate enough never to suffer during her monthlies, but it was occasionally convenient to pretend that she did.

She took her place, noting without surprise that the gentlemen on either side of her seemed not a whit concerned by her absence. No-one ever was. What would they say if she told them what she'd just done? She could hardly believe it herself now that she was back at the table. She hadn't planned it, and even when the idea formed in her mind while she was enduring the first course, she didn't really intend to go through with it. But as she counted the hours and hours of tedium stretching before her, she calculated that if she was going to do it, then the best time would be right now, when everyone—guests, her parents, the servants—was occupied with dinner. After that it was as if a little devil inside her was urging her on. Up until the moment she stepped out onto the parapet, she'd told herself she could turn back at any point. She was so glad she hadn't. The knowledge of what she'd done, and the fact that not a single other person here knew, was like champagne fizzing around inside her.

The gentleman opposite her was staring at her. Even though she had already checked her face for dirt or cobwebs, Mary quickly wiped her cheeks. He raised his brow at her, and seemed to be on the brink of breaching all the rules of etiquette to speak to her across the table, before changing his mind at the last minute, shaking his head, and looking away with everyone else towards the huge baron of beef which followed the haggis. The roast was borne aloft by two footmen and drew a sigh of approval from the gentlemen guests which the poor haggis had failed to elicit. No-one would turn the pudding down; but in the many banquets Mary had sat through here at Drumlanrig, she had observed that very few sampled it, never mind consumed it with relish. She personally enjoyed it much more than the slabs of rare beef which everyone was licking their lips over; and Jamie, knowing her tastes, accordingly served her a large portion.

"You are partial to haggis?" the gentleman on her right side, a politician friend of her father's, asked as he eyed his own morsel askance.

"Almost as much as crappit-heid," Mary replied, deadpan. "That is haddock head stuffed with oats and suet. Don't tell me you have never tried it?"

"I have never even heard of it," he answered her with a shudder. "I have a strong suspicion, Lady Mary, that it is an invention of your own and you are pulling my leg."

"Actually, no, it's something that Sir Walter Scott had served to King George when he visited Edinburgh some years ago."

"Ah, a most auspicious occasion for the capital and the nation."

"Indeed it was." And an oft-recounted episode in her family's history. Accordingly, she informed her companion that King George had resided at Dalkeith Palace, the Buccleuch family home near Edinburgh, for the duration of his visit as a guest of her father who, though he had already inherited his title, had been but a child at the time.

"As was I," the gentleman said, nodding and smiling, "but it has entered the nation's folklore."

He launched into a long and rambling anecdote about the king's visit which Mary had heard many times, leaving her happily free to smile politely and study the man across the table from her. Unlike almost every other male guest, he was not kitted out in plaid, but wore evening dress in plain black, with a pristine white shirt and necktie. He was rather handsome, with strong features that included a cleft in his clean-shaven jaw. Short-cropped black hair, a strong nose, a full mouth like her own, and heavy-lidded dark-brown eyes that gave him a sleepy look that Mary decided was deceptive. She guessed him to be in his thirties. There was a fan of lines at the corner of each eye and deeper grooves on his brow that could be attributed either to age or to his having endured some sort of trauma or suffering. Was that being fanciful? For some reason, she suspected not.

He must have arrived earlier today, presumably for the first shoot, when she had been out visiting with her mother. She didn't recognize him as one of her father's coterie, which was unusual in itself. Intrigued, she continued to study him from beneath her lashes, making a vague comment to her dinner companion about her distant relative Sir Walter Scott. The real object of her attention was not eating, but carefully rearranging his dinner on his plate.

"It is a shame that Sir Walter cannot be here tonight to hear his work performed in Gaelic." Once again her neighbour interrupted her thoughts. "Such a thoughtful commission for your father to make," he continued.

"It was my brother William's idea. Last year was the centenary of Sir Walter Scott's birth, you know."

"I did. I attended the celebrations in Edinburgh at the time and spoke to your brother, the earl. He is a fine ambassador for the duke, and for our native language, too."

"You mean the Gaelic? You speak it yourself, I assume?" Mary enquired.

As she expected, the reply was equivocal. "Not exactly, but heritage and all that, you know? The proud Highlander that your relative Sir Walter writes of, and Her Majesty so reveres. Even those of us who don't actually speak it can appreciate the—the lyrical beauty of it, eh?"

"Oh yes," Mary said with one of her most demure smiles. "Like this example?" She rhymed off the long Gaelic curse, which John-Angus, the under-gardener from the Isle of Lewis, had taught her, in the soft lilting accent she had learned to mimic, which made the vicious words sound like a soothing lullaby.

"Beautiful," her companion said. "May I ask the meaning?"

Across the table, the man had set down his cutlery, his meal almost untouched. He had not taken more than a sip of his wine either. "Do you know that gentleman?" Mary asked, in an effort to avoid answering.

"Who? Oh, that is Colonel Trefusis," her companion informed her, sounding less than enthusiastic. "Formerly of the Scots Fusiliers, but I believe he is now some sort of administrator."

"Perhaps that's why he's not wearing his uniform."

"Aye, very plainly dressed he is indeed. Not a scrap of tartan on him. We've all made an effort, too, for your father was eager to put on a show to mark the opening of the black grouse season. It's a shame that the Prince of Wales cancelled at the last moment."

"Postponed, not cancelled. His Royal Highness was required to deal with an urgent matter of state," Mary said tactfully, having overheard her father's furious speculation as to the real reason. "Is the colonel married?"

"No, no, he's an army man, no wife. His brother is Lord Clinton, I think his estates are in Devon or Cornwall. Somewhere in the West Country."

"Lord Clinton? I don't recall ever meeting him, and I have most certainly not met Colonel Trefusis before, but I believe they must both be distant cousins."

"Aye, I reckon between your father's and your mother's illustrious lineage, you're connected to every family of note in the land. Perhaps Colonel Trefusis will honour his Scottish heritage by donning a kilt for the reels later. Which reminds me, Lady Mary, that I would be very much obliged if you would honour me with a dance, if I'm not too late to put my name down on your card? I'm told I execute a competent schottische, if you have a vacancy?"

"I am not sure where I've put my card, but when I find it . . ."

To her relief, her mother signalled the change for the next course, and she turned dutifully to converse with the guest on her other side. Slanting a look across the table as she did so, she momentarily met Colonel Trefusis's eyes. He raised his brow at her again; and this time, though he did not ask it, the question seemed to her writ loud and clear on his face. *What on earth have you been up to?*

CHAPTER TWO

Reeling at the Ceilidh

Drumlanrig Castle was the least grand and imposing of the Buccleuch family stately homes, used primarily for shooting parties in the summer. Impressive though it appeared on the exterior, it was sparsely furnished inside and the rooms were bitterly cold in the winter. It was also a most inconvenient residence, with access to the second floor limited by the spiral staircases in the four towers, which were so narrow that a one-way system was in operation.

Drumlanrig had no ballroom, which meant that the annual ceilidh was held in the drawing room on the first floor. Though all the furniture had been removed, the carpets rolled back, and the musicians crammed into the far corner, there was still very little room for dancing. Fortunately, the reels at the Drumlanrig ceilidh were sedately danced, featuring none of the gusto that prevailed at the less exalted gatherings Mary had illicitly attended on the estate with her friend Stuart, the head gamekeeper's son. Tonight, the steps to each dance were carefully executed, with a caller standing at the side of the accordionist to describe the more complicated manoeuvres. Strict time was kept, hands were neatly placed, and heads were correctly turned at each step or change of direction.

Years of practice made it easy for Mary to dance without the need to concentrate, and since every one of her partners lacked her experience, it was an added bonus that conversation was sacrificed as they endeavoured not to tread on her toes. She engineered her current partner into the polka section of the "Balmoral Schottische," earning herself a grateful smile, and surveyed the room once more for Colonel Trefusis, but he was nowhere in sight. She couldn't see her father either. The duke hated to dance, but he was a stickler for propriety, and it wasn't at all like him to disappear in the middle of his own ceilidh. Were the two men closeted together? What on earth could they be discussing? It must be something more important than a polite chinwag.

The dance ended and Mary was dropping the requisite curtsy when her mother appeared at her shoulder. "If you will excuse us," the duchess said, smiling graciously at Mary's partner, and taking her arm in a firm grip, "I require a quiet word with my daughter."

Oh dear heavens! Her mother must have noticed how long she had been away from the table. "Mama, the next dance—"

"Does not begin for ten minutes." The duchess led her out of the drawing room to the window embrasure of the adjoining sitting room where several guests were recovering from their exertions on the dance floor. "Now tell me honestly," she said, "should I be worried about you?"

"No!" The denial sounded panicked. Mary reminded herself that her mother could not possibly know what she really had been doing. "I mean, no, of course you needn't worry, Mama."

"You were gone from the table for at least twenty minutes. To leave in the middle of a banquet like that, you must have been feeling terribly ill."

"Oh no, I promise you I am perfectly well," Mary said guiltily. "My monthlies arrived early, and I had to attend to the matter, that is all."

The duchess winced. "Oh. Yes, I see."

"I really didn't mean to worry you."

"No, I'm aware, Mary, that you never do. You think that having one daughter causing me sleepless nights is more than enough for me to endure" was the surprisingly accurate and wry reply.

"Margaret is very happy now in New York. She said so in her last letter; and you know, Mama, one thing about Margaret is that she never pretends. If she says she's happy, then she is."

"That is very true: one always knows exactly where one is with Margaret. In that sense you are very different from her. I never know what is going on in that head of yours. You are my only little fledgling left in the nest."

"I thought you were eager for me to take flight," Mary replied, taken aback by her mother's unaccustomed whimsy.

"What makes you think that?"

"Wasn't that the whole point of me spending the last two Seasons in London? I'm sorry I've proved so difficult to dispose of."

"Dispose of! What a way to put it. I wanted you to enjoy yourself. A new wardrobe, parties—it was a chance for you to meet new people, make new friends. You have been too much alone, and I am aware that to a large degree that is my fault. You are shy, and that first Season was something of a trial to you, but I hoped you would enjoy this Season more."

"Well, I didn't," Mary said baldly. "Are you really saying you didn't take me to London to find me a husband?"

"I thought my motives were obvious. I hoped you would understand, Mary, that I have learned from my mistakes regarding your sister." The duchess pursed her lips. "This is not a topic we should be discussing at the moment. We should rejoin our guests."

There was much food for thought in her mother's words, but over her shoulder Mary spied Colonel Trefusis and her father re-entering the drawing room. Colonel Trefusis had clearly spotted her, for he made his way quickly across the floor and made his bow.

"Your Grace. Lady Mary. I believe this dance is mine?"

Mary knew full well that it was not and so did her portly partner, who was barrelling his way towards her, but she allowed him to take her arm. "The Lord Provost has his name down for this reel, you know."

Colonel Trefusis smiled and shook his head. "If he attempts a strip the willow he'll have an apoplexy. You'll spare him and the good people of Dumfries by dancing with me instead."

He led them to a set of three couples which had formed nearest the front door. Obviously a man with no regard for the strict rules governing a ceilidh, he then positioned them at the head of the line, which meant they would be the first to dance rather than the last. "We should be at the back," Mary hissed, trying to free her arm.

The colonel, however, linked arms with her, securing her firmly to the spot. "I've been waiting all night to dance with you, and cannot bide my time a moment longer."

"Waiting all night! Where? I haven't seen you since dinner."

"I was otherwise engaged."

"I wasn't looking for you. I simply noticed . . ."

"That I had disappeared?" he queried. "As indeed you did during dinner."

"I left the table to attend to a—a personal matter," Mary said, colouring, "as I was just explaining to my mother."

Any gentleman would have immediately turned the subject. Colonel

Trefusis simply raised his brows. "A personal matter. An interesting way of putting it."

What did he mean? He could not possibly have seen her. It was strictly against all the rules of etiquette to leave the table half-way through a banquet, as she had done. The band struck up. Mary tried to tug her arm free. "I cannot possibly offend the Lord Provost."

"If the Lord Provost is offended, it is my fault. As for the dance, I think you'll find I'm reasonably competent," Colonel Trefusis replied, urging her into a spin exactly on cue.

There was nothing at all sedate in the way he did it, almost whirling her off her feet. She was so giddy when he released her, she almost missed her own step as she danced her way down the line of gentlemen. At the bottom they spun together again, but she was ready for him this time, and enjoyed flying around. It was the colonel's turn now to make his way up the line, birling each of the ladies. At the top, he took Mary's arms for one more turn, this time spinning her so wildly she staggered, unaware that he had danced them out of the drawing room until he came to a sudden halt.

"What on earth are you doing?" Mary gasped.

"I thought you needed some air. You look a little giddy."

"Thanks to you!"

"We need to talk, and it's impossible to do that while dancing."

Still holding on to her, he hurried her past the two footmen standing at the top of the main oak staircase, through a door which led to one of the small balconies on the southern façade of the castle, and down the stone steps into the gloom of the garden.

"We can't be long, or we'll be missed," Colonel Trefusis said, letting go of her arm.

"We've probably already been missed. That was hardly a subtle manoeuvre," Mary said pointedly, completely thrown by his high-handed behaviour. "My mother . . ."

"Tell her you felt faint."

"I've already worried her enough tonight by disappearing at dinner. Anyway, I never faint."

"You should cultivate the habit. It can be a most useful method of escaping from tricky situations."

"Such as this one?"

"I would have thought the situation you placed yourself in earlier was much tricker."

Her heart skipped a beat. *Don't panic.* He could not possibly have seen her. Diversion, Mary thought, clutching at straws. "I still don't understand why you didn't simply put your name on my dance card, if you were so set on dancing with me."

"I had not planned to join in the dancing."

"Now you have singled me out, it will look very odd."

"Then I will make a point of dancing with at least two other ladies when we go back to the ceilidh, which will have to be soon. Let us come to the point, shall we, Lady Mary?"

Her mouth went dry, but she managed what she hoped was a bland smile. "Which is?"

"The astonishing exploit you performed during dinner."

She considered trying to deny it, but there was something in the colonel's expression that made her change her mind. A subtle change that she couldn't put her finger on, but it made her feel rather like a junior officer caught in the wrong. "You saw me."

"I saw you. What the devil were you playing at, risking your neck like that?"

"I wasn't risking my neck!"

"Really? You seemed very unsure of your footing as you set out."

"Once I'd got my balance, I— Where were you? You can't possibly have seen me from the dining room, so you must have been in the garden. It's considered very ill-mannered to leave a table in the middle of a banquet, but you know that."

His mouth tightened. "I came out for a breath of fresh air between courses."

"You seem to require a lot of fresh air," Mary retorted, recalling belatedly that attack was the best form of defence. "Perhaps you live on it, for you don't eat much, or drink much either."

His eyebrows shot up. "You were watching me?"

"I notice things about people, that's all. You didn't eat any food; you merely rearranged it on your plate."

"I wasn't hungry. Stop trying to change the subject."

Mary crossed her arms, her mind racing. Could she brazen it out? "So, we both escaped dinner for a few moments—what of it?" she demanded, trying desperately not to let her panic show. "It was most improper of *both* of us, but no harm was done. Now, may I go back to the ceilidh?"

"You terrified the life out of me," the colonel said, ignoring this gambit. "I came charging to your rescue, though what I thought I would do if you fell, I have no idea."

"Tried to catch me?" Mary said, resorting to flippancy. "I'm no lightweight; I would probably have crushed you to death." A vision of herself plummeting to the ground made her shudder. She shook her head to dispel it. "Fortunately for you, I didn't fall."

"No, you looked as if you relished every moment, after a faltering start. Do you enjoy courting danger?"

She glowered at him. "That is none of your business."

"I'm interested," he continued, "because the young woman dancing her way across the parapet was such a contrast to the insipid creature at the dinner table. You still haven't told me what you were doing up there."

"You wouldn't understand," Mary retorted, wondering now if she understood either. "It doesn't matter why I did it. I did it, and now I wish I had not."

"Is that true?"

She opened her mouth to agree, then changed her mind, shrugging instead.

"It was such a very extraordinary thing to do at any time, but right in the middle of a dinner party! I can't think of a single reason why you would do such a thing."

In the starlight, she couldn't see his face properly, but he sounded genuinely baffled. She didn't need to explain herself, but it was so rare for anyone to wish her to, that she was sorely tempted. "I didn't mean to go through with it. I was only imagining it at first, while I was being talked at. Picturing myself leaving the dining room, running upstairs to change, and walking out onto the parapet."

"And at some point your imagination gave way to action?"

"Are you laughing at me?"

"I am—I am confounded by you, to be honest.

"Confounded," Mary repeated, quietly pleased.

"Do you make a habit of alleviating the tedium of a dinner party in this way?"

She gave a snort of laughter. "Of course not! That was the first time."

"And the last, I hope, now that you have proved yourself, if that is what you were doing."

"Perhaps I was," Mary said, surprised.

"How on earth did you acquire such a remarkable skill? It's not exactly a normal part of a young lady's education."

"One of the kitchen garden apprentices comes from a circus family.

He taught me how to walk a tightrope a few years ago, though I've never done that more than a few feet off the ground. I have practised on the Long Wall on the terrace countless times, but never before walked on the parapet. I hadn't quite appreciated how far down it was. I shouldn't have looked down—it almost overset me."

"It almost killed you," the colonel said grimly.

"But it didn't," Mary said, repressing a shudder. "Thinking back now, however, I will admit that I don't really know what possessed me."

"The thrill of a dangerous act, combined with a fervent desire to thumb your nose at everyone present, without anyone guessing was what you were doing."

"Oh!" Her jaw dropped. "How did you know that, when I didn't?"

He laughed softly. "'When I was being talked at,' is what you said. You must have been fairly sure that neither of your dinner companions would remark upon your absence."

"I was right! What about you?" Mary said, once again on the back foot. "You must have been absent from the table for almost as long as I was. How did you explain yourself?"

"As I said, I went out for a breath of fresh air."

Clearly he did not like her questioning him. A burst of muffled laughter came from the dining room. The staff would be setting the table for supper. "I ought to get back in," Mary said. "My mother— Oh God, are you going to tell her? Please, I would really rather you did not. It would place her in a dreadful position."

"What on earth do you mean?"

"I can't explain, but if you tell my mother, then she will be obliged to inform my father. Colonel Trefusis, you can have no idea how much I truly, deeply, most fervently do *not* wish her to have to do that—" Mary broke off, mortified, as the full extent of her wilfulness dawned on her. "I can't explain, there's no time now, we simply can't stay out here any longer. Could we meet tomorrow morning before breakfast? I usually go for a walk about six. We could accidentally bump into each other."

"I am not sure that would be appropriate."

"Please!" She could hear footsteps. "Meet me at the Heather House," Mary hissed. "It's in the wilderness beyond the bowling green, you can't miss it. Please, Colonel Trefusis."

"Very well. As it happens I'm also in the habit of taking an early morning walk." The footman whom her mother had obviously sent to find her appeared, and Colonel Trefusis took her arm. "If you are feeling better now, Lady Mary, I think we should return to the ceilidh."

CHAPTER THREE

The Dormouse

Drumlanrig Castle, Sunday, 25 August 1872

IT WAS A BEAUTIFUL START to the day. The sun had just risen and the last of the ceilidh stragglers had finally gone to their beds when Mary set out for her meeting with Colonel Trefusis. Thanks to her earlier lie about feeling unwell, her mother had insisted she go to bed relatively early, at two. She had spent most of the night lying wide awake, replaying the events of the evening, trying—and failing—to imagine the conversation which was to follow this morning. Turning at the half circle in the garden to look back at the castle, her walk across the parapet seemed like a dream—or perhaps that should be nightmare?

She was torn. If her mother became embroiled, then she would never forgive herself, but if she could persuade Colonel Trefusis that it was more expedient that they keep her exploits between themselves . . . Mary smiled, hugging herself. Then she would not regret it, for she had enjoyed it so very much.

The colonel had been as good as his word last night. Returning to the ceilidh, he had first handed her solicitously over to her next dance partner before seeking out a partner for himself. He had executed an

intricate schottische with elan, and taken part in three other reels. This
proved what she had already surmised, that he was an honourable man,
but the decorum with which he had danced, the restraint which he had
not shown when partnering her, was confusing.

She didn't know what to make of him. He looked and dressed like
the most conservative of men, yet the method he had used to secure a
conversation with her was reckless. Then there was his excuse for having left the dinner table. Why had he needed a breath of fresh air? Was
he ill? That would explain why he was pushing his food about his plate,
but it wouldn't explain the energy he'd shown on the dance floor. The
contradictions intrigued her. His interest in her, his having actually noticed her in the first place, intrigued her, too, though they also baffled
her. What mattered this morning, however, was that he was giving her
a chance to explain herself, and she had better make sure she made the
most of it. Which was going to be challenging, since she never spoke
about herself or divulged her inner feelings.

She had reached the Heather House, a recent addition of her mother's to the garden, and one of Mary's favourite places. It was a quirky
little round pavilion built of wood standing on a grassy mound surrounded by trees, with a pretty view of the Marr Burn and the water-
fall. Inside, the walls were decorated with the Buccleuch family crest
and various other heraldic symbols and mottos, all of them cleverly
constructed from lime-soaked moss and heather. She took a seat on
the bench which encircled the outside, facing away from the path, and
closed her eyes to listen to the Marr tumbling through the woodlands
as if, she always thought, the burn was in a dreadful hurry to get somewhere. The sound calmed her nerves, until the soft crunch of a twig
breaking made her eyes fly open.

"Good morning."

Flustered, Mary jumped to her feet. "Colonel Trefusis. You are early."

He was clad in a dark lounging-jacket and matching waistcoat with buff-coloured trousers, his shirt plain and blindingly white. The dress was casual, but he wore it with an elegance that made Mary horribly conscious of her own, hastily assembled toilette. She was wearing one of her favourite morning gowns of white cotton embroidered with little blue flowers, pretty but unexceptional, and her long unruly hair was only roughly combed, hanging down her back and casually tied with a ribbon. The colonel's hair was neatly combed and he was freshly shaved, the only sign of informality the lack of a hat.

She had thought him handsome last night. Today, she realized with dismay that she also found him extremely attractive. Memories of her excruciating first Season flitted into her head, making her toes curl. She had never enjoyed being the focus of attention. She had no idea how to make conversation with the gentlemen her mother rounded up to dance with her. The more attractive the man, the more tongue-tied she became. She was not a success, and at first mortified by her gaucheness until it dawned on her that failing to attract a potential husband was exactly the outcome she wanted. After that, she mastered the art of being tongue-tied and awkward, of looking downcast and demure, and easily overlooked. She succeeded, on her own terms, in repelling any advances, and spent much of the time observing the progress and the setbacks of the other debutantes. Predicting what would happen had become a game with her. She had discovered that she was adept at it. It seemed that one of her few skills was to be intuitive when it came to people. Typical of her that her one attribute was useful as a parlour game but not much else.

"Shall we make ourselves comfortable?" Colonel Trefusis said, with a hint of a smile that made her wonder how long she'd been staring at him.

He waited until she sank back onto the narrow bench before sitting down beside her. His boots were highly polished, not even a blade of grass marring their perfection. Mary tucked her dew-damp feet beneath the hem of her gown, clasped her hands together, and smiled brightly. "Thank you for taking the time to come here and talk to me."

She sounded like her mother addressing one of her least favourite dinner guests, but the colonel, gazing out at the tumbling Marr, seemed not to notice. "On such a beautiful morning, it's no hardship. I'm an early riser, and I like to be outside in the fresh air at the start of the day when I can."

"And during dinner and in the middle of a ceilidh, too," Mary quipped, immediately regretting it, recalling too late how defensive he had been when she had attempted to quiz him last night. "At least we have established that we have something in common," she said, striving to make amends. "A love of fresh air, I mean. It is one of the things I disliked most about London—the lack of fresh air. And not being able to enjoy the air anyway, without a chaperone. That was another thing I hated. All the chaperoning. I am *never* permitted to go anywhere alone." Mary cringed inwardly. "Sorry, I'm talking too much."

"You've no need to be nervous."

"I have every need. Last night, I agreed to explain myself, but I am not used to explaining myself, and I hardly know you, so it's difficult—oh, do shut up, Mary." Blushing furiously, she stared down at the ground.

"Then let me start with an explanation of my own. I left the table at the banquet last night because I had a bad headache."

"Why didn't you say so? You covered it up very well when you danced with me."

"Seeing you up on the parapet served to cure me of it. You were a balm to my fevered brow."

She smiled at the deliberately flamboyant compliment. "I am happy to have been of service."

Colonel Trefusis angled himself on the bench to face her. "One good turn deserves another. I don't know why you got it into your head that I would go telling tales to the duchess, but I had no such intention. I understand why you were up there. I consider myself privileged to have witnessed your daring. Let that be an end of it."

"Really?"

"Really."

"Thank you. Oh, thank you so much. If my mother knew—I've been castigating myself all night for being so selfish."

"I am happy to have been of service."

She smiled at his deliberate use of her own words. "I am very, very much obliged to you."

"Then indulge me, and tell me why it matters so much."

Her relief gave way to wariness. "What do you wish to know?"

He studied her for a moment, mouth pursed. "Never mind, I should not have asked. My decision wasn't made with conditions attached."

He made to rise, but she caught his arm. "No, wait. You have been very generous, I owe you some sort of explanation."

"You don't owe me anything."

"That's why I'd like to explain." Mary twined her fingers together in her lap. "Though I'm not sure where to start. What do you wish to know?"

"Well, I suppose—yes, I'd like to know, if it was not for your worries about your mother finding out, do you regret it?"

"Honestly?" Mary closed her eyes, reliving that moment when she recovered from her stumble and began to walk along the parapet. "I am not sure that I do. It was thrilling," she said. "Like I imagine flying would be like. I felt like a hawk, surveying the world from on high. Everything looked so small, and I felt—I felt free, and powerful. As if nothing could touch me, as if no-one could reach me. It was the most exhilarating experience. I've never felt anything like it. Sorry, I'm babbling on and being fanciful."

"No, you are being entrancing."

There was a warmth in his voice, a look in his eyes as she met his gaze that made her hot. Not uncomfortable but self-conscious and aware of him once more as a very attractive and sophisticated man. Who could not possibly be interested in her, save perhaps for her novelty value. Mary looked away.

Colonel Trefusis shifted marginally on the bench and crossed his legs. "Why is it so important that your parents don't find out about your high wire act last night? It sounded as if it was more than just not wanting to get into trouble."

The change of subject brought her abruptly back to earth. "Because of Margaret, my sister." How to explain Margaret? "She is everything I am not." Pretty, assured, and defiant, Mary thought ruefully. Margaret would handle this conversation so much better than she was doing. She would get straight to the point. "She caused a huge scandal by running away from the ball where her betrothal was to be announced. 'The Buccleuch name dragged through the mud,'" Mary continued in her father's sonorous tone, "'our dirty laundry washed in public.' The duke was mortified."

"Good God, I'm not surprised. What an awful thing to have done."

"Yes, but not so awful as to try to force a person to marry a man she found loathsome in the name of duty."

"Force? This is the nineteenth century. A woman cannot be compelled to marry."

"Her life can be made very difficult if she refuses. My father packed Margaret off to Dalkeith, which is our family home near Edinburgh, to teach her a lesson in obedience. I was sent here with my governess to keep me away from her influence. When she still refused, she was exiled to Ireland and all mention of her forbidden, and now she is settled in New York. I haven't seen her for six years."

"Good God."

"Exactly," Mary said, somewhat astonished by her outpouring. "The duke won't even have her name mentioned. My mother writes to her, and so do I, but we are obliged to pretend we don't."

"That places you in a most invidious position."

"And my mother, much more so."

"Perhaps, but—you must have been very young when all this turmoil was going on."

"I was almost fourteen when I was sent here from Dalkeith with my governess."

The colonel frowned. "I thought it was your sister who was being punished with exile."

"I love Drumlanrig. My parents were keeping me out of harm's way. They had more important matters to attend to," Mary said, though there had in fact been occasions when she'd wondered if anyone remembered her existence. "I was very well looked after here."

"Wait! You mean you remained here for—for how long?"

"Until I came out, two years ago." It sounded dreadful, saying it like that. "You must not be thinking that I was unhappy. There were times when my parents were in residence. For the shoot and—and other times. And I was always with my family at Christmas, too. Besides, I am perfectly content in my own company."

The colonel looked appalled. "Forgive me, I do not wish to malign my host and hostess, but it sounds to me as if you must have had a very lonely existence."

She wanted to deny it, but it was the truth, though she had not permitted herself to think so. How had the conversation taken such a personal turn? Mary tried to shrug, but to her horror, a lump rose in her throat. No-one had ever asked her how she felt. It had taken this complete stranger to point out what ought surely to have been obvious to her mother. To her further embarrassment, a tear escaped from her eyes. She brushed it impatiently away. "I'm sorry."

Colonel Trefusis shook his head, handing her a handkerchief.

"Thank you." Mary dabbed at her eyes, striving frantically for self-control. "The only thing worse than a human watering pot is one who doesn't carry a handkerchief."

"I may be wrong, but you don't strike me as someone given to displays of emotion."

"I'm not. I almost never cry and I never pour my heart out to anyone, let alone a stranger. I do beg your pardon, I don't know what came over me."

"A long overdue relaxing of your stiff upper lip," Colonel Trefusis said dryly. "You were at a very impressionable age when you were sent here. You must have felt as if you were being punished along with your sister."

"I didn't really understand what was going on at the time. I knew that Margaret had done something terrible, but when I asked, my parents . . ." Mary shuddered. "The subject was forbidden. So I learned not to ask."

"And to make no demands?" When she said nothing, he shook his head, pursing his mouth. "To be perfectly frank, it sounds to me as if you were very badly treated."

Tears burned her eyes again. Mortified, Mary blinked furiously. "I learned to be self-sufficient."

"You had no choice."

She had herself back under control now. "I made a true friend in Stuart, the head gamekeeper's son. As I said, I'm very self-sufficient."

"You're also admirably loyal." The colonel touched her hand lightly. "And you don't like to talk about yourself, either."

"Never. I don't know why I'm telling you all this. You must think— I've no idea what you must think of me."

He was silent for a moment, allowing her time to compose herself. "I think, whether you admit it or not, that your sister's exploits have cost you dear."

"It cost my parents even more. The whole episode put a terrible strain on them."

"And you are determined not to add to their woes. You must have been terrified of making any faux pas."

"That is it exactly! I was. I still am," Mary admitted, astonished. "My mother is in a very difficult position. I feel for her."

Colonel Trefusis looked unconvinced. "I would not be so presumptuous as to judge either of them, but you are completely innocent in all of this. Now I understand your anxiety last night about not wishing to be the cause of any further trouble."

"It's not Margaret's fault, but she has caused a great deal of—of disharmony in our family."

"I suspect that is your biggest understatement yet," the colonel said, smiling grimly. "So, your sister is living her own life in America, while you have been forced into playing the dutiful and dull daughter who no-one takes much notice of."

"When it comes to dutiful and dull, my eldest sister, Victoria, wins hands down. She is the perfect daughter, as far as my father is concerned. Her idea of rebellion would be to have two sherries before dinner."

"While yours is to walk a parapet in the middle of the banquet. Kicking over the traces, that's what you were doing last night, isn't it?"

The lump was back in her throat. Her eyes were once again full of unshed tears. "Yes," Mary whispered. "I am so sorry, Colonel Trefusis, I truly am not in the habit of crying." She tried to smile. "Colonel Trefusis! How formal that sounds, when I am crying all over you. What is your name?"

"Walter."

"No!" Mary gave a watery laugh. "Oh, good heavens, I'm already surrounded by Walters—my father, brother, various cousins. Anyway, even if I wanted to, it wouldn't be appropriate for me to be so familiar, given you are significantly my senior."

"I am only thirty-four."

"I am just turned twenty-one, though at the moment I expect I look about forty. Tears don't suit me."

"No, you look much better smiling. My friends call me Trefusis."

"Are we friends? I am not sure that would be considered proper either. What about Tree, like an oak? Or no, what about Tre as in tray? I like that."

"Tre. Why not?"

"Excellent. Then you must call me Mary, when we are alone, at any rate." She blew her nose and patted her cheeks dry. "I hate self-pity. I truly am sorry for crying."

"Don't apologize, please."

She studied him carefully, but could see no sign of pity or embarrassment. She should feel humiliated at having laid bare her innermost thoughts like this, but what she felt was enormous relief at having *relaxed her stiff upper lip.* At last, someone had listened to her side of the story. Until now, no-one had even acknowledged her right to *have* a point of view. She *had* been abandoned. She *had* been lonely. All those feelings that had been pent up inside her for so long were legitimate after all. "You got more than you bargained for, all the same," she said.

"I got exactly what I hoped for."

"Oh. Well, I'm not sure if that is a good thing or a bad thing, but . . ."

"I think a great deal more of you, not less."

"Oh." His smile was doing odd things to her. She felt awkward, too hot, though not embarrassed exactly. "Thank you, Tre."

"Tre. I rather like it." He took his watch from his pocket then frowned. "I had no idea that was the time. I don't want to get in the duke's bad books by being late for breakfast, and I'll have to change for church. Shall we risk walking back together?"

"If you don't mind, I'd like to take a few moments to compose myself, then I'll go and see Mama before she goes to mass in Dumfries. My mother converted to the Catholic faith when I was a child. It is another topic that is not discussed in our family."

"So the duchess, like her two daughters, has her own method of rebelling."

"Goodness, I've never thought of it like that. What an extraordinary thing. It is as well that she has Victoria, straight as the proverbial die. Upright, proper, compliant—and the apple of my father's eye, I would like to say, and so she would like to be, but alas, she is a mere female. Fortunately the duke is well provided for with sons. And I'm rambling on. How do you do it? Get me to spout like a faucet, I mean, when I'm usually clam-like."

"It's a useful knack in my line of business."

"I'm curious, what is your business?"

He spread his hands. "It can be none of yours, I'm afraid. I hope you're not regretting what you've confided in me? I meant it, Mary, when I said I am honoured by the trust you place in me." He took her hands in his. "It must have taken a great deal of courage to speak as you did."

"I didn't intend to say so much. Or to cry on you either. Thank you, Tre, for listening."

He lifted her hand to his lips, kissing it lightly. "It was a pleasure."

CHAPTER FOUR

The Shooting Party

Drumlanrig Castle, Monday, 26 August 1872

T HE DUKE OF BUCCLEUCH ANNOUNCED at breakfast that he would not be able to make this morning's grouse shoot, thanks to the arrival of a certain Captain Beckman of the 15th Hussars. The captain had lately travelled from India, where he had been serving alongside the duke's third son, Captain Lord Walter Scott, from whom he brought a folio of letters. His Grace was sure the company would understand that he was anxious to peruse them.

"If you will excuse me, I will leave you in my wife's capable hands." The duke got to his feet. "Colonel Trefusis, now would be a convenient time to have the discussion you requested, if you would care to join me," he said, and departed the dining room, causing Tre to abandon the breakfast he had only just served himself and follow in his wake.

"I am afraid I was not expecting to attend the shoot," the duchess said, looking rather put out. Mama, Mary knew, had been looking forward to taking a number of interested guests on a tour of her beloved kitchen garden. Poor Tre hadn't even had a chance to drink his first cup of coffee, and he liked to drink at least two, she had noticed. It was typical of her father to take no account at all of anyone else's plans, save his own.

"I can take charge of the shoot, Mama," she said impulsively, pushing aside her own half-eaten eggs and hastily gulping the last of her tea. "You go ahead with your tour."

"Oh no, Mary, that is most thoughtful, but His Grace . . ."

"Would not wish you to disappoint those of our guests who have been looking forward to seeing all the changes you and Mr. Thomson have made to the gardens in the last few years. I am more than capable of hosting the shoot, but I would be a very poor substitute for you when it comes to horticulture."

"If you will excuse us." The duchess got up from the table, indicating that Mary should follow her out of the room. "I very much appreciate the offer," she said, "but you cannot possibly take on such an important and onerous task."

"I've assisted you with the arrangements every year since I was fifteen."

"Yes, but you have never taken sole charge."

"You have already done most of the hard work, haven't you?"

"I suppose that is true. It is mostly a question of supervising."

"Which I can do," Mary said eagerly. "In fact, why not let me take over now, and then you are free to concentrate on your own arrangements for once, rather than leaving them to the last minute."

"That would certainly be a novelty," the duchess said wryly. "All the same, I am not sure it is fair of me. You will be obliged to act as hostess at lunch."

"It is not like a dinner party," Mary said, refusing to be daunted. "The talk will be all about the shoot; it will take care of itself. All that I'll need to do is make sure everyone's plates and glasses are full."

"If all does not go exactly to plan, your father will be furious. He takes such pride in everything running smoothly."

"Please, Mama, I'd like to feel useful for once."

"For once! I had no idea you lacked occupation."

Her mother had no idea that she didn't take sugar in her tea, but it always seemed so churlish to point it out. "I'd like to help," Mary said, "and I know how eager you are to show off the kitchen garden."

"That is certainly true. Mr. Thomson has gone to a great deal of trouble to arrange the tour, and luncheon is to be served in the pinery."

"That settles it. You cannot possibly upset your head gardener, especially since Mr. Thomson is famous, now that he has published his book. You make an excellent team."

Her mother smiled indulgently. "We are lucky to have him."

"You have great plans, don't you, for next year?"

"We do." The duchess looked much struck. "We certainly do but—oh dear, I don't know, it is a great deal to ask of you to pick up the reins today."

"You didn't ask, Mama, I offered. Please, won't you trust me? I won't let you down."

"Let me down? I think you and I must talk later. But for now, thank you, Mary, I am extremely grateful."

MARY HAD OFTEN HEARD HER parents describe the grouse shoots at Drumlanrig as small and informal events, which indeed they were in comparison to the shoots which Their Graces regularly attended with the Duke of Sutherland at Dunrobin Castle and at Balmoral, too, with Prince Albert when he was alive, and hosted latterly by the Prince of Wales. Mary discovered, however, in the next three hectic hours, that a "small and informal" shooting party still required a gargantuan amount of effort from an army of staff.

She had offered to help on impulse, as a way of silently atoning to her mother for the parapet walk, and for having so entirely misunderstood her motives in launching her in society. Was that what her mother had meant, when she said they would talk later, an unusual remark in itself, for they rarely did talk. Not in the sense she and Tre had talked yesterday. She had never talked to anyone like that. It had given her a great deal to think about. Though now, as her mother had pointed out, was hardly the time.

In the kitchen, Cook was presiding over the assembly of lunch on the long deal table that stretched the entire length of the room. It looked as if it would feed an army. There were four huge pies cooling, the perfectly browned crusts glistening, each decorated with a different element of the Buccleuch arms. A flock of roast poultry was laid out in descending order, a goose at the head, followed by chicken, pheasant, grouse, pigeon, and ptarmigan. There were elaborate savoury jellies fresh out of the copper moulds with delicate morsels suspended in their gleaming depths, looking far too fragile to survive the jolting journey to the luncheon location. There was a whole salmon with cucumber scales, and a pig's head with an apple between its jaws. There were cream horns and strawberry tarts, a Stilton wheel and several of the small crowdie cheeses fresh from the Drumlanrig dairy. And of course there was a tower of pineapples waiting to be carved into exotic shapes.

Urquhart, her father's butler, was counting out the bottles of champagne that were to be kept cold on the blocks freshly cut from the ice house. The claret was already boxed, and he would personally bring the brandy and malt whisky with him. Out in the kitchen yard, the first of the brakes was stacked high with the boxes containing the glasses, plates, serving dishes, silverware, and damask tablecloths and napkins, while the trestle tables and chairs had already been despatched to be set up in readiness. Three footmen and three maids would travel in the first brake.

Feeling like a beleaguered general, but surprisingly relishing the challenge, Mary rushed from the kitchen up three flights of the spiral staircase to her bedroom to change quickly from her morning gown into the more fitting attire which her maid had laid out for the shoot. Though Mary would not take part in the sport, she dressed the part in a jacket of mossy-green Shetland wool and a matching skirt, the hem of which was trimmed with leather to protect it. Into the oversize pockets she crammed her notebook, several handkerchiefs, her penknife, a pair of scissors, two pencils, a small mirror, and a comb, while Clara, her maid, tidied her hair into an elaborate bun and secured her hat.

Grabbing her brown gauntlets, Mary flew back down the stairs to oversee the transport. To her relief Mr. Irvine, her father's trusted head gamekeeper, was already in place and in charge of the distribution of guns for those who had not brought their own. She set about allocating places for the guests in the carriages, taking due regard of their status.

Stuart was with his father. "Look at you," her friend hissed in her ear, "lady of the manor. Who'd have thought!"

Mary threw him a comical look. "I'm auditioning for a new role, I think I might be rather good at it."

Hurrying the last two gentlemen along and asking them to extinguish their cigars, Mary stood back as Mr. Irvine explained the rules for the carrying of weapons while in transit and instructions for guests on how they were to comport themselves when they arrived on the moor. Then they were off, and the initial part of her duties complete, she took the shortcut through the offices under the terrace for one last check of the kitchens before jumping up into the brake carrying the plates and glasses.

MR. IRVINE HAD SOLE CHARGE of the actual shoot. The beaters, who roused the grouse from the heather and drove them towards the shooting positions known as butts, and the pickers up with their dogs who retrieved the game, were experienced men who joined the shoot every year. Stuart and some of the duke's other tenants would act as loaders and unofficial watchmen in the butts for Mr. Irvine, to ensure as far as possible that the participants didn't shoot too high or too low, that they didn't poach each other's targets, and that everyone understood the rule: a bird should never be shot at unless the sky could be seen behind it.

Arriving at the edge of the moor as the echo of the first gunshot cracked, Mary concentrated her attention on the vital task of getting lunch ready on time. The al fresco dining room was set up in a clearing about a mile from the shooting positions. By twelve o'clock, she felt as if she had been in a battle but one that she was winning. It was a novel feeling to achieve something tangible and most satisfying. The trestle tables were set, the chairs arranged, the silverware polished, the glasses gleaming. The wine had been decanted, the champagne was chilling, and another long trestle table lay ready for the food which would be set out before the hungry party arrived back from the moor, but not so early that the sultry weather and the accompanying flies would spoil it.

The first of the food carts appeared in the distance on the track from the castle, and Mary was allowing herself a small pat on the back when she noticed that it was carrying two passengers squashed onto the bench beside the driver.

The gentleman was the first to jump down and make his bow. "Captain Christopher Beckman— No, forgive me, but you cannot possibly be the Duchess of Buccleuch."

"I am Lady Mary Montagu Douglas Scott, Captain Beckman, the youngest daughter of the duke and duchess. My mother is otherwise engaged this morning. How do you do?"

"Very well, Lady Mary, thank you. I'm so sorry to arrive like this with little notice, but His Grace insisted it would be no trouble for me to join the shoot."

"You are very welcome, Captain Beckman, and it is no trouble at all. We have enough food to feed another hundred," Mary replied, taking an instant liking to the young man. His blond hair flopped over a high forehead, under which were a pair of wide-spaced green eyes, a snub nose, and the kind of mouth that looked as if it was smiling even when it wasn't. It was a likeable face, giving the impression of boyish openness, though she reckoned he must be at least five or six years older than she was. "I take it my father won't be joining us this afternoon?"

"I don't think so. I left His Grace with Colonel Trefusis. Oh, do excuse me," the captain said, turning back to the cart to help down the woman who had been seated beside him. "Lady Mary, may I introduce you to Mrs. Fitzherbert-Smythe?"

"We are already acquainted," Mary said, belatedly recognizing the other passenger with a sinking heart. Tall and sparse, with deep-set brown eyes and a long quivering nose, she was a vile woman, the type who flourished in male company and had little time for her own sex. Lacking beauty, she had set herself up as an arbiter of fashion, with a vicious tongue she employed without discrimination or mercy. "How do you do?" Mary said, extending her hand.

"I am very well. Thank you, Lady Mary," Mrs. Fitzherbert-Smythe replied. "I came a day early; I was sure it would not be an inconvenience. My husband has been detained in London and I am afraid unlikely to join me now. I do not see Her Grace?"

"My mother is conducting a tour of the kitchen gardens," Mary replied, shocked by the casual liberty the guest had taken. Mrs. Fitzherbert-Smythe was a mere acquaintance, invited to Drumlanrig because her husband was involved with one of the duke's philanthropic causes and not by any means a close friend.

"Mrs. Fitzherbert-Smythe is looking forward to bagging some birds this afternoon, she tells me," Captain Beckman informed Mary.

"As you see, I am dressed for the occasion," the lady said, granting the captain a thin smile. "Though I have not my own guns," she added, turning to Mary. "I presume that is not a problem?"

"Mr. Irvine, the head gamekeeper, will attend to that. You will not be offended, I know, if he enquires about your experience, for—"

"I am to be answerable to an estate worker?"

"It is standard practice, Mrs. Fitzherbert-Smythe, as he is responsible for the safety of everyone out on the moors, and I am sure—"

"I will not answer to a servant."

The woman glared at her, clearly expecting her to back down. Mary braced herself. The fact that the woman was questioning Mr. Irvine's authority proved to her that Mrs. Fitzherbert-Smythe was an inexperienced markswoman. How would her mother handle the situation? "Here at Drumlanrig we pride ourselves on never having had a shooting accident during the grouse season. For our guests who have less experience, we can offer some assistance with loading and aiming."

"I hope you are not asking me to prove myself adept before you allocate me a gun."

She did not need to, for Mr. Irvine would. She doubted that Mrs. Fitzherbert-Smythe could manage to hit that ridiculously ostentatious brooch she wore on her coat lapel at ten paces, never mind a grouse on the wing at twenty yards. "The guns are in Mr. Irvine's charge," Mary said, in her mother's firm tone. "My domain is purely domestic, and I shall be more than happy to hand you a glass of champagne, if you wish."

"That would be wonderful," Captain Beckman interjected with a warm smile. "It's a hot day, isn't it, Mrs. Fitzherbert-Smythe, and a refreshment would be most welcome. I'll tell you what, since we arrived late together, why don't we stick together, eh? I'm not such a bad shot myself, and more than happy to look after you. Consider the matter resolved," the captain said, with a conspiratorial smile at Mary. "I must say, Mrs. Fitzherbert-Smythe, that is a most unusual brooch."

"Why thank you, Captain." The lady preened. "I'm surprised you noticed it. Gentlemen are not usually much interested in jewellery."

It was, Mary thought uncharitably as she signalled to Urquhart to pour the champagne, impossible to miss. A huge piece, with a massive diamond at the centre, surrounded by emeralds and rubies, it was both vulgar in her opinion and utterly unsuited to a shoot.

"I couldn't help but notice," the captain was saying.

"I have just had the catch repaired. You see, it is a most ingenious mechanism." Mrs. Fitzherbert-Smythe took the champagne from the silver tray offered to her by Urquhart without a thank you. "It is an heirloom, you know, and worth a small fortune. That is why I am wearing it. I find it safer to keep such valuable items close, when one is away from home."

Mary let out an indignant gasp at this insult. Urquhart looked mortified, and Captain Beckman blushed scarlet. "I am sure that you did not intend that as it sounded, madam."

"Oh. No. Of course not. I mean no offence to your parents, Lady Mary."

She could not bring herself to say that none was taken. "If you will excuse me, our guests will be returning from the moor. I must see to the food," Mary excused herself, seething. Thank goodness her mother had not heard the insult. It would be all over the servants' hall by dinner time, though, and she didn't rate Mrs. Fitzherbert-Smythe's chances of hot water or tea in her bedroom tomorrow morning.

ATTENDING TO THE HUNGRY SHOOTING party made Mary forget all about Mrs. Fitzherbert-Smythe. Captain Beckman, proving himself the perfect gentleman, continued to sacrifice himself to that lady's demands, much to Mary's relief, leaving her free to attend to the needs of the other guests, though Urquhart and his well-trained team left her very little to do. There were general noises of approval as the hungry shooters began to load their plates up from the vast array of cold meats and pies which adorned the long trestle table.

"A little of the pork pie, if you please, and a sliver of the ham. Perhaps a smidgen of the chicken if it is in aspic, and—yes, I think I might also manage a little of the turkey pie," Mrs. Fitzherbert-Smythe commanded, holding out her glass for a refill of champagne.

Mary grimaced inwardly, then retreated to check that the beaters and loaders, along with Stuart and his father, were also enjoying their well-deserved repast, which had been set out a few yards away behind a screen of gorse. Stone flagons of beer and ginger beer, hearty pork pies, plain chicken, and a large cheese along with a number of fresh loaves and a moist fruitcake were being very well-received. Stuart, she noted without surprise, was watering the dogs including his own precious pointer, Boo, who as usual, when she tried to pet him, turned his back on her. Boo was very much his master's faithful hound.

"Two new guests have joined us for the afternoon shoot," Mary said, taking Mr. Irvine to one side. "Captain Beckman of the Fifteenth Hussars has his own guns and is I believe a good shot."

"My Stuart says you're the best shot he's seen."

Mary blushed. "He was a very good teacher. You must be very proud of him."

"Aye, he's a good lad."

"I'm afraid Mrs. Fitzherbert-Smythe has rather an inflated opinion of her prowess."

"She'll resent being put to the test, in other words, my lady?"

"Precisely. Fortunately, Captain Beckman has offered to keep an eye on her."

Mr. Irvine pursed his lips. "I'll have to put them in the Whins, then," he said.

The shooting butt was named for the yellow, sweetly scented gorse-like bushes which all but surrounded it. Safely out of range of the other butts, it was always assigned to the least experienced marksmen. "Poor Captain Beckman, but it can't be helped."

"I'll give her Stuart as a loader, just to make double sure, my lady."

"Oh, poor Stuart. Thank you very much, Mr. Irvine."

"Not a problem, my lady, and if you don't mind my saying so, you're doing a sterling job here. I know you're not one for taking compliments, but credit where it's due. Her Grace will be proud of you."

"Thank you," Mary said, touched and surprised. "But really I had little to do. My mother had made all the arrangements, it was merely a question of executing them."

"Aye." Mr. Irvine unbowed for a moment, grinning at her. "Like I said, you're not one for compliments."

CHAPTER FIVE

Mayhem on the Moors

THE SECRET TO HER MOTHER'S slim figure, Mary decided after lunch, lay in her determination to be an attentive hostess. The small slice of turkey pie which Mary had served herself lay untouched on her plate as she saw the guests off to the afternoon shoot. The table was cleared, the dirty crockery, silverware, and glasses packed onto a cart, and the clean dishes set out for afternoon tea which was already arriving on the cart which had just ferried the remains of the lunch back to Drumlanrig, driven by . . .

"Tre! Were you hoping to join the shoot? They left about half an hour ago."

"Ah, well, never mind." He jumped down, handing the reins to the waiting footman. "I'll just have to wait until they come back for tea. What are you doing here? Are you helping your mother? The duke sent his apologies to the duchess. Business detains him."

"My mother took the ladies on a tour of her kitchen garden. I stepped in for her— Oh, I remember now, that was after my father had ordered you to abandon your breakfast before you'd had a chance to eat it. Did you manage to have lunch?"

"I had a ham sandwich while I was waiting for them to load up the cart."

"Why are you driving it?"

"Because the lad who was supposed to bring it back hadn't turned up, and I was keen to join Captain Beckman. I take it he's out on the moor?"

Mary grimaced. "With Mrs. Fitzherbert-Smythe, who I am convinced has never aimed a gun in her life. Captain Beckman most kindly offered to look after her and spared me and Mr. Irvine the embarrassment of testing her mettle."

"That was good of him. He has the reputation of being a crack shot."

"I suspected he was being modest when he said he wasn't a bad shot. Do you know him, then?"

"I know of him, but I've only just met him. The duke was kind enough to introduce us." Tre frowned down at a pebble which he was rolling under his boot. "He is in the Fifteenth Hussars, the regiment your brother serves in. He's an interesting chap. Comes from very humble stock. Worked his way up the ranks impressively, which is something that few men do, and he's very well-liked by his fellow officers, too."

"I am not surprised. I liked him. He makes me think of a friendly, lolloping Labrador."

Tre laughed. "I know what you mean, but don't be fooled. He might look eager to please and gormless, but he's far from that."

"You seem to know a lot about someone you've only just met."

"It takes a lot for our entitled officer class to accept a man like Beckman into their midst. The officers' mess is an exclusive club, and they like to keep it that way. One must behave like a gentleman, and if one is not *born* a gentleman, that's a difficult thing to pull off. Unwritten rules, pointless traditions—" Tre broke off, biting his lip.

"You sound as if it's an exclusive club you would rather not belong to," Mary said, puzzled by his tone.

He opened his mouth to say something, and changed his mind, simply shrugging. "Ought you to go and check on tea?"

Mary glanced over at the table. "Urquhart seems to have everything in hand. Stop trying to change the subject, please—I am not so easily diverted. Why are you so interested in Captain Beckman? Has my father asked you to cultivate him?"

"Not at all. The idea was entirely my own."

"So you *are* interested in him, then? But your interest isn't linked to whatever it was you were discussing with my father this morning."

"It is in a way."

"So you're not at Drumlanrig simply for the shoot?"

"The duke is the reason I'm here. As you have already surmised, I have something of a—an important matter—a proposition to put to him."

"What sort of . . ."

"Mary, I've already said far too much."

"Fine! Keep your secret," she exclaimed, disproportionately hurt. "I had better go and check on the tea after all. The boiler can be temperamental."

As she turned, Tre caught her arm, pulling her to the other side of the cart, out of sight of the staff. "Please don't take umbrage. It's not that I don't trust you."

"What is it, then?"

"It's not my secret to share, Mary. Look, it's early days, but I am hoping to speak to the duke about an initiative of mine. Something I believe will be of enormous benefit to the army."

"Good heavens!"

"I know!" Tre grinned. "I don't even know precisely how we will operate. This is highly confidential—do you understand me?"

"I trusted you to keep my secrets, Tre. You can trust me to keep yours."

"Thank you. You've no idea how much this initiative means to me."

"A chance to escape from your administrative post and be useful."

"Yes." He met her eyes, and laughed. "I can see you have a hundred questions, but there really is no point asking them."

"What about my father? May I ask what role he plays in this mysterious undertaking?"

"Your father is a very influential man with impeccable connections. His support could be crucial to ensuring that my plans are implemented—and I can't tell you what I mean by that, I'm afraid."

"You don't need to! Impeccable connections can only mean one thing. Are you going to be very important?"

"No, but the work will be. That is why I must not—I *must* not let myself down."

"I am sure you won't," Mary said, puzzled by his change of tone.

"I wish I had your certainty. Just between us, I'm glad to have missed today's shoot, but there will be another in a couple of days. I would much rather not join in, though I must, for it would cause great offence if I excused myself."

"That is very true. My father believes he confers a great honour on any gentleman he invites to take potshots at his grouse."

"Do you shoot, Mary?"

"I can, rather well in fact, but I hate to kill anything. Stuart taught me to handle a gun when I was sixteen, shooting targets off a wall. I have a good eye, my father has a vast selection of guns, and I had plenty of time to practise. Stuart said that I couldn't call myself a crack shot unless I took out a bird on the wing, but it was so horrible I've never done it again. I suppose," she added hesitantly, "being a soldier, you have had more than your fill of shooting. Is that it?"

"Guns and flogging, bullying, pointless rules." Tre swore softly under his breath, staring off into the distance for a moment. Then the sound of the shooting brakes trundling over the moor reached them, and he let go of her arm. "I think your guests are arriving for their tea."

Tre remained by the cart as Mary rushed to check that everything was ready. He was shaken by the strength of his desire to confide in her, not about his new possible future but about the cloud of his past which hung over him. His illness, if that's what it was, was shameful. *Unmanly* was the word whispered in shocked tones that miserable evening in the mess. *Humiliating!* He winced. Best not to recall that time.

He never talked of it. Never! And yet a few moments ago, he had considered doing just that. What would he have said? How could he possibly describe something that he couldn't even put into words himself, to anyone, never mind an innocent young woman like Mary? Though he hadn't ever met a young woman quite like Mary. Thank God they had been interrupted.

A loud shriek startled him, sending him running towards the tea party.

"My brooch is missing! My precious brooch has been stolen!" The sharp-nosed woman staggered backwards, her fall conveniently broken by a chair. "That brooch is a family heirloom. It's worth a fortune."

"Fetch some brandy," Tre ordered the transfixed butler.

"Yes, please, Urquhart," Mary said, "brandy. Mrs. Fitzherbert-Smythe, I am sure your brooch—"

"It has been stolen! Stolen, I tell you." The woman was clutching dramatically at her bosom, looking as if she had been shot through the heart. "I am going to faint."

Failing to fulfil her own prophesy, she sent up a wailing lament. Her nose quivered, her prominent brown eyes welled up with tears. Mary, looking quite aghast, took the tumbler of brandy from the butler and handed it to her prostrate guest. "Your jewellery must have fallen off. I shall have someone search the shooting butt."

The crystal tumbler of brandy was snatched from her hand and a large gulp taken before Mrs. Fitzherbert-Smythe continued with her lament. "The catch was perfectly secure. I had it checked only last week, Captain Beckman!" She snapped her fingers. "You will back me up on this. I particularly remember your admiring my brooch before lunch. The catch was perfectly secure, was it not?"

"Well, I can't say for certain," the captain said, looking deeply un-comfortable, "and you know, it's possible that it came undone while we were walking to our shooting positions."

"Nonsense! It could not have fallen off by accident. Besides, I am certain it was still attached to my coat when we arrived at the butt. It has been stolen!"

"Let's not jump to conclusions." Mary looked as if her day was un-ravelling in front of her eyes. "I will arrange to have the grouse butt searched. I am sure—"

"It has been stolen!" the woman shrieked, making Mary recoil. "My precious, precious brooch has been stolen, I am absolutely certain of it." Mrs. Fitzherbert-Smythe glowered at the circle of guests, every one of whom was now looking deeply uncomfortable. "Someone has taken it. I am distraught." Emitting a loud wail, she proceeded to sob into a handkerchief, her shoulders shaking. "What will my husband say! It is an heirloom."

Mary, it seemed to Tre, was rather more concerned with what her parents would say, for the commotion was embarrassing everyone, and the sobbing woman seemed to him determined to make as much fuss as possible, brushing off Mary's attempts to soothe her. "Serve the tea, feed her some cake," he said softly to her. "Let me speak to Mr. Irvine."

"Thank you," Mary said, throwing him a grateful look. "Mrs. Fitzherbert-Smythe, gentlemen, if you would like to be seated? There is more champagne for those who don't want to take tea, and I can personally vouch for the quality of our cook's Dundee cake."

To her obvious relief and Tre's, the summons was answered. Captain Beckman stepped in with a charming smile and an offer to serve the wailing woman a few choice slivers of cake. He succeeded where Mary had failed, being granted a tearful assent, and Tre's good opinion of the man increased.

The head gamekeeper was standing with his loaders and beaters. "Mr. Irvine. A word if you please," Tre said. "Will you have the grouse butt where Mrs. Fitzherbert-Smythe was shooting searched, please?"

"I've already sent two men off to do that, Colonel Trefusis. The lady was shooting from the butt where my son Stuart served as loader," he said, nodding over to the tall young man whom Tre knew was Mary's friend. "They were placed in the Whins, which the lady did not like, though I doubt she could have hit a grouse if I'd held it up in front of her nose," Mr. Irvine said quietly. "Were it not for the captain there keeping an eye on her, I'd have refused to give her a gun."

"I'm sure the item will be found. It's an ostentatious piece, I gather?"

"Aye it is, you couldn't help but notice it. Why she wore it on a shoot I have no idea. If it's not found, Colonel Trefusis . . ."

"It will be found, I'm sure. In the meantime, get your men to take their tea; they'll need the sustenance. I believe that there is to be duck-shooting at the end of the day."

"There is. Will you be joining us?"

"Not today," Tre said, suppressing a shudder.

He would wait until Mary was free, then suggest they walk back to the castle together, he decided. He was quietly looking forward to this as he watched the cakes, pastries, and sandwiches disappear at an impressive rate from the table, when the head gamekeeper approached him again, looking extremely troubled.

"I'm sorry, Colonel Trefusis, but there was no trace of the brooch to be found."

"Are you sure, Mr. Irvine?" Mary, who had obviously been on the lookout for the men's return, appeared at his shoulder.

"I'm afraid so, my lady. My men combed the path to the grouse butt and the butt itself—every bit of bracken, every nook in the stone, every blade of grass underfoot. They found nothing but spent cartridges."

"What is to be done?" Mary turned to Tre, looking panicked. "It cannot possibly have been stolen. She must have mislaid it somewhere."

"Well?" Mrs. Fitzherbert-Smythe, fortified by copious amounts of brandy, champagne, and cake, had pushed back her chair. Her voice was strident. "You haven't found it, have you? I was right: it has been stolen."

"I am sure it has simply been misplaced," Mary said. "It could have been lost on the drive over the moor, or—"

"It most certainly was not. I was wearing it at lunch. Everyone here will recall it?" Mrs. Fitzherbert-Smythe said, glaring at the faces around the table until several of the men nodded. "Captain Beckman has already verified that the catch was not loose . . ."

"Well, actually . . ."

"So I did not lose it. It must have been taken deliberately. It is a most valuable item, the rubies in particular are very rare, it is—"

"An heirloom," Mary said, through gritted teeth, a very distinct quiver of anger in her voice. "How on earth could it have been stolen without your noticing?"

"It was attached to my coat. Naturally I removed my coat before shooting commenced." Mrs. Fitzherbert-Smythe pointed at Stuart. "He was the only other person present in the butt, beside Captain Beckman, and I know that the captain is not a thief."

The implication stunned everyone. Mary's jaw dropped, then her face turned bright red. "You cannot possibly be accusing Stuart of stealing your brooch."

"It seems very obvious to me that he did," was the haughty response. "There *is* no other explanation."

The woman was already acquainted with Mary, and clearly thought that she would back down. Having heard her loyal defence of her wilful sister and parents, however, Tre wasn't in the least surprised when Mary refused to be cowed.

"That is a very serious allegation. Stuart is Mr. Irvine's son. His family have served the Drumlanrig Estate for generations. I would trust him with my life. You cannot possibly imagine that he is a common felon."

"Clearly *you* cannot, but I think we would all agree that you are somewhat biased," Mrs. Fitzherbert-Smythe said with an acid smile. "Not to say extremely naive. If Her Grace, your mother, were in charge here, she would not be so quick to leap to that young man's defence."

"I am very sure that my mother would say exactly what I have said. I have no idea what has happened to your brooch, but I know Stuart did not steal it."

"Let him prove it, then. Have him turn out his pockets!"

"No!" Mary exclaimed, mortified, but Stuart was already doing as requested.

"It's for the best," Tre whispered. "It will likely prove the boy innocent."

But when his jacket had been searched, his pockets turned out, and his gun bag checked, and no brooch uncovered, Mrs. Fitzherbert-Smythe was not satisfied. "He will have hidden it out on the moor for an accomplice to retrieve while we are here taking tea."

"That's a preposterous thing to say," Mary burst out, obviously reaching the limits of her self-control. "If you had done what any sensible woman would, and left it at the castle—but, oh no, I forgot. You don't trust our servants, do you?"

"I think it's only fair," Captain Beckman stepped in, "that I too should turn out my pockets as I was also present."

"There is no need for you to do any such thing," Mrs. Fitzherbert-Smythe exclaimed.

"On the contrary, madam," the captain said, "there is every need."

"There!" The woman once again turned to Mary as soon as the captain's pockets proved empty. "The evidence is now inescapable. I demand—"

"I wonder," Tre said, before Mary could respond, "if we should form a bigger search party and go back over all the ground. We should end the shoot now and let Mr. Irvine organize a more methodical search. What do you say?"

Over the general murmur of approval came the strident voice. "Irvine is the boy's father."

"And so has a vested interest in finding the item," Tre pointed out.

"It is not lost," Mrs. Fitzherbert-Smythe insisted, though more quietly now.

Out of the corner of his eye Tre could see that Mary was struggling to contain herself. Whether she was going to lose her temper or burst into tears, he couldn't tell, but he was determined to spare her either, if he could. "You will desist from making these accusations, madam. They are quite without foundation and, what's more," Tre continued ruthlessly, when the woman made to speak, "they are grossly insulting to your host. You are embarrassing us all and in danger of causing a most unnecessary scandal."

"Hear, hear," Captain Beckman whispered.

"Well!" Mrs. Fitzherbert-Smythe looked satisfyingly cowed. "I certainly have no wish to upset the duke and duchess."

"I am relieved to hear you say so. I will speak to Mr. Irvine."

"I will escort Mrs. Fitzherbert-Smythe back," Captain Beckman said valiantly.

"Thank you." Tre took Mary to one side. "I think you had best head back to the castle and let your mother know what has occurred."

She nodded, still struggling to regain her composure. "He didn't steal it."

"You're quite the lioness, when it comes to defending your own, aren't you?"

She managed a shaky laugh. "Thank you for stepping in and for addressing that woman as if she had turned up on parade with her buttons tarnished."

"You should be proud of yourself. She assumed you were a doormat for her to trample on."

"Dormouse. That's how I think of myself," Mary said, colouring.

The confession touched his heart. "Perhaps," Tre said, fighting the urge to hug her, "it's time for a rethink."

CHAPTER SIX

Repercussions

*T*ODAY, ON MY LITTLE IMAGINARY *island*, Charlotte, the Duchess *of Buccleuch, wrote in her diary, I walk through an archway into a walled garden. The air is thick with smells, jasmine, lavender, and roses; lemongrass, mint, and lemon verbena. The paths are marked out by low box hedges. Beyond the walls of the garden I can hear the busy river bustling towards its destiny. I perch on the steps of the little potting shed set on wheels. I am safe here. I have pulled up the draw-bridge. No-one can reach me in this idyllic place. . . .*

With an impatient sigh, Charlotte set down her pen. She had turned sixty-one in April, long past the time for indulging in such whimsy. Where had the years gone? She had already lived four years longer than her mother. She had been married for forty-three years—not that her husband was counting anymore. He hadn't even acknowledged the anniversary two weeks ago.

Walter was so distant these days, distracted by his many political and philanthropic causes. It was hard to believe that theirs had once been a love match. Children and dedicated public service had left no room for romance. How long had it been since Walter told her she looked well, never mind beautiful? How long since he had paid her a compliment of any sort? Last night he had informed the Lord Provost that he could trust her to keep an eye on the accounts, and the day before she'd overheard him praising her foresight and tenacity in having gas lighting installed at Drumlanrig, but she'd heard him say something very similar about their clerk of works, who had been the real driving force behind that project.

She was fortunate, very fortunate, she knew that. She had her children and her grandchildren and her charities and her friends and her faith now, too. She had no reason at all to feel so—so bored, so purposeless, and so invisible. That was the worst of it. A woman in her sixties ought not to be concerned with her looks, nor with her husband's waning interest.

Charlotte wandered over to the window, throwing it open to embrace the soft, late-afternoon light. In her mind, she stepped back onto her island, to the fresh smell of summer, the earth stirring, coming to life, ready to burst into bloom. A knock on the door forced her to abandon her reverie. She had hoped for another half hour of peace and quiet contemplation. The person at the door was not one of her staff, however, but her daughter.

Her heart sank, seeing Mary. Something had clearly gone wrong at the shoot. "Come in," Charlotte said, ushering her daughter to a chair.

Mary was twisting her clasped hands together, a sure sign that she was upset. "Mama, I'm afraid something dreadful has happened. No-one has been shot," she added hurriedly. "It's not that."

"Thank goodness," Charlotte said, her mind racing through the other possibilities. She could see Mary's toe tapping, another very rare sign of strong agitation. Was not the plan to go duck-shooting later?

She ought to have checked on Mary as soon as she returned from the kitchen gardens instead of daydreaming alone here in her bedchamber. "As long as everyone is safe, whatever it is can't be too awful," she said, wincing at her tone, for she sounded like one of those dreadfully patronising women talking down to a charity case.

"It is awful. So awful that I am not sure what can be done to limit the damage. That vile woman . . ."

"What vile woman?" Charlotte asked, with a sense of foreboding. This was not a case of a drunken guest or a disputed kill. Mary was as white as a sheet, too.

"Mrs. Fitzherbert-Smythe. She arrived when you were out with the other ladies, and she insisted on coming to the shoot." Mary caught sight of her tapping foot, and pushed it out of sight under her skirt. "Mrs. Fitzherbert-Smythe has lost her brooch. It is a most valuable item, an heirloom worth a small fortune," she said, capturing that woman's tone perfectly. "I am sure that she misplaced it, despite all her rantings about the catch being secure, but—but you should know that she has accused Stuart of stealing it."

"Do you mean Stuart Irvine?" Charlotte exclaimed.

"He was her loader, Mama. You know Stuart— there isn't a dishonest bone in his body, he would never, ever— Oh God, you should have seen his face when she accused him. And Mr. Irvine, too, he was mortified!"

"I should think he would be. Tell me the whole story from the start, if you please."

She listened with growing horror as the tale unfolded, cursing her own selfishness for having allowed her daughter to take on her duties. If only she had been there!

"I tried to calm her down, but she wouldn't listen," Mary said.

"When someone like Maria Fitzherbert-Smythe wants to cause a commotion, no-one can stop her." Certainly not poor Mary, Charlotte thought wretchedly, who would not, as they said, say boo to a goose.

"She was so determined to accuse Stuart of theft. But I insisted that she was mistaken."

"Did you?"

"She said that I was 'somewhat biased' and you would not be so quick to jump to Stuart's defence."

"And what did you say to that?" Charlotte asked, in some astonishment.

"That I was certain your reaction would have been identical to mine. That whatever had happened to her brooch, there was no question of Stuart stealing it," Mary said, her grey eyes flashing with anger. "Stuart is my *friend*. Surely, Mama, you are not going to say I was wrong to defend him?"

"No." Charlotte looked at her daughter askance. "No, you were quite right. Stuart is not a thief."

"She forced him to turn out his pockets. I tried to stop him, but Colonel Trefusis said it was better done straight away."

"In front of witnesses. A very sensible precaution," Charlotte said, struggling to picture the scene.

"Of course the brooch wasn't in his possession, but that woman was determined to blame Stuart all the same."

"What is happening now?"

"We cut short the shoot. Colonel Trefusis and Mr. Irvine are organizing a thorough search of the moor. Captain Beckman is escorting Mrs. Fitzherbert-Smythe back. I came ahead to warn you. I am so sorry, Mama. My father will be furious with you for trusting me to take charge."

"The duke left for Balmoral this afternoon." Without any notice, abandoning his own shooting party, Charlotte recalled, momentarily distracted. Simply expecting her to sweep up after him, as he always did! "He had urgent business to discuss with Her Majesty. I have no idea what."

"So there is a good chance this will all have blown over by the time he returns?"

"If he returns. Once Her Majesty has him at Balmoral— Oh, never mind the duke."

"But he's such a stickler, you said it yourself, and he wouldn't believe for a moment that I was capable—" Mary broke off, looking stricken. "I am so very sorry."

"Please, stop apologizing. If anyone is at fault, aside from Maria Fitzherbert-Smythe, it is the duke. It was his shoot, and he was not in attendance. You have handled a very difficult situation extremely well."

"It was Colonel Trefusis, really, who calmed things down."

"You did well, Mary. To stand your ground as you did—I confess, I didn't think you capable."

"Nor did I, but I couldn't stand by and let her malign Stuart like that. Mama, what if the brooch isn't found?"

The possibility was so appalling that Charlotte winced. "It will be, I am sure," she said, sounding entirely unconvincing. "If it isn't found, then our guest must accept that it has been lost. If she sees reason, I shall compensate her with a similar item from my own jewellery collection. From what you've described I am sure I have an equally garish brooch that my aunt Lucy gave me when I came of age."

"But then she'll assume that you are buying her silence."

"She would not be so indelicate as to say so," Charlotte said uncomfortably. "So you see, the matter will be resolved one way or another without having to involve the duke."

Mary dropped her gaze to her entwined hands. The knuckles were showing white. She hid them in the folds of her skirt. "What about Stuart?"

"What about Stuart?" Charlotte asked, her heart sinking. "I know the two of you have been close in the past, but . . ."

"He was my friend when I had no-one else, Mama. He deserves my loyalty."

It was a rebuke. A very gentle rebuke, but it was the first Mary had ever delivered. And it was well-deserved. Charlotte, as ever, resorted to dealing with the problem in hand. "He won't go to gaol, if that is what concerns you, once I have come to an accommodation with Mrs. Fitzherbert-Smythe."

To her shameful relief, her daughter seemed much more concerned with her friend than any further recriminations about the past. "Mud sticks," Mary said. "That woman has accused him of theft in front of your guests, his father, and a host of men from the estate. Someone will talk, and some people will choose to believe what is said. Besides, why should Stuart be any different from my father, mortified by the slur on his good name?"

"Oh, for goodness sake, Mary, you know perfectly well that the two cannot be compared. We may all be equal in the eyes of God, but in the eyes of the world . . ."

"The Buccleuch name must be protected, while Stuart's name can bear a few slurs! That isn't right."

Charlotte sighed wearily. This extraordinary conversation was exhausting. "No, it's not, but that's how it is. We will look after Stuart. If he decides he'd like a change of scenery, then I am sure we can find him a role at Boughton."

"It will look as if he's been sent there in disgrace."

"Mary! For goodness sake, it won't come to that." *Though it might,*

Charlotte acknowledged to herself, and Mary was right: it wasn't fair. She sighed inwardly. "One step at a time. Let us wait and hope for the brooch to be found. Now, I shall go and attend to our guest. I think I shall suggest that it is better for her nerves to dine in her room tonight."

"I think you would do better to suggest she packs her bags and never comes back."

"I confess, I'm tempted, but . . ."

"You can't," Mary said, looking utterly dejected. "I beg your pardon. I am so very, very sorry that the afternoon turned out as it did. Is there anything else I can do to help?"

"Stop apologizing, I beg you. This mess is not of your making. Let us hope that the brooch is found by the time dinner is served. Now off you go and have your bath."

The door closed on her daughter, and Charlotte sank back onto the chair in front of her desk. What on earth was she to do about Mary? Her own child was an enigma to her, which was going to make it horribly difficult to make up for all that pain she had glimpsed. Pain that she had inflicted, and which Mary had made it very easy for her to ignore. Who would have thought that quiet, shy, retiring young woman could speak out so fiercely on behalf of her friend? That at least was one thing she didn't need to worry about, thank goodness. Stuart Irvine was her *friend*. Charlotte smiled grimly to herself. Another of Mary's tacit messages: Don't worry, Mama.

Oh dear, but there were so many reasons to worry. Poor Mary. One of life's most painful lessons was accepting the injustice and inequality in the world. It was a lesson that Margaret still struggled with as did she herself, if it came to it. If only she really could escape to her little island, pull up the drawbridge, and keep the world at bay.

Alas! Charlotte picked up her diary and locked it away in the secret drawer at the side of her desk. Mary had proved herself useful, and clearly *wanted* to be useful. It would be a relief to have someone she could rely on, especially if Walter remained at Balmoral for a time, as she suspected he would. Perhaps, if she allowed Mary to shoulder some responsibility, it might even bring them closer. She pulled the bell to summon her maid. It might be a good idea to retrieve Aunt Lucy's brooch from her jewellery case. Just as a precaution.

CHAPTER SEVEN

Machinations

Drumlanrig Castle, Tuesday, 27 August 1872

THANK YOU FOR MEETING ME, Tre," Mary said, racing up the shallow flight of steps to the Heather House the next morning. "And more importantly, thank you for yesterday. I don't know what I'd have done if you hadn't been there."

"You would have managed perfectly well without me, as I told your mother last night. You have greatly exaggerated my role and minimized your own."

"You are very kind and very modest."

"Mary, the duchess was clearly very proud of you."

"She said I handled a difficult situation extremely well." Mary frowned down at her hands. "She didn't say she was proud of me, though, and I doubt she would have confided any such thing to you."

"Not in so many words," Tre replied. "She is of a generation and a class who are raised not to sing anyone's praises."

"She sings Margaret's. No, no, that was unworthy of me. I am sure Mama only sings Margaret's praises so loudly to me because she cannot voice them to anyone else."

"Shall we sit down?" Tre waited until she did so, then took a seat on the bench beside her. "You said you wanted to discuss yesterday's events. It seems to me, though, that the duchess has the situation well in hand."

"As far as Mrs. Fitzherbert-Smythe is concerned, she does. Everyone at dinner was delighted to accept that the brooch was lost, and my mother will bribe her with a brooch from her own collection. Though, of course," Mary added, curling her lip, "we must pretend it's not a bribe, it's a gift."

"It's a small price to pay for her silence, though, isn't it?"

"But the point is, Tre, she wasn't silent, was she?" Mary exclaimed indignantly. "She stood there in front of all those people and accused Stuart of stealing! And because he's *only* the head gamekeeper's son, then she will get away with it."

"Nothing is going to happen to Stuart Irvine. Aside from anything else, there's no evidence against him."

"But mud sticks. That's what I said to Mama yesterday. What about his good name? Why doesn't anyone care about that?"

"You obviously do, a great deal."

"He was my friend when I had no-one else. I said as much to my mother, who didn't take it well."

"She should have thought about it before now. She left you to fend for yourself when you were not much more than a child. She should be grateful that at least you had Stuart to befriend you."

"All she wants is to hush this whole stupid affair up, before my father returns, and that's what I want, too. Except . . ."

"Except it doesn't clear your friend's name."

Mary heaved a sigh. "Exactly. Thank you. I knew you'd understand. Unless the brooch is found, there will always be a tinge of suspicion hanging over him. That he is the head gamekeeper's son will make him a popular scapegoat in some quarters. Mr. Irvine is as honest as the day is long, but part of a gamekeeper's duties is to prevent poaching, and that, as you can imagine, doesn't exactly make him universally popular around here. My mother's solution to that is to pack Stuart off to Boughton."

"Packing a person off to another house and forgetting about them seems to be your mother's modus operandi."

"Tre!"

He shrugged. "It's the truth."

"Yes, but—I suppose it is. It sounds so shocking, though, when you say it like that."

"It *is* shocking." He pressed her hand briefly. "However, raking over the past isn't going to get us anywhere."

"What do you really think happened to that brooch? It was such a huge piece, and Mr. Irvine's men practically combed the entire moor and the tracks without success. I find it difficult to believe that it was simply dropped, don't you?"

"I do," he agreed reluctantly. "I spent half the night going over and over events after I spoke to Beckman last night. You're not going to like this, but he confessed that he took himself off for a cigar at one point during the afternoon shoot. His aim was out, he said, and he thought a smoke would calm his nerves. He was gone about fifteen, maybe twenty minutes at most, but your friend was alone with Mrs. Fitzherbert-Smythe for that time. If you are determined to pursue the matter, Mary, you're going to have to face the fact that there may be consequences you don't find palatable."

"You mean that by drawing attention to the fact that he had the opportunity, I'll be encouraging some people to believe him guilty? I don't want to make things worse for Stuart, I want to clear his name, but I don't want to undo all my mother's hard work in clearing up this mess either. What shall we do? Is there anything we *can* do without stirring up a hornet's nest and bringing my father back into the fray?"

"I must admit, I'm struggling to think of anything. Yet something isn't right. Why hasn't the blasted brooch been found? Because it's not meant to be found, is the obvious answer." Tre got up, digging his hands into his pockets. "If it wasn't Stuart Irvine, though . . ."

"Then it must have been Captain Beckman?"

"My instincts tell me he's honest."

"And I agree, but can we trust our instincts? We only met the man yesterday. He could have stolen the brooch and hidden it while he claims to have been having a smoke. And he did seem uncommonly keen to demonstrate he didn't have it about his person."

"A distraction tactic? I don't know."

"Wait! There's something else. Something Clara, my maid, said to me last night. I can't believe I've forgotten. The oddest thing. When one of the maids went to turn down Captain Beckman's bed, while we were all at dinner, the door was locked."

"There could have been a perfectly legitimate reason for that."

"Yes: that he has something to hide. A stolen brooch, perhaps?" Mary jumped to her feet. "We need to check if he locks it again when he comes down for breakfast, and if it is still locked, we need to break in."

"For God's sake! We can't—"

"Not both of us. Me. If I can get hold of the housekeeper's keys, then I won't need to actually break the lock, though that may prove tricky, for she keeps them on a chatelaine attached to her belt."

"Mary! You are jumping to all sorts of conclusions."

"I'm not! Well, perhaps I am, but if Stuart didn't do it—and we know he didn't because that horrible woman made him turn out his pockets. And if we can prove that it wasn't Captain Beckman either, then where does that leave us?"

"I don't know. Perhaps the blasted thing really was lost. Let's concentrate on eliminating Beckman before we worry about that, and let us do it as discreetly as possible."

"You don't need to caution me on that front, I promise you. We can't risk letting anyone else know that we are still suspicious, for Stuart's and Captain Beckman's sake. Does that mean you're going to help me?"

"I'll help, but I'm not breaking into Beckman's bedroom. I'll have a word with him later this morning, see if I can find out why he keeps his room locked, without arousing his suspicions."

"What will I do?"

"Have a little patience?"

"The problem is that if we eliminate Stuart and Captain Beckman, that leaves us—Tre!" She clutched his arm. "The lady herself."

"Why would she steal her own brooch?"

"'It's an heirloom, worth a small fortune. The rubies are particularly rare.'"

"You have a real talent for mimicry," Tre said, laughing. "Good lord, though, do you seriously think . . . Surely she wouldn't dare? If Stuart Irvine was arrested—but then without the brooch, the authorities would be unlikely to pursue the case."

"Unlikely, but it is not certain!"

"Remember what I said about jumping to conclusions."

"I know." Mary fought for control, her hands furling into fists. "I know, I must not, but if it is true . . ."

"The scandal doesn't bear thinking of," Tre said grimly. "I doubt even someone as influential as your father would be able to keep it out of the papers."

"Oh, dear heavens! That was the most unforgivable aspect of Margaret's breaking her engagement so publicly. It was in all the papers, and my father . . ." Mary sat down abruptly on the bench, aghast. "Mrs. Fitzherbert-Smythe must have been counting on that all along. She must have known that my mother would do everything in her power to hush the matter up. And now she has not one but two brooches!"

"Mary, for heaven's sake, this is only speculation. We don't know it was her." Tre sat back down beside her, frowning heavily. "We have absolutely no evidence."

"The brooch must be somewhere. You said it yourself earlier. If it hasn't been found, it's because someone doesn't want it to be found. She must have hidden it."

"Even if by some miracle we found it, though, what could we do without causing a scandal? Your father's good opinion of me matters a great deal to the men who have offered me this new role."

"I didn't think of that. I shouldn't have involved you."

"I'm not going to abandon you now. We're in this together."

"No, no, no, you can't—oh curse that woman! If it were not for Stuart, I would happily leave her and her horrible heirloom to live happily ever after together. Though of course she's probably going to sell it at the first opportunity."

"I wonder what she needs the money for."

"Something she wants to keep from her husband, presumably. What shall we do?"

"Let us take it one step at a time. We'll eliminate Beckman from our enquiry, and then . . ."

"The maid! Of course! I should have thought of that. A ladies' maid always knows everything about her mistress and, more importantly, her clothes. If the brooch was not stolen but hidden—that's it!" Mary jumped to her feet. "You talk to Captain Beckman, and I will talk to

Mrs. Fitzherbert-Smythe's maid. Discreetly, I promise you. I shall do it at breakfast, when she is putting her mistress's room to rights."

"I'm not sure that's a good idea."

"It is an excellent idea. I shall think of some excuse, and be very, very careful. I have no more desire than you to have my father's wrath descend on me."

"My real worry is what we'll do if we discover we're right."

"Nothing, if it means a scandal, or it puts your future in danger. I could not be responsible for either of those, not even for Stuart," Mary said. "Let's take your own advice, and proceed one step at a time, shall we?"

CHAPTER EIGHT

Lady Mary Investigates

Drumlanrig Castle, Wednesday, 28 August 1872

Mrs. Fitzherbert-Smythe was not an early riser. Mary had plenty of time, as she spun out her own breakfast, to question whether she was capable of going through with her plan, never mind whether or not it would work. The weight of responsibility made her feel sick. Would it be better to let the matter rest? Mrs. Fitzherbert-Smythe would be delighted if she did. Her mother would be spared any further friction. Her father would never know about the affair at all. But Stuart would be left with a cloud hanging over him. It wasn't fair! And if she didn't try, then she'd have failed. And Tre—no, Tre wouldn't judge her harshly or even at all. He was the only person who had ever looked beyond the dormouse. Was there another creature hidden inside her, a braver person, a more confident person? One thing for sure, she had never felt less like a lioness in her life.

Mary toyed with a slice of bread while, at the head of the table, her mother was conducting the breakfast conversation, ensuring that all the guests had something to occupy them for the day. Tre was drinking black coffee and eating what was for him a hearty breakfast of two boiled eggs and a roll, casting her the occasional encouraging smile.

"Good morning, Your Grace. You will be pleased to know that I slept well after our little chat." Mrs. Fitzherbert-Smythe stalked into the dining room and Tre leapt to his feet to offer her the seat he had kept free between himself and Captain Beckman. She gave him a tight smile, obviously still resentful of his tone at the shoot, but the captain was treated to a simper.

"I will take coffee," she said, in reply to Urquhart's questioning look. "And I will have some hot rolls, eggs, devilled kidneys, and a kipper."

The duchess hated the lingering smell of kippers and never served them, and another guest had most inconsiderately eaten the last of the devilled kidneys. As the butler offered kedgeree, sausages, and liver instead, Captain Beckman poured Mrs. Fitzherbert-Smythe a cup of coffee, a footman offered the rolls, and the duchess recommenced her interrupted conversation about the efficacy of milk for the treatment of aphids on roses. Mary muttered her excuses and rose from the table.

"Good luck," Tre mouthed as she passed his chair.

She felt light-headed as she raced up the spiral staircase to her own bedchamber on the second floor to change hurriedly into a new day dress of powder-blue silk before taking a moment to stop and go over the plan they had carefully constructed together. Why was Tre so intent on helping her when it would be so much easier and safer for him and his own future to do nothing? Something wasn't quite right, he'd said. He shared her disgust at the way Stuart had been used, but Stuart wasn't his friend. Was it for her?

What on earth did Tre see in her? She had no idea, but he did see her, she knew that, in a way that no-one else did. Was it possible that he was attracted to her? The way he looked at her sometimes, those looks she'd told herself she must have imagined or misinterpreted—oh for heaven's sake, what on earth was she doing asking herself such momentous questions now!

The overskirt of her gown was liberally adorned with a dark-blue beaded fringe. With the aid of her pocket knife, Mary cut the first few tiny stitches, before ripping a stretch of it ruthlessly free, then made good her escape, back down the spiral staircase to the first floor, where Mrs. Fitzherbert-Smythe had a bedchamber in the west wing. She tapped lightly on the door and peered in. To her relief, Mrs. Fitzherbert-Smythe's personal maid was there, sitting at the dressing table where a plethora of jars and bottles were scattered over the surface. "Excuse me."

"Oh!" The maid jumped to her feet and dropped a curtsy. She was a stern-looking woman who could be anywhere between forty and fifty, dressed in a plain, iron-grey gown which matched her hair. "I am afraid my mistress is at breakfast."

"It was you I was looking for actually," Mary said, closing the door behind her and smiling bashfully. "I hope you don't think me too presumptuous, but I was trying on this new gown, and I have somehow managed to tear the beading. I wondered if you would be good enough to mend it for me?"

"Surely your maid . . ."

"I would rather she didn't know," Mary said, lowering her eyes and making a silent apology to Clara. "I should have waited for her to help dress me, but I was so excited to try my new gown on. My mother has asked me to escort the ladies on a shopping trip to Dumfries. I wanted to look especially well since I shall be her deputy, which is a huge responsibility. And now look what I've done in my hurry. I'm so terribly clumsy, I can't imagine how I ripped this."

"Let me take a look." The maid frowned. "It looks to me as if the stitching wasn't quite finished off properly. A poor job, if you don't mind my saying so, but it won't take me a minute to fix."

"Oh thank you—it's Smith, isn't it? I'm Lady Mary."

"Yes, my lady, I know."

"'Mary, Mary, quite contrary.'"

"Which I am sure you are not, my lady."

"Thank you. I don't think I am. Or am I?" She waited, but the maid either had no sense of humour, or else her joke was decidedly poor. The latter, most likely. Calm down. Stick to the plan. Flatter her. Don't rush in. Take your time. Gain her confidence. She could hear Tre's voice in her head.

"You know," Mary said, "I couldn't help but notice Mrs. Fitzherbert-Smythe's hair. Such a beautiful rich colour, for a woman of her age. She is very fortunate. I don't think I'll be so lucky. My mother has some silver in her hair."

"The duchess looks most distinguished," Smith said, her eyes on the needle she was threading.

"Yes, but silver is so very aging, isn't it? I mean, Mama and Mrs. Fitzherbert-Smythe are about the same age, I believe, yet your mistress looks years younger," Mary said, with another mental apology, this time to her mother.

"Her Grace has a natural beauty. My mistress requires rather more in the way of assistance. Now, if you would stand on this little stool it will make it easier for me to—that's perfect, thank you."

"Mrs. Fitzherbert-Smythe is fortunate in her choice of lady's maid if I read you correctly, Smith. To enhance what nature has provided, I mean."

"Especially when nature has not been very generous." Smith, reattaching the fringe with perfect, tiny stitches, smiled thinly.

"Really? My goodness, you'll be telling me next that her complexion is not naturally flawless."

"Well now, my lady, I'm flattered to hear you say so, for that is exactly the impression we like to give."

"You are a woman of many talents. A magician as well as a seamstress. What an asset you must be. Mrs. Fitzherbert-Smythe must be on tenterhooks that you might succumb to one of the lures that must surely be constantly cast your way."

Smith snipped the thread, her expression hardening. "There, that should hold properly now, my lady."

"Oh thank you. You stitch quite beautifully. I am extremely grateful." And disappointed. Mary slid the guinea without much hope into the maid's hand.

Instead of discreetly palming the coin, Smith stared at it for enough time to allow Mary to panic. "You have done me a great favour, I didn't mean to offend you."

"No, it's not that. It's very generous of you," Smith said, tucking the coin away. "The thing is, you see, I haven't been paid since I started with her. So I'm very grateful, my lady."

"Good grief," Mary exclaimed, genuinely shocked, for one of her mother's cast-in-stone tenets was to always pay her staff and her bills on time. "How long ago was that?"

"A year next month. I'm only staying with her until she gives me what I'm owed."

"She owes you a whole year's wages! Granted, you have a roof over your head and food on the table, but that doesn't mean you don't have a whole host of personal obligations."

"Well, my lady, you are very much in the right of it," Smith replied bitterly. "I haven't been able to send more than a few scraps of my savings to my mother."

"Would you like me to have a discreet word with my mother?" Mary asked, forgetting all about the plan she had agreed with Tre in her concern. "Though she is perfectly happy with her own maid, the duchess has a number of friends who I am sure would be delighted to employ a woman of your talents."

"Thank you, my lady, you are very kind but it's not necessary. I already have a position lined up. I should not have mentioned my troubles to you, it was very indiscreet of me, but you caught me at a low ebb."

"My goodness, I am not surprised."

"As I said, I shouldn't have been so indiscreet. My mistress has assured me that she will be in a position to pay me within the next week or so. All being well, I shall be with my new employer next month, October at the latest."

"That is excellent news for you, and you may rest assured that I will not mention this to anyone."

"I appreciate that, my lady."

"You have saved me from Clara's wrath by repairing this gown, Smith. I owe you a great deal."

"It was nothing, my lady. I am happy to have been of assistance to you."

"I am sure Mrs. Fitzherbert-Smythe will find you difficult to replace," Mary said, trying to buy herself a little more time

Smith smiled sourly. "Or impossible, more like. I'm the second maid she's lost in a short period."

"Really?" *Really!* "What—may I ask—do you mind telling me what you mean by that?"

She all but held her breath while Smith mulled this over before shrugging. "I don't see why not. The last maid left under a cloud, is what I was told at the time. Stole a necklace from the mistress, apparently.

Perhaps she did. If she hadn't been paid, same as me—of course I don't condone it, my lady, but you can understand it."

Appalled, for she was now sure she understood all too well, Mary felt sick, not with nerves but with fury and disgust. "What happened to her?" she asked, desperately trying not to let her feelings show. "Was she sent to gaol?"

To her relief, Smith shook her head. "From what I understand, the mistress thought it was punishment enough to dismiss her without a reference. Which it was, I suppose, if I'm right, and she was owed."

Though if Mary was right, the poor woman had been left with neither a character nor any compensation. The sound of footsteps in the corridor made them both gaze anxiously at the door, but they went slowly past without stopping.

It was time to go. "Thank you again, Smith, you have been truly invaluable." Quickly checking that the corridor was clear, Mary slipped out and fled to her room.

CHAPTER NINE

Accusations

Drumlanrig Castle, Thursday, 29 August 1872

A T BREAKFAST, THE DUCHESS READ out a telegram from her husband informing his guests that he would be unavoidably detained
at Balmoral until early the next week. Unfortunately Her Majesty also
required the duchess to join him as soon as possible. This meant that the
party would break up tomorrow, with Saturday's shoot cancelled, along
with Friday's expedition to the little market town of Moffat. Today's entertainment, she was pleased to say, would proceed as planned, with bowling and tennis this morning and an archery competition this afternoon.

AN HOUR LATER, MARY STOOD in the shelter of the long low pavilion
which formed one end of the rose garden, watching Tre attempting to
coax Pug into retrieving a ball. Tre hadn't noticed her yet. The dog had
been an unwanted gift to the duchess some years ago, and the two had
taken each other in mutual dislike. Pug was cared for by one of the
grooms and was supposed to live in the stables, but he was forever escaping in search of Urquhart, the butler, the only person at Drumlanrig
who found the fat, slobbery animal endearing.

Tre threw the ball again and Pug sauntered after it, very much with the air of a dog doing a man a favour. *We are in this together*, Tre had said when they arranged to meet here this morning. He didn't mean anything by it, save that they were united in their efforts to prove Stuart blameless and to ensure that horrible woman did not use and abuse anyone else in future. *We are in this together*. He didn't mean anything more than that, but no-one had ever said that to her before.

Tired or bored with the game, Pug wandered off to burrow his corpulent body into the soft soil of one of the rose beds. Mary waved, and Tre smiled, making his way down the path to join her.

"I didn't see you there," Tre said.

"You and Pug seemed to be having fun. I didn't want to disturb you. Tre, I know you said yesterday that we needed to be cautious, but now that the party is breaking up . . ."

"I agree, if we don't do something now, we'll have missed our opportunity."

"So you still think that after what I discovered from Smith, we've reached the right conclusion?"

"I'm afraid so. I spoke to Beckman. There's not been time to tell you and no time now to explain, but his locked bedroom door has nothing to do with this so-called crime. I fear we've no alternative but to confront the woman and, if she denies it, to find some way of tricking her into a confession."

"There's so much we don't know, though," Mary said. "Why didn't Mrs. Fitzherbert-Smythe do the obvious thing, have the brooch copied in paste before she sold the original?"

"It's an heirloom," Tre said wryly. "I suppose there's a good chance that her husband would notice. Besides, it's clear from what you gleaned yesterday that she doesn't give a damn about casting aspersions on people like your friend Stuart."

"Or her previous maid," Mary said grimly.

"So we are agreed: we have to put a stop to her because if we don't, she'll very likely use the same trick on another unsuspecting member of the lower classes the next time she's in need of funds. You know, there is still one other option, Mary."

She shook her head vehemently. "Poor Mama has more than enough on her plate at the moment; and if we tell her, then she'll be obliged to inform my father, and—oh, we've been over all this."

"Very well, then, a confrontation it shall be. I think it will be best if it's just one of us," Tre said, touching her shoulder lightly.

She covered his hand with hers briefly. "I know you're not going to like this, Tre, but it has to be me."

"No," he said flatly, snatching his hand away.

"Listen to me. We know what she's done but we can't prove it. We can lie, pretend that we have evidence, but if we fail to convince her and she sticks to her story, we'll have no option but to let her get away with it."

"I don't see why that means it must be you, and not I, who confronts her."

"Even if she denies everything, she'll want to protect herself. I know I would, in her shoes. There's a good chance she'll tell my mother she has been accused, and my mother will then almost certainly feel obliged to inform my father. So if it's you who confronts Mrs. Fitzherbert-Smythe . . ."

"The duke will wonder what the devil I'm doing, confronting his guests with unfounded allegations when one of the key elements of the role I'm up for is discretion," Tre said, blanching.

"Exactly. Therefore it can't be you, which means it has to be me."

"I don't like it."

"I don't like it either, but that woman has used and abused my mother's hospitality in the most underhand, vile way. Whether she took advantage of me, too—my being in charge of the shoot, I mean—assuming that she could cow me into accepting her accusations against Stuart is a moot point."

"She certainly under-estimated you," Tre said, looking troubled, "which might work to your advantage."

"I am also, if I say so myself, a good judge of character. I honed my skill observing the marital merry-go-round of the London Season. I'll know if she is lying when I confront her."

"Don't be flippant, Mary. This is extremely serious."

"I know it is. I'm not taking it lightly."

They were still in the shadow of the pavilion. He clasped her hand between his, studying her face intently. "It will be tricky. We can agree on a script, but if she doesn't stick to her part, then you're going to have to think on your feet. You've proved you can do that when you were talking to the maid, your instincts are sound, but Mrs. Fitzherbert-Smythe will be a very different proposition."

"You think she'll try to intimidate me?"

"Browbeat, threaten, harangue."

"So you don't think I can pull it off?"

"I wish there was another way, that's all, so you didn't have to put yourself through this ordeal. I don't doubt you can do it, Mary, not for a minute." Tre lifted her hand to his lips. "What you need to ask yourself is, do *you* think you can?"

MARY'S NOTE HAD ASKED MRS. Fitzherbert-Smythe to meet her at noon in the summer house, which was at the opposite end of the gardens from the bowling green. It was much plainer than the Heather House from the outside, though inside, the walls were a mosaic of wood which was meant to represent a basket of flowers, but which Mary privately thought bore more of a resemblance to a patchwork quilt.

She and Tre arrived ten minutes before the appointed time and waited inside, where the doorway and the front windows gave them an excellent view of the approach. "She's coming," Mary hissed, spotting the tall, sparse figure of Mrs. Fitzherbert-Smythe picking her way along the woodland pathway towards them. "Oh, dear heavens, she's coming."

"There's still time to change your mind."

"No, I'm going through with it. I can do it." Mary smoothed her gloves and straightened the bow of her bonnet. "I'll get a sense very quickly if we have this all wrong, and find a way to back out. If she is lying or posturing, I'll know."

"Put yourself in her shoes if she does. You've already proved you can do that. Try to keep a step ahead of her."

"And remember the power of silence. I know. Now you'd better make yourself scarce before she spots you. No, don't go out the door, you'll have to climb . . ."

But Tre had already leapt with surprising grace through the arched window frame. "Good luck."

He disappeared behind the window, leaving her momentarily alone. And utterly terrified. Mary sat down on the circular bench which ran all the way around the summer house, positioning herself in the centre of the back wall.

This was going to have to be the performance of a lifetime. If things went wrong—but they would not. She could not allow herself to think that way. Tre believed she could do this. She believed she could do this. She *would* do it! She must remain calm, and play the part they had rehearsed, and—and it was too late now, for here she was.

"Mrs. Fitzherbert-Smythe," Mary said, getting to her feet. "Thank you so much for coming."

"Lady Mary. I must confess I was most surprised to receive your note. I presume, when you requested my discretion, that you did not wish your mother to know, and that it is therefore something to do with that gamekeeper's son you are so fond of."

"I have known Stuart all my life, but there is nothing in our friendship that my mother would object to," Mary said, immediately placed on the back foot by this very direct attack.

"Such friendships must always be of a concern to a mother when a young lady is out in Society. Even a duke's daughter, as your mother knows only too well, is not immune from the stain of scandal. However," Mrs. Fitzherbert-Smythe continued with a condescending smile, "your mother and I have between us agreed to let the matter drop. I am happy to reassure you that I will not be pressing charges against your friend."

"Without any evidence, I doubt you would succeed, even if you wished to," Mary said pointedly. "Shall we sit down?"

"I have been most magnanimous in the matter," Mrs. Fitzherbert-Smythe said, frowning. "Your mother . . ."

"Is, like almost everyone else, labouring under a misapprehension."

"What do you mean?"

"She believes that the brooch has been misplaced. You and I know, however, that it has been stolen. Won't you sit down?"

Mrs. Fitzherbert-Smythe remained standing. "You have changed your tune, young woman. You were quite adamant that the boy . . ."

"Oh, I don't mean that Stuart stole it. I never thought that for a moment. I did wonder about Captain Beckman."

"An officer in Her Majesty's army! Certainly not!"

"No, I am as sure of that as you are, but for a different reason, which is none of your concern," Mary said, her confidence growing as the woman glaring at her became defensive. "It wasn't Stuart or Captain Beckman who took the brooch. It was you, wasn't it?"

"I! How dare you!"

Mrs. Fitzherbert-Smythe sat down on the bench. If she was innocent, she'd have walked away in disgust by now, threatening to inform the duchess, but she sat down. She was as guilty as sin.

"I dare because I know it's the truth," Mary replied with barely a tremor in her voice. "Why on earth did you wear the brooch to the shoot? That's what I simply couldn't understand from the outset."

There was no need for Mrs. Fitzherbert-Smythe to justify her actions, but she chose to. "I prefer to keep that particular brooch close. It is an heirloom, and means a great deal to me. I have been quite devastated by the loss."

"And your husband, too, I expect he will be devastated."

"Of course he will be. The piece is extremely valuable."

"So valuable that if you were careless enough to lose it—and on a grouse-moor, of all places—I imagine your husband would be very angry with you."

"The catch was secure. I had it checked. The brooch wasn't lost."

"Because you couldn't risk your husband's ire. That's why you had to claim it was stolen and to place the blame on someone in no position to defend themselves. Such as a gamekeeper's son." Or a maid, Mary added to herself.

"I think you have been out in the sun too long. This tone you are taking with me, your manner, hurling these wild accusations around. Perhaps I should go to your mother, inform the duchess how her daughter speaks to her guests."

Feeling as if she was standing on the edge of a precipice, Mary smiled politely. "Please do. I will be happy to accompany you."

Mrs. Fitzherbert-Smythe pulled off one of her gloves, studied her wedding ring, and then put the glove back on. "Well now, there is no need for that. This has all been a misunderstanding, a—a figment of your imagination, though I have no idea how you reached such a conclusion. However," she said, preparing to rise, "I am sure you did not mean to upset me. If you will apologize, then we will consider the matter closed."

"I'm not sorry. I know you faked the theft of the brooch."

Mrs. Fitzherbert-Smythe sat down again. Mary clasped her hands together, recalling Tre's advice. Seconds passed that felt like hours. She curled her toes tightly together to stop herself from tapping her feet, and began to count in her head.

"What evidence do you have to back up that extraordinary accusation?"

She had reached twenty-six. "I searched your room. I know where you hid it."

"You cannot have. I know for a fact that it is still— What I mean is, I cannot believe that you would dare rifle through my personal belongings without my express permission."

Mary said nothing.

"You are merely speculating wildly."

The first time that Mrs. Fitzherbert-Smythe had spoken the truth, albeit unwittingly. Mary began to count again. This time she only reached fifteen.

"I have never been so insulted in my life."

She wasn't going to admit to anything, but she wasn't making any attempt to leave. "I didn't ask you here to trade insults," Mary said carefully. "I asked you here because I believe there is a way out of this situation that allows you to save face."

"Not that I am admitting to anything, far from it," Mrs. Fitzherbert-Smythe said warily, "but the last thing I wish is to cause trouble."

"You have caused a great deal of trouble already."

"Your mother's intervention has already brought a satisfactory end to the matter."

"But it's not satisfactory." You are a thief and a liar, Mary thought.

Don't antagonize her if you can avoid it. Tre's words. He was right. "You have cast a slur on an innocent young man," she said. "Until your brooch is recovered, that slur will remain."

"So it is all about that boy after all!"

"It is also about the fact that you have taken advantage of my parents' hospitality, and taken a very valuable gift from my mother under false pretences. Last but not least, it is about the fact that if you get away with your ruse this time, you are almost certain to try it again, and next time your victim may not be so lucky."

"So you are setting yourself up as judge and jury!"

"No, I'm simply trying to right the wrongs you have committed."

"How on earth do you propose to do that, pray?"

"I want you to go back to the castle," Mary said. "Retrieve the brooch from its hiding place and tell my mother you have just found it."

"Preposterous. Found it where?"

"I don't care where. Make something up, you have a fertile enough imagination."

"I will look like a fool."

"Better a fool than a liar and a thief. I am offering you the opportunity to retain your reputation. If you clear Stuart now and offer him your abject apology, you have my word that the matter is closed."

Mrs. Fitzherbert-Smythe bristled. "I will do as you say, but I am not going to apologize to that boy!"

"I'm afraid that's non-negotiable, and it's the very least you can do. I will keep the content of this conversation to myself, but I warn you, if I ever hear that you have attempted to repeat your odious trick, I will speak up." Mary got to her feet. "Do we have an agreement?"

"Lady Mary and the Case of the Missing Heirloom," Mrs. Fitzherbert-Smythe said sardonically, ignoring her outstretched hand. "What a shame you can't boast of your achievement."

"It is a secret I am more than happy to keep, if you adhere to our terms."

She didn't need to begin counting again. Mrs. Fitzherbert-Smythe nodded. "You are intriguing. I have under-estimated you, something I rarely do. It is a useful quality. You should cultivate it."

When she had gone, Mary sank onto the bench with a huge shuddering sigh. Shaking, she took several minutes to regain control of herself before getting to her feet and setting off purposefully in the direction of the castle.

CHAPTER TEN

A Heart to Heart

IT WOULD BE PREMATURE TO celebrate until Mrs. Fitzherbert-Smythe had fulfilled her side of the bargain. Exhausted by the confrontation and feeling deflated rather than triumphant, Mary had no time to reflect on her success, as her mother had tasked her with organizing the archery competition. Accordingly, she rushed to the bowling green, where the targets were already being set up while lunch was being served at the castle. The targets, consisting of concentric rings with an "inner" at the centre, were placed at regulation distances, as required by the official rules of the sport. A long table was laden with a selection of bows, belts, and quivers along with gauntlets and finger guards for those guests who had not brought their own equipment.

The competition would follow the well-established York Round format, which specified the number of arrows each participant would release at the targets. For the gentlemen, these were set out at sixty, eighty, and one hundred yards, while the ladies shot at targets set fifty and sixty yards distant. Her mother would award the prizes, the traditional arrow incorporated into the Buccleuch shield, one in silver for the lady victor and gold for the gentleman.

Her sister Margaret had found the sport tedious beyond belief, but Victoria, Mary's eldest sister, excelled at it, and had a collection of little silver arrows she had won in various competitions over the years. Though Mary had an excellent eye and unfailingly hit the inner, even from the farthest distance, she found the repetitive nature of the competition rounds tedious. She was making her final checks of the targets when the first of the competitors arrived and began to arm themselves. Practice shots were fired. Captain Beckman, who had apparently once given the Grand National champion a close match, volunteered to act as scorer. The rest of the guests had seated themselves on the wooden garden chairs arranged safely at the edge of the bowling green, but there was no sign of the duchess. Or of Mrs. Fitzherbert-Smythe, Mary noted. Nor Tre either. Butterflies began to flutter in her tummy. She resolutely ignored them, called everyone to order, and the competition began.

It was a full twenty minutes later that her mother arrived and instead of joining the spectators, made straight for Mary. "A word, if you please," she said.

Her heart sank as she followed the duchess to the far side of the bowling green. She should have known something would go wrong. Her first impulse was to apologize immediately, but she remembered, just in time, Tre's advice about the value of silence.

"I see you have everything in hand with the competition," the duchess said. "You have been a great help to me these last few days with your father away, and I know it doesn't come naturally to you, to be the centre of attention."

"No, but I like to be useful."

"Yes. More useful than you would have me know," her mother said wryly. "Mrs. Fitzherbert-Smythe has just been to see me."

Mary's mouth went dry. "She has?"

"Remarkably, her brooch has turned up. It was in the inside pocket of the coat she wore to the shoot. She had completely forgotten, she said, that she had put it there for safekeeping. What do you think of that? I wonder."

That the blasted woman could have tried a little bit harder to come up with a more plausible explanation was Mary's first thought. Her second was that her mother smelled a rat. "Really! That is wonderful news."

"You don't sound particularly surprised. It's strange, isn't it," her mother continued without giving her a chance to answer, "that her maid didn't discover it before now."

"Surely the most important thing is that it has been found? It means that Stuart is off the hook."

"Mrs. Fitzherbert-Smythe informed me that she owed Stuart Irvine an apology. She has gone in search of him now."

"I wish I could watch her delivering it."

Her mother's mouth twitched. "I don't know how you managed to persuade her to act as she did. It was you, though, wasn't it?"

Mary opened her mouth to deny it, then closed it again. She had succeeded. They had succeeded, she and Tre. Her mother had guessed only half of it.

"Your silence speaks volumes," the duchess said. "Our guest is leaving to catch the train in an hour. An urgent summons from her husband, she tells me, though I was not aware that any telegram had been delivered. You need not fear that I will do anything to undo your efforts. I told her to keep the brooch I gave her and to consider it a gift, so no-one will be any the wiser. Not even the duke. Or I should say, especially not the duke, for it was he you wished to spare, I assume."

To Mary's astonishment, her mother pulled her into a tight embrace.

"I am very proud of you. And," she added, releasing her, "I must admit somewhat confounded."

Two people confounded in the space of a few days, Mary thought, thinking of Tre. "I enjoyed it, although it was unknown territory for me. I can only say that, now that it's all worked out for the best. I didn't expect you to guess. I feel as if I've done something useful. Not like helping with the shoot, or this competition, but something that matters. Oh, I don't mean they don't matter—"

"You're right," her mother interrupted dryly. "They don't, not in any real sense."

"Mama! That is practically heresy!"

"Yes, I suppose it is. Don't look at me like that, Mary. I'm not taking leave of my senses but rather coming to them. Today has proved that I barely know you, far less understand you. We are not close, and that is almost entirely my fault. This is not the time for such a conversation, but there never seems to be a right time. I abandoned you here, and neglected you for Margaret, and now I am summoned to Balmoral and must leave you again."

"I'll still be here when you return."

"Yes, but what then, that is the question. I thought that you would enjoy London, but you hated every moment of it, did you not?"

"I don't wish to have a husband found for me."

"And I have no intention of forcing one upon you. I thought that was so obvious it didn't need saying. Another thing I got wrong, it seems."

A cry of delight and a smattering of applause made them both look round. The conversation was so very strange, it made the competition being played out in the distance look like a painting. "What about my father?" Mary asked.

"I don't know. I had better go and watch the last few rounds," the duchess said. "I wonder if I might take a leaf out of Her Majesty's book, and tell the duke that I would like to keep you by my side, as a companion in my winter years."

"Like poor Princess Beatrice, you mean? You're not old, Mama."

"On days like today, I feel every one of my years. I really must go and join our guests now. I'm sorry there is no time for us to talk properly. When I return from Balmoral."

"I will be here." The sense she'd had of a change beginning to develop between them burst like a bubble. Waiting? As her mother hurried across the grass, Mary noticed Tre standing on the perimeter of the party. They had done it! They had righted several wrongs, and they may even have prevented another being done in the future. Whatever happened now, she was done with waiting.

CHAPTER ELEVEN

The Slings and Arrows of Outrageous Fortune

I T WAS LIKE A FOG creeping up on him, a grey mist insidiously enveloping his brain, squeezing it so painfully that the backs of his eyes ached. He couldn't pin down when it had started. When leaving Mary to face that woman in the summer house alone? The waiting, wondering how the confrontation had unfolded. The growing doubts that the confidence he had shown in her had been misplaced. He told himself that she would have overcome her stage fright and given a virtuoso performance just as she had on the parapet when he had first set eyes on her. He castigated himself for doubting her. It felt like a betrayal.

Mary wouldn't fail. She reminded him of the more subdued of his men, who had none of the bravado displayed by others as they prepared to go into battle. The men who were quietly terrified; who understood exactly what they were facing; who braced themselves for the test; and who, when the call came, always rose to the occasion. Those were the men who he could most rely on under enemy fire. The silently brave. The unrewarded heroes. Exactly like Mary.

Should he have refused to have become embroiled from the start in what was a tricky but essentially domestic situation? It was too late for that now. As events unfolded, he'd been as furious as she at the injustice they had uncovered, and even more at the abuse of power at the heart of the crime. But it was Mary who had drawn him into it. From that first sighting he'd had of her up on the parapet, then shortly afterwards transformed into the demure woman at the dinner table, he had been—fascinated? Intrigued? Enthralled? Despite the dormouse she was to everyone else, the subversive, rebellious, crusader spirit inside her resonated strongly with him. She made him laugh, throw off the restraints he'd placed on himself, become the man he had been once and had almost forgotten existed. She'd made him forget that he was damaged. Broken. He had flippantly said she was a balm to his fevered brow after seeing her on the parapet had cleared his headache. He now realized it was true. She was good for his soul. He had not permitted himself to imagine she could be more than that, but he had come close, dangerously close, to crossing the boundaries of propriety, surrendering to the temptation to kiss her. Thank the stars he never had.

Now he never would. Now his curse was back, taking vicious root, worsening with every arrow that whistled through the air to embed itself with a dull thump into targets of the archery competition. Like a bullet piercing human flesh, a sickening sound he would never forget. Worse still was the haunting, brief silence that followed, before being broken by the sound of screaming.

What had brought it on this time? He had no idea. None at all. Tre swore under his breath. The truth of the matter was that he never did. Every time he thought he'd got to the root of it, he proved himself wrong. Was it the sound of the arrows thudding home? But it had started earlier. He didn't know.

Retreat! He knew he should obey the clarion call. Leave now, make for his room, lock the door, hide away until it passed. But on the other side of the bowling green there was Mary in conversation with her mother, and he didn't want to retreat. He had found sanctuary in her company that first night at Drumlanrig. If he could talk to her, walk with her, the mist would clear and spare him the embarrassment of fleeing to his room like a frightened child. Spare him the lies he'd have to tell. Spare him the excuses he'd have to invent. Spare him the burning shame.

At last, the duchess and her daughter had ended their tête-à-tête. If the conversation with the Fitzherbert-Smythe woman had gone badly, or if they had been just plain wrong, Mary would be in very hot water. But, no, the two women were smiling. And Mary, to his utter relief, was making her way towards him.

"We did it," she whispered gleefully. "It was the most nerve-racking and difficult thing I've ever done in my life, but that horrible woman is apologizing to Stuart even as we speak, and her maid is packing her clothes. They leave within the hour. Oh, jolly well done," she added loudly, joining the applause as the last of the ladies fired two bull's-eyes in a row.

Only one more round to go, from the last of the gentlemen, and the competition would be over. Tre averted his eyes from the target, but each arrow he heard land felt like a hot needle behind his eyes. "Your mother—you were talking to her for quite a while."

"Yes. Are you all right, Tre? You are very pale."

"One of my headaches. It will pass," he said with grim determination. "Was the duchess surprised that the brooch had been found?"

"Actually, she guessed that I had something to do with it, on account of Stuart. Don't worry, she has no idea of your involvement, and she's sticking by the story we came up with."

"Well done."

"She finally said she was proud of me, too, and that she had neglected me, and that she would speak to my father, try to protect me from any efforts he might make to marry me off."

"Really? That sounds like a very momentous conversation to have in the middle of an archery competition."

"There was no time for it to be had elsewhere," Mary said with a twisted smile. "She is off to Balmoral, remember? I have been a great help to her, but my father and our queen need her now, so it's back to hibernation for me."

"Mary . . ."

"Except I am done with that, Tre. I don't know what I am going to do, so don't ask me, but I need to do something. I understand what you mean now, completely, about whatever your new opportunity is and needing a sense of purpose. It's such a marvellous feeling, isn't it? I am so glad I met you."

She beamed up at him, and for a moment he forgot everything as an overwhelming urge overtook him to take her into his arms and to kiss those soft, generous lips, to lose himself in her. A pinprick of pure pain made him wince. Mary wasn't a substitute for laudanum! It was selfish of him, quite wrong of him, to let her imagine she could be anything to him at all. "I need to talk to you."

"You look quite shaky. The weather is horribly sultry, which I know is not suited to people who suffer regularly from sick headaches as you do."

"I never said . . ."

"No, but I guessed. I think you had better go inside."

"A walk. I should go for a walk. I won't be thought an invalid."

"An invalid! It's a headache, that's all. Isn't it? Tre, are you ill?"

Walter, are you ill? Sibilla's voice resonated so clearly in his head that he started. She wasn't there. It was Mary, her big grey eyes wide, gazing at him with concern. "Not ill. I just need some fresh air."

"Well if you're sure . . ."

"Positive." The competition was over. The spectators burst into applause. He managed a grim smile. "It's easing already," he said, silently ordering his head to co-operate. "A walk will have me right as rain."

"I'd like a walk, too. I'll come with you," Mary said, smiling brightly and taking his arm, obviously as unconvinced as he was that he would be right as rain but determined to indulge the lie. "If we go now, while my mother is presenting the prizes, no-one will notice. If we follow this path we will end up at the kitchen garden, and I can show you Mama's precious pinery, though I am not so sure you should walk that far."

"I'd like to see the pinery," Tre said. A purpose, a destination, that's what he needed, to clear his head. And then he could make his excuses. "Lady Rolle, my aunt Louisa, would like to hear about it. She's a keen gardener. Palm houses are her speciality, but she also has a small pinery, and the one here at Drumlanrig is famous."

"Yes, we call it a poor year if we produce less than one hundred pineapples for the table." Mary came to a halt, forcing him to stop, too. "Stop pretending you're well, Tre, I can see by that frown between your eyes that your head must be aching."

"Talk to me," he said desperately. "It will help me forget it."

"Don't you think that you'd be better taking some laudanum and sleeping it off?"

"Doesn't help. I've tried, believe me. It's not that sort of headache." He took her arm, urging her forward. "Walk and talk. That's what I need."

"If you are sure."

She cast him a worried look, but did as he asked. He considered hanging on to her arm, but he didn't want to cling to her like a drowning man or a lost child. He didn't want to drag her down with him. "Pineries," he prompted her.

"Pineries." Mary talked and he listened, not to the content of what she said but to the tone of her voice, letting it flow over him, trying to tell himself it was like a cool, calming stream. She was wearing a little hat with an emerald green bow that matched the trim on the hem of her gown. The fabric was soft, fluttery, cream, embroidered with little sprigs of something—mint? The fragrance she wore was subtle. Citrus. Not lemons or lime. "Orange? Your perfume, what is it?"

"It's Bouquet Opoponax. Bergamot, with citrus and vanilla amongst other things, I believe."

"It smells of you." He stumbled, and Mary grabbed him. He looked around, dazed, at the row of cottages and outbuildings. A huge wall which must protect the famous kitchen gardens. Glasshouses. One of them must be the pinery. If he could reach it, he would be safe. He knew he was being irrational, but he had lost the power to be anything else. His head ached. He pinched his nose. When he looked down, he could see stars.

"Tre," Mary said, clutching his arm.

"Pinery. Which way?"

"Tre, you are not well."

"Get me there," he said, gritting his teeth. "If you can just get me there . . ."

"This way. Come on."

He had no option but to cling to her now, forcing her to bow under his weight as she all but dragged him forwards to the nearest glasshouse and pulled open the door. The smell of warm, damp earth hit him, the lush sweetness of tropical plants that took him straight back. "Like Bicton," he said, reeling. "Mistake." The fog enveloped him, he felt the blood rushing in his ears and he surrendered to oblivion.

CHAPTER TWELVE

Alone Again, Naturally

MARY WAS BEGINNING TO PANIC, wondering if she ought to seek help after all, when Tre finally opened his eyes. "Oh, thank goodness. Stay still, don't try to move."

He ignored her, pushing himself upright and dislodging the damp handkerchief she had placed on his brow. "Where . . ."

"You are in the pinery. You fainted."

He was ashen, his eyes unfocused. Mary handed him a cup of water. "From the fountain. It is perfectly fresh." She watched anxiously as he sipped. "I was on the verge of calling for help, but I thought you wouldn't want . . ."

"No. Thank you." He picked up the damp handkerchief and dabbed at the sweat glistening on his brow. "Please accept my abject apologies." Staggering to his feet, he had to clutch at the brickwork of the pinery beds, shooing her away when she made to help. "I am perfectly well now."

"You look perfectly dreadful," Mary said frankly. "There is a bench here." She took his arm and all but dragged him to it. "Sit, before you fall."

"I'm fine," he protested, even as his knees gave way and he dropped onto the bench. "The heat in here must have made me light-headed."

He dabbed at his brow, which was already damp with sweat again. Though he was seated, he was swaying slightly, and his pupils were pinpricks. He looked as if he would swoon at any moment. "Shall I rinse your handkerchief in the fountain?" Mary asked, reaching for it.

Tre snatched it away brusquely. "I really wish you would—I would appreciate it if you left me alone to recover."

He sounded strange. Stilted and formal. Angry. No, he was embarrassed, that's what it was, of course it was, mortified at having fainted in front of her. As if she cared about that! She was about to say so, but caught herself just in time. What he needed was to be distracted, not to have attention drawn to what had just happened.

"Where is Bicton?" Mary asked, studiously looking away as he continued to dab at his forehead. "You muttered something about Bicton."

"Bicton? Bicton House is my aunt Louisa's home in Devon."

He obviously didn't remember saying the name. She decided against asking him what he'd meant by *mistake*. "Lady Rolle is such a wonderful name," Mary equivocated. "I am imagining a fat, jolly woman with at least twenty chins who smells of barley sugar. Am I right?"

From the side of her eye, she saw Tre manage a very faint, crooked smile. "Only four chins, and she prefers peppermints."

"Are you close, you and your aunt?"

"Yes." He nodded, frowning as if he was having to concentrate very hard. "Though she is a great deal older than me. Must be in her seventies."

"And is there a Lord Rolle?"

He shook his head, wincing. "She's been a widow for about thirty years. If I ever met her husband, I don't remember."

"Goodness, did he die very young?"

"He married very old," Tre said. "Think he was nearly seventy. My aunt not quite thirty. Something like that."

"Good heavens, how extraordinary."

"She is extraordinary," Tre said, sounding marginally better. "Least conventional woman I've ever met, until I met you."

"I rather like the sound of Lady Rolle." Mary eased the damp handkerchief from his hands.

"You'd like her, and she'd like you, I reckon." Tre closed his eyes, leaning back on the bench, allowing her to quickly refresh the linen in the cold fountain. He took it from her when she sat back down, dabbing at his brow. "That's good. Thank you."

His colour was very slowly returning. Mary decided to keep him talking. "Do you visit Lady Rolle often?"

Tre shook his head, then winced. "I've not been to Bicton since— since I went there to—not for a while." Easing himself more upright on the bench, he opened his eyes. "The smell in here reminds me . . ." He shook his head. "I do see her quite often though, in London. She has a house in Upper Grosvenor Street. Aunt Louisa is something of an epicure, and fortunately for me, she does not like to eat alone."

"Ah, but the real test of her fondness for you is surely whether or not she shares her peppermints?"

Tre, to Mary's delight and relief, managed a small laugh at this sally. "She doesn't share her peppermints with anyone."

"Tre!" He had turned ashen again. "Tre," Mary repeated sharply as his head began to loll back, "please don't faint again."

He snapped upright. "I won't. I'm perfectly fine."

"You're not fine." She could no longer pretend, nor contain her panic. "I'm going to fetch some help."

"No!" He winced. "I don't want—it's bad enough that you are here. I wish you would just go."

"I can't leave you like this, but if you would rather I had someone else fetched—Captain Beckman, perhaps?"

"No! For God's sake, have you any idea—no, why should you." He dropped his head in his hands. "Look, I don't need help. If I could just sit here, if you'll just leave me alone, I beg of you."

"I can't."

He swore under his breath, then sat up again, mopping his brow. "Then talk to me."

She stared at him, feeling utterly helpless, terrified that he might lose consciousness again, and that by obeying his request she was putting him in danger. "Only if you promise not to die on me."

"I promise."

"How can I be sure you mean it?"

"It will pass. It always does."

"Is there nothing you can take for it?"

"I've tried everything, but nothing works, except riding it out. I'm sorry."

Mary took his hand, gripping it tightly. "You will be, if you apologize to me one more time. You are ill—it is nothing to be sorry for or ashamed of."

"I wish that were true." He returned the pressure on her hand before disengaging and shifting away from her on the bench. "You must be delighted with your morning's work."

"What? Oh, you mean Mrs. Fitzherbert-Smythe? I had almost forgotten. Our morning's work. My mother is pleased, and my father will never know, and that is all I wished for. I couldn't have done it without you."

"Nonsense. All I did was act as a sounding board. It was you who got the maid to speak up, and you who worked out what must have happened, and you who confronted the culprit in such a masterly way."

"Your trick of using silence helped me considerably."

"You should be very proud of yourself."

"I was terrified, but thank you." Quite bewildered by the change in him she absent-mindedly pulled off her gloves and twisted them around her fingers. Tre got shakily to his feet and refreshed his handkerchief at the fountain. She watched him through her lashes, completely at a loss as to what ailed him and what to do about it.

"I'm feeling a lot better now."

To her utter relief, he seemed to be. "You've stopped looking like a ghost, at any rate."

"I'm much improved. You'll ruin those," Tre said, indicating her gloves.

Mary smoothed them out on her lap. The atmosphere between them had shifted subtly. She felt awkward. Nervous. "You never told me why Captain Beckman keeps his bedroom door locked."

Tre folded his handkerchief up and tucked it into his coat pocket. "Beckman smokes opium."

"Opium!"

"Not everyone who smokes opium is an addict," Tre said spikily. "Used with due care, it can help a person to sleep, that's all. Beckman didn't wish any of the staff to find the pipe and paraphernalia. That's why his room was locked. He didn't want them to leap to the same conclusion that you did. Plenty of people take laudanum drops, which is a different form of the same thing."

"I didn't know that." He was angry again—was it anger? "Have you tried it—smoking opium, I mean?" Mary asked.

Tre shrugged. "I have but it didn't agree with me."

He was avoiding her gaze again, his eyes fixed on the mound of pineapples piled in the corner. She was completely out of her depth, and for once quite unable to glean what was going on in his head. She was missing something, but what? His throat was working, his fingers flexing. He didn't want her to press him, yet she couldn't pretend that all was well when it so very, very obviously was not.

"Tre?" Tentatively, she put a hand on his arm. "Can't you tell me what is wrong? It's more than a sick headache, isn't it?"

He flung her hand away, turning his back on her. "It's a curse is what it is."

Staring at his straight back, his rigid shoulders, Mary had never in her life felt so helpless or so forlorn. Something between them was broken, and she had no idea how to fix it. "I am very sorry," she said stiffly. "I have been horribly presumptuous in remaining here with you when you wished to be alone."

He let out a long, shuddering sigh and turned back to face her. "As you can see, I have myself perfectly under control now."

By a supreme effort, she thought, forcing a smile. "Yes, I can see that."

They both knew it for a lie. He was waiting for her to leave, but it felt wrong for them to part on such strained terms, especially after what they had achieved together earlier. "I felt useful today," Mary said. "I felt as if I actually had a purpose. I wish I could feel like that more often. You at least have a vital job of work to do, even if you can't talk about it. My only occupation of late has been to smile insipidly and dance sedately, while my pedigree and lineage are discussed. Honestly, there were times when I felt like a brood mare, being trotted out at parties for inspection."

"I have never come across a brood mare at a party. Do they dance?"

He was humouring her, but if he was humouring her, it surely meant he didn't want her to go. That he cared about her in some way. Oh God, was she really that desperate! "Certainly they dance," Mary replied, "on their hind legs, like circus horses, only wearing bustles and swathes of ruffled silk. A circus horse has about as much conversation as a young and eligible lady, too."

She jumped up from the bench, aware that she was acting the fool, unable to stop herself. "We must never venture an opinion of our own, and merely respond to orders and observations. We must never walk but must glide everywhere, as if we were on wheels under our gowns. Heads straight, shoulders back."

She picked up one of the pineapples, which were doubtless intended for tonight's dinner table, yanked off her hat and balanced the fruit on her head. Walking with arms outspread, as if she were once again high on the parapet, she managed ten steps before the pineapple toppled, and she caught it just in time.

"Very impressive." Tre took it from her hands and replaced it on the pile. "We need to talk, Mary."

Her heart sank. "Yes." Tears smarted in her eyes. She dipped her head to hide them.

The touch of his finger, light as a feather on her cheek, made her look up. There was something in his gaze that made her breath catch. For a wild moment she thought he was going to kiss her, and she stood rooted to the spot, entranced, waiting. Then he let her go and stepped back. "Now that the matter of the brooch is resolved, I have decided to take a leaf out of Mrs. Fitzherbert-Smythe's book and return to London as soon as possible. It's imperative that I devote myself to my new role, assuming that it actually comes to pass. I can't afford any distractions. The party is to break up tomorrow anyway."

"You're going," Mary said flatly. Of course he was going, and he was making it clear their paths wouldn't cross again. Everyone always left her, in the end. She had been foolish, stupid—no, beyond stupid—to imagine that Tre was any different. She had not considered the future, nor whether there might be a place for him in it, but she hadn't thought of there being a future entirely without him either. The possibility of that was gone now, and she didn't know how it had been lost.

"It's for the best," Tre said.

His words were clipped, but she thought there was something, just a glimmer of regret or wretchedness in his eyes. No. It was she who was regretful. She who was wretched and she was *damned* if she would let him see it. "I understand."

He winced again. "I doubt it."

And whose fault was that? Mary thought, with a flicker of anger. A curse, he said, and that was it. Stiff upper lip. Don't let on that you're suffering. Colonel Trefusis had regained control of Tre. Well, he wasn't the only one well practised in the art of keeping a stiff upper lip. Her entire focus now was on holding herself together. She mustn't cry. She mustn't let him see how much his goodbye was hurting her. He had never said there wouldn't be a goodbye. He had not once given her any reason to imagine that he might wish to further their acquaintance. Nor had he ever given her any reason to believe that it was anything more than an acquaintance.

If she was hurt, it was her own fault, not his. Her own fault for thinking, for daring to imagine that a man like Tre would be interested in a dormouse. He had been bored, and she had amused him for a while, and now it was over, and he had more interesting and much more important matters to attend to.

"Well, then," Mary said, with a brittle smile, "I wish you the very best of luck with your new endeavour."

"Thank you. And you, Lady Mary, I wish you luck, however you decide to occupy yourself in the future."

Lady Mary! "I expect I'll join a circus and walk the high wire, thus confounding everyone's expectations, not only yours, Colonel Trefusis." He flinched at her use of his title, as she had expected him to, but it made her feel worse, not better. She clasped her hands behind her back. "Goodbye, Colonel."

"Goodbye, Lady Mary."

He turned away, and she bit her lip, determined to cling to the remnants of her dignity. She watched him walk steadily out of the pinery. The door closed behind him.

"Goodbye, Tre," she whispered.

Once again she was alone at Drumlanrig. Once again she had been abandoned, and soon she would be forgotten. It had happened before, but this time the pain was much, much worse. She'd thought she'd found a kindred spirit. She'd thought she'd met someone who understood her. Who cared for her enough to wish to know her better. She was wrong. Wrong, wrong, wrong, and it hurt!

She wasn't ever going to let it happen again. Not ever. Mary's knees gave way under her. She dropped onto the bench and burst into a flood of wretched tears.

PART II

Newburgh Priory, Yorkshire

1875

CHAPTER THIRTEEN

We'll Meet Again

Newburgh Priory, North Yorkshire Moors,
Tuesday, 9 February 1875

THE WHITE DRAWING ROOM WAS an elegant chamber, with high, elaborately corniced ceilings and a large bow window flanked by two columns, facing south out to the park. Being evening, the curtains were drawn, obscuring the view. Two mirrors with intricate gilt frames hung on either side of an imposing arched alcove on the other side of the room. The chamber was an obstacle course of occasional tables decked with fine china, gilded chairs, and footstools.

Sir George Orby Wombwell, the 4th baronet, the priory owner, and host of this gathering, was holding court by the bow window. "I had not one but two horses shot from under me," he was saying. "I managed to reach the Russian guns all the same, and then the villains captured me, five of them with sabres drawn, but they didn't hold on to me for long. In the midst of the battle and confusion it was Lord Cardigan himself who gave me the idea of how to rescue myself. 'Catch a horse, you young fool, and come with us!' he yelled at me. So I did. I escaped their clutches, managed to catch one of our riderless horses, and galloped back to our own lines. How I made it, I still don't know to this day, for it was all but impossible to see more than a foot in front of my nose, what with the mayhem, smoke, and chargers running loose in all directions. But I did it, and I lived to tell the tale, as you see."

The baronet, a stout man with a full head of hair, copious side-whiskers, and a large, drooping moustache, paused for a moment to allow his small circle of guests to make the appropriate noises of admiration and encouragement before he continued with what was clearly a well-rehearsed tale. "Man's best friend is his horse. I knew that before, of course, but that day as I rode out of that Valley of Death it was brought home to me, and it's something I've never forgotten. I brought the horse that saved my bacon back from the Crimea with me, you know. Kept the beast here at Newburgh, let him enjoy his retirement, breathing in the good Yorkshire air, eating the sweet Yorkshire grass. Least I could do. He's here still, buried in the park with a monument to mark his final resting place, which you can take a look at if you care to venture out in the snow tomorrow. I remember Lord Cardigan saying to me—I was his aide-de-camp, you know—I remember his lordship saying to me . . ."

Tre edged away from the group, making his way to the other side of the drawing room where he stood at the mantelpiece, pretending to study the huge portrait of his host which hung above it. The inscription on the little brass plaque informed him that it had been presented to Sir George by his tenantry in 1859, in recognition of his gallantry in the Crimea. Sir George was painted in his military uniform, a foot resting on a canon, his trusty black charger, possibly the very one buried in the grounds, by his side. Though the scene was intended to represent the aftermath of a battle, both the officer and his steed were impeccably turned out, horse brasses and medals gleaming.

Were the noble six hundred who took part in the Charge of the

Light Brigade gallant, deluded, or simply obediently following orders? By the time Tre had been posted to Sevastopol the next year, Lord Cardigan had already departed on his yacht, claiming ill health. Sir George had lived to tell the tale. What did it matter whether the tale he told was the truth or the legend that Tennyson had helped to create with his poem? The problem, Tre thought wryly, was not that he doubted his host, like his precious charger, had earned his acclaim and his string of medals. The problem was that those who deserved the most acclaim were the ones who often received none.

Which was hardly the point, Tre reminded himself. The point was that bluff Sir George wished to be useful to his country once more, and he had the contacts and influence to ensure that Tre would be expected to do his level best to give the man what he wanted. Despite the fact that all his instincts, when he was informed of his task, were that he was being sent on a fool's errand.

"The powers that be have insisted we give Sir George a hearing," he had been informed by his superior. "If I must refuse, I need solid grounds for doing so."

Tre had already identified the ideal candidate for the assignment, a man who was a perfect fit for the job, despite his lack of blue blood, officer ranking, and unbroken pedigree. It was going to be an uphill struggle to award it to him now. Gold braid still trumped ability, unfortunately.

"Your Grace!" Sir George exclaimed, interrupting Tre's musings.

"Sir George. Please forgive our tardy arrival."

That voice! He was sure he recognized it. Tre whirled around so quickly that he caught his foot on the fender. As he grabbed the mantelpiece to regain his balance, his host and hostess hurried across the room to greet the woman standing in the doorway.

The Duchess of Buccleuch was dressed with customary elegance in an evening gown of mauve silk. "We missed our train connection to York," she was saying as her host and hostess made their respective bow and curtsy. "I did send a telegram, but your butler informed me that it arrived only five minutes before we did; and since I did not wish to delay dinner, I asked that we be shown straight to our rooms to change."

Our rooms? The duchess was trapped in the doorway by the line of guests jostling to be introduced and to make their bow or curtsy. Behind her, in the shadows, was another figure. Though he couldn't see her, the hairs on the back of Tre's neck stood on end. He knew it must be she, even before her mother ushered her forward.

"My youngest daughter, Sir George, who I know you will be pleased to meet."

"Indeed, yes. Welcome to Newburgh Priory, Lady Mary. Let me introduce . . ."

Mary. It had been almost three years since his mortifying display in the pinery at Drumlanrig. Watching her standing in her mother's shadow, he recalled the first time he had seen her, prancing across the parapet in her tunic, her face alight with sheer joy. He remembered her face dark with anger and lit up with laughter, the touch of her hand on his arm, the gloves she was forever pulling off and twisting around her fingers, the tilt of her head, that fierce way she had of looking at him when she thought he was trying to fob her off. He remembered her attempt to make him laugh by walking with a pineapple on her head that last day. He remembered the look on her face when he told her he was leaving, the hurt quickly disguised. He remembered the effort it had taken for him to walk away, not to look back, forcing himself to recall just exactly why there was no other option.

Their paths had not crossed since. He would have seen the announcement in the press if she had married. That she had not was the limit of what he knew of her. He had never permitted himself to enquire, though he had often thought of her. In the three years since he'd cut such a pitiful figure at their last meeting, he had helped to launch the new department, and had contributed significantly to its growing importance. He had regained much of the respect he'd lost. He was settled. He didn't want to be un-settled.

Un-settled! Tre made his way across the room. For heaven's sake, it had been almost three years, and their acquaintance had lasted a matter of days.

"Colonel Trefusis! How do you do?"

"Your Grace." Tre made his bow over the duchess's extended hand, but his eyes were on Mary. "This is an unexpected pleasure."

"You remember my daughter, Colonel?"

Their eyes met, their gazes held, and in that instant the pleasure of seeing her again subsumed all his other feelings. "Lady Mary." Tre made his bow.

"Colonel Trefusis." She was elegantly dressed in a dark-blue evening gown with a low-cut bodice that made the most of her figure. Her hair was piled high on her head, showing off her long neck and high cheekbones. She looked elegant, sophisticated, and distant. "I hope you are well."

"I am, thank you," Tre replied, nonplussed. "And you? You look very well."

"Thank you." Mary moved to the side in order to allow Sir George to introduce another guest to her mother, smiling thinly at him. "Accepting compliments gracefully is one of the many things I have learned since we last met."

"I, on the other hand, have not changed," Tre replied, hurt by her tone, though he had no right to be. "It was not a compliment, it was the truth."

Her smile faltered. "And has your mysterious assignment proven a success? You need only nod or shake your head, Colonel, I am aware that you are not at liberty to do more."

The barb hurt, but it hurt him more to think that she had been nourishing the resentment which had generated it. "It is still early days, but it is proving to be a success, yes."

"Then I am glad for you Tre—Colonel Trefusis."

Tre. No-one else called him that, though it was how he always thought of himself now. "And you, Lady Mary? Since I have seen no mention in the press of the famous 'titled tightrope walker,' I presume you decided against joining the circus."

She remained stony-faced. "I have not wasted my time."

"May I present Mr. Glover, my wife's cousin, Your Grace, Lady Mary."

"It never occurred to me that you would," Tre said softly, before stepping back politely out of the way.

CHAPTER FOURTEEN

The Dog Kennel Garden

Newburgh Priory, Wednesday, 10 February 1875

BREAKFAST WOULD NOT BE SERVED until ten. Mary took tea in her bedchamber, waiting impatiently for daylight. While her mother had been given a large state bedroom with a view to the north out over the lake known as the fish pond, her own considerably smaller, though very comfortable, room faced out to the parkland on the south frontage. She had ample time to dress without Clara's help, pinning her thick locks into her favourite chignon. The gown she chose was made of pale-blue velvet with a polonaise-style double skirt, trimmed with dark-blue satin ruching. Her shape had subtly changed in the last few years, and she was now, wholly unintentionally, fashionably curvaceous, though as she studied herself in the mirror, she was as ever struck by the absurd contrast between the narrow circumference of her waist and the swell of her bosom, which she had covered by means of a lace fichu under the bodice of her gown.

It was just after half past seven when dawn began to break, and Mary used the buttonhook to fasten her boots, trying to ignore the butterflies which were beginning to flutter in her stomach. She had no right to be nervous. She was going for her usual early morning walk. If she happened to bump into Colonel Trefusis, it would be an excellent opportunity for her to affirm that they were nothing more than distant acquaintances. She was here for a specific purpose, and she could not be distracted by his presence. There had been an awkwardness between them last night that she would rather dissipate, since they would be under the same roof for the next few days, eating at the same table, taking part in whatever entertainment their hosts had planned.

So! Mary checked her reflection in the mirror and stuck another pin into her hair. If she bumped into Tre—*Colonel Trefusis*—that would be one less thing to worry about. Though the chances of her bumping into him were slim. Even if he recalled her penchant for early morning walks, he would in all likelihood decide against taking one himself, and then she would know for certain that she had misinterpreted him completely last night when she thought he was glad to see her. Until she made it clear she wasn't glad to see him. Which she wasn't. She didn't feel anything for him at all, not after the way he had so brutally severed contact with her.

Mary wound the long blue scarf round her neck that her niece Cecil had knitted for her and pulled on her cloak and gloves. The snow had melted overnight and the sun was making a valiant attempt to shine. She left her room and made her way down the stone staircase. Very little light penetrated, and in the gloom, she felt as if the eyes of the subjects of the many portraits in their gilded frames were following her as she descended. A tapestry rippled as she passed. A draught, that was all, she told herself, feeling foolish, but hurrying away from it all the same.

A wood-panelled, stone-flagged hallway connected two separate entrances, the main door, where their carriage had deposited them last night, and the famous King James's Porch. Where, through the glass panels in the door, she could see a male figure standing. She knew it was he. Was he waiting for her? There was only one way to find out.

"Oh!" Mary said, pulling open the door and feigning surprise. "Colonel Trefusis."

"Lady Mary, good morning."

His smile was tentative. He clearly wasn't at all sure of his welcome. This bolstered her. "I thought I'd take a walk down to the lake—or the fish pond, as I believe it is called."

"May I walk with you? Last night's meeting was a shock—a pleasant one, for me, at any rate, but I sense in you— What I'm trying to say is, Mary—Lady Mary—that I owe you an apology for the circumstances under which we parted. Your remark about my fierce reticence regarding my work is something else I would like to remedy, though if you would rather be alone . . ."

"No. It would be sensible for us to take the opportunity now that it has presented itself to us." She knew she sounded odd, stilted, and he had noticed, but that couldn't be helped. "Shall we?"

However, as soon as they escaped the shelter of the porch, an icy wind tugged at them. "If we dispense with the view," Tre shouted, clutching at his hat, "I believe there is a walled garden which will give us some shelter. For some bizarre reason it is known as the dog kennel garden. It's this way, I think."

Mary, head bent forward, followed in his wake. By the time they found the entrance to the high-walled garden her carefully arranged chignon was a tangle of escaped tendrils, her cheeks were red, and her eyes were streaming.

Tre pushed the door closed, and the wind immediately abated. She pulled off her gloves to dab at her eyes and cheeks, while he pushed his hair back from his brow and replaced his hat. His skin was glowing from the cold, his eyes bright but, unlike hers, not in the least bit watery.

"I must look a fright," Mary said, tucking several loose strands of hair behind her ears.

"Windswept. It suits you."

"I see you are still fond of paying odd compliments."

"It wasn't a compliment. It wasn't an accident that I met you on the porch either. I was waiting for you."

She would not allow herself to be pleased by this. "You could easily have missed me, if I had left by one of the other doors."

"I would have seen you coming through the hallway if you'd used the main entrance. If you'd gone out by the other door on the south side, I'd have seen you on the path."

"What would you have done if I had decided not to take a walk at all?"

"Then I'd have been forced to conclude that either you've changed even more than I thought, or you were avoiding me."

"Why would I do that?" He looked at her for a moment, his dark-brown eyes fixed on hers. No-one looked at her like that, as if they were trying to read her thoughts. She dropped her gaze. "It's surprisingly mild in here now that the sun is up."

"Mary— Lady Mary, I am sure you have not forgotten the circumstances of our last meeting. I behaved—my conduct—my lack of self-control was deeply embarrassing. It has been a source of deep mortification to me that you witnessed it. Please accept my abject apologies."

That is what he meant by the circumstances of his departure! His illness, not his abrupt termination of their acquaintance. "You were not well," Mary said. "There is no need to apologize."

"I placed you in a very difficult and embarrassing position."

"When you fainted, do you mean?" she interrupted him. "I was worried—terrified, actually—that you were going to die on me, but embarrassed? If that is what you're apologizing for then there is absolutely no need."

"I should have done as you suggested, and retreated to my room until it passed."

"Yet you insisted on getting a breath of air, Tre—Colonel Trefusis. As I remember it, you were actually eager for my company at first."

"I thought it would pass. I thought that if we talked—but I should have known better."

"And if you had retired to your room to suffer in solitude, when it had *passed*, would you still have made your excuses and left post-haste, as you did?"

"My reason for returning to London was genuine. The party was breaking up early."

"Yes, I remember. Never mind. Since you seem to think it important, then I will accept your apology and consider the matter closed. That looks to me like a pond at the end of the path. Shall we go and investigate?"

She started to walk without waiting for him, hurt and angry in equal measure, and irked with herself for having let him see she felt anything at all after three years. By the time he caught up with her a moment later she had herself in hand. The path leading to the pond was set between two borders of wooden trellises around which wisteria grew. "This must be glorious in the summer," Mary said, using her mother's tone. "The duchess would have it planted with rambling roses, though."

"The duchess is still a keen gardener, then?"

"Gardening, Her Majesty, her charities, and of course the duke take up as much of her time as ever. She divides what is left between my sister and her latest project, which is her health."

"Your sister—you mean Margaret, I take it?"

"She currently lives alone in a town house in Edinburgh, much to my father's chagrin. The duke can no longer ignore her existence, for not only has she dared to set up home by herself only seven miles from Dalkeith Palace, she has the nerve to publish her writings under her own name. However, she has redeemed herself slightly by becoming betrothed to a very respectable man of whom our father approves."

"And you? How do you feel about being reunited with your sister?"

They had reached the large round lily pond at the end of the walk. Mary stared down at it, thrown by the question. No-one had ever asked it. She wished he had not, for it reminded her that it had been one of the things that had drawn her to him the first time around. How do *you* feel? What did *you* think? He always wanted to know, except when it came to the question of himself. The leaves in the pond were tinged with brown. She counted three large silvery-scaled fish swimming sluggishly in the cold water. "I don't see a great deal of her," Mary said, "but of course I'm proud of her, as is my mother."

"You mentioned the duchess's health?"

"It is no more your concern than my relationship with my sister," Mary said vehemently. Perhaps too vehemently. "You've given me a quite unnecessary apology. If you've changed your mind about remedying your—what did you say?—yes, your reticence regarding your work, then please say so, and don't prevaricate by asking me questions. If you were interested in my well-being or my mother's, you could have asked at dinner last night."

She was aware of him studying her again, but she kept her eyes trained on the fish, furious at herself for the flash of temper. Beside her, Tre had taken off his hat and was smoothing back his already smooth hair. It was one of his habits, especially when he was thinking.

He caught her looking, smiled wryly, and put his hat back on again. "I'm sorry," he said. "I was prevaricating—you're quite right. Last night, when I was imagining this conversation, it was with a different person. I've thought of you over the intervening years, and I've often wondered what you were doing; but I never took account of how you might have changed, which was stupid of me. And patronising. You have changed significantly is what I'm trying to say. So much so I don't know you."

And didn't wish to? At each compass point of the pond's circle grew some strangely shaped topiary that looked like standing stones. Confused by her see-sawing emotions, Mary set off through them.

"Wait!" Tre caught her arm. "I seem to have acquired the knack of saying completely the wrong thing, and you seem determined to take everything I say amiss. Do you think we could start afresh?"

"What would be the point?"

Tre sighed. "Will you at least allow me to explain about my work and why I was so guarded at Drumlanrig?"

She said nothing but followed him to a wooden bench set against the wall next to a small glasshouse which was in full sun, and sat down, careful to keep herself as far away from him as possible. He had removed his hat again. She had thought him unchanged, but in the bright sunlight she thought that the dark shadows under his eyes were considerably diminished, and the fan of lines at the corners of his eyes not so deep. "You do look well, Tre—Colonel Trefusis," she said, softening. "Your work, whatever it is, obviously suits you."

"It does. I am useful again. I am making a difference." He dug his hands into the pockets of his greatcoat and stretched his legs out, another sign, she recalled, that he was gathering his thoughts. "It has been a long time since I've felt either of those things. Long before I secured my promotion to lieutenant colonel back in sixty-five, and my move to the Department of Topography and Statistics."

"The administrative position?" Mary asked, wondering if this was another form of procrastination. "I didn't realize that was your choice."

His expression clouded. "It seemed the best option at the time. The department was set up after the debacle of the Crimean War in an attempt to make sure that if—when—we went into the next conflict, we'd be better armed—with maps and information, I mean, as well as guns."

"That certainly sounds sensible."

He laughed shortly. "But very far short of what we really needed. There are enormous gaps in our knowledge of other countries—their armies, leaders, political landscape, even the climate. We know next to nothing, for example, about Russia."

"Ought we to?" Mary asked, feeling both woefully ignorant and completely baffled.

"If we wish to keep the tsar out of Afghanistan, and ensure that India remains part of the British Empire, then, yes, we ought."

"Couldn't you simply ask Prince Alfred? Since he is married to the tsar's daughter, I mean . . ."

"Mary, I'm not talking about the kind of information that might come up in a dinner conversation between His Royal Highness and one of his father-in-law's courtiers. At least, I am talking about that kind of information but not only that."

Mary. He hadn't corrected himself this time. She found it difficult to think of him as Colonel Trefusis. *Wait a minute!* "What did you say? Good God, Tre, are you a spy?"

"Not exactly."

"Then what are you, precisely?" Mary asked, turning in astonishment to face him.

"It's difficult to be precise. I'm not supposed to talk about what I do at all, but provided I don't tell you any detail, I don't think I can be accused of being a traitor."

"A traitor! I can't think of a less likely person."

"But treachery is how it would be seen all the same, if I let slip any names, for example. My old department has become the Intelligence Branch of the War Office. Our existence is an open secret, but what we do and how we do it is not. I am responsible for recruiting intelligence agents. Or rather, I am responsible for deciding whether an individual is worth recruiting."

"Good grief! Don't tell me you are here to recruit Sir George?"

"Mary! I've just told you that I can't possibly comment on specifics."

"Sir George! No wonder he wishes—" Mary broke off abruptly. "And at Drumlanrig, too. Captain Beckman?"

"Mary!"

"Sorry. I'm sorry, but— Good heavens, Tre, how does my father fit into this?"

"He used his influence in Parliament and with Her Majesty to promote the value of gathering intelligence. That was why I was at Drumlanrig, to lobby your father to support our idea. It turns out the Queen was already on board, and they finally persuaded the government to take us seriously. And so the new department was born."

"So when my father went off to Balmoral, that was at *your* behest?"

"Not wholly. The timing was very convenient for me, however."

"I cannot imagine Sir George as a spy," Mary said, diverted.

"I didn't say that was why I was here. I am simply a guest at a house party."

"Of course you are! I am the soul of discretion—you must remember that at least about me, and it hasn't changed. But Sir George! He is so upright and honest."

"Is he?"

"He was an officer in Her Majesty's army. One expects certain standards."

"Ah, yes, of course. I thought you were speaking from personal experience."

She was, to a degree, though she wasn't going to let Tre know that. "Oliver Cromwell is supposedly buried here at Newburgh Priory," Mary said. "Wasn't he famous for having spies work for him?"

"He had a second-in-command, a lawyer called John Thurloe, who looked after a network of spies for him. I don't do anything like that. I assess whether a man is fit for purpose, that's all."

"So there are no female spies? You are missing a trick there, Tre! Are they all officers?"

He snorted. "Most officers pride themselves on being gentlemen, and would consider spying dishonourable. We do make use of some military men, but we also employ explorers, archaeologists, merchants, academics. Botanists are also an excellent resource. They travel the world collecting exotic specimens and at the same time can collect all sorts of other useful information."

"What sorts of useful information?"

"Everything and anything. Train networks, maps, troop movements, political unrest—there's no limit to the amount of stuff that comes our way, in letters and diaries, reports and newspapers, maps, drawings—a mountain of paperwork."

"What happens to it?"

"It's sifted and sorted and summarized and sent to the appropriate men in the army, if it's of interest to the military, and then—oh, some use it, some file it away, some most likely burn it."

"And my father? Does he play a part in all this? I find it very difficult to believe he would be involved in anything so interesting."

"Half the time, it's not interesting at all. As I said, sifting information. Paperwork, in other words."

He wasn't lying, but he was prevaricating, she was sure of it, and he hadn't answered her question about the duke. He had, however, entrusted her with a great deal more than he ought to have. "Why are you telling me all this now?"

Tre sat up on the bench, angling towards her. "It was never about my not trusting you, Mary. That August when we met, there was still a good chance that the whole idea would go up in smoke. It wasn't solely my proposal, but I was central to its succeeding. I *needed* to make it happen."

For the first time that morning, she felt as if he was trying to be honest with her. That he wanted her to understand. That it mattered to him. But she didn't understand; there was a thread she was missing. "To have a sense of purpose?" she asked, recalling her own words that day.

"And to prove myself   to prove my idea would work."

"Which it has? Are you frightfully important now?"

He laughed. "In a frightfully quiet and unobtrusive way, which is how I like it."

"Is that why you decided against transferring back to your regiment and active duty? I wondered, you see, if you were so bored with your administrative post, why you didn't consider that as an option?"

It was an obvious question, Mary thought, but Tre's brow clouded. "An army in peacetime can be a tedious place to be."

She had heard her brother Walter say so, too, but once again she had the sense of hearing half the truth. She had, however, heard a great deal more than she had expected from him. "Thank you, Tre. Needless to say, you can trust me not to breathe a word of this to a living soul."

"I told you, that was never the issue. I was—I'm not superstitious, not usually, but in this matter I was."

"You thought if you said the words out loud, it somehow might not happen?"

"Something like that," he said sheepishly. "Am I forgiven?"

"For being discreet? Of course."

If he guessed she was equivocating, he chose not to say. "Am I permitted to ask you what you are doing here with the duchess at Newburgh Priory?"

"I am sorry," Mary said primly, "I'm not at liberty to divulge any aspect of my top secret and extremely mysterious work."

Tre burst out laughing. "You've waited a long time to deliver that rebuff."

"It was worth the wait."

He checked his watch and grimaced. "We'd better get back, they'll be serving breakfast soon." She hesitated, then took the hand he held out to help her up. "It's good to see you, Mary."

Her fingers curled involuntarily into his. She snatched her hand away. "The sky has quite clouded over. I think it's cold enough to snow again."

CHAPTER FIFTEEN

Relics

Newburgh Priory, Thursday, 11 February 1875

SIR GEORGE WOMBWELL AND HIS wife were extremely attentive and thoughtful hosts, providing a range of entertainment for those guests who wished to occupy themselves, equally happy for them to idle away the hours in front of the fire engaged in gossip, or reading in the library. For most of yesterday and all of this morning, Mary had been occupied with the very particular reason for her visit to the priory, a reason which only Sir George and to a limited degree her mother were party to.

She had a great deal to think about, as the puzzle she was faced with solving was extremely taxing; but the problem which occupied her mind at the moment, as she sat in Sir George's study at Sir George's desk, was Tre. If he had taken his morning walk as usual today, he had also taken care not to bump into her. She hadn't expected him to. He had avoided her last night, too, in the drawing room before dinner; and after dinner he had been closeted with their host, adding fuel to her suspicions that he was here to assess Sir George's potential future as an intelligence agent.

Mary indulged herself, imagining bluff, portly Sir George in action. The man was as honest as the day was long, as they said. Explaining the situation which brought her here, he had turned bright red and begun to stutter with indignation. He was also an extremely fond husband and father, his desk crowded with informal photographs of his family, his wife and children at the beach, in the garden with dogs, or on horseback. She tried to picture him in—let's see, Saint Petersburg? Yes, his experiences with the Russians would make that an ideal destination for him, and he had a history of escaping their clutches which would serve him well when he had to flee with a handful of revealing letters which he'd stolen from a beautiful countess whose lover was the head of the Russian army. *Picture yourself in this situation*, she imagined Tre saying to Sir George. *What would you do?* Eat the letters would be the most likely answer. Mary giggled. Tre would say . . .

Stop! She was not going to share this silly bit of whimsy with Tre. She was *not* going to make the mistake of thinking that Tre was anything more to her than a fellow guest. Yes, he had at last explained the mysterious occupation which meant so much to him, and, yes, she understood a little of why it meant so much to him; but the more she picked over their conversation yesterday, the more unexplained gaps she found in it. There were the questions he had carefully—and cleverly—avoided answering, such as whether or not her father was embroiled in this new department. More interesting, though, than the who and the what, was the why. *Why* did he feel that he had to prove himself? *Why* had he transferred from such a prestigious regiment as the Scots Fusilier Guards to a department that made maps? *Why* did he call his illness a curse? *Why* was he so determined to devote his life solely to his career? And *why*, if that career was so important to him, had he allowed himself to be distracted, to possibly even compromise his career, by helping Mary resolve the issue of Mrs. Fitzherbert-Smythe's brooch?

Another thing. *Why* was such an attractive man of thirty-seven not married?

Mary closed her notebook, then locked the papers she had been studying back in Sir George's desk. Tre was an attractive man. There was no harm at all in her admitting that fact to herself. He was handsome, and he was successful, and he was interesting, in the sense that a puzzle was interesting. Solving puzzles was something she was very good at. It was why she was here.

Tre was avoiding her because he thought that was what she wanted. Was it? She was no longer the naive little dormouse who craved understanding and who had so very nearly fooled herself into thinking that understanding might lead to something more meaningful. She wasn't in the least bit interested in a meaningful relationship with any man. She enjoyed his company, admittedly, but she didn't *need* it. They had a lot in common, and there were few people she could say that about. If any. He had a wry sense of humour that appealed to her and a subversive way of looking at people and situations that chimed with her, too. She liked him. There was nothing wrong with admitting that. She liked a challenge, too. And Tre—yes, she did rather like the fact that she had piqued his interest. It might be fun to continue to do so. Sauce for the goose, in fact, and it would result in him revealing more of himself. The real Tre which he kept well hidden. Smiling to herself, Mary left Sir George's study. Now she had two cases to solve instead of one.

THAT AFTERNOON, GUESTS WERE OFFERED a choice of activities. Sir George led a walk in the park to view the monument erected to his charger, and for the more adventurous the walk would continue a few miles to the little village of Kilburn for a view of the famous White Horse which was carved into the chalk hill, with a carriage arranged for the return journey. His wife was to have conducted a tour of the priory's more macabre and interesting exhibits, but unfortunately she had wrenched her foot on the stone staircase that morning, and instead offered the pleasure of her company in the library to those of a leisurely inclination. The Duchess of Buccleuch chose to join her, having discovered to her delight that the bookshelves contained some rare drawings of André Le Nôtre's parterres for Louis XIV's gardens at Versailles.

Mr. Dacre Glover, Lady Wombwell's cousin, had stepped in to conduct the tour of the house, and Mary, with two of the other guests, Mr. and Mrs. St. John Aubyn, immediately expressed an interest in joining him. Tre, who had missed his morning walk, was on the point of attaching himself to Sir George's walking party when Mary, to his surprise, appeared at his side.

"I thought you might find the house tour interesting," she said.

He eyed her warily. Yesterday morning, in the garden, though there had been moments when she let down her guard, most of the time it was firmly in place. His attempt to heal the breach he had created between them had not succeeded; and on the whole, he had almost persuaded himself, this was for the best. Almost. Her deliberate attempt to intrigue him had been effective, but what fascinated him were the changes in her. He didn't recognize her, but there had been glimpses of the woman he thought he knew, a brief pulling back of a curtain before it was drawn again.

"Tre?"

Tre. A step forwards, a step back, a deliberate ploy or a slip of the tongue? It could be any of those—he had no idea. "I was planning to join the walking party. I missed my walk this morning."

"Because of me?"

"You made it pretty evident you'd had a surfeit of my company."

"I—it was a shock, seeing you after all this time. And I've been otherwise engaged."

"With Sir George?"

"He allowed me the use of his study. I had some correspondence to write, and there is no desk in my room. I didn't wish to be disturbed."

"One reason would have been sufficient, Mary. Two raises suspicion. But three?" Tre shook his head. "Three tells me that you have something to hide."

"Is that the sort of advice you dispense to your recruits?"

"Absolutely. It's rule number five in the spy handbook."

She chuckled. "Do come on the tour, Tre; there is a room that I think will be of most particular interest to you."

Her big grey eyes lit up when she laughed. Another thing that hadn't changed. "How can I resist," he said, wondering if he should.

They joined the small party, which began with a tour of the formal rooms on the ground floor. Mr. Dacre Glover was a good-looking man, clean-shaven, with guinea-gold hair worn rather too long, and dark-brown, thickly lashed eyes. His coat was tailored to show off a good pair of shoulders, though it was, in Tre's view, cut too tight. He judged the man to be in his early thirties. *Charming*, he reckoned would be the epithet Glover would like to have ascribed to him, the type who liked to be liked.

Mrs. St. John Aubyn seemed to be succumbing to Glover's charms, hanging on his every word, and to Tre's surprise, so, too, was Mary. Since he knew her for an excellent and intuitive judge of character, he was immediately suspicious. As Glover led them from room to room, from picture to tapestry, Mary encouraged him to expound, asking question after question. Glover, to his credit, never failed to answer.

The Worcester tea service was a gift from King George III to Henry, the last Earl Fauconberg, and Sir George's great-grandfather. The quill pen displayed here in the Small Drawing Room belonged to Oliver Cromwell. Glover seemed to have a genuine reverence for the priory's history. It was in the dining room, when the man stood aside to allow the St. John Aubyns to examine the carving above the fireplace, that Tre first noticed the change in their guide. Thinking himself unobserved, a deep frown furrowed Glover's narrow forehead, his mouth pursed. Tre wasn't the only one who noticed. He caught Mary's eye and raised his brows at her. She threw him a bland look.

On the tour went, upstairs to the three state bedrooms which were not occupied, and on again to the attics. He assumed, because Mary's attention for once wasn't on Glover, that this was the room which she reckoned he would be particularly interested in.

"Ladies and gentlemen," Glover announced, "we are about to enter a shrine. I beg you will treat it with due reverence."

The door creaked as Glover opened it. A gust of cold air made Mrs. St. John Aubyn exclaim in surprise and clutch at her husband's arm. The room was small and very austere, as befitted its single occupant, the bare brick walls painted white, the only piece of furniture an old trunk.

"Here," Mr. Glover intoned in sepulchral tones, "lies the mortal remains of Oliver Cromwell, whose New Model Army defeated the Royalists and who, famously or notoriously, was responsible for the execution of King Charles the First."

The vault containing the body was built into the wall under an arch, which Tre presumed must be part of the original priory, and marked by a plain plaque. The little room was musty and icy cold, though the only window was closed. Tre edged over toward the trunk to allow Mr. and Mrs. St. John Aubyn to inspect the vault more closely. "When you told me that Cromwell was buried here," he whispered to Mary, "I didn't realize you meant inside. What a macabre place."

"I thought you'd like it," she answered with a smug smile.

"How did Cromwell's body come to be interred here?" Mr. St. John Aubyn asked, running his hand over the covering of the vault.

"Sir," Mr. Glover said, grabbing his wrist, "I beg you do not touch. The family have taken an oath never, ever to open this vault."

"I should hope not! Why would they want to do any such thing?"

"The contents have been disputed," Mr. Glover said, folding his arms over his chest. "Though we are certain that Oliver Cromwell lies here, others have questioned it."

"Really? Why?"

"The corpse interred here is headless," Mr. Glover declared, edging towards the door.

"A headless corpse!" Mrs. St. John Aubyn shrieked. "Good heavens, my dear, come away from there."

"Don't be foolish, my love," her husband replied. "He's not going to jump out at me. Is he, Mr. Glover? I mean there's no ghost here, is there?"

"Not here, no."

"Oh my goodness." Mrs. St. John Aubyn cowered against her husband. "Do you mean he's lurking somewhere else?"

"No, no, there is no ghost of Cromwell at the priory, as far as I know. Only the corpse."

"The majority of the corpse," Tre corrected. "How *did* it come to be interred here?"

"Well, now, as to that, legend has it that his daughter, who was Countess of Fauconberg and lady of this very manor, had her father's remains stolen from the walls of the Tower of London where they were displayed at the command of Charles the Second."

"Ah yes, I remember now," Mr. St. John Aubyn said. "Charles had the body dug up, didn't he, when he was restored to the throne. Dug up, and beheaded. Isn't that the case?"

Glover shuddered. "So I believe. And then the, er—the corpse was displayed on the walls of the Tower."

"What a vile thing to do," Mrs. St. John Aubyn exclaimed.

"Well, when you think about it," her husband said, "the man *was* responsible for beheading Charles's father."

"All the same. One would expect better behaviour from a king. Petty vengeance—it is not a good example to set. I am not surprised the countess wished to retrieve her father."

"Well, I hope she took her smelling salts with her," Mary quipped.

"She did not attend to the matter personally," Mr. Glover replied, frowning slightly.

"Lady Mary," Tre said, shaking his head gravely, "picture the scene. The body would have been positioned high up on the Tower, a lesson for all who passed by of the consequences of defying the monarchy. In order to retrieve it, a person would have had to be brave enough to walk boldly out along the parapet, with the River Thames rushing far beneath."

"'Don't look down,'" Mary said, her own voice suitably hushed, "'don't look down,' they would be telling themselves, for to do so would be to plunge to their death in the cold, stinking, roiling river."

"Ah, but our bold perpetrator would not have looked down. She—I mean he—would be enjoying the danger. Knowing that his accomplice was watching, his heart in his mouth . . ."

"He had an accomplice?"

"He could not have managed the body alone," Tre pointed out.

"I didn't think of that. What about the guards?"

"Asleep in the guard-room?"

"Or drunk on the brandy our brave man had thoughtfully provided them with?" Mary suggested, her eyes again alight with laughter.

"Oh yes, that is excellent," Tre said. "I like that."

"And the body, Colonel Trefusis?" Mr. St. John Aubyn asked. "How was that—er, retrieved? One would have to be mighty strong to haul it up."

"By the chains from which it was suspended," Tre said.

"And placed in the large hessian sack he had brought," Mary added. "I think there must have been a sack, don't you?"

"You are in the right of it, Lady Mary. A sack would have been very necessary, depending on how long the body had been buried," Mr. St. John Aubyn agreed, grimacing. "Putrefaction, you see. The stench would have been overwhelming. No wonder, really, that he forgot the head."

"Yes, but without the head," his wife replied, "how could he be sure that he had the correct body?"

"A very good point, my dear. *Now* I understand why there has been pressure to open this vault." Mr. St. John Aubyn ran his hands over the cover again. "It's tempting, is it not? What might we find here, do you think, after all this time? Bones or just dust."

"My dear, I beg you do not—"

"Sir! Do not—"

A creak, as of a rusty hinge, was followed by the loud thump of wood falling on wood. Mary jumped. Mrs. St. John Aubyn screamed. Her husband leapt back. Mr. Glover turned white as a sheet and slumped against the wall.

"I do beg your pardon," Tre said. "I was curious as to the contents of this trunk. I thought it might be important, since there is nothing else in the room but the vault. The lid was so heavy, it slipped from my grasp. I didn't mean to startle any of you."

"What did you expect to find?" Mary demanded. "Cromwell's missing head?"

"The trunk was empty save for a couple of spiders. As I said, I do apologize."

"I think—I think we should end the tour here." Glover straightened up, mopping his brow. "Lady Mary's portrait hangs in the Long Gallery—Cromwell's daughter, that is, not this Lady Mary. I had intended that to be the next stop on our tour, but I think—yes, I really do think it is time for tea."

"Good God," Mr. St. John Aubyn exclaimed, "you've gone quite green about the gills, Mr. Glover."

"You poor man." Mrs. St. John Aubyn surged forward, glowering at Mary. "This ghoulish tale has been too much for your sensitive disposition. Let me help you."

"No, no." Glover rallied. "I am perfectly fine. A cup of tea is all I need."

"It is what we all need. A cup of tea, and perhaps a slice of cake. Or even two." Mrs. St. John Aubyn tucked her hand into Glover's arm, urging him towards the door.

"I have heard," Mary said, "that Mrs. Hare, the cook here, is famed for her chocolate cake."

"Chocolate cake! Now that is an offer I do not wish to refuse."

The three departed, and Mary made to follow, but Tre caught her arm. "A word, if you please."

"I have my heart set on chocolate cake."

"You don't like cake." Tre waited until the clattering of the footsteps receded. "Why are you so interested in Glover?"

"What do you mean?"

"Another classic mistake, Mary. Your response is far too defensive and merely arouses suspicion. You should have said, 'Oh. Glover! Didn't you find the depth of his knowledge intriguing?'"

"It was odd, though, wasn't it," Mary said. "He sounded as if he'd digested a catalogue. Or as if he was compiling a catalogue for himself?

But the items he treated with the most reverence were far from the most valuable."

"The Lord Protector here, for example," Tre said, indicating the vault.

Mary shuddered. "You frightened the life out of poor Mrs. St. John Aubyn."

"I really didn't mean to."

"I thought Mr. Glover was going to faint."

"He's certainly on edge."

"You noticed it, too! Though anyone would have. It wasn't that I was particularly—" She broke off, flushing, and made a point of reading the plaque on the vault.

"Glover has that story all wrong, you know," Tre said, deciding not to push her. "Cromwell's body was dug up and hanged at Tyburn. Then it was decapitated, and the head put on a spike at Westminster Hall, not the Tower. Eventually the spike broke, and the head was recovered and sold, believe it or not. The rest of the body was dumped in a pit at Tyburn, and no-one knows for sure what became of it."

Mary edged away from the vault, grimacing. "Whatever is in there, it's a horrible thing to have in one's attic. I had better go—my mother will be wondering where I am."

"You haven't answered my question."

"I am not one of your potential recruits, Tre. I am not obliged to answer your questions."

"I wish we did recruit women. You would make an excellent spy."

Mary gave a huff of laughter. "Is that another of your odd compliments?"

"You have all the qualities, and a rare ability to put yourself in another's shoes, to read what is going on in their head."

Her smile faded. "I am not infallible," she said curtly. "When it comes to you, for example, and your curse, as you called it. I never did understand that."

Tre flinched, not only at the direct reference to his most shameful secret but that she had quite deliberately broken the mood, pushing him away. His instinct was to turn the subject, to protect himself, but she was so prickly, she may not give him another chance. Did he want another chance? Whatever she was doing here, and however it connected with Glover, Sir George must somehow be embroiled. If he was to do his own job thoroughly, he was obliged, then, to discover what Mary was up to.

"Never mind," she said. "I shouldn't have brought it up."

"It's not that I don't want to explain. I simply can't. I don't understand it myself." The words were matter-of-fact, but to his horror, his voice trembled.

"Oh, Tre." Mary covered his hand with her own. "I am so sorry, that was unkind of me. I hate to be unkind."

"As I remember, you went out of your way never to be. To spare your parents, that was your whole raison d'être for the hoops you jumped through with Mrs. Fitzherbert-Smythe."

"And you helped me, at such a critical point in your career, too, to take such a risk . . ."

"Justice had to be done somehow."

"You thought so, too, I remember."

"How is your friend Stuart?"

"Oh, he decided that he wanted a change of scene, despite having his name cleared, and moved to Boughton at the end of that summer. He's married now, very happily."

So Mary had once again been abandoned at Drumlanrig, losing her parents to the queen and, as far as he could make out, her only friend to another household. And he had left her, too. He had missed her. Looking into her eyes, the touch of her hand in his, gave him a pang of pure longing. She still wore the same fragrance. Citrus. Not lemon or lime. Orange, he remembered all of a sudden, and bergamot. "I missed you," he said, the words torn from him.

Her expression hardened. She extracted her hand from his. "It was your choice to end our acquaintance, not mine. I must go—my mother will be wondering where I am."

CHAPTER SIXTEEN

Lady Mary, Quite Contrary

Newburgh Priory, Friday, 12 February 1875

T HE LONG GALLERY WAS IN the east wing of Newburgh Priory and was indeed a very long narrow room, with polished wooden floors and a great deal of oak wainscotting and panelling, augmented by a number of heavy oak chests and coffers. Despite the lead-paned windows that ran along one wall, it was an extremely gloomy chamber, well suited to the dark and austere portraits which bedecked the walls. The boards creaked as Mary made her way along in search of the portrait of her namesake. The thick brocade curtains in one of the windows swayed gently as she passed. The casements must be badly fitting, she told herself. There was a musty smell here that reminded her of the attics at Drumlanrig. The likeness of Mary, Countess Fauconberg, was positioned half-way along the gallery. Oliver Cromwell's daughter was a rather terrifying-looking woman, with the air of someone perfectly capable of scaling a building and stealing a desiccated corpse if she had to.

Mary shivered, wishing she had thought to bring a shawl. A floorboard creaked behind her, making her whirl around. "Tre! You scared me. What are you doing here?"

He shrugged, walking towards her down the gallery, stopping in front of a large glass case. Inside was a dark-blue tunic with white cuffs, a pair of pale-grey pantaloons, and a cap. "'The uniform worn by Sir George Wombwell of the Seventeenth Lancers in the Charge of Bala-clava, October twenty-fifth, 1854,'" he read. "And by the looks of it, it hasn't been cleaned since."

"Is this another chapter from your handbook? The one headed Diversionary Tactics?"

"You could write that particular chapter. Change the subject. Pretend to misunderstand. Walk away."

"You mean yesterday in the attic? Why on earth would I believe that you missed me, when you made no attempt to seek me out, and in fact you made it very clear that when you left Drumlanrig you were going to make sure our paths didn't cross again."

He flinched, then sighed heavily. "Would you rather I left the priory and returned another time to conclude my business?"

His secret business, she almost threw at him, remembering just in time that she had been even more secretive. His suggestion was a sound one, for he was proving to be a distraction, one way or another. "Your business is of national importance," Mary said. "It would be very wrong for me to obstruct it."

"It's not a life-or-death matter. It can wait. To be honest, I think it will have to wait. Sir George has little enough time to give me, with all his various other concerns. Until you resolve whatever matter it is you're here to assist him with, I'm going to struggle to get his attention. If I make my excuses, say I'm called back to London on business, I reckon he'll be relieved. And you will be, too, unless you think I can be of some assistance to you, as I was the last time?" Tre said diffidently.

"Assuming that you are here to resolve some sort of similar problem? I know you don't need my help, but . . ."

"I don't. I've been acting on my own for almost three years now."

"Good grief, am I in the presence of a lady detective?"

"No, you are not," Mary said, flustered. "I solve problems, that's all, the sort of things you would consider trivial. They are trivial, compared to what you do, but in my own way, I make a difference. What's more, discretion is vital to my success. Not even my mother knows the details."

"Discretion is every bit as vital to my activities, Mary. In fact it strikes me that what we do requires the same set of skills. We worked together very well before, didn't we?"

She crossed her arms, caught his eye, and immediately uncrossed them. "Your time is far too important for you to embroil yourself in this essentially domestic matter."

"Sir George clearly considers this matter—whatever it is—of primary importance. But as to myself—yes," Tre said sardonically, "you're quite right, I am far too high and mighty to get my hands dirty."

"I only meant—"

"That you would rather work alone. Or is it that you would rather work with anyone other than me?"

Both, she thought, quelling under his direct gaze and taking refuge by pretending to study one of the paintings, a particularly vile still life of raw meat and barely dead fish. She was being illogical and obstructive. She didn't need Tre, but he needed her to complete her work before he could conclude his. There was no reason why they couldn't collaborate one last time, for Sir George's sake and for Tre's and for the good of the country! Then they could go their separate ways, and if they never met again— which they most likely wouldn't—no harm would have been done.

"You think it's a bad idea," Tre said, appearing at her shoulder.

"Forget I suggested it. I thought we could make a fresh start, but if you don't trust me . . ."

"It's not that," Mary said.

"Then what is it?" Tre asked.

Good question. There had never been any question of her not trusting him. She had confided in him more than she'd ever confided in anyone. Recalling just how candid she had been could still make her toes curl. Poor little lonely, needy Mary, he must have thought. But three years had passed, and she wasn't that person now. Tre's proposition made perfect sense. She was about to say so, when he turned away.

"I have put you in a most embarrassing position. Forgive me. I'll go and make my apologies to Sir George."

"What! What do you mean by embarrassing? Tre, wait a moment, I truly don't understand."

"You consider me too much of a risk."

It took her a moment to understand his meaning, but when she did she was appalled. "Your—your illness. It never crossed my mind."

"You have always been very tactful—kind—but I quite understand . . ."

"Has it prevented you from doing your job these last three years?"

"No."

"If you believed it would be a risk, would you have offered to help me?"

"No, but . . ."

"It didn't cross my mind, Tre, not for a second," Mary said, shaking his arm. "Besides, I thought you were cured."

"I have it under control; it's not the same thing." He freed himself, brushing an imaginary piece of lint from the sleeve of his coat. "However, given the circumstances of our last meeting, my condition—I will quite understand if you consider it a risk you don't want to take."

What she wanted was to ask him what he meant by "under control." What she wanted to do was reassure him that she didn't think him weak or in any way unmanned by his condition—condition now, not curse, she noticed. Impossible for her to do either. She didn't wish to embarrass him further. She didn't want him to imagine her overly concerned. "My only worry is that you might steal my thunder by solving my case," Mary said, in an attempt to lighten the mood.

He smiled faintly. "Yes, I forgot your penchant for having praise heaped on you. If I promise to keep out of the limelight and allow you centre stage at all times, do we have an agreement?"

"Perhaps. If you will teach me some tricks of the trade. I'm an amateur with a talent for solving puzzles and reading characters. I've become more adept at getting answers to questions without asking them than I was three years ago, but I'm not an expert. I'd dearly love to see a copy of that handbook of yours."

Tre laughed. "It doesn't exist."

"Don't you think it should, though?"

"I can just imagine the uproar if it fell into the wrong hands. I don't mean the enemy, I mean our government. Obtaining information by stealth is really not acceptable, you know."

"Ah yes, it is ungentlemanly. There you see, that's another argument for using women."

Mary made her way down the gallery, and Tre followed her. "Are we to be partners in crime, then?" he asked.

"Only for this particular crime, which may not even turn out to be a crime. After that, you will go back to making the country a safer place, and I will carry on with my own modest attempts to make a difference." She took a seat on one of two very uncomfortable-looking oak chairs set under the window.

"Am I permitted an insight into how you have spent the last three years?" Tre asked, sitting down in the other chair. "What is your own particular way of making a difference, as you put it?"

"It's nothing compared to what you do. Small affairs, though they do matter to the people involved. Tracing misused funds in a charity that my mother is involved with was one of my early successes. The sort of thing that would usually be covered up." Mary grimaced. "In a way, that's exactly what I do. Resolve the problem and deliver some minor form of justice in a way that ensures everyone involved can pretend that nothing untoward has occurred."

"You are as self-effacing as ever. So you avoid scandals and set wrongs to right, is that it? And you can do so discreetly because you're Lady Mary Montagu Douglas Scott. A society insider, in other words."

"Yes," Mary said, secretly impressed, "that's exactly it."

"How do people engage your services? You can't exactly put an advert in the *Times*, and those you have helped are hardly going to broadcast that fact."

"Those I have helped will occasionally recommend me, but usually it's word of mouth through the network of servants who run the big houses. You know how it is: the staff behind the green baize door know everything that is going on. Most of the senior staff travel from house to house with their employers, and they inevitably talk. No-one at Drumlanrig knows the full story of Mrs. Fitzherbert-Smythe and her precious brooch, but it came to be known that I was involved and somehow responsible for saving the day."

"Covert exchange of information," Tre said, grinning. "Our work is much more similar than either of us would have imagined. We both work alone; we're both required to be invisible. We study people. We make judgement calls. May I ask how Sir George came to engage you?"

"His man of business once worked in my father's offices at Drumlanrig, and he is still friendly with Mr. Irvine."

"The head gamekeeper, your friend Stuart's father. You have your own little network of contacts. I find it difficult to believe that no-one in your family save the duchess has any idea what you do. Isn't it galling sometimes, to be so consistently under-estimated?"

"It suits me that they still think me the shy, boring, dispensable sister."

"And of course, now that the outgoing, scandalous troublesome sister has returned from America, you will feel obliged to play the dormouse, even though you've shed that skin."

This was precisely what she found unsettling about Tre: his ability to read between the lines of what she said. "We are all very proud of Margaret."

"So you said the other day. Does she get in the way of your playing Princess Beatrice to your mother's Queen Victoria?"

"My mother has a great many calls on her time, not least Her Majesty. My father isn't the least bit interested in where I am or what I am doing. To be honest, he seems to have very little interest in my mother's whereabouts either these days, provided she is there when he needs her. Annie, my brother Walter's wife, is my more usual companion; and that suits me very well, for she is short of wit and utterly lacking in curiosity. My mother accompanied me to Yorkshire because she wishes to take the waters at Harrogate. She is leaving me in Lady Julia's charge tomorrow, for a few days, and I believe two of the other ladies in the party will be joining her."

"Is the duchess ill?"

"I think she imagines herself so. She is very fond of spa treatments. Homeopathy, hydrotherapy, galvanism. Anything that involves being immersed in a bath of mud, or having various parts of the body bombarded with ice-cold water. Something called a needle douche is the newest treatment she is intent on trying. One stands in the middle of a contraption of water pipes and is bombarded with needle-like sprays of water."

"Dear heavens, you have painted an extremely vivid picture, and one I would happily have forgone."

Mary chuckled. "We had better go; it's time to change for dinner. Shall we meet in the morning to discuss my remit? If you still want us to collaborate, that is?"

"It makes sense. It is to our mutual benefit after all," Tre said, lifting her hand to his lips and brushing the lightest of kisses on her fingertips. "The scent of citrus," he said, releasing her. "You told me the name once, but it escapes me."

"Bouquet Opoponax." She recalled the occasion exactly. That last day. The walk to the pinery. He had been on the verge of collapse, clutching her arm, clinging to her words as if she would save him. "Bergamot, citrus, vanilla."

"It smells of you," Tre said.

Exactly what he'd said that August day almost three years ago. A lump rose in her throat. "We can't be late for dinner," Mary said, hurrying away.

CHAPTER SEVENTEEN

I Get a Kick Out of You

Newburgh Priory, Saturday, 13 February 1875

TRE WAS ALREADY WAITING IN the King James's Porch when Mary appeared the next morning. She was wearing a cloak, her hair covered by the blue scarf she had been wearing around her neck the last time they had gone for a walk, rather than a hat. The stitching on the scarf was extremely uneven, and he could see at least one hole in it. Had she knitted it? Was he maligning her, imagining her absent-mindedly dropping stitches while her mind was focused on something else? If it was her poor handiwork, though, she wouldn't wear it, she'd hide it away in a drawer, which meant that the scarf must have sentimental value. A handmade gift from one of her many nieces, most likely.

"Will we walk round to the fish pond?" Mary asked, setting out without waiting for him.

She was on her guard again, businesslike, launching straight into an account of the circumstances she had been invited here to investigate. Tre was becoming inured to this, the reserve, followed by a slow thaw. The moments when she forgot herself, when their eyes met in a shared joke or a memory. Or when she allowed herself to acknowledge what had been there from the first between them, an affinity. Kindred spirits. Then she recovered her ground with a sardonic remark, consulted her watch, and announced that her mother would be wondering where she was.

She was different, more polished, confident, and at times haughty. Yet behind the veneer—was it a veneer?—the essence of her was the same. The wicked sense of humour, the instinctive understanding of people that allowed her to put herself in their shoes, her ability to disappear into the background, to make herself invisible. One of the reasons for his success in his new role was his own ability to read people accurately, to assess and weigh them up; but this new Mary was a challenge. It was in his interests to assist her, just as he'd said yesterday, but he wasn't going to pretend it was a hardship. He was fascinated by her and disconcertingly, persistently, extremely attracted to her. He was fairly sure she felt the same, though she had been quite adamant about placing boundaries around their acquaintance. This, and no more, she had said, in different ways, several times yesterday. He couldn't argue with her logic. His new career had been everything to him these last three years. It hadn't cured him, but he had his condition under control. This, and no more, made perfect sense. Yet every time he looked at Mary, every time their eyes met, every time she called him Tre—every time, he wanted this, and more.

"I don't think you were listening to a single word I was saying," Mary said, interrupting his thoughts.

"He ought to have known there would be an audit at some point," Tre said. "That's one of the reasons Sir George is unsure of his guilt." The weather was cold and very overcast, the dull slate-grey sky lowering to meet the pewter waters of the fish pond, completely obscuring the view of the hills and the White Horse. A slow but persistent mizzle was falling. "Let's go and find some shelter before we get soaked."

MARY TOOK THE LEAD, WALKING briskly back up the slope from the fish pond to the dog kennel garden, and hurried into the little glass-house just in time. She perched on the gardener's stool, and Tre pushed aside a stack of terra-cotta pots, which had been washed ready for the coming season, so that he could lean against the potting table before removing his hat, smoothing back his hair, and digging his hands into the pockets of his overcoat. Whatever he had been thinking, he wasn't going to share his thoughts. It didn't matter, Mary told herself, the only thoughts she was interested in were on the subject in hand.

"So, let me get this straight," Tre said. "Two hundred pounds has been siphoned off over the last two months from the charity that Sir George established to care for Crimean veterans and their families, paid out to a person who doesn't exist. And this was discovered by Sir George's man of business, when he was doing an audit of the accounts."

"Who once worked in my father's offices at Drumlanrig and is still friendly with Mr. Irvine, Stuart's father, which is how I came to be involved."

"And Dacre Glover, who is Lady Wombwell's cousin, is the principal suspect. Tell me what you know of him."

"Mr. Glover has been staying in one of the estate cottages for the last six months or so. 'Had a bit of bad luck in a business deal,'" Mary said, pleased with her imitation of Sir George's gruff tones. "'Not his fault, my lady wife assured me. Chap was badly advised, his partners took advantage.' Basically, Mr. Glover lost his capital and his reputation, Sir George took pity on him, when the rest of his family wanted nothing to do with him, and invited him to the priory. Thinking that the best thing to restore his self-esteem would be to make him feel useful, Sir George then handed over his own role as chairman of the board of trustees of his charity. Amongst his other duties, he is responsible for assessing new claims and paying out if he thinks they are worthwhile."

"And it looks as if Mr. Glover considers himself a worthwhile cause," Tre said. "You're right, though, there's something that doesn't add up about that. He must have known there would be an audit, and it's such a blatant breach of trust. Biting the hand that feeds him, so to speak."

"All the same, Mr. Glover is worried about something—you noticed that yourself. He is extremely well turned out, I'd say he was quite vain, yet his nails are bitten right down to the quick. If he has taken the money, why hasn't he absconded with it?"

"I assume he doesn't know he's been caught out yet. Could be he's planning to take more. Sir George hasn't confronted him, I take it?"

"No. Poor Sir George." Mary pulled off one of her gloves and began to twist it around her fingers. "He is such an honest, good-hearted man. He has kept his suspicions from Lady Wombwell; and even that small deceit, which is done for the best of reasons, is cutting him up. If you are intending to ask him to gather covert information, Tre, I'm not sure he'll be able to square it with his conscience. Though, of course, that may not be what you want from him. Indeed, you may want nothing from him at all."

"Mary . . ."

"I'm teasing you, not castigating you," she said, with a mocking smile. "You have already admitted to your business with Sir George. Yesterday, in the Long Gallery, remember?"

"I'd forgotten, actually. Now I'll have to find out one of your deepest, darkest secrets in order to bind you to silence." Tre got up, taking the twisted glove from her hand. "Or maybe I'll hold this to ransom and at the same time save it from ruin."

"Give me that back!"

He slipped it into his coat pocket. "So Mr. Glover is the chief suspect, because he looks guilty."

"He's guilty of something, that's for sure, but I prefer to have proof to back up my instincts; and Sir George would very much prefer me to discover that someone else entirely is guilty. He trusted Mr. Glover when no-one else did, and he doesn't want to be made to look a fool for having done so. He's furious about the money, 'food from the mouths of widows and orphans,' to use his own words, and if it is Mr. Glover, Sir George will not let it go unpunished, but he needs to be certain."

"Understandably," Tre said, "but there's no other likely candidate, is there?"

"Sadly not, but the case against Mr. Glover really isn't as watertight as it appears. Remember, he has already been duped in his business dealings. It could be that history is repeating itself. According to Sir George, he is trying hard to prove himself, but he's not particularly bright when it comes to business. That's why there was an audit, to make sure he hadn't been making any foolish mistakes. But two hundred pounds constitutes more than a silly mistake. Then there is the fact the claimant is fictitious. So it is a premeditated act of fraud."

"What is our plan, then, aside from waiting and watching? If Mr. Glover hasn't stolen the money, someone else has, either for pure avarice or perhaps because they want to frame Mr. Glover. We could try and establish if the man has any enemies."

"I asked Sir George about that but he was not aware of anyone Mr. Glover had upset. So the most obvious way of investigating that . . ."

Tre rolled his eyes. "I think I can guess what you're going to say."

"You're right! Ask the servants, who see and hear everything, though which ones, and how to go about it without arousing suspicion, is the problem. I can hardly barge into his cottage and demand to speak to his valet, and he doesn't have any other staff of his own."

"What does he do for food?"

"He eats his dinner at the priory most nights," Mary said.

"Dinner isn't the only meal of the day, and a good valet won't deign to do more than make a pot of coffee."

"You're right. There's the cleaning, too, which must be done by one of the maids. I should have thought of that," Mary said, getting to her feet. Her scarf was soaking. She took it off to shake it out.

"A gift from one of your nieces?" Tre asked.

"Yes, Cecil, who is Victoria's daughter. She knitted it for my Christmas present. How did you know?"

Tre shrugged. "A lucky guess."

Mary wound the scarf around her neck. Tre was rearranging the stacks of terra-cotta pots into a neat square on the potting table. "The result of careful observation, more like. I feel like you are assessing me. Why?"

He turned, smiling ruefully. "Because you intrigue me."

"You can't solve me. Concentrate on the puzzle of the missing money, if you please, Tre. And give me back my glove."

"It's not a question of solving you. I'd like to understand you better."

Mary glared at him. His hair had flopped over his brow. He was smiling faintly at her, the merest quirk of his mouth. It raised her hackles, that look, and it also raised her pulse. "Why?" she demanded. "As soon as we have resolved this matter, I shall be off to—to . . ." Where? Drumlanrig, to await another cry for help? Or she could take Victoria up on her invitation to spend a lengthy visit with her. "It doesn't matter where," she said. "It's of no interest to you, since we won't see each other again."

"Unless we take matters into our own hands," Tre said.

"Why would we do that? You have your work," Mary said. "I have mine," she added, with slightly less conviction.

"You're right," Tre said, brushing some fragments of compost from the skirts of his overcoat. "There's no reason for us to meet. The nature of my occupation requires me to work alone. I enjoy that, I'm solitary by nature, but it is—it's a pleasant change to work with a like-minded person."

"It does make a pleasant change," Mary said. "Just this once, I mean." There was no harm in admitting that much. It was the truth. So long as she remembered that when their work together was done this time, she wouldn't see Tre again.

"We'd better get back," Tre said.

"Yes. My glove?"

He took it out of his pocket. She reached for it, and his fingers closed over hers. She could have snatched it away, but she let him pull her closer, all the time her eyes locked on his. Her heart began to hammer. She was close enough to smell his shaving soap. He murmured her name. He hesitated for a fraction. She felt him inhale sharply. He pulled her towards him. Her hand fluttered over his cheek.

And then they both came to their senses. The glove dropped onto the floor of the glasshouse. Tre stooped to pick it up. Mary turned away. "As you say, we'd better go," she said.

He picked up his hat. "Yes, we had. Your mother no doubt will be wondering where you are."

CHARLOTTE HAD NEVER ENJOYED BREAKFASTING in company, but her mother had taught her it was rude and inconsiderate to take anything other than tea in her bedchamber, whether she was a guest or a hostess. She had never had much of an appetite for food before twelve either, but once again, her upbringing contradicted her wishes. Seated at a table, she was required to eat, or at least make a pretence of eating, lest she insult her hostess or encourage concerned enquiries regarding her health. Even if such an enquiry was valid. She really did feel squeamish this morning. And tired, extremely tired, though she had fallen into a deep sleep the moment her head hit the pillow last night.

She sipped her tea and cut a small finger from her slice of bread and butter. Was she ill? This perpetual sluggishness was a relatively new symptom. Perhaps she was simply getting old. She took a tiny bite of the bread and butter, but her stomach made it clear it would not accept any more. If Mary were here, she would be able to slip the rest onto her plate. Where was she? Surely not out walking in this weather? This Yorkshire drizzle was even more insidious than the Highland version, soaking through even the heaviest of outer garments. Mary always dismissed her concerns about her health, but she had been the least robust of Charlotte's babies. No, not the least robust, for there had been poor, darling little Francis. It was hard to believe he would have been thirty-five if he had lived. She counted herself fortunate to have lost only one of her children so young, but even after all those years, the pain of that loss was sharp. When Victoria lost her own little one, seeing her daughter's suffering brought it all back to her. And then just last year, Henry had lost a child, too. Was it easier for men to bear such losses, or was it simply more difficult for them to express their grief?

Charlotte caught the footman's eye, and without having to ask, had a second cup of tea poured. Lady Wombwell's servants were very well-trained. There were scarce half of her guests seated around the table this morning. At least she was spared the need to make conversation. She poured more milk into her tea. She used to take it with the merest splash, but nowadays she couldn't drink it if it was too hot. She would never resort to Her Majesty's habit of having two cups and saucers, pouring the tea from one to the other until it was cool enough, which in anyone other than a queen would be viewed as extremely vulgar. The tea was still too hot. She stirred it in an effort to cool it. The tinkling of the spoon against the porcelain made her head ache.

Was she ill or getting old? She would soon be sixty-four. Looking in the mirror, she barely recognized herself. Though she ate like a sparrow, she was putting on weight. Both her sisters were dead now, and four of her eight brothers. Would she be missed if her turn came soon? It was wicked to think that way. She was still useful. If she hadn't stepped in and relieved Walter of the burden, the project to upgrade all the estate cottages would have come to nothing. The gardens at Drumlanrig would never be finished. Then there was the Refugee Benevolent Fund and the Poor Servants of the Mother of God, and all the other charities.

Her children no longer needed her, though her grandchildren seemed fond enough of Granny B. It was such a joy to have Margaret back. Her second daughter was so generous-hearted, so open with her affections, she had made it easy to heal the wounds of the past and to establish a new warmth and closeness. Charlotte was delighted to see Margaret happy, looking forward to her marriage, embracing life with such enthusiasm, but Charlotte's pleasure was bittersweet, knowing she would be losing her all over again.

At last, Mary arrived, making her apologies to Lady Wombwell as she took her place beside Charlotte.

"Your hair is wet."

"I was out walking, Mama." Mary smilingly accepted a cup of tea and a hot roll.

"With Colonel Trefusis?" she asked, for that gentleman had just entered the room and taken a vacant seat at the other end of the table.

"Aren't you feeling well?" Mary asked. "You've not touched your bread and butter."

"I was waiting for you." Charlotte picked up a tiny piece of her breakfast and forced herself to eat it. Mary went to the sideboard, where there was an array of covered platters. She would take eggs if they were scrambled but not fried, and mushrooms, however they were cooked, Charlotte knew. She might take a sausage if they were pork but not beef. She would not touch the kedgeree or the liver. She would have three cups of tea, though she would only add milk to the first one.

Charlotte placed her napkin over her plate as her daughter sat back down beside her. How could it be that she knew all these minutiae about her youngest child but so very little about the essence of the woman she had become? Was there something brewing between her and Colonel Trefusis? There was no point in asking. Mary would either change the subject or give her a bland, meaningless answer. She never lied, but she never volunteered information of any sort, especially not about herself.

It was her own fault, Charlotte castigated herself. The damage had been done all those years ago when Mary had been all but abandoned at Drumlanrig, and she and Walter and the rest of the family were fully taken up with Margaret and with their own many civic duties. She had no right to expect Mary to confide in her, or even to like her particularly. They were entrenched in their positions now, and she had no idea how to change that. Nor the energy, these days, to try.

Mary was eating her breakfast, her attention fastened on her plate, but every now and then Colonel Trefusis slanted her a look. What did those glances mean? They seemed far too intimate for two people who barely knew each other. What did Trefusis do? An administrative post of some sort? Or had that changed? Yes, she recalled now, Walter had mentioned something about a new assignment, though he'd been very unforthcoming about it. How Walter loved to be important! And how, it seemed to her more and more often of late, he enjoyed making her feel very unimportant—or at least most unnecessary to his well-being. He had no idea she and Mary were in Yorkshire.

Did Trefusis have intentions? Mary had never shown any sign of being interested in any man, though she'd had her share of interested parties in the last two years, since she came out of her shell. Not an ounce of encouragement had she given any of them. Walter had begun to evidence some interest in finding her a husband. Heaven forfend that he discover what she'd been doing behind his back. Their marriage had survived the rift between them that Margaret had precipitated, but another rebellious daughter, aided and abetted by her mother—which is how he would see it. Dear heavens, it didn't bear thinking about.

The room was stifling, thanks to the huge fire which blazed under the marble edifice that was the fireplace. Diana and Apollo stood one on either side of the carved overmantel, with Venus in the centre. Every one of them naked, and though the male and female characters had strategically placed hands and drapes, it was clear that they were very eager to remove them. She could barely remember Walter looking at her like that, but he had once. When they were first married . . .

"Mama?"

Charlotte opened her eyes to find Mary looking at her anxiously. "Eighteen twenty-nine," she said.

"Mama, it's eighteen seventy-five. I don't think you are well enough to go to Harrogate."

"Nonsense." Charlotte took a sip of her tea. It was stone cold. Mary's plate was empty. "Nonsense," she said bracingly. "The show must go on. I have made commitments, I cannot let the other ladies down."

CHAPTER EIGHTEEN

The Water Garden

Newburgh Priory, Monday, 15 February 1875

MARY HAD EXCUSED HERSELF FROM the expedition Lady Womb-well had organized to a nearby beauty spot, feigning a head-ache. A morning spent poring over the charity account books once again had given her lie credibility. She was sitting on a wooden bench under a window on the south side of the priory, enjoying the weak winter sunshine, when Tre found her.

"I've just spent the last hour with Sir George." Tre sat down beside her. "He was under the impression that he was being considered for a position as military attaché and, on reflection, had decided that it wasn't for him. He wished to let me know, so that he didn't waste any more of my precious time."

"Oh." Mary bit her lip hard. *Oh!* She pasted a smile onto her face. "So, you'll be off, then?"

"No," Tre said. "No, I'm not leaving. There was never any question of offering him such a position. Though I must say, I very much enjoyed his take on why he was so unsuited. Moscow, he informed me, was too far from home and he didn't speak the language. He likes Paris, he likes the food . . ."

"But he doesn't speak the language?" Mary interjected, recovering from her shock.

"Berlin . . ."

"Oh, let me guess. He is a great admirer of Prussian discipline, but sadly doesn't speak the language? Poor Sir George. Was he disappointed when you told him what it was you actually wished from him?"

"I don't know who came up with the idea of sending him off in the company of a cartographer to the Crimea, but, as you can imagine, he was appalled by the prospect."

Mary narrowed her eyes. "Is that a joke?"

"Sadly, not."

"Sir George is a family man, and he's immersed himself in local affairs. He's a Justice of the Peace, for goodness sake! I'm surprised at you, Tre. You must have known from almost the moment you met him that he would never have consented, even if he was suited."

"I did, of course I did, but it wasn't that simple," Tre said, frowning. "There's a great deal of pressure on me to utilize fellow senior officers wherever possible, even if they are retired, regardless of whether or not they are the best fit to the requirements. I meet a lot of resistance if I put a non-commissioned soldier forward, for example."

"Whereas Sir George is a hero who was aide-de-camp to Lord Cardigan?"

"Lord Cardigan! Whom some people still insist on believing a hero despite the evidence to the contrary."

"So if a man like Sir George wishes to serve his country, then there is pressure on you to give him what he asks for—is that it?" Mary asked. "Even if he's not a good fit?"

"That's it. Though ironically, I think that now I know him better,

I may be able to offer Sir George a different role. Whether he'll take it or not is another question. If Mr. Glover is guilty, then Sir George will have to assume responsibility for managing his charity, and it's a substantial undertaking."

"The fraud was very crudely executed," Mary said. "So crudely, it's as if whoever did it wanted it to be uncovered. Which means it could be that Mr. Glover was duped, but equally it could be that he's completely inept."

"You don't like him, do you?"

"No, but that doesn't make him guilty."

"They don't like him in the servants' quarters either, according to my valet," Tre said. "He's high-handed, you know, talks down to them."

"Yes, Clara, my maid, said the same, but, again, it doesn't mean he's guilty. He's in an odd position being Lady Wombwell's cousin but living in a cottage on the estate."

"And all too aware that the staff will know something of his history, if not the detail. I don't like him either," Tre said, "but I'm not sure where that leaves us."

"I am going to find a way to speak to the maid who cleans his cottage. I thought I might contrive to bump into her when she is on her way back, tomorrow if I can. Otherwise, I'm at a loss, and Sir George may have no option but to confront Mr. Glover."

"Don't despair. What you need is a walk and some fresh air."

Mary smiled. "Your cure for everything. Perhaps you're right. There's a water garden in the woodlands over there, I believe. If you have nothing else to do . . ."

"Nothing else I'd rather do," Tre said. "Shall we?"

They walked together in silence, heading away from the house across the parkland. Tre matched his pace to hers. Back in Drumlanrig, she would have put her hand on his arm while they walked. That last walk they had shared together to the pinery, he had clung to her like a man drowning. He had his condition under control now, he said. Did that mean he no longer suffered? That his suffering was not so extreme? Did he know now what caused it? Guns, she had eventually surmised, or weapons. The arrows, that last day?

"What will you do," Tre asked, disturbing her thoughts, "I mean after you solve this mystery? Do you have another assignment?"

"If this mystery is resolved and, no, I don't," Mary replied tersely. "I am not in your fortunate position of being occupied full time."

Tre smiled faintly. "So what will you do, Mary?"

"I don't know, Tre."

They had reached the edge of the woodland. He caught her arm, forcing her to stop walking. "What's wrong? Have I offended you in some way?"

"No. It's nothing. I don't know what I will do next, but that's no business of yours. I very much enjoy what I do, when I do it, but it's not a career. If I were a son and not a daughter, it would be different."

"Yes, you could find yourself packed off to the army."

"Is that what happened to you?"

"My father paid just over two thousand pounds for my lieutenant's commission when I left Sandhurst at seventeen and was sent to the Crimea. I'm a younger son. I had a choice, if you consider it a choice to serve Queen and Country or God."

"Seventeen, and you were sent to war!"

"The siege of Sevastopol was my—my baptism of fire. Shall we carry on? The path is quite narrow. Do you want to go first or will I?"

"I can't imagine what it must have been like," Mary said, standing her ground.

"It's better you don't try."

Yet she wanted to. She really wanted to know what he had endured. "Sir George said that the horses were treated better than the men."

"Did he?"

"That story he tells of the charge, it's so—so sanitized. And the picture in the White Drawing Room, too—he looks as if he has just stepped off the parade ground, not out of the heat and chaos of battle."

"It certainly doesn't represent the reality of war, I can assure you of that."

"I asked him," Mary said, "the other day, when we were discussing the case, I asked him what the real story was. He wouldn't tell me. He said it was best to forget such things."

"He's right."

"Yes, but what if you can't forget, Tre?" He was avoiding her gaze now, looking over her shoulder. She tugged his arm. "Is that what it is? The sound of guns reminds you?"

"No." He freed himself. Turning his back on her, he took off his hat, smoothed his hair. "I know you want an explanation. I want an explanation, too, but there is none," he said, turning back to face her.

His expression was strained, his mouth set in a firm line, the fingers of his left hand curled tightly around the brim of his hat, the knuckles showing white. Tre was a man who liked answers, just as she did. How would it feel, to live with whatever ailed him and never to have an answer? She smoothed her hand over his coat sleeve, desperate to comfort him and utterly at a loss.

"I live with it," Tre said. "I have found a way to live with it. My work—" He broke off, shaking his head. "As I said, it gives me a purpose."

"I understand that, Tre. I do."

"Yes, I know you do." His mouth softened. He ran his finger down her cheek, tucking a strand of her hair which had become loose behind her ear. "I've never met anyone like you," he said softly. "You are so . . ."

He was wearing gloves, but his touch was making her shiver with anticipation. Their gazes were locked. "So?" Mary asked.

"So, this."

Their lips met. Her eyes fluttered closed. For a moment they stood motionless, and then she stepped closer, and he slipped his arm under her cloak, around her waist, and he kissed her. She had been kissed before. Chaste, tentative kisses. She had been kissed before, because she had wanted to know what kissing was like. It hadn't been like this.

She put her hand on his shoulder. His lips moved on hers gently, urging her to open her mouth; and when she did, he sighed, his arm tightening on her waist, pulling her closer. She kissed him back. She smoothed her gloved hand over his cheek. Her heart was hammering. She was glowing from the inside.

Then with a muffled groan, Tre lifted his head, and it was over. He stared at her, looking as dazed as she felt. "Was that wrong of me?"

Mary shook her head.

"Are you sure?"

Nothing about that kiss felt wrong. It made her realize that all the other kisses—not that there had been many—hadn't been right. It made her realize why kissing was so dangerous. Not yet trusting herself to speak, Mary nodded, turning towards the path leading to the water garden. It was narrow, forcing them to walk single file. Tre led, and she followed.

She rarely considered the rules of propriety. She broke them regularly, but since she took care to ensure she was discreet, she didn't concern herself too much with the fact. To be compromised was the ultimate crime for a young, single woman. At her next birthday, Mary would be twenty-four, yet in the eyes of the world she was still an innocent. Had she been *compromised*, kissing Tre? She had relished every moment of it. She was still tingling with the effect, the thrill of it, the way her body seemed to sing in response, the breathless feeling she had even now, just thinking about it. She would happily—very happily—kiss him again. And again. Was that wrong?

It was wrong in the eyes of the world, because they were not be-trothed, nor did they have any intentions of becoming betrothed. But no-one would ever know. A person could not be compromised, if no-one ever knew, and discretion had been her watchword since she was fifteen years old. Besides, Mary reminded herself, it wasn't as if her family actually cared about her, save as a—a commodity! A bargaining chip in the eternal game of Power and Influence.

Oh, dear, there it was, the huge insurmountable wall that she kept coming up against in the early hours of the morning when she woke won-dering, with increasing frequency, what was to become of her. Her mother was getting old. What if she actually was ill? And Margaret, the rebel of the family, even she was settling down and getting married. At some point soon, the duke was going to realize he still had another daughter to utilize. If her father found out that she was here, alone, with Tre, that she had kissed him—it would not only be Mary who was in trouble. The duke had had a hand in establishing Tre in the Intelligence Branch; he would have no qualms about removing him. Or worse, he might try to force Tre to marry Mary, in a horrible, horrible echo of his ruthless attempts to force Margaret and her first, despised suitor into wedlock.

For heaven's sake! She was letting her imagination run away with her. Her father was in London. She and Tre had kissed. It had been wonderful. She wanted to kiss him again. Whatever her eventual fate, she was free now; and if she was vigilant, and discreet, there was no rea-son why she shouldn't enjoy spreading her wings just a little bit.

TRE CAME TO A STOP. The path had led them to a circular pond of dark, brackish water surrounded by mossy stones. The pond fed a series of little waterfalls and smaller pools which trickled over boulders and rocks, the path meandering alongside. The trees above them were bare, but the branches formed a thick canopy through which the weak winter sun danced, making the water glitter and sparkle. The air was lush with the smell of damp leaves and rich earth.

"It's beautiful," Mary said, coming to a halt beside him. "Like a fairy glen. Magical."

"It's treacherous underfoot. I'm not sure we should risk going any farther."

"Oh, don't be so prosaic!"

Tre watched her, cloak flying out behind her, her blue scarf unwinding. The path was slippery, consisting of sodden earth and large boulders, but she was sure-footed. Aside from the trickle and burble of the water, and the noise of their footsteps—soft, dissonant thuds— there was silence. No birds, no rustle of other creatures. He had kissed her. He shouldn't have kissed her, he'd had no intentions of kissing her, but he'd been unable to resist. The moment her lips met his, he was lost. He wished that it had been a bad kiss. A disappointing kiss. He wished that Mary had been horrified or shocked or disgusted. No, he didn't wish any of those things. What he wanted was to kiss her again.

What the hell was he doing here alone with her in this most magical, romantic of places, ideal for illicit kissing! He hadn't kissed anyone in so long; perhaps that was it? And there was the second chance effect, too. The kiss they hadn't shared in Drumlanrig. Though that would have been wrong; and it wasn't that young woman he wanted to kiss again, it was this woman, traipsing at a dangerous speed down the muddy path, whom he wanted to kiss again. Perhaps if he did kiss her again, it wouldn't be such a good kiss?

Tre laughed inwardly. There was a limit to how far he could delude himself. Mary had reached the bottom of the hill, where the cascades fed a small stream that tumbled along the floor of the valley. A series of flat stones had been laid across the stream to form a narrow crossing. She stepped out, ignoring his cry of warning. He watched her, jumping sure-footedly from stone to stone, his hands dug deep in his pockets. She reached the last stone, leapt onto the bank, turned and gave a flourishing curtsy.

The performance was as much for her own benefit as his. She was embarrassed and at a loss, and there wasn't a pineapple at hand for her to balance on her head. What the devil was he doing here with her! He wasn't busy enough, that was it. Back in London he was far too busy to need distraction. Far too busy to miss female company. Far too busy to succumb to his condition. He wasn't lonely. There was no time. Here at Newburgh Priory he had too much time on his hands. And there was Mary.

She was crossing back now, arms outstretched, making an unnecessary show of it. One last leap to the bank, but her foot caught on a branch that had lodged between the stones. She lurched, wobbled frantically, tipped forward, and by some miracle ended up not in the icy stream but in his arms.

"Are you hurt?" he asked.

"Only my pride."

She looked up into his eyes, and he groaned, and she said his name, and her arms went around his neck, and their lips met. He forgot to be gentle, but she kissed him back fervently. Their tongues touched, and he felt her shiver, nestling against him, and even through the layers of their clothing his body reacted to the warmth of her, the sheer delight of having her in his arms. He wanted her.

Tre came to his senses. His hat had fallen onto the path. Mary's scarf had unwound. Her cheeks were flushed. Her big grey eyes were heavy-lidded. And her mouth. Don't look at her mouth!

"I'm sorry," he said, "that was . . ." Wonderful. Wrong, wrong, wrong. He stooped down and picked up his hat. "I'm sorry."

"Are you?"

He winced. "Trying to be."

"I expect I should try, too." She smiled crookedly. "But I'm not going to."

"Mary . . ."

"Don't you dare walk away from me like that!"

Tre whirled around, but there was no-one in sight.

"Did you hear me, Dacre? Stop ignoring me!"

Tre's brows shot up. "Glover?" he mouthed.

"For pity's sake! Stop following me. It's becoming embarrassing." Glover's voice carried to them from somewhere farther down the valley.

"What else am I to do? There's never a chance for me to speak to you in private," a female voice pleaded.

"I can't talk now. Perhaps later."

"You never used to have a problem finding time. I'm at my wit's end. Please!"

"Not now! I'm busy." Glover swore. The voices began to fade.

"There must be another path beyond the trees," Tre said softly. "I wonder who the woman is."

"I don't know, but I'm going to find out," Mary whispered.

She was smiling, happy to be distracted, Tre guessed, but also relieved to have some sort of breakthrough. Failure had been weighing on her mind. The obvious reason for the confrontation they had overheard was an age-old one, and if he was right, Mary was getting herself into a quagmire that may have nothing at all to do with the missing money. But how to caution her?

Tre brushed the mud from his hat and put it back on. There was little point now in any further discussion about whether the kisses they had shared had been right or wrong. He was thankful for this small mercy.

CHAPTER NINETEEN

Maybe This Time

Newburgh Priory, Wednesday, 17 February 1875

D ISCRETION REQUIRED MARY TO PLAY her part as a guest. Lady Wombwell, oblivious of the suspicions hanging over her cousin and eager to ensure that the Duchess of Buccleuch's daughter was not neglected while her mother took the waters at Harrogate, had unwittingly prevented Mary from spending very much time on her investigations over the last few days. She had at last managed to "bump into" the maid who cleaned Mr. Glover's cottage this morning. It was a disappointing encounter, for though she had confirmed what Mary already knew, that he was not popular below stairs, she was not the regular maid. Henrietta, or Henny as she was known, always went to the local market with Mrs. Hare, the cook, on a Wednesday morning.

"So I'll have to try and waylay her tomorrow," Mary informed Tre as they walked together down the Long Gallery where they had taken refuge from the weather which had turned stormy. "Unless I can think of another way to speak to her privately. My mother returns from Harrogate tomorrow with the other ladies. I had hoped to have made real progress before then. We are due to leave on Monday."

"I thought you had no other plans at the moment," Tre said.

"I don't, but my mother is expected in London at the end of next week, and it would look very odd if we extended our visit." They had reached the end of the gallery. Mary leaned her forehead against the windowpane. "I hate this kind of weather. Aren't you anxious to complete your business with Sir George, and return to London?"

"I'm not in any rush." Tre was half-way up the gallery, gazing at the portrait of the other Lady Mary. This was the first time they had been alone for more than a few minutes since the water garden. "Have you thought about what that conversation might mean, Mary? The one we overheard?"

"The woman had a strong local accent. Pleasant, but not educated. She sounded young, but voices can be misleading." Mary turned around. "What do you think?"

"It could be that Mr. Glover has taken advantage of her."

Mary's eyes widened. "You mean he is a seducer?"

"It's the obvious conclusion to reach, unfortunately," Tre said. "He's avoiding her. She's at her wit's end. I could be wrong. I hope I am."

"But you don't think you are?" Mary sank onto one of the uncomfortable oak chairs. "I should have thought of that possibility. Oh no, surely he would not?"

"It happens," he said, taking the other seat, frowning heavily, "much more often than it should."

"But—but—do you think the woman might be expecting his child?" Mary asked, horrified. "If she is, and he is washing his hands of her—oh, the poor, poor woman. What will become of her?"

"If we have guessed correctly—and we don't know that—then I'm afraid she's in a very invidious position."

"He'll need money, won't he, either to pay her off or to—to clean up his mess? Money he doesn't have. The poor woman, what a terrible predicament to be in."

"It might be that he has legitimate reasons for avoiding her. We have no idea who this woman is. There might not even *be* a child. Whatever the circumstances, the unfortunate young woman's dilemma is not your problem. You're here to trace some missing money, not get embroiled in strangers' lives."

"You cannot expect me to simply forget all about her!"

"What do you know of such matters, Mary? Have you any experience at all of dealing with an issue like this?"

"No, of course I haven't, but— Margaret! My sister would know what to do."

"Your sister isn't here." Tre heaved a sigh. "I do have experience of similar situations. In the army, I'm sorry to say it's a common problem. When men are posted away from home— This isn't a topic for your ears. I'm sorry I brought it up."

"I'm glad you did. I should have worked it out for myself." Mary sank back onto the chair. "I know—I am aware that the army has camp followers," she said, twisting her hands together. "But this woman didn't sound like a—a streetwalker. Not that I have ever met one, to my knowledge, but if she was . . ."

"She'd know how to take care of herself," Tre said grimly. "I'm not talking about that sort of woman. I really don't think we should be discussing this."

"But then who should I discuss it with? I can't ask my mother or Lady Wombwell—they would be horrified. *And* even if they could answer my questions, they wouldn't because my innocent ears must remain unsullied. I'm nearly twenty-four, Tre, my ignorance is embarrassing."

He sat down in the other chair, digging his hands into his pockets. "Every story is different, but the gist of it's the same. An army man. A local woman. Sometimes it's a case of two people genuinely falling in love. Sometimes it's lasting, and on a very rare occasion, if the man in question is free, it ends in a marriage. More commonly, though, the liaison ends when the army moves on."

"And the women?" Mary asked, after she had taken a moment to digest this.

"Are left behind to deal with the consequences," Tre said bluntly. "Sometimes with financial assistance from the man. Sometimes not. It's not right, it's utterly wrong in fact, but that's how it is, and if we've guessed correctly about this case . . ."

"You mean he'll get away with it? And the woman . . ."

"It's very unlikely she'll be able to keep the child, if there is a child. If she needs to earn a living, she'll have no option but to give it up, though first she's going to have to find a way to avoid the shame of her condition being discovered by her family or her employer."

"Give it up to the parish, do you mean?"

"We're speculating needlessly, Mary."

"It's so unfair!"

"We could be completely wrong."

"I hope so," Mary said fervently. "I truly hope so."

"And it's very unlikely to have anything to do with the missing money."

"At least now I am more aware of how the world works. I appreciate you telling me."

AN HOUR LATER THE RAIN had abated. After tea, restless and unsettled by their earlier discussion, Mary paid another visit to the water garden. The rain had caused the waterfalls to turn into cascades, and the path to mud. The stepping-stones she had crossed earlier were submerged under a torrent of water.

"Great minds," Tre said, picking his way down the path to join her. "I hope you're not contemplating trying to cross again."

"I wasn't, but now you're here to catch me if I fall—" She broke off, recalling what had happened the last time.

"I shouldn't have kissed you," Tre said. "I don't mean that it was improper, though it was. I mean I shouldn't have done it because now all I can think about is doing it again."

"Oh."

He smiled faintly. "Precisely."

"No. I mean, oh," Mary said, blushing, "I am having the same problem."

"I wish you hadn't told me that."

He made no move to touch her. He wouldn't, unless she encouraged him. She knew she shouldn't but she couldn't *not* touch him. She smoothed her hand over his cheek. He shuddered in response. "But I have told you," Mary said. "So now you know."

She was in his arms before the sentence was finished. He murmured her name. She lifted her face to his, wrapped her arms around his neck, and their lips met. This kiss was very different from the earlier kiss. This kiss swept her away, made her forget everything except Tre, the taste of him and the smell of him and the feel of him. She kissed him back, wanting to be closer, needing to be closer. He murmured her name, his hands on her back, on her waist, pulling her closer still. She smoothed her hand over his short-cropped hair. She felt restless and hot. She could feel her heart hammering.

He swore under his breath, dragging his mouth away from hers. His lids were heavy, his eyes dazed. He groaned. Their lips met again, but only for a second.

"Stop." Tre let her go. "We can't—we have to talk."

Conversation was the last thing she wanted. She had no clear idea what the first thing was, but it certainly didn't involve speaking.

"For heaven's sake, don't look at me like that." Tre turned away. "Sorry. Not your fault."

Mary was still beyond words, trying to catch her breath. She should be mortified, shouldn't she, at losing control like that? It was very wrong, wasn't it? How could it be wrong, though, when her body was so alive?

"I want you to know, I am absolutely not in the habit of kissing any-one like that." Tre's cheeks were still flushed, but his expression made her heart sink. "I won't insult you by apologizing," he said flatly.

It wouldn't happen again is what he was going to say; and this time he would mean it, and Mary rather desperately didn't want him to mean it. She had a horrible feeling of teetering on the edge of a precipice, be-fore she pulled herself back. "Don't worry, Tre. I'm not imagining that a few kisses mean anything more significant."

"Aren't you?"

"You are wedded to your work, and I am no more interested in finding a husband than I was three years ago." Which was the truth, wasn't it?

"You haven't thought about it at all? I wondered, you see, when you seemed to imply that you were reconsidering—that you weren't sure of your plans. And with your sister marrying, too . . ."

"I have never had any wish to follow in Margaret's footsteps." To her horror, Mary found herself on the brink of tears. She *hated* to cry. "If I'd known that your conscience would trouble you, I wouldn't have kissed you. I thought we understood each other."

She turned to start back up the path, but Tre stopped her. "You've misunderstood me. I'm not trying to talk myself out of a tricky situation, I'm trying to establish if you feel as confused as I do. You must know that wasn't simply a few meaningless kisses."

Mary was beginning to wonder if she knew anything. Confused. She was certainly confused. "Nothing has changed," she said, as much for her own benefit as his.

"Do you think that? I don't know if I do. I'm not making any sense, am I?"

"Not really."

He smiled crookedly. "If you'll listen, I'll try."

She waited, an ominous feeling settling in the pit of her stomach as she watched him pick up a stone and throw it into the stream, bracing himself. For what? To tell her that he had compromised her and felt obliged to present himself to her father? To tell her that he had been one of those men, when he served abroad, a seducer? Both were laughable. Then he was going to tell her that he was leaving now, he wasn't waiting until she had solved the issue of the missing money. And of the young woman Mr. Glover had seduced. *If* he had seduced her.

"It goes back to Sandhurst," Tre interrupted these jumbled thoughts. "That was the first time that I remember, anyway."

"Your condition," Mary said, after a shocked moment. "Is that what you mean?"

Tre winced. "My curse, or whatever label you choose to put on it." He dug his hands deep in his pockets. "There was a cadet, a man—a boy—completely unsuited to the army in every way. He was clumsy, inept, terrified of guns, the type who dropped his weapon when it discharged. On the parade ground one day, he almost shot one of the officers. They don't flog officer cadets, but he was flayed in a different way. Bullied. Ridiculed. Insulted. The butt of every stupid, predictable joke. It went on for weeks, until one day he broke down in the mess during dinner. Fell apart. Lay curled up on the floor, sobbing like a child." Tre stopped, swallowed several times. "No-one helped him. Everyone sat, watching in silence, until he stopped. And then they carried on talking while he picked himself up and left. They found him later on the parade ground. He had shot himself in the head with his Adams revolver." Tre put his head in his hands. "It is one of my biggest regrets that I sat with the others, in silence. I didn't try to help him."

"Oh, Tre."

He shook his head sharply. "A few days later, during firing practice, I had the first of my episodes. I fainted. They put it down to the heat. I was a good officer cadet, you see. Not weak. Not—not *sensitive*. So they put it down to too much sun."

He stopped, but Mary, sick with pity and horror, knew now not to interrupt.

"The next time was in the Crimea," he continued a few tense moments later. "The men were starving and freezing. Tents in tatters, uniforms, too. Boots frozen to their feet. But standards had to be maintained." He swore viciously under his breath. "So many pointless rules and regulations, you'd think that there would have been enough suffering to go around without flogging those who failed to stick to them. I tried to intervene and was disciplined for my trouble. It was afterwards, the headache set in, but by then I knew when to hide. Retreat until it passed. I forget how many more times it happened. Three or four. Never during battle. Always afterwards."

Tre paused once more, picked up two more stones, turning them over and over in his hand before hurling them into the water. "Then peace came. Guard duties. Marching drills. Parades. Rifle practice. It was then that I met Sibilla."

The hairs on the back of Mary's neck stood on end. "Sibilla?"

"Countess Sibilla Ruspoli. We were to be married."

This is what he had been leading up to. She had never imagined for a moment that she was the first woman Tre had kissed but to hear he had gone so far as to propose made her feel sick. *Countess Sibilla Ruspoli.* Italian? Exotic. Sophisticated. Alluring. Mary fought the absurd impulse to cover her ears and run away. "When was this?"

"Sixty-four. Almost eleven years ago."

Was she beautiful? "Was she aware of your condition?" Mary asked.

"I kept it from her. Until the night in the mess. Ladies dinner. I can't recall what it was that set me off earlier in the day, but I knew I shouldn't go. She wanted to, though. Sibilla. She wanted to go. So she was there, in the mess, when history repeated itself, though they didn't leave me on the floor. I was escorted out. The next day, my commanding officer informed me that an opportunity to purchase a promotion had come up. The lieutenant colonel role was in a War Office department I had never even heard of—the Department of Topography and Statistics. He clearly wanted me away from the regiment, and the role would make me virtually invisible."

"So the promotion was a punishment? They forced you out of the regiment!" Mary burst out furiously. "Didn't they realize you were ill?"

"It's not an illness. An illness can be cured. It had happened before, Mary, though never so publicly. I was an embarrassment, a liability to my regiment."

"And Sibilla?" Mary asked, though she already knew the answer. Tre wasn't married.

"Later the same day, she ended our betrothal. She'd done her homework by then, and discovered that I'd been lying to her."

"Not lying, Tre. You were protecting her."

"No. It's part of me, my condition, and I kept it from her. I deceived her, but I couldn't lie a second time. I couldn't promise her that it wouldn't happen again. She couldn't cope with that."

"She abandoned you, on the same day when you had been abandoned by your regiment!"

"I don't blame her."

"But you loved her," Mary said flatly. "That's why you won't ever marry again. You still love her."

"Not anymore. Sibilla is the reason I decided never to marry again, but it's not because I'm still in love with her. It didn't go away, you see. After that debacle, I still suffered. You saw me at Drumlanrig. Usually I have enough warning to hide myself away until it passes. That day—well, I didn't."

Why not? she wanted to ask, but Tre spoke before she had the opportunity.

"Since then, in the last three years, it's not been so bad. I have it under control. I think it's because I feel I'm not doing my penance in that other job, I've got a purpose. Which brings me to the point of this very long-winded confession."

There was another long pause. This time Mary waited, sick with apprehension, though she had absolutely no idea what he was about to say.

"Maybe this time," Tre said. "If I'm not being presumptuous, maybe this time, if you wanted to—not that I'm asking you to make any sort of commitment or promise or even to take a risk, if you don't want to."

"Take a risk?" He could have been speaking a foreign language for all the sense he was making.

"Explore the possibility of a future together, or at least not reject it outright, which is what we've both been doing. I wouldn't have said anything, I know your feelings on the subject, or thought I knew them. Until we kissed."

It was too much. Her head was reeling. Her instinct was to flee. "What do you want from me?"

"To keep an open mind to the possibility that we might come to mean something significant to each other," he said. "I know it's a lot to ask. Too much perhaps. Certainly too soon, I can see that from your expression. Will you think about it?"

Mary blanched, feeling a rising sense of panic. "I don't know what to think, Tre. You asked if you could help me, but throwing all this at me right now is not helpful in the slightest, frankly. I need to focus on the reason I am here. So I need to speak to Henny." She turned her back on him. "As a matter of urgency," she said, taking off up the path.

CHAPTER TWENTY

A Maid All Forlorn

MARY CLOSED THE DOOR OF her bedchamber and turned the key. Her heart was racing. How dare Tre attempt to change all the rules, force her to think about things she didn't want to think about. Couldn't afford to think about, right now. He was wrong! It was just a few kisses. They meant nothing at all.

Shaking, she tottered over to the bed and lay back, her feet still on the floor. How did he imagine they would explore the possibility of a future together? And where? London? Drumlanrig? *Please, Mama, would you invite Colonel Trefusis to stay, so that we can explore the possibility of a future together?* The moment her father got wind of any exploring of any nature, he'd summon Tre, who would find himself on the other side of an interrogation into his circumstances and his intentions. Did Tre have an income? A house? She knew nothing at all of his life, none of the important things a future wife should know.

What were the important things? Mary pushed herself upright. Income and property are what her parents would say, and lineage, of course, which was the one thing Tre did have. Connections, power, influence. Did Tre have those? He certainly had power and influence, but was it the right type of power and influence?

She sighed impatiently, and began to pace her bedchamber. If a man had all those things, would a woman be a happy wife? Margaret hadn't thought so. Margaret's most heinous crime had been her inability to stomach the man who had all those things. Surely Margaret was right—what mattered most was the man himself. Tre. Whose kisses made her feel as if she were melting and burning at the same time. Whose kisses made her want to forget everything—yes, absolutely everything—and lose herself in his arms. Whose kisses made her want more than kisses. He made her laugh, too, and he understood her own dark, wry sense of humour. He was the only person she had ever met who almost never asked, what do you mean? He was interested in her— another rarity—in her thoughts and her opinions and in how she felt.

She picked up a hideous porcelain statuette of a simpering little boy dressed in blue velvet and his equally simpering dog from the mantelpiece and stared at it. "Honestly, Mary," she said to it, "you're going to miss him when this is over."

True, but when it was over the last time, she had recovered. She had made a life for herself. She was perfectly—happy? No, but she was perfectly content. When she was resolving other people's problems, at least. There were times when she was lonely and bored and restless, but . . .

She replaced the statuette with an impatient sigh. If only she hadn't met Tre, she wouldn't have to ask herself all these questions. Well, yes, she had been asking some of them before, but he had made the questions much more difficult to answer. *Explore the possibility*, he'd said, which meant that it was possible he could change his mind. He'd abandoned her before. Though he had explained why.

"Oh, Tre." She sank onto the bed again. What must it have cost him to bare his soul like that? And she had turned her back on him! Walked away. No, she'd fled. Just like Sibilla. Beautiful, exotic, traitorous Sibilla who had broken Tre's heart.

Maybe this time, he had said. Was Mary second best? If *maybe this time* became definitely this time, she wouldn't be able to walk away. Tre would still have his precious work, he'd continue to serve his country, but what would she have if she took a chance and found that it was a mistake?

It was too much. He shouldn't have asked her. She had no time for maybes at the moment. What she needed was certainty. Who stole the money from Sir George's charity? That's the reason she was here, not to exchange a few kisses with Tre. Tomorrow, she would position herself on the path that led to Mr. Glover's cottage, and she would hopefully waylay Henny. Tomorrow her mother would be back from Harrogate. Tomorrow, Tre would be expecting her to give him an answer to the question he shouldn't have asked her. Mary gazed at the statuette. It really was vile. An idea came to her, and she smiled. The ruse had worked with Mrs. Fitzherbert-Smythe's maid, there was no reason why it shouldn't work again.

She picked up the ornament and hurled it forcefully at the fireplace. It shattered with a resounding crack, scattering shards across the hearth. She picked up several of the larger body and animal parts and crushed them with her boot, and then scattered them over the floor. She took out her dark-blue evening gown and tore a long stretch of the pleated flounce from the skirt. Then she rang the bell, unlocked her door, and waited for Clara.

"My lady?"

"I have had an accident," Mary said, indicating the broken statuette. "Will you please get Henny to come and clear it up?"

"I'll do that, my lady."

"No, Clara, I need you to repair my gown, look. I want to wear it this evening, but someone trod on my hem. Please, take that away and fetch Henny to clear up this mess."

IT WAS ONLY A FEW moments later when the maid tapped on the door. "Clara said you wanted me, my lady?"

"Henny?" Mary recognized the voice immediately, but the leap of excitement quickly subsided as the young woman came into the room. Gently does it, Mary cautioned herself, as she ushered the maid into her bedchamber. "I'm afraid I've been very clumsy. Do you think it can be mended?"

Henny was a very pretty young woman with abundant dark curls, big blue eyes, and a generous mouth. She stared doubtfully down at the dust and shards. "I don't think so, my lady. It looks quite beyond repair to me. Why don't you sit yourself down, and I'll tidy it up."

"I'll help." Mary knelt down beside her, and the two of them began to gather up the bigger pieces. "It was on the mantelpiece. A little boy in blue with a dog."

"Oh yes, I remember it." Henny picked up a fragment of the boy's face. "I always thought he looked like he had eaten a lemon."

"I must admit, I thought it a horrible piece, but I'm so worried that it might be a favourite of Lady Wombwell's."

"I doubt she'll be too bothered, my lady. This house is so full of china and porcelain. If it was really valuable, it would be in one of the cabinets."

"That's true. Mr. Glover led us on a tour of the priory the other day. He was extremely knowledgeable about everything on display. I must say, I was very impressed, especially when I learned he'd only been living at the cottage for—four months, is it?"

"Six," Henny said quickly. "He arrived at the beginning of September last year. We'll wrap the pieces in newspaper, but I don't think this can be saved."

"Thank you. You clean his cottage, don't you?" Mary said, trying to remember the little she knew about pregnancy. How far on before a woman's condition began to show? It was one of the many topics that wasn't discussed with unmarried women. And there were corsets, special corsets to disguise the evidence—she recalled Victoria mentioning one in an unguarded moment. Three months? Four? Five? As Henny finished clearing up, Mary tried to study her shape, but her waist looked neat, and her apron covered her stomach, and anyway maids wore corsets, too.

"Mr. Glover seemed quite out of sorts during the tour. Distracted by something, or worried." Mary waited hopefully, but Henny simply took up the hearth brush and began to sweep some of the smaller fragments into a pile. How long before a woman knew she was expecting a child? That was the more pertinent question, but infuriatingly it was another she had no answer for. At least two months. So working back, assuming that it had taken Glover at least a month to seduce her—if he had seduced her.

"Do you enjoy working at the cottage?" she asked. "I mean, having to go there every morning, rain or shine."

"I enjoy the walk."

"And Mr. Glover?"

"My lady?"

This was ridiculous. If she and Tre were right, then Henny wouldn't dream of letting anything slip in a casual conversation with one of her employer's guests. Beneath that bright smile she must be terrified of being found out. Mary decided to change tack. "Talking of walking, I took a stroll in the water garden on Monday morning."

"Monday morning?" Henny stopped sweeping.

"It must have been just before midday, I think. It is astonishing, isn't it, how sound travels through that little valley."

"Does it?"

Mary removed the brush from Henny's hand. "It does. One can even make out voices, snatches of conversation, believe it or not."

Henny scrambled to her feet. "I had better go and help Mrs. Hare prepare dinner."

Mary jumped up, catching her by the sleeve of her uniform. "Please, wait just a minute."

"I don't know what you heard, or thought you heard, but it's best you forget it, my lady, if you please."

"I heard enough to guess that Mr. Glover might have taken advantage of you. Am I right?"

Tears started flowing from Henny's big eyes. "Please, my lady, I beg you, you'll only make things worse."

Tre had guessed correctly, judging by Henny's reaction. "I promise I won't say a word to Lady Wombwell," Mary said, "and I also promise you I will . . ." What? What on earth could she promise? "I will do everything I can to help you."

"You can't help me, my lady." A tear rolled down her cheek. "And Dacre didn't take advantage. It's not like that. *I'm* not like that, my lady. We're in love."

"In love!"

"And he's going to marry me," Henny said determinedly.

"Marry you!" The words were out before she could stop them, Mary's shock all too apparent.

Henny scrubbed at her eyes and glared. "Yes!"

Marriage! Mary floundered. Nothing she had heard added up to marriage: quite the contrary. And a marriage between Mr. Glover and his cousin's maid? "But from what I overheard . . ."

"I don't care what you heard. He's going to marry me."

"Henny, that is—I—how can you be so certain?"

"Because he has to, because I'm going to have his baby."

The words hung in the air in the shocked silence that followed. Tears gushed from Henny's eyes. She covered her face with her apron. "There, are you happy now?"

Mary was almost as distraught as Henny. She had no idea what to say or do. Wretchedly, she recalled Tre's words of caution, but it was too late now, far too late to tell herself this was none of her business. She had made it her business. She gently urged the sobbing maid over to a chair.

"You won't breathe a word of this, will you, my lady?" The young woman scrubbed at her cheeks. "If his lordship finds out before I can— before Dacre and me—please, don't say anything. Promise me."

"I won't. I promise, I won't do or say anything you don't wish me to." A promise easily made, but how was she to keep it if she was going to help Henny? And just how did she imagine she could help Henny?

"Dacre—Mr. Glover, he's already mad enough at me. If he finds out that you heard us argue and I told you what it was about—please?"

"I can't ignore what happened, Henny. I want to help."

"You can't." Henny wrapped her arms around her waist and began to rock back and forth. "You can't help me. Only he can. He says he won't, but he will. I've just got to persuade him—I know he will in the end."

Her eyes were bright with tears, her pretty mouth working in an effort not to shed more of them. Henny was terrified, and rightly so. Whatever she believed, whatever promises Mr. Glover had made her, there was no way he would be allowed to marry her, even if he wanted to, and recalling the words Mary had overheard, he most certainly didn't want to. Her helplessness gave way to a simmering, impotent fury.

What on earth should she do? If her mother were here—but she couldn't tell her mother; she had promised Henny she wouldn't tell anyone. She needed to think. And she needed to establish a few more facts. Mary took a clean handkerchief from her drawer and handed it to the maid, kneeling down at her feet. "Might it make you feel better to talk about it? I know I'm a complete stranger, but that might make it easier, don't you think?"

"You can't have any idea—it's not you I need to talk to, it's him. Only he won't listen." Henny dabbed at her eyes. "I'm fine now, my lady. If you'll excuse me, I'd better get back to the kitchen. Mrs. Hare will be wondering where I am."

My mother will be wondering where I am! "Tell Cook that I detained you. If you go now, it will be very obvious that you're upset, which will only raise questions as to why. As you've already said, it's much better that no-one else knows of your—your situation just yet."

Henny's eyes widened in horror. "No-one does know. Only him. And my brother, but Tommy would never say."

Mary squeezed her hands, then got to her feet lest her doubts show on her face. If only she wasn't so ignorant. Think!

"Dacre is the only person who can help me, my lady. He has to marry me. He told me he loves me, and I love him. I do love him, even though he's being—and he does love me, I know he does, but he's frightened. Sir George . . ." Henny shuddered. "Sir George took him in when no-one else would, you see, that's what he's forever saying, and he can't let him down. But what about me? He can't let me down either, can he? Not now."

He absolutely *damned well* could and by the sounds of things, would. Though Henny was so certain. What if she was right and Mary was wrong? She mustn't let her dislike of Mr. Glover prejudice her, even if Tre disliked him, too. It could happen. One of her mother's brothers had married a toll-keeper's daughter. Though he'd been forced to live abroad, and the marquess, Mary's grandfather, had tried to disinherit him. *Think, Mary.*

Money. That's why Sir George had invited her here, to find out where the money had gone. Mr. Glover had a very clear motive for defrauding the charity, if he intended to pay Henny off. But two hundred pounds was a great deal of money, and if he really was set upon not letting Sir George down, it didn't make sense.

She pulled a chair over and sat down again. "Henny, you have to trust me. I'm on your side."

"Why? I'm nothing to you . . ."

"We're both women, aren't we?"

"That's the beginning and the end of it, if you don't mind my saying, my lady. You're not a servant expecting a child out of wedlock. You probably think babies are found under a gooseberry bush."

"I am not quite so ignorant as that." Though she wasn't much better informed.

Henny blushed. "Sorry, my lady. I'm not quite myself."

"No wonder." Mary slanted another glance at Henny's stomach. A *love child* was one of the politer terms for such babies. Would the child be loved? Had it been love which had created it? Or passion? Or lust? What was the difference? Did it matter? The result was the same and, she realized with dull horror, easily achieved. Those *few kisses* she had dismissed could easily have led her down that path. Not that Tre would have—and she hoped that she would not have—but she had been close to not caring. She had always assumed, because it was what she had been raised to believe, that passion was wrong, that only women with no morals found themselves in Henny's condition. It wasn't true. What to do about Henny, though? She had to do something. First things first: establish whether or not Mr. Glover was a crook as well as a seducer.

"Henny, I'll be honest with you," Mary said. "I have no idea at present how I can help you, but I am determined to try. Will you trust me?"

"I don't have any choice now, do I?"

It was hardly an enthusiastic endorsement, but under the circumstances, Mary had no right to expect anything more. Right, first things first. Acquit Henny of any involvement in the crime. "Tell me, can you read and write?"

"Write? A letter, you mean?" Henny's face brightened. "I never thought of that. You think he'd read it? Would you help me, my lady, only I'm not good with reading and writing—it's my brother who has all the brains in our family. Numbers and letters, they dance about when I look at them. But if you think he'd read a letter . . ."

"No, that wasn't what I meant. Bear with me. May I ask what your brother does for a living?"

"He's a clerk in the estate office." Henny's mouth trembled. "He's worried he'll lose his job if they find out about me. He wants to send me away before I—before it's obvious." She wrapped her arms around her stomach again. "He said he can make arrangements to keep me comfortable, out of the way, but when it's over, he says I'll have to give away my baby to someone else."

Mary stared at her helplessly, feeling horribly inadequate. The solution was practical, and it would preserve Tommy's job and Henny's reputation. She'd be able to find work afterwards, whereas if she persisted . . .

"Don't tell me it's for the best," Henny said. "I'm not giving my baby away. Dacre's just scared, that's all. He's worried about what they'll all say. But he'll come round."

Mary bit her lip, torn. "If he doesn't, though . . ."

"He will. You're as bad as my brother, but he's wrong, too. Dacre will do the right thing. He just needs time to get used to the idea."

"How much time has he already had, if you don't mind my asking?"

"He's known for a couple of months, as soon as I was sure. I reckon I've got another month before anyone—before I show." Henny wiped her eyes and blew her nose, then folded the handkerchief up neatly. "I'll wash this, my lady, and get it back to you."

"Keep it."

The sharp, distinctive crack of a gunshot made them both jump. Henny was the first to recover. "His lordship must be trying out his new guns," she said. "There's to be a shooting competition in the morning. Dacre is a—a crack shot—is that the right phrase?"

"Did he tell you so?"

"He tells me lots of things, my lady. I know all about his family, and how they disowned him for being too trusting, and everything. He wouldn't talk to me like that, about personal things, would he, unless he loved me? No," Henny added softly, "no, he wouldn't."

She smiled at Mary, a bright, generous smile that lit up her pretty face. "Thank you, my lady. You were right—it's done me good to talk. I see now I was just getting myself in a right state. Things will work out, I know they will. With your permission, I'd better get back to the kitchen now."

With a brief bob, Henny left the room. As soon as the door closed, Mary picked up the largest of the fragments which had been left in the newspaper and stamped on it, then ground it under her foot for good measure. What was she going to do? This was not the crime she had been asked to investigate, but it was a much more monstrous one. *Leave it well alone*, she could hear Tre cautioning her, but that was impossible. Besides, if the two crimes were linked, it was very much her business.

Tre. What was she going to tell Tre? She had no idea. She didn't want to think about it. She didn't have time to think about it. The clock was ticking for Henny. Forget Tre, Mary told herself. He would have to wait. There were more pressing matters for her to attend to.

CHAPTER TWENTY-ONE

The Shootist

Newburgh Priory, Thursday, 18 February 1875

A SHOOTING RANGE HAD BEEN set up on the south lawn after break-fast, consisting of a row of bottles set on a plank supported by two ladders. Distances of twenty-five, fifty, and one hundred yards had been marked with stones. Tre joined Sir George, Mr. Glover, and Mr. St. John Aubyn at the table where the guns were laid out. He couldn't remember the last time he had fired a shot. He picked up one of the rifles.

"They were made by Greener's of Birmingham," Sir George said proudly. "A new cross-bolt mechanism that he has patented, which he calls a—what is it, Glover?"

"It's Greener's new choke-bore gun." Glover was studying the pistols. "Colt forty-five," he said. "Made for the United States Army, I believe. Have you experience of shooting with it, Colonel Trefusis?"

"No, I've used that Webley Bull Dog, but I've never fired a Colt. May I?" Tre took the pistol and weighed it in his hand. No trace of a headache. His hand was steady as a rock. But it was always afterwards the problems started.

"Forty-five calibre," Glover was saying. "They call it the Peacemaker."

"Glover here is something of an expert," Sir George said. "Why don't you try out one of the rifles, Colonel? You're an army man like me, show Glover how it's done?"

Tre looked at the rifle. He felt perfectly well, but why tempt fate? Take a chance, he'd said to Mary yesterday. Explore the possibility. His toes curled, recalling the words he'd used. He shouldn't have launched in like that, should have taken the time to phrase his thoughts more elegantly. He hadn't planned it, and as a result he'd scared her off. She had avoided him ever since, refusing to meet his eyes over dinner and breakfast. He picked up the unloaded rifle. He raised, sighted it, felt the familiar heft of it. Still perfectly fine. "We'll start with fifty yards," he said to Glover. "At fifty yards it would be hard for any but the merest beginner to miss, even with an unfamiliar weapon."

"Certainly." Glover picked up the other rifle and followed Tre's lead in loading it. "Best of four, and then we'll go to one hundred?"

MARY WATCHED, STANDING UNNOTICED BESIDE Sir George as the two men shot at the bottles. Glover was an excellent shot, but Tre had the edge. Twenty minutes into the competition, with the bottles being replaced again, and the distinctive smell of gunpowder in the air, he looked as if he was thoroughly enjoying himself. Only when Glover, obviously accustomed to winning, suggested that they continue with pistols did Tre notice her.

"Lady Mary."

She had been avoiding him, and he knew it. She still had no idea what she thought of his proposal or suggestion or whatever it was, and she didn't want to think about it. "Colonel Trefusis. You look as if you are enjoying the competition."

"I am looking forward to trying out this Colt revolver," he said, picking up the handgun and loading it.

He looked perfectly well. Since he could easily have excused himself, Mary could only assume that he had deliberately chosen to shoot this morning. Was he testing himself? The two men chose a revolver each, Tre taking the Colt and Glover an older gun that Mary recognized as a Webley, and the four men with Mary in tow went up to the twenty-five-yard marker.

"I was informed that you are a crack shot," Mary said to Glover as he prepared to shoot. "I am looking forward to seeing if you can do as well with the revolver as the rifle."

"Ha!" Sir George exclaimed, rubbing his hands. "Go on then, Glover. This young lady has put you on your mettle."

"How do you know he's a crack shot?" Tre whispered, as the party moved back to the next marker stone.

"I have it on very good authority. Henny's."

"The maid? So you spoke to her this morning?"

"Yesterday. After we—in the afternoon. Tre, it's Henny we overheard arguing with Glover."

"What!"

"Ready! Aim! Fire!" Sir George shouted. Glover fired. The middle bottle on the shelf shattered. "Oh, bravo! Excellent. Now Colonel Trefusis with the Colt."

Tre took careful aim, shattering the next bottle. He seemed quite unaffected by the gun or the noise. Gunshot wasn't the sole cause of his condition, but he knew it was a factor. She was now convinced he was testing himself. Or proving his point?

"Lady Mary," Sir George said, "you are fortunate to be in the presence of two expert marksmen, if I am not mistaken."

"What do you say to that, Colonel Trefusis?" Mr. Glover asked. "Would I be an asset on the battlefield?"

"It's difficult to tell," Tre replied. "Bottles don't shoot back."

The men swapped guns. Two more shots were fired and two more bottles shattered.

"Let us have a decider," Mary said. "A smaller target." She took two apples from the fruit bowl on the trestle table which had been set up with refreshments. "What do you say, Sir George?"

"Ha! I like your thinking, Lady Mary. An excellent idea."

"Shall I do the honours?" Tre asked.

"No. Mr. Glover is eager to set them up," Mary said, handing over the fruit. "May I take a look at the Webley while he does so, Colonel Trefusis?"

Tre glared at her, but handed over the pistol. "What the devil are you up to?" he said under his breath.

"Mr. Irvine thinks I am one of the best shots he's ever seen. You've never seen me shoot, though, have you?"

"There's no need to prove it to me. You've never fired that pistol before."

"Not this one, but I've fired the same make. How well does this one perform?"

"Perfectly straight, no kick to it. What the devil are you doing?"

"You were right," Mary said. "Glover is a seducer and a liar. The one thing I am still not sure about is whether he is also a thief." She aimed the gun. Sir George cried out a warning. Glover, who was placing the second apple on a bottleneck, swung around. Mary squeezed the trigger. The other apple, already positioned, exploded. Glover screamed, leaping back. "Thank you, Stuart," Mary said under her breath, smugly satisfied before crying out in a very different voice, "Oh my goodness! I am so very sorry. I didn't mean— My finger slipped on the trigger. Oh pray tell me, Mr. Glover, that I did not hit you."

"By some miracle, my lady," the gentleman said grimly, wiping fragments of apple from his cheek, "you did not."

"Indeed," Sir George said, sending her a puzzled look. "For a moment there, I thought . . ."

"Best not to think too much about it," Tre said. "An accident but luckily no harm done. Lady Mary is understandably quite overcome. I will concede the contest and restore her to her mother," he said, taking a firm grip on her arm and marching her off. "That was a damned foolish trick to play. You could have wounded him."

"I wouldn't have done it if there was any risk of that."

"You'd never used that gun before." He gave her arm a shake. "For God's sake, Mary, killing him isn't going to help anyone."

"I didn't intend to kill him, only give him a fright."

"And make him suspicious of you."

"Do you think so? I never thought of that—but, no, I think you're wrong there. What on earth would he suspect?"

"Nonetheless, you shouldn't have done it."

"No," she admitted, deflated. "Of course, I shouldn't have. It was a spur-of-the-moment idea. I didn't come out here with any intention but to watch you. I was very surprised to see you shooting."

He shrugged. "I haven't fired a gun in a while. I was curious." They had come to a halt at King James's Porch. "Mary, I spoke on impulse yesterday. Ought I to have held my tongue?"

She stared at him helplessly. "I don't know. I can't think about it at the moment. After what Henny told me, I can't think of anything else."

"Then you'd better tell me what she said."

"I promised that I wouldn't say anything to anyone."

"Come on—we'll head round to the other side of the house. You know that nothing you tell me will go any further."

"Yes, of course I know that. It's such a dreadfully sad story. Glover told her that he loved her. He may even have promised her marriage. I am so very angry on her behalf."

In fits and starts, she managed to recount her conversation with Henny. Tre listened in grim silence until she had finished, by which time they had reached the fish pond. "I know your promise to help her came from the heart, but it was foolishly made. What do you imagine you can do?"

"I have no idea, but I'll think of something."

"The best solution is the one her brother is proposing."

"To give her child away!"

"I can't think of any solution that would allow her to keep it, unless Glover marries her and that seems unlikely in the extreme."

"Why must Henny be the one to pay the price for what Glover has done?"

"He didn't do it on his own."

"Tre! You can't possibly be on his side!"

"Of course I blooming well am not. I know you're outraged, but you have taken that young woman's part without even knowing the full story. You only have her word for what Glover did and what Glover promised. No, wait a minute, I'm not finished. Glover has abused his position, but unfortunately it's a common enough occurrence. That doesn't make it right, but I ask you again, what do you think you can do about it?"

"It seems so unfair."

"I am not disputing that, but on this occasion I'm afraid that Lady Mary won't be able to dispense any sort of justice."

"Don't mock me."

"I'm not mocking you, I'm trying to make you see sense. You can't fix this, Mary, but if you interfere, you may well make things worse. This is not the crime you've been asked to investigate."

She jerked her arm free. "I am aware of that, but it must be connected. Glover has a real motive for stealing now, though I cannot understand why he'd steal from Sir George who, by Henny's account, he is determined to impress and feels greatly under obligation to."

"She told you that?"

"Glover confides in her—or he did. She sees it as evidence of his love for her."

"The man is a— No, I don't need to say it. We both know what we think of him."

"The pertinent question, though, as you have pointed out," Mary said tightly, "is whether he is also a thief. And the even more pertinent question for me now is what on earth do I do next."

"The pertinent question for *us* is what do *we* do next."

"You're still going to help me?"

Tre stared out across the small lake to the hills where the horse carved into the chalk could for once be clearly seen. "You don't think it would be better to lay what you know in front of Sir George? You said yourself—he's a kind man, and a good one, behind that bluff façade. He'd make sure that Henny was looked after."

"In the same way as her brother will."

"He's going to have to find out eventually, whatever happens, Mary."

"If I can at least resolve the matter of the funds, then he'll know whether he has been nurturing a thief as well as a seducer in the bosom of his family."

"Poor Sir George. And before you say it, poor Henny."

Mary heaved a sigh. "I know. Yesterday, listening to her, I realized how ignorant I am. 'You probably think babies are found under a gooseberry bush,' she said to me. Which I don't," she added hurriedly, blushing, "but I felt so inadequate. Compared to Henny's problems, finding out what happened to two hundred pounds seems almost trivial."

"Two hundred pounds wouldn't seem trivial to Henny."

"I know that, but since she can barely read and write, we can exclude her from our investigation."

"Her brother can read and write, though," Tre said. "He's an accounts clerk."

"And he's already made arrangements, according to Henny, so he must have put money aside." Mary's face fell. "But if he's an accounts clerk, then surely he would have done a better job of covering his tracks?"

"I agree. Two hundred pounds is far more than he would need for Henny," Tre pointed out. "Why steal so much? I think we'd better find a way to speak to Tommy, don't you?"

"I do." Mary grimaced. "If we continue to eliminate suspects, we'll have no-one left but Sir George."

"I do understand, you know, why you feel so strongly." Tre took her hands. "The world is neither kind nor fair to women like Henny. That's how it is, but it's still cruel and wrong. It is to your credit that you want to help. Most people would look very determinedly in the other direction. I'll help you, but you must understand there may be nothing we can do to help Henny."

"I do. I'll try. How is your head, Tre?"

"All I've proved is that I am still a crack shot. Better than Glover, but I'm not so sure I'm better than you, after your little exploit with the pistol. Isn't it time you looked at your watch and informed me that your mother will be wondering where you are?" Tre took a quick look around, then pulled her close, wrapping his arms around her. "Don't despair. We're in this together."

Mary closed her eyes, allowing herself the comfort of resting her head on his shoulder for a moment. It felt good. Too good. She freed herself. "The York train is due in at Coxwold at twelve. I'd better be at the house to greet the carriage."

CHAPTER TWENTY-TWO

A Little Digging

Newburgh Priory, Friday, 19 February 1875

THE SUN HAD COME OUT, and Mary's mother said she would like to take a walk. Together, they made a slow circuit of the dog kennel garden, with the duchess studying each of the beds in turn, speculating on the likely planting, inspecting the pruning and the condition of the few early shoots which had been brave enough to peek through.

"This will be very pretty in the spring," she said as they made their way along the wisteria terrace, "but personally, I prefer rambling roses. You find that amusing?"

"No, only that I said—thought as much—when I first took a walk here."

"Lady Wombwell informs me that you take a great many walks."

"You know that I like to get out before breakfast, Mama."

"Normally, though, you prefer to walk alone."

"There is a little pond here which is confusingly not what they refer to as the fish pond. It's very soothing, seeing the fish dart about," Mary said. "I wonder that you haven't thought of having one dug in Drumlanrig."

"Are we to have one of those conversations, where I make a comment in the hope that you will confide in me, and you instantly turn the subject and hope that I won't notice? I'm getting old, but I'm still in full possession of my senses."

Startled, Mary glanced down, but her mother's gaze was fixed straight ahead. "Colonel Trefusis shares my habit of walking before breakfast. We bump into each other now and then. Mama, are you ill? I ask because you hardly ate a thing at breakfast."

They had reached the pond. The duchess stood at the edge, stirring the water with the stick she had taken to carrying of late. "I will be sixty-four in April. My appetite is not what it was."

Nor was her stature, Mary noticed suddenly. She seemed to have shrunk several inches. When had that happened? What's more, despite the fact she ate barely enough to keep a mouse alive, she had put on weight. In fact, she was beginning to look very like her friend, the rotund Queen Victoria. Mary took her arm, earning herself a surprised look, which shamed her. "You can't afford to be ill, Mama. Your gardens aren't anywhere near finished."

Her mother sighed, patted her hand, then disengaged herself. "I am not the only one of us getting on in years. You will be twenty-four in August. At your age, I had been married for seven years and already had three sons."

Mary stiffened. "Has my father spoken to you about me?"

"The duke has said nothing as yet, and I have no intentions of instigating any discussion concerning your nuptials. Or lack of them." The duchess set off slowly down the path again, forcing Mary to follow her. "His Grace has been reticent, not as you think because he has forgotten about you, but to grant you the time to find a suitable husband without his intervention." Her mother slanted her a sly smile. "I see I have managed to surprise you."

"You have managed to astonish me," Mary retorted.

"He has no idea of how you have actually been occupying your time, before you ask. Though I must say, Mary, that he has not heard anything is nothing short of a miracle."

"My father would never listen to servant's gossip, and besides, the whole point of what I do, Mama, is to prevent talk."

"Indeed, but your success is beginning to generate talk above stairs. It is only a matter of time before someone somewhere sings your praises to him."

Mary gave a snort of laughter. "He would think them either mistaken or deluded."

"No, he would ask me what was meant by it."

"Oh," Mary exclaimed, stricken. "I would not for the world put you in that position."

"I have never lied to your father, Mary, nor have I ever gone counter to a single one of his express wishes. I take my vows to love, honour, and obey very seriously. When I decided to write to Margaret, it was with his tacit consent, as you know, and that was painful enough, with neither of us able to be open with each other."

"I have not forgotten, I assure you," Mary said, with a horrible sense of impending doom and a mild sense of panic.

"I am very sorry to have to have this conversation," the duchess continued in an even tone, her eyes focusing straight ahead. "You are an extremely astute observer of human nature. Sadly, you don't seem to be able to apply that scrutiny to yourself. I had hoped that you would have reached the obvious conclusion."

"What conclusion?"

The duchess stopped, raising her straight, fine brows. "That you must put an end to your—goodness, I have no idea how to refer to it. These investigations you carry out. You are proving too successful for your own good."

"As to that, I am not at all sure this particular case will have a satisfactory ending."

"I do not wish to hear the details, but if you must tell people that you are shopping for me, please think of some better lie than embroidery silks. I don't even think that there is a shop in Coxwold that sells them."

"There isn't. I had to go there yesterday because—"

"I don't want to know, Mary. Now, I think I have seen more than enough of this garden. Why it is referred to as the dog kennel, I have no idea, but I must say, I do rather fancy having a little pond. Not at Drumlanrig but perhaps at Bowhill. It's getting cold now that the sun has gone in. Do we understand each other, Mary?"

"I had already been considering my position. With regards my—my work."

"Work! You make it sound as if you take a wage."

"If I did, then I wouldn't have to consider my position," Mary retorted. "Don't worry, I wouldn't do anything so vulgar as to take paid employment."

"You sound just like Margaret."

"You know, I'm beginning to think that we might be more similar than I thought," Mary retorted. "We neither of us wish to be forced into the same mould that you were cast from."

"I beg your pardon?"

"I'm sorry, that was very badly put."

"There is no question of the duke and I forcing you into a marriage with a man you cannot like or respect."

"I know that, but that's not why I don't want to get married," Mary said desperately. "Can't you understand, Mama? I don't want to be a dutiful wife. I don't want to have to love, honour, and obey a husband at any price. I don't wish to be an—an appendage to my husband. I want to be something more than simply a wife."

"There is no higher aspiration for a woman than to be a wife and a mother," the duchess said stiffly.

"Perhaps not, but must it be the only aspiration? This *work* I do, that you don't wish to know about, it's not only that it gives me a purpose. My opinion is sought and taken seriously by people like Sir George and his ilk. What other single young woman can claim to be listened to, respected?"

"It makes you feel important, you mean?"

"No," Mary said dejectedly. "Valued. I don't want to give that up yet to become a dutiful wife."

The duchess opened her mouth to speak, then changed her mind. "I have said enough. I will leave you now to think about it. Despite your reservations about matrimony, I can assure you that if Colonel Trefusis wishes to call on your father, he will be well-received."

Mary watched her mother leave the walled garden, then, thoroughly depressed, set off alone on another circuit, oblivious of the drizzle that was falling like a mist over her coat and hat. The duchess had said very little Mary hadn't been aware of herself, but then she had had no idea that her mother was equally aware! Or that her father was attempting to grant her the freedom of choice none of her sisters had enjoyed. Reparation for how he had treated Margaret? Of how he had treated Mary? Or not that at all, but merely her mother's rose-tinted interpretation of his behaviour? The last time she had been in the duke's company was at Christmas, when he had been his usual distant self, closeted in his study with his sons, avoiding Margaret like the plague and looking at Mary, on the odd occasion when they were in the same room, as if he couldn't quite remember her name.

No, her mother was being generous, because the duchess did feel guilty about Mary's parentless childhood. What did it matter now! She had reached the pond again. The fish weren't at all soothing. They were horrible, silvery, glassy-eyed whiskery things lurking in the fronds. Tre would be a welcome suitor for her hand, it seemed. Clearly, Lady Wombwell had been checking up on her, and her mother, too. They were only doing their duty, protecting the innocent young woman in their care. She didn't like the idea of Tre being deemed acceptable by her parents. It implied he was conventional and dull. Contrary Mary!

Tre wasn't dull. Those who thought he was didn't know him, or didn't choose to look beyond the gentle, quiet façade he presented to the world. They really were kindred spirits. Mary knelt down to stir the waters. If that was true, why was she so resistant to *exploring the possibility of a future* with him? Because it seemed so prosaic, and so conventional, and because ultimately, she thought gloomily, she simply wasn't sure she would ever want to get married.

The rain was becoming persistent. The decisions looming over her were too momentous to be considered. She checked her watch, and saw with surprise that the time was a great deal more advanced than she realized. Tre would be waiting.

CHAPTER TWENTY-THREE

To Catch a Thief

MARY FOUND TRE ON THE upper floor of the western wing of the priory outside the door to the Cursed Room, which was kept locked. Sir George had given her the keys when she had expressed an interest in seeing it, offering to escort her but refraining from questioning her when she declined his kind offer. His continued trust in her ability to resolve the matter she was investigating for him was touching, but it weighed heavily on her. He had made it clear he required no progress reports, only a definitive answer. As she put the key in the door, she hoped that this upcoming conversation with Tre would finally provide her with the information she needed.

"Did you enjoy your tour of the garden with your mother? How is her health? I know you've been worried."

"I enquired, but she dismissed it as age, and I didn't pursue the matter."

"That's not like you."

Tre was dressed as usual in sombre colours, his shirt pristine white, his waistcoat today olive green. Though he was clean-shaven, there was a bluish-black shadow on his chin. The grooves which ran from his nose to his mouth were more pronounced than usual. There were shadows under his eyes. "Didn't you sleep well?" she asked.

"I'm perfectly fine, Mary. I've not been sleeping particularly well but it's not one of my headaches that's been keeping me awake at night." He took her hands, pulling her towards him, studying her face. "It's all been so sudden, hasn't it? Not seeing each other for so long and then being closeted here in the priory unable to avoid each other. Now the clock is ticking, and we'll both be going our separate ways on Monday and we have no idea when or if we'll see each other again."

"If only we could continue like this, without having to think about the future or make any momentous decisions."

He caught her hand, pressing a kiss to her palm. Her breath hitched. Their eyes met. His mouth was soft on her skin, warm. He kissed her again, soft kisses moving across her palm, licking into the space between her fingers, making her pulse race. She whispered his name, closing the gap between them, her eyes drifted shut and their lips met in a slow, deep kiss that went on and on. His hands cupped her face, his thumbs caressing the line of her jaw, and still the kiss went on.

"This isn't the purpose of our arrangement to meet up here," Tre said ruefully, when the kiss finally came to an end. "Sir George would be shocked to his portly core if he knew what we were doing, and rightly so. The problem with these sorts of kisses is that they make one want more, and crossing the line is a very easy thing to do."

"Crossing the line." She was only hazily aware of what that was. Had he crossed the line with Sibilla? Was it acceptable if one was betrothed? Henny. She recalled abruptly that Henny had crossed the line, and look where that had got her.

"Do you know the history of this room?" she asked Tre, turning her back on him to wipe the dust from a windowpane. "Sir George told me.

It goes back to the eighteenth century, when the Fauconbergs had the priory and were making some changes to the building. A fire broke out in one of these rooms, apparently a bedchamber belonging to Henry, one of the sons, and he fled to safety. The story is that he heard a maid screaming for help but failed to return for her. While she lay dying, she put a curse on the room."

"That's a horrible story. The poor woman—what a terrible way to go."

"Sir George finds her curse extremely inconvenient. She declared that if the room where she perished was not left exactly as it was, then the sons and heirs of the family would all meet an untimely death. Honestly," Mary said in Sir George's gruff tones, "you'd think she could have come up with something a bit more imaginative than preventing us from giving the rooms a lick of paint."

"They need more than a lick of paint," Tre said. "Shall we take a look?"

Gas lighting did not extend to this part of the priory, and the fires were never lit. The rooms were damp, musty, and icily cold. There were no shutters over the windows, but the light which filtered through the cobweb-covered panes was dim, the sky outside as ominous as the atmosphere inside. Smoke damage, mould, and damp patches were everywhere. Crumbling holes peppered the ceilings, and the window frames were nothing more than a skeleton of rotten wood. The floorboards creaked underfoot as they explored, and scuttling noises came from behind the wainscotting, through which the mice had gnawed holes—Mary sincerely hoped it was mice. The walls were in a sad state. Some consisted merely of raw brick, with huge cracks beginning to show. Others had been lathed but not plastered; on others the plaster had been cross-hatched, awaiting its final skim. The mice had been chewing on the horsehair, too, bringing down chunks of wall in the process.

A door lay propped against the wall at a drunken angle. One room had been painted chalky red which had faded to pink, the paintings in their frames set against it waiting to be hung. A thick dark line of soot stained the wallpaper above the fireplace and also coated the window frames and shutters. She shivered, looking askance at the row of paintings. "Have you noticed that the subject in every portrait in this house seems to watch you?"

"Not especially," Tre replied. "If this wing is left to decay much longer, it will fall down, and then the curse will no longer hang over the Fauconberg heirs. Sir George is very fond of his children. Perhaps that's his intention, to let the wing fall down and thus free them from the curse."

"Which is the room where the maid died, do you think? And where was Henry, the son who saved himself? It's odd, isn't it, now that you look at them—why were they here in the first place, when the wing wasn't nearly finished?"

"There's an obvious answer," Tre said dryly. "To be alone together for an illicit tryst."

"Oh goodness. I never thought of that. And now history is repeating itself."

"What! Mary, I would never—"

"I was referring to Glover and Henny."

Tre coloured. "Of course."

"You are thirty-seven years old, Tre. When you say you would never, do you mean that literally? You're not married, you've never been married, but you are not an *innocent*, are you—you have had experience. No-one expects you to live like a monk." Mary broke off. The subject was embarrassing, and she lacked the vocabulary to continue it. "Never mind."

"What you are trying to say is that it seems unfair to you," Tre said thoughtfully, "that women are judged so much more harshly than men? That it's acceptable for unmarried men to have experience that is utterly unacceptable for women to have? The reason for that is why we are here. It's the woman who bears the consequences. Quite literally, in Henny's case."

Mary's shoulders sagged. "You're right. I'm distracting us. I think I've worked out what happened to that money, but it's such a tangle."

"Then why don't you tell me what you know. Sometimes all you need is to talk a problem through, and the solution suddenly becomes clear."

"I said something like that to Henny the other day, and unfortunately the solution she came up with was the one least likely to happen." The whistle of the wind and the sudden darkening of the room made them look up. Mary peered out of the window. "It's snowing. I hate the snow."

"Then turn your back on it. Here." Tre pulled over a workman's bench and brushed the worst of the dust from it. "Sit down, and tell me all about the Case of the Missing Funds."

Tre propped himself up against the casement, after carefully checking to ensure that it was not so rotten he'd fall through it.

"I have to tell you," Mary said, "I have no solid proof or evidence at all to back up my conclusions, and that is one of the things which worries me most."

"Tell me first what you have concluded, and then we'll deal with your concerns."

"Very well, then. First of all, Mr. Glover may be many things, but I don't believe he's a thief. It simply doesn't fit. He is not a businessman—we know that because he's been duped before—but he is not a complete idiot. He is responsible for deciding whether a cause is worthy or not, therefore any new case must have been authorized by him and can be traced ridiculously easily back to him. Which makes me think that's precisely what someone else wants us to believe."

"So he could have been fooled into believing it is a worthy cause and has handed the money over in good faith?"

Mary nodded. "Then there's the fact that he's still here, and hasn't run off with the funds. There's also what Henny said about his feeling such an obligation to Sir George and wishing to prove himself to take into consideration. Though how he can reconcile that with what he's done to Henny—but I won't let my disgust of him cloud my judgement."

"I think I agree with you," Tre said, frowning. "Glover is not our man, and Henny is not a woman scorned seeking vengeance because she's barely literate."

"And she loves him."

"Which means," Tre continued, "someone else wishes Glover harm, and that brings us to your trip to Coxwold yesterday to visit Henny's brother, Tommy. Which is what I presume you were doing and not shopping for embroidery silks for the duchess?"

Mary smiled. "My mother told me this morning that I lacked imagination in my excuses. She hates to embroider."

"Under what guise did you speak to Tommy, the clerk with the means and the motive?"

"I knew Henny was working yesterday, and that he had the afternoon off, so I simply called on him at his cottage. When I explained that I knew about his sister's condition and that I wanted to help, he was naturally extremely defensive. The fewer people involved, the more likely it was he could keep it quiet, and he didn't appreciate my interfering, thank you kindly."

Tre smiled. "In other words, you took a liking to him?"

"Yes, I did, though I am not acquitting him on that basis."

"You are acquitting him, though?"

"It turns out Henny had a beau before Mr. Glover appeared on the scene. A good friend of Tommy's as it happens—or he was. He also, as it happens, works in the local bank where the charity has an account. According to Tommy, Michael Baxter—that's his name—and Henny had an understanding. Then along came Mr. Glover, and Henny only had eyes for him."

"How much does Mr. Baxter know?"

"Only that Henny is in thrall to Glover, to use Tommy's words. Michael still loves her. He blames Glover for casting a spell over her, and basically leading her down the garden path."

"So he doesn't know that she's expecting Glover's child?"

"No, Tommy's sure of that. Michael thinks that Glover has ruined his life, that if he had never come to Newburgh, Henny would be his wife. He might be right."

"So Michael Baxter *is* our man?"

"He has the means and the strongest possible motive." Mary looked quite dejected. "But I have no proof unless I confront him, which I obviously can't do without betraying Sir George's trust in me to be discreet."

"We don't even know what he's done with the money. If he is a thief, there's a chance he might have spent it. Alternatively, if he is not a thief, but framed Glover as a kind of revenge, he may have hung on to the money. The law will come down heavily on him, though, either way."

"If Sir George decides to invoke it. I don't know, Tre, it feels all wrong that he should be the only one punished. Apart from Henny, I mean."

"Mary, you've untangled what has in all probability happened. The best and simplest thing now would be to lay the truth before Sir George and let him decide what to do. You could point out to him that he's already living in a house cursed by one wronged maid, and he might not wish to incur another."

He meant to make her laugh, but Mary shivered. "It's rather a horrible coincidence, isn't it, if the poor maid who died here had been seduced? I *wish* I could think of a way out of this mess. I may even, as you cautioned me, be about to make it worse. It's all so awful."

He couldn't disagree. Disgusting as it was, the chances were that Henny would be shamed, she'd lose her child, probably her job. The clerk would go to gaol. And Glover? "Sir George is going to find himself in an awkward position, his wife's cousin revealed as a seducer."

Mary jumped up, wringing her hands. "It would have been better if I hadn't come here and meddled."

"You've not been meddling. You have the best interests of everyone involved at heart."

He could see tears glinting in her eyes, but she would do everything she could to stop them falling. "My mother was right," she said. "This must be my last case. I *have* to find a way to prevent it being an abject failure."

"What did the duchess say to you?"

"A great deal. Food for thought, but I don't have time to talk about it now."

He was beginning to wonder if she would ever have the time to talk to him about personal matters. Had it been a colossal mistake to open up to her? When would he get another or better opportunity? It wasn't fair to press her, though. She had taken this unpleasant case to heart, so the best thing he could do was try to make the solution a little more palatable.

CHAPTER TWENTY-FOUR

Ready to Run!

Newburgh Priory, Saturday, 20 February 1875

S O THERE YOU HAVE IT, Lady Mary," Sir George said, with a heart-felt sigh. "Your suspicions confirmed. I won't go into the detail of how young Michael Baxter embezzled the money, but I'm going to put measures in place to make sure that it can't ever happen again."

They were in the library before dinner. One of the most idiosyncratic of the priory's many quirky rooms, the library had a dome set in the ceiling directly in front of the huge carved marble mantel where the central figure was most disconcertingly naked. Mary was seated on one side of the hearth. Sir George, who had been quite incredulous when she had first spoken to him yesterday, now wandered restlessly about the room, deeply affected.

"At least the charity is no worse off," he said. "Baxter hadn't spent a single penny of the money. Stupid young man; he planned to make an anonymous donation of the whole amount back to us once the fraud had been discovered and my wife's cousin summarily dismissed."

Sir George took out a handkerchief and mopped his face, dropping heavily back onto his chair. "I must confess, Lady Mary, that I was very much inclined to hand him over to the law. I pride myself on being an upright citizen. I like to set an example, especially as I am the Justice of the Peace for North Riding, and it goes much against the grain to bend the rules, to use your own words. However, it was, as you also pointed out, a crime committed not for personal gain but out of passion. I am coming round to your way of thinking that that mitigates his action somewhat, misplaced though it was."

"I am so sorry. I wish there were a better solution."

"So do I—indeed. I had no notion that you would uncover such a tragedy, right here in my own household, too. I inadvertently put a great burden on your shoulders. I must confess, I feel extremely guilty to have exposed you to such a sordid tale. My wife would be horrified if she knew, and as for your mother, the duchess—" Sir George broke off, shuddering. "She would, quite rightly, be extremely angry with me."

"Please don't apologize. This is not an uncommon situation, I'm very sorry to say."

"Alas, you're in the right of it. It's not uncommon, but your solution is extremely unconventional."

"You've decided to go along with it?"

"I've already put the wheels in motion, so to speak. I've spoken to Baxter and informed him that I'm going to take no further action with regards the fraud, on the understanding that he makes an offer for Henrietta. Whether she'll accept or not is a matter for her."

"Poor Henny."

"At least she'll have a choice," Sir George said gruffly. "If she doesn't take it, then I'll make sure she's looked after—and the child, too. We'll see what we can do to find it a good home, and Henrietta will have her job here to come back to if she wants it."

Marriage would allow Henny to keep her child and her reputation, as Tre had pointed out. But marriage to a man she didn't love, and who would very likely see the child as a cuckoo in the nest, seemed to Mary a dreadful choice to have to make. She couldn't imagine how Henny could be happy. Though she had been happy enough with Michael Baxter before she met Dacre Glover, as Tre had also pointed out.

"When will you speak to Henny?"

"It's a dreadful business. Normally the sort of thing that would be better coming from a woman, but of course in this case I can't get my good lady wife involved. I'll wait until this little house party breaks up. Her brother, Tommy, is a good chap with a sensible head on his shoulders; he has agreed to look after her in the short term while she considers her options. I'll put it about that she's sick until she has made her decision. As to Glover . . ."

Sir George mopped his brow again. "That is one interview which I would happily have avoided. I spoke to him this morning. That he could have abused my trust to such an extent! And then prove himself to be such a coward, too—for at first he denied everything. If he had but owned up! I cannot abide a sniveller or a coward, and he proved himself both. He's had his chance. He won't get another from me."

"When will he be leaving?"

"As soon as he can think up an excuse that my wife will believe." Sir George got to his feet again. "That's the devil of it—excuse my language—the invidious position he's placed me in. My wife and I don't have secrets from each other, but if I tell her the truth about that disreputable cousin of hers we've been harbouring—no, it doesn't bear thinking of." He poured himself a snifter of brandy, swallowed it, then poured another. "After a great deal of reflection I have decided to keep the truth from her. I shall resume my responsibility for the charity, needless to say. And of course your role is known to no-one but myself."

He crossed the room once more, and handed Mary a glass of sherry. "I am very much in your debt, Lady Mary, as is Henrietta, though she will never know it. If there is ever any way I can be of assistance in the future, with anything at all, you know you only have to ask."

"Usually I would say my reward is in resolving a problem to everyone's satisfaction, but unfortunately, in this case no-one can be satisfied."

"This is a sad business, but it would have been a scandalous mess were it not for your intervention." He touched his glass to hers. "You are a most intriguing young lady. Thank you."

"I am glad to have been of assistance, though I am not sure, to be honest, that anyone but yourself would think I've helped."

"You have come up with a creative solution that I would never have dreamed of."

Much of the creativity had been Tre's, and all of the pragmatism. As far as Mary was concerned, everyone involved would be diminished, save Tre. Henny would be broken-hearted. Michael Baxter would probably be forced into supporting another man's child. Glover lacked the gumption to either take responsibility or recover from his disgrace. Sir George was being forced into lying to his wife. Mary had failed.

"There now—don't look so downcast," Sir George said, "I'm a tough old bird, one of life's survivors. Did I tell you the story of how I escaped the Russian forces at Balaclava?" He swallowed his brandy in one gulp. "Hell hath no fury like a bank clerk scorned, what! Now then, we'd best join the party before my wife comes looking for me. I'll go first, you stay and finish your sherry."

Sunday, 21 February 1875

It was early, and the sky looked leaden with snow as Mary recounted her interview with Sir George to Tre, who was propped up against the potting table in the glasshouse of the dog kennel garden. It occurred to her it had become their little office, or perhaps *campaign headquarters* was more apt.

"So it's not exactly all's well that ends well, but all's as good as it can be, given the terrible situation," he said when she had finished.

"Thanks in no small part to you," Mary said.

"You'd have got there in the end without me."

"No, I'd have been quite lost. This has been an extremely sobering experience for me." Mary tried to smile, but her mouth trembled. "I've been up most of the night thinking."

"That sounds ominous," Tre said, adding, when she made no attempt to deny it, "I see. It's all too much of a risk for you, I take it."

Round and round and round in circles her mind had roamed, testing out argument after argument, and failing every time. She felt battered and bruised, as if she had been in a fist-fight with herself. "Yes," Mary said sadly, "I'm afraid it is."

"I understand. That day in the pinery, the display I made of myself . . ."

"No, you don't understand at all. My decision has nothing to do with your condition, as you call it. How could you possibly imagine I would let that influence me?"

"You forget, I have a painful prior experience."

"I didn't forget. I don't know your Sibilla, but I know myself and I know you. Condition, curse, however you wish to refer to it, it's part of you."

"I am hoping that is no longer true."

"It doesn't make a difference to me, Tre." She wanted to shake him. She wanted to embrace him, but she dare not risk touching him. "I don't think it's a weakness, it's not something to be ashamed of, and it doesn't make you pathetic or pitiable either. What is shameful and pathetic is how you have been treated because of it by the army, your fellow officers, and by the woman you love."

"I have long since ceased loving Sibilla."

Mary tucked her chin into her blue scarf, frowning hard. This was so difficult. "But you're not sure, are you, what you feel for me?"

Tre was silent for so long that she was forced to look up. Like her, he was frowning deeply. Like her, he had taken off his gloves. "I am not sure if what I feel for you is deep enough or likely to last," he said, finally looking up. "That's what I would like to discover." He grimaced. "That sounds extraordinarily pompous. I'm trying to be honest with you. When I'm with you, I feel certain, but when I'm not with you, when I make myself think about the reality of the situation, our total acquaintance extends to less than a month."

"What if, after spending more time together, we find that our feelings for each other don't run deep enough? What then?"

"I don't know. I hadn't considered that. I had assumed that we would discover the opposite."

Mary got up, using her glove to wipe the condensation from one of the panes. The air was speckled with falling snow. "My mother told me the other day, here in this garden, that my father would be pleased if you called on him. If we explored—pursued our acquaintance, people would know. Assumptions would be made—the same assumptions that my mother is already making, that you have intentions and that I am pleased to receive them. There couldn't be any changing of our minds without a scandal, without one or both of us being maligned. And as far as my father is concerned, a case of history repeating itself. That's not a risk I'm willing to take, for both our sakes."

She turned back around to face him. "But that's not the main reason, Tre. It boils down to one simple fact. It feels wrong." Now she had said the words, there was a terrible sense of relief, though it faded immediately when she saw his expression. "I'm sorry."

"May I ask what you mean by wrong?"

"Seeing Henny so helpless, with next to no say in her fate, gave me pause for thought. I don't want that. If she marries Michael Baxter, what are the chances of her being happy?"

"A lot lower than the chances of us being happy."

"I can't risk it." They were both on their feet now, facing each other. "For once in my life, I'm putting myself first. I don't want to be obligated to my husband. What would I do if we married? You would have your precious intelligence work, but I wouldn't have any meaningful purpose, forced to occupy myself with gardening or some other pursuit, just like my mother."

"You'd have me."

"That's not enough." Tears smarted in her eyes. "There, I've said it. It's not enough. I just can't do it." Mary picked up her gloves and pulled them on. Her hands were shaking.

"I see." He turned his face away from her. "What will you do now?"

"I don't know. I am concerned about my mother's health."

"So, Lady Mary, nursemaid will be your next reincarnation, will it?"

"Tre!"

"I apologize. I'd hate to be another altar for you to sacrifice yourself on. I'm glad we've cleared that up."

He picked up his gloves. The door of the glasshouse squeaked shut after him. Mary stood motionless, watching him disappear into the snow. It was over, but she knew in her bones that she'd done the right thing.

IT HAD STARTED THIS MORNING in the glasshouse, though he hadn't noticed it until this afternoon, when he was closeted in the library with

Sir George. A walk before dinner had eased it, but now with his head feeling as if it might explode, his entire focus was on getting through the rest of the evening unscathed. Dinner. Nine interminable courses to celebrate the last night of the house party. Tre toyed with the food on his plate, aware of Mary's covert glances over the table. She'd be thinking she'd had a lucky escape. Counting her blessings. His head was as thick as a London fog by the time the ladies left the gentlemen to their port. He made it through the ordeal by counting, over and over, one to a hundred, one to a hundred, one to a hundred, going ever more slowly but sticking doggedly to the sequence.

Rising from his chair he staggered, and caught the back of it. "A tad too much port," he muttered to his neighbour, whose name he couldn't recall.

"Fresh air is what you need." Sir George came to his rescue, taking his arm firmly and marching him out of the room. "You didn't touch a drop, Colonel Trefusis," he said. "Are you . . ."

"Well. Perfectly well. Absolutely—what you said. Fresh air."

"You don't think that you'd be better retiring? I can make your excuses."

"Fresh air. All I need." He knew it wasn't true, but he clung desperately to the hope.

Sir George, to his relief, took him at his word, helping him across the hallway to the door of the King James's Porch. "Stay here. You've no coat and it's snowing. Are you sure . . ."

"Fine now. Go. Back. Guests." The mist swirled. Tre sank onto the wooden bench against the wall, waited until the door closed behind Sir George, and then the blackness enveloped him.

THERE WERE TO BE CHARADES after dinner, but Tre did not appear with the gentlemen to join in. Sir George had been late joining them, too, Mary had noticed. Tre was having an attack. She'd watched his condition take hold of him over dinner. This time she knew exactly what had triggered it. She had. It was all her fault. Where was he? Had he collapsed? If so, it had not been in front of the other gentlemen. Had Sir George escorted him to his room? Oh, Tre, she thought wretchedly, imagining his mortification.

No, he'd have done anything to prevent that. The last time—the only time she had witnessed it, what he'd wanted was fresh air. That's what he'd have done now, not retired to his bed. He'd have gone outside and done absolutely everything in his power to ensure that his host left him alone. But what if he had fainted, as he had done the last time? It was snowing heavily now. If he had fallen . . .

She had to find him. As the rest of the guests laughed and teased each other, sorting through the collection of clothes, hats, and feathers that Lady Wombwell had supplied for the game, Mary whispered an apology to her mother, waving vaguely at her stomach, and left the room.

If Tre was safely in his bed, she was on a wild goose chase, but she was as certain as she could be that he was not. Rushing to her own chamber, she grabbed her cloak and scarf. Racing back down the stairs, she stopped at the library for the decanter of brandy and a glass. Which door? Which way would he have gone? From the dining room, the most obvious exit was the King James's Porch. Mary wrenched open the heavy door.

He was seated on the bench, his head bent forward resting in his hands. "I'm fine," he muttered. "Just need a few more minutes."

His voice was slurred. Mary sat down beside him and poured a tiny amount of the brandy into the glass. "Take this."

"You!" Tre swore and jerked upright. "Should have known."

"Yes, you should have." She held the glass to his lips. "Sip."

He took it from her, his hand shaking violently, but did not drink. "Not cured after all."

"Tre, drink the blasted brandy."

He threw it into his mouth, choked, swallowed. "Sir George?"

"Said nothing. I guessed you were here."

"You were watching me," Tre said, holding out the glass. "At dinner."

"Of course I was." Mary wrapped her scarf around his neck, then poured another tiny tot of brandy. "You should be in your bed."

"So mine host told me." Tre took a cautious sip, grimaced, then set the glass down. "How did you know I was here?"

"Fresh air, that's your solution to everything."

He gave a grating laugh. "Pot and kettle, Mary."

"I know. The air is rather too fresh tonight, though—you'll freeze. Come inside."

"No!" He took a shuddering breath, pushing his hair back from his brow. There was a lamp lit in the porch, the gas making his complexion look green rather than ashen. The frown between his brows was a deep furrow. "It's none of your business. I am none of your business anymore. You made the right decision."

"It wasn't for this reason."

"I think you're scared. That's what I think. But I'm not your parents or your sister. All the people who have abandoned you. I'm not leaving you—you're making me go." Tre forced himself to his feet. "You've had a narrow escape, mind you, given the wreck of a man you see before you. I'm leaving on the early train, so I'll bid you good night and good-bye. Oh yes, and good luck."

He turned away, opened the porch door, and disappeared inside.

Mary got up and made her way slowly back up the stairs to her room, where she sat in the window, and watched the snow fall. In another room, Tre was suffering while confronting his demons. She had forfeited any right to comfort him. She had left him, just as Sibilla had. This time she was the one doing the abandoning.

PART III

Carlsbad and London

1876

CHAPTER TWENTY-FIVE

Taking the Cure

Carlsbad, March 1876

THE SPA TOWN OF CARLSBAD nestled in a beautiful verdant valley in the foothills of the Ore Mountains in West Bohemia where the Teplá, Ohře, and Rolava rivers converged. The main part of the town followed the winding flow of the Teplá in the floor of the valley, where a charming series of little bridges had been constructed to allow traffic to cross from one bank to the other. The buildings were on a grand scale and, it seemed to Mary, in a constant state of upheaval, expansion, and improvement to cope with the ever-increasing influx of visitors arriving to take the waters and enjoy the baths.

After a year spent largely in the duchess's company, Mary was convinced that her mother's ailments owed less to genuine illness and almost everything to the vast variety of treatments and regimes she inflicted on herself. When in Scotland, they had become regular visitors to the Strathearn Hydropathic Hotel in Crieff, where the patients were required to follow a strict diet as well as endure the various water treatments. The accommodation was luxurious, but the copious green and brown food served was vile—the more disgusting it was, it seemed to her, the healthier it was deemed. Water was drunk by the gallon. The patients were also pounded with vast deluges of it. One of her mother's favourite treatments, the Vichy douche, required her to lie, draped only in a thin bath sheet, under the relentless jets of three large showerheads.

The duchess had come to Carlsbad in search of variety, and Mary had come along because she had become exactly what Tre had predicted, her mother's nursemaid. It had not been a deliberate tactic but a role she had fallen into through a combination of inertia and lack of other options, for she had no money of her own and still was what she had always been: her father's daughter to dispose of as he chose. He had chosen to ignore her, and she wished to keep it that way.

Bruised from what she still saw as her abject failure to resolve matters satisfactorily in Yorkshire, particularly with regards to Henny, she had decided that her amateur sleuthing days were over. After her last "case," her instinct had been to retreat from the world and lick her wounds. By playing Princess Beatrice to her mother's Queen Victoria, she could do this and be of service to the duchess. She had not, however, imagined that she would still be in this position more than a year later.

It was a beautiful morning, the blue sky contrasting with the emerald-green pines which grew on the slopes of the mountains. The buildings gleamed and sparkled, as if they, too, had been taking one of the many water cures. In the crisp, fresh mountain air that was reputed to be so healthy, a tang of sulphur from the springs was noticeable. They had been in Carlsbad for three weeks, and Mary was on the verge of despair. She could not continue like this, but what else could she do? Marriage was the obvious solution, but even now her every instinct rebelled. She would not bind herself forever to a husband who would expect her to mould herself into a dutiful wife. Not even if her husband was Tre. As usual, thinking about him brought on a mixture of guilt and longing, so she pushed him from her mind.

She and her mother were making the slow promenade they made every morning, from the Czech Hall Hotel to the Mill Colonnade, which was built over the famous springs and was currently being significantly upgraded. Inside, the air was heavy with the sulphurous steam hissing up through the railed-off openings in the floor, through which the waters were retrieved by attendants and eagerly consumed by patients. The long hall was already busy. The duchess had made many acquaintances, kindred spirits who enjoyed battling for supremacy in the pursuit of suffering, Mary thought. People came to Carlsbad from all over Europe with endless combinations of symptoms, sharing wealth and lineage as well as a deep obsession with their health.

Her mother made her first stop to take a glass of the waters. There were people here who were real sufferers, people whose pain was etched on their faces, who shuffled along the colonnade leaning heavily on canes and crutches or were pushed along in Bath-chairs, but they were in the minority. Too much money. Too much time. Insufficient occupation. Two out of the three most certainly applied to her.

She had wasted another year of her life, and if she didn't do something, take some sort of action, then she would waste another, and another. Inertia didn't suit her. There was far too much time, living this sedentary life, to reflect. It was bad for her, and it was bad for her mother, too. Every day over tea, every night over dinner, the talk was all of ailments and treatments and doctors and cures. Dressing for their morning walk, dressing for tea, dressing for dinner, dressing for the occasional evening concert occupied a good part of the time. For her mother, undressing and enduring her treatments took up the rest. Why was it acceptable here for a woman to display herself in only a bath sheet—a wet bath sheet!—in front of complete strangers of both sexes?

Why was it appropriate for men and women to share the same hot baths? Did illness preclude any notion of being in a compromising situation?

"Your Grace!" An elderly woman, as round as she was tall, dressed in scarlet, waddled over to them. "I'm right, am I not, in thinking that I'm addressing the Duchess of Buccleuch?"

Her mother stiffened. "I do not believe I have had the pleasure, madam."

"No, we haven't met," the woman admitted, unabashed. "I know, I ought to find a common acquaintance to introduce us, but I've never understood why one is expected to go to such a bother, when I'm perfectly capable of introducing myself. Louisa," the woman said, holding out a hand swathed in expensive calfskin gloves, "Lady Rolle. I'm—"

"Tre's aunt," Mary said, immediately colouring. "Colonel Trefusis, I mean." *Dear heavens, Tre's aunt.* "This lady is his aunt Louisa."

"My nephew Trefusis is a distant relative of your husband, Your Grace, which is why I knew you wouldn't mind my introducing myself."

"Of course. How do you do, Lady Rolle?" Mary's mother accepted the extended hand. "May I introduce my youngest daughter? Mary, you obviously recall Colonel Trefusis very well."

This was said with a pointed look. Hoping that Tre's aunt would attribute her hot cheeks to the steam, Mary dropped a curtsy. "How do you do, Lady Rolle?"

"I'm very well, though I must say, from the little I've seen of this place, it's enough to make the most hale and hearty individual feel as if they are at death's door. I do most sincerely hope, Your Grace, that you have not drunk any of those noxious waters?"

"I take two glasses every day, from two different springs. It is most beneficial."

"Beneficial! Are you a steam engine in need of water in order to run? That stuff will rot your innards, if you don't mind my saying. And even if you do," Lady Rolle added, "it's too late as I've said it. What we need, Your Grace, is a cup of tea, and I know just the place."

Giving the duchess no time to refuse, Lady Rolle took her arm and began to head off towards the main entrance. "Extraordinary" is how Tre had described his aunt. As Mary followed in their wake, she could think of several other words. *Rumbustious. Intimidating. Overpowering. A force of nature.* What was she doing here, especially as she seemed to have nothing but contempt for the treatments? Had Tre confided in her? He'd once described his aunt as the least conventional woman he had ever met. *Until I met you,* he had added. What would he think of Mary now, traipsing around hanging on her mother's coat-tails, playing the companion to a determined invalid? No trace of the tightrope walker, or even the righter of wrongs, remained, just a bored, tedious nursemaid. He wouldn't have mentioned her to his aunt, why would he? He'd have forgotten all about her, or erased her from his memory, the woman who was too scared to grasp the possibility of a very different future. He'd been right, too. She had told him she didn't want to be beholden to a husband and yet here she was, beholden to her mother.

She was lagging behind. This meeting was a complete coincidence. It was ridiculous to think it could be anything else—but there was a faint possibility that Tre had happened to mention Mary's name, and therefore the chance that when Lady Rolle next saw her beloved nephew, she might mention that she had met Lady Mary. She needed to ensure that what Lady Rolle reported back was *not* that she'd met a dormouse or a nursemaid. As she caught the other two women up, Mary wondered if she dared ask her new acquaintance for a peppermint.

THE TEA-SHOP WAS BUSY, BUT Lady Rolle commanded one of the best tables. Slightly dazed, Charlotte accepted a cup of tea and a pastry filled with honey and almonds which would normally have made her feel nauseous just to look at. It did smell delicious, though. She took a small bite. It tasted even better.

Lady Rolle's face was as round as her body, and exceedingly tanned. Her mouth was rather on the large side as was her nose, and her hair, iron-grey and wildly curling, like the rest of that bountiful woman, looked as if it was about to burst forth from the cap she wore under her hat.

"Pineries," that lady announced after she had selected three pastries for herself. "We have one at Bicton, which is my home in Devon, but nothing to compare with what you have at Drumlanrig, Your Grace. Tell me, how many pineapples do you harvest in a year?"

"We call it a poor year if we have less than a hundred fit to eat," Charlotte replied.

"Well, well, that is quite something My own gardener . . ."

Charlotte listened as Lady Rolle launched into a highly technical exposition of her gardener's techniques, well enough versed in the process to maintain the conversation while studying the extraordinary woman who had all but commandeered her. Truth be told, she had been happy to be commandeered. She was frightfully bored, and just as weary of poor Mary's company as Mary was of hers. Her daughter, sipping her tea and imagining herself unobserved, was studying their companion closely. She never mentioned Colonel Trefusis of her own volition. When they left Yorkshire a year ago, all she would say was that she thought it highly unlikely they would meet again. Charlotte had tried to press her, only to be informed, in that tight little voice that was the only indication Mary was upset, that her mother had been mistaken in imagining there was ever anything between her and the colonel.

"'Practical Hints on the Culture of the Pineapple,' it's called. But you have not eaten a thing, Lady Mary." Lady Rolle rounded on Charlotte's daughter.

"I am not hungry, thank you, Lady Rolle."

"You have a very good figure, you're obviously not one of those young women with the appetite of a sparrow. Are you ill? Is that why you are here?"

"No, I am in rude health, thank you very much."

"Hmm, I'd say you've a peaky look about you. What you need is to get away from the miasma of those baths. There's nothing like fresh air, I always say. Cures all ills. And you, Your Grace"—Lady Rolle turned back to Charlotte—"If you don't mind my saying, you're looking quite washed out. Too many of those water cures, I expect. They can't be good for you, draining away all the body's vital elements."

"The idea is to wash away impurities and to revitalize oneself," Charlotte said, taking umbrage. "Medical science has proven—"

"Piffle. Twaddle. Balderdash. If you ask me, those so-called medical men are making a great deal of money out of people like you."

"I did not ask you, and I am not sure what you mean by people like me . . ."

"With too much money and too much time on their hands," Lady Rolle said. "There, Lady Mary agrees with me."

Mary's eyes widened. "Do I?"

Lady Rolle gave a snorting laugh. "Don't you?"

Seeing her daughter, most unusually, at a disadvantage, Charlotte forgot her own displeasure. "Well, Mary?"

"I think that Lady Rolle delights in setting people at odds," Mary replied.

"Ha! That I do, you are quite right. And I like to speak my mind, too, you know, I'm known for my bluntness. You will always know where you stand with me, Lady Mary. In that way, I'm very different from my nephew."

Mary's smile did not falter, but Charlotte was watching her closely. Whatever had happened between her daughter and Trefusis, she was not indifferent. She said nothing, however, as was her way, but picked up her tea-spoon and began to stir her tea.

"I see something of my nephew when I am in London," Lady Rolle persisted. "As you can detect from my figure—or rather I should say, my lack of figure—I am very fond of my food, but I don't like to eat alone, and Trefusis indulges me by enduring my company."

"Are you putting up at the Czech Hall for your stay, Lady Rolle?" Mary asked. "I'm afraid an epicurean such as you will find the food rather disappointing."

"I'm at the Saxon Hall. Well now, ladies, if you are finished with your tea, I have a fancy to try out one or two of these treatments, in the name of research," Lady Rolle said with a twinkle in her eye. "What would you recommend, Your Grace?"

"Have you ever had any hydropathic treatments before, Lady Rolle? No? Nor has my daughter, who shares your scepticism. Come, I shall speak to my personal physician and we will arrange for you to enjoy a few choice cuts, as you epicureans might say. An amuse-bouche for the body. And Mary," Charlotte said, smiling serenely at her daughter, "shall accompany you."

THE CORRIDORS OF THE BATH house were thick with steam, the walls running with condensation, and the air an unpleasantly tangy mixture of sulphur, minerals, mud, pine, and sweat. Mary and Lady Rolle were escorted by a female attendant to a changing room where they were given a plain chemise, a bath sheet, and a robe, then left alone in cubicles separated by curtains to undress.

Taking off her coat and walking dress, Mary's mood swung back and forth. She was irked at her mother for forcing her into taking the baths and annoyed at herself for being so easily pushed into a corner. She was intrigued and amused by Lady Rolle, huffing and puffing, muttering and creaking in the next cubicle, but she was also very wary. Lady Rolle had been studying her carefully over tea and, if the duchess had not played into her hands, would without doubt have found another way to closet herself away with Mary. What did she want? Tre must have said something, but what? They were close, aunt and nephew, she recalled him saying, but how close? And what did it matter anyway, because she had burned her bridges well and truly with Tre.

Tre. His face, his smile, the smell of his shaving soap, the rough smoothness of his cheek, assaulted her, making her stop in the act of unbuttoning her boots. She tried not to think of him.

"Lady Mary! I am very sorry to have to ask you, but I simply cannot unfasten my corsets and I have no desire to call an attendant to assist me. Ah, thank you. I know I should be able to manage myself, but my fingers are too clumsy these days. Tell me, do you think one keeps one's drawers on?" Lady Rolle lifted her petticoat to survey her own pair, startling crimson silk trimmed with black lace. "No, I don't think so. Well, when in Rome!"

Mary beat a hasty retreat as Lady Rolle recommenced her undressing, and hurriedly finished her own. Her undergarments were modest, white lawn and cotton lace. She rather liked Lady Rolle's style, though it did seem odd to go to such expense only to hide it under a petticoat. The chemise which had been provided for their treatment was thin, made of very cheap cotton. She wore more clothes to bed.

"It is certainly not a case of one size fits all." Lady Rolle poked her head through the curtain. "I can scarcely breathe in this chemise. I hope the baths are more accommodating. Do they come back for us or

are we—ah no, here is our expert. Once more unto the breach, Lady
Mary. I must say, I'm rather looking forward to this now."

Mary hastily pulled on the robe, picked up her towel, and followed
the attendant in the wake of Lady Rolle's undulating form. In the corridor, they passed several other patients clad in the same robes. Men
and women, barefoot, some bright red and beaded with sweat, others
coldly dripping, others looking, as Mary was beginning to feel, extremely anxious.

The first treatment her mother had arranged was a peloid mud bath.
There were two sets of two baths set out in the tiled room, separated
by a low wooden partition. One of the pair of tubs contained clean
water, while the other contained a mixture of what looked like brown
mud and brackish water. It stank. On closer inspection, Mary found a
dismaying quantity of decaying matter which she hoped was mineral.
The mixture was gently, repulsively steaming.

Over the partition, Lady Rolle was inspecting something on the
end of her finger, her nose wrinkled in disgust. She looked over, caught
Mary's eye, and the two of them burst out laughing.

"Well, my dear," Lady Rolle said, her chins trembling, "I sincerely
hope I'm right when I say that things can only get better. Deep breath,
and in we go." She held on to the rope which dangled from the ceiling
to steady herself; and as she disappeared from sight, there was a loud
sucking sound and a muttered curse. "A moment if you please while I
arrange myself," Lady Rolle snapped at the attendant, standing ready
with a cover intended to keep the heat in. "Now, now, yes, you're going
to have to press down a little—ouf."

Trying to smother her fit of the giggles, Mary stepped gingerly into
her own tub. The mud oozed between her toes. The tin underneath
was slippery. She clutched at her chemise in an effort to prevent it from

sliding up as she eased herself gingerly down, the mud sucking at her skin. It was hot. Beads of perspiration broke out on her forehead. The attendant was already standing impatiently by to put the lid on her. Mary sank down, shivering as the mud slithered over her body, and was immediately locked in place by the lid. Only her head poked through the half-circle cut for it.

"Are you in, Lady Mary? How do you find it? I feel like a large salmon in a fish-kettle."

"I feel hot," Mary said. Perspiration was rolling down her forehead into her eyes and her nose, but her arms were trapped under the wooden lid. She tried to blow the beads away, and encountered a blob of mud on her lip which made her want to retch. "How long must we endure this?" she asked.

"No idea." Lady Rolle's disembodied voice was slurred. "It's really rather soporific. I think I'll just close my eyes."

A gentle snore came from the other side of the partition. Mary wriggled lower in the bath, and laid her head back. She closed her eyes. And slept.

THEY WERE ROUSED FROM THE peloid baths, dipped in the clean bath to take off the worst of the mud, and then stood, still half asleep in their clinging chemises, under a warm shower to rinse off the remaining detritus. Then they were placed in another contraption made of circular bands of pierced piping which sprayed them with sharp needles of colder water. Wide awake now and shivering, Mary and Lady Rolle were conducted to another tiled room and placed in two more wooden boxes, these ones set upright with a narrow seat. The doors were closed on them and the attendants left.

"Well!" Lady Rolle's iron-grey hair was a wild fizz of curls. Her face was almost the same colour as her crimson drawers. Her eyes twinkled with merriment, and she was smiling broadly. "Your mother's little joke has backfired. I'm enjoying this immensely."

"It has a certain novelty value," Mary admitted, "though I wouldn't like to put myself through it again."

"No, indeed, I'm going to look like a very wrinkled russet apple at the end of all this. We have half an hour before they douse us again, so I won't beat about the bush. As I have no doubt you've already surmised, for you are a very bright young woman, it was no accident that I bumped into you and your mother this morning."

Steam was being fed into the box Mary was locked into through a pipe located somewhere around her ankles. There was something jabbing into her stomach, trapped under her chemise. A pine needle, best case. She was dripping with perspiration, her hair was probably every bit as frizzy as Lady Rolle's. Looking across at her fellow sufferer, Tre's aunt, a year of pent-up emotions welled up inside Mary. Tears mingled with perspiration on her cheeks, and she asked the most important of many questions first. "How is he?"

CHAPTER TWENTY-SIX

Home Truths

Carlsbad, March 1876, Two Weeks Later

T HERE WAS STILL SUFFICIENT SNOW for Aunt Louisa and Mary to take a sleigh-ride through the Slavkov Forest. Wrapped up well against the chill with cloaks, hats, and blankets, they huddled together behind the driver and their guide, in a low sleigh pulled by two horses. It was early in the afternoon. The sky was clear, their breath forming clouds in front of them, and the bells on the horses' harnesses jangled as they travelled. A few miles from the town, along the Ohře River, their driver came to a halt to allow them to admire the Svatoš Rocks, which their guide informed them was a wedding party, turned to stone by a spurned lover with supernatural powers.

"Yes, yes," Aunt Louisa said, looking singularly unimpressed, "but we mortals are in need of our dinner. Onwards, driver."

The Hans Heiling Guest House stood on the opposite bank of the Ohře River, on the edge of the forest. It was a large stone building, the windows shuttered against the cold. Inside, the stone walls were decorated with antlers and exposed wooden rafters, giving the impression that they would be dining in a barn. The warmth from a roaring fire was most welcome, the heat making their cheeks sting. The gloomy candlelight, too, was welcome, after the achingly bright light of the sun glinting on the snow. With some difficulty, Aunt Louisa squashed her rotund body onto the bench, informing the waiter that she did not expect him to show any other diners to the table.

"For I wish to talk in confidence to you," she said to Mary, as the waiter poured frothing beer from a stone jug. "I am always delighted to sample peasant food and drink. Now, first things first, tell me how your mother is?"

Mary sat, took a sip of the beer, which was cold, yeasty, and rather pleasant, and obediently tried to construct an honest answer. Since Aunt Louisa had arrived, Mary had spent a part of every day in her company and one of the first things she had learned about the redoubtable old woman was that she would not accept what she called flim-flam. It was Aunt Louisa who had talked the duchess into a consultation this afternoon with a new doctor who specialized in digestive problems. Aunt Louisa had also insisted on accompanying her, *to make sure you don't shilly-shally about,* adding ominously, *bowels.* The word had made the duchess's cheeks turn scarlet.

How was her mother, then? "When I asked her how the consultation went, she said that she had never endured such a mortifying experience in her life."

"Nonsense, the woman has had eight children."

Of whom only seven were living. "My mother told you about Francis?" Mary asked, surprised at the mention of the brother who had died of measles as an infant, long before she was born. "She almost never speaks of him. I only learned of his existence when my sister Victoria's little boy died, almost six years ago."

"The death of a child affects one profoundly. It is a tragedy that most prefer not to talk about, for it's simply too painful." Aunt Louisa took a long draught of her beer "I know, you see, because I had a little girl who died. Barbara, we named her. She was six months old when she was taken from me. Even now, after all these years it affects me." She dabbed at her eyes, then took another drink.

"I am so sorry," Mary said. "I can't begin to imagine how dreadful that must have been for you. At least my mother had other healthy children."

"Ah, I don't think it works like that, my dear. I am sure your mother grieved every bit as abjectly as I did. She doesn't talk of her loss, but that doesn't mean she has forgotten. Women like your mother were raised to keep their feelings to themselves; but I am of the belief that it's better not to bottle things up, and I never wish to forget my little Barbara. I think it did your mother good to talk about Francis with someone who understands." Aunt Louisa reached across the wooden table to pat Mary's hand. "What have I said to make that pretty brow of yours furrow?"

"I was thinking about Henny."

"You mean the girl you encountered in Yorkshire you told me about? What aspect of that unfortunate young woman's life is occupying you now?"

"Her baby arrived too early to survive. Sir George said in his letter that it was a blessing, but . . ."

"A mixed blessing, is what I'd call it. If you're asking me, would she have grieved for the child, then the answer is yes, of course she would. She was a mother, her child died—it's simple enough." Aunt Louisa pursed her lips in a way that always reminded Mary disconcertingly of a recently landed haddock. "But you have to ask yourself, as you so obviously have, whether it will be easier for your Henny in the long run, not to have her lover's child foisted on her husband."

"I wish I could persuade myself that she will be happy."

"Her fate is in her own hands now."

"But it's not! She's Mrs. Michael Baxter. She married him to give her child a name, and now she doesn't even have the child."

"I think it's about time we put this subject to bed once and for all. We will need more beer first, though." Aunt Louisa topped up their glasses and sat back down. "Life goes on, Mary, and one must make the best of what it serves up to us. Your Henny is a respectably married woman with a good job. I know she made a real impression on you. I understand why she did and why you have such sympathy for her predicament, but there's no more you can do for her. It's up to her to make the best of her situation. We must count our blessings, not dwell on our misfortunes and mistakes."

"Did you tell Mama that?"

"Your mother is fortunate enough to have seven healthy children and a gaggle of grandchildren into the bargain. You understand me well enough by now, Mary, to know I would be blunt." Aunt Louisa's face creased into a smile. "In Bicton, they call me a benevolent despot, though no-one has yet dared say so to my face."

Mary chuckled. "A benevolent despot. My mother would certainly agree with that. I think the consultation did her good, to answer your earlier question. She said that the doctor eliminated a number of her more serious concerns."

"Your mother had got it into her head that she was in a terminal decline, and by carrying on the way she's been this last year, indulging her fears with no-one to contradict her, it would have become a self-fulfilling prophesy. And you, young lady, have not been helping. I am very fond of you Mary, I hope you realize that. We've only known each other a short time, but I've known of you for longer."

"Tre said that we'd like each other, when he first told me about you."

"He was right. I like you very much indeed and it saddens me to see you wasting your life. No, don't worry, I'm not about to play the benev-olent despot with you. It's your life—you have to decide how you live it. What I can do, however, is give you the benefit of my vast experience. But first, my stomach is telling me that it's time we ate."

THE LOCAL FOOD WAS PLENTIFUL and extremely filling, which ex-actly suited Aunt Louisa's taste. A thick soup made with potatoes and mushrooms was served with sour cream and quails' eggs. This was fol-lowed by a huge platter of roast and smoked pork, sausages, dumplings, bread, more potatoes, red cabbage, and sauerkraut—the local pungent pickled cabbage—which Mary tasted sparingly and which Aunt Lou-isa partook of heartily. A hard pale-yellow cheese with an orange rind was served with more bread and a side dish of boiled greens.

It was getting late by the time they had finished their meal. Replete and cold in the sleigh, they completed their return trip in silent appreci-ation of the scenery, driving through the Slavkov Forest and following the Teplá River back to Carlsbad and Aunt Louisa's hotel, where she ordered coffee to be served in her sitting room.

"I shall be eighty next birthday," she said, stirring sugar into her cof-fee. "I'm not ready to go yet, but if I were to meet my maker tomorrow, it would be with the knowledge that I've made every day count." She took a sip of coffee, grimaced, and stirred in another lump of sugar. "You never know if it might be your last."

She took another sip of her coffee. "I was twenty-five when I mar-ried Rolle, and he was forty years older than me. There was a lot of speculation at the time, as you can imagine, for Rolle was an extremely wealthy man. 'Louisa took the Rolle for want of bread.' That's one of the lines from a poem published at the time of our marriage. It wasn't entirely true, though. I married him because it suited us both very well.

It wasn't a love match as such, but it was a very good match, and we had twenty very happy years together. You're wondering what this has to do with you, I can see."

"Your stories always have a point," Mary said, putting down her own coffee-cup.

"You're a good listener. You don't rush a person, and you take your time before you speak. Trefusis is the same," Aunt Louisa said with a tender smile. "The point to my story is that at twenty-six I'd had plenty of time to think about what I wanted to do with my life, and as a single female with very little money, Rolle was my best chance of doing it. Between us, we spent a great deal of his money on good causes; and since his death, I've put a great deal more of it to good use. Not only church building, but helping those who can't help themselves. Almshouses, that sort of thing. One day, I'd like my gardens at Bicton to be open for everyone to enjoy.

"I am not telling you this to boast about my achievements, Mary, but to explain my marriage to you. Rolle and I were honest with each other from the start, and there was a—a rapport between us. By which I mean, my dear, that we were well-suited in matters of the bedchamber. Do you understand what I mean by that?"

If anyone could enlighten her, it would be Aunt Louisa. Would it be embarrassing? Undoubtedly, but better to be embarrassed than to remain clueless. "No," Mary said, meeting her eyes shyly, "but I would like to."

"Oh, you remind me so much of myself at that age. My mother told me to lie back, close my eyes, and imagine that I was asleep, which was about as much good as—ach! Well, Rolle and I were well-suited, though of course as he got older—but by then I had all my other interests. My gardens. Politics—now that has always been a big part of my life, but being a female—and that's really the point of this little story, Mary.

We must face facts, we females. There are so many things men want to prevent us from doing, so we have to go about achieving them in a more roundabout way, without their realizing that's what we are doing. Or in my case, aided and abetted by my husband. Not all men are the same, you know. Rolle was happy to let me go my own way if that's what suited us both best, to help me along the way if required. Now despite my best intentions, I really have lost the thread of what I meant to say."

Aunt Louisa eased herself to her feet and crossed the room to sit beside Mary. "Ah, I have it. Put yourself first, Mary, that's it. Stop worrying about your mother, stop worrying about Henny. You put all your energy into solving other people's problems, into trying to right the wrongs done to others, but what about you? Who is Lady Mary? I wonder if you can answer that question."

"I know what I'm not," Mary retorted. "I'm not like other women."

"Then stop behaving like them. Be yourself, for goodness sake. Be the young woman whose company I've so vastly enjoyed for the last few weeks. Ask yourself, what does this young woman want from life? Then find a way to achieve it. That's it in a nutshell."

Mary burst out laughing. "Now why didn't I think of that!"

"Because you're far too selfless."

"And what," Mary asked, more serious now, "has this got to do with Tre?"

"Tre? You mean Trefusis, I presume. Now there's a question. Perhaps it has nothing to do with my nephew at all. If you're asking me what I would like, then that's easy enough. I think you are perfect for each other. I think of him as the son I never had. I would very much like you to be my daughter-in-law, but we're not discussing what I want, we're talking about what you want."

"It's not only a question of what I want," Mary said. "Tre—he wasn't even sure himself what he wanted or that he wanted me."

"And, like you, has had a year to take stock. I don't know, before you ask, what conclusions he's come to—and even if I did I wouldn't tell you—but I do know he's not happy. He's stuck, is what I reckon, just like you are."

"I am stuck, I'm in a rut, but I'm not at all sure that marriage is the way out of it. I want to be useful, I want to make a difference to people's lives in some way. How would marriage enable that?"

"Then ask yourself how you'd achieve that without getting married." Aunt Louisa sighed. "Don't limit yourself to what you think is possible or acceptable. Aim for the stars, and then build yourself a ladder to reach them. Once you're there, you can decide whether you want my nephew to climb the ladder and join you."

"He won't want to. Despite what I said to him, he's probably convinced himself that I ran away from his—his condition."

"His curse, he used to call it in the early days. At Bicton, after he came back from the Crimea, he was—I suppose *broken* is the best way to describe it. He used to hide in the palm house when it was at its worst. He wouldn't take kindly to your offering for him out of pity."

"I wouldn't! I don't pity him. And it wouldn't be up to me to offer for him," Mary said, torn between laughter and outrage.

"Why shouldn't a woman ask for what she wants? It's what I did."

"You proposed to Lord Rolle?"

"I put a proposal to him. As I said, I know what I wanted, and by then we were both sure of—of the other side of things."

"Aunt Louisa, are you blushing? Good heavens, are you telling me that you and he were intimate before you were married?"

"We made love. It's a lot more common than you think. For heaven's sake, Mary, I was twenty-six years old. I've always had a lust for life. Food. Clothes. Passion. I knew how to look after myself; and my husband, luckily for me, knew how to help me enjoy myself. Now I can see that I really have shocked you—your cheeks are burning."

"I am shocked, but I'm also fascinated."

Aunt Louisa gave a hearty laugh. "Then there's hope for you yet. But to return to the point," she said more seriously. "Change is frightening, my dear. But if you don't embrace it, what are you left with? Nothing but a wasted life."

"I've realized that, and I'm determined to do something about it."

"I'm very pleased to hear that, but it's not a question of giving up playing the nursemaid and becoming a wife and mother—that's just another role. What else do you want?"

"Excitement. I want to wake up in the morning and wonder, what will happen today?" Mary laughed. "I want the impossible."

"You don't know it's impossible unless you try. What about Trefusis?"

"I miss him. Aside from you, he's the only person who really knows me, though I don't think he understands what you do—that I don't want what other women want."

"Have you told him that?"

Mary shook her head. "I tried to, but I didn't really understand it myself at the time."

"Don't look so dejected. Did you think I had all the answers? I'm sorry, I simply pose the questions; only you have the answers."

"What if Tre isn't part of the solution? What if he doesn't want to be?"

"Do you want him to be?"

His half-smile. The feel of his cheek. His kisses. The way he listened to her. The way he looked at her. No-one looked at her like that. No-one made her feel like that. "But what if he doesn't want me? What if I change my mind? What if—"

"What if the moon were made of cheese. At least you'll have tried," Aunt Louisa said.

"One can't try out a marriage like a new corset to see if it fits."

"No, but you can make sure that the marriage you're proposing entering into is going to give you what you want. And if it isn't, then you can make sure you can find what you do want somewhere else."

"You make it sound so straightforward."

Aunt Louisa gave a gusty laugh. "Not a whit of it, but it's exciting, isn't it? Now you have something to think about, to plan for—admit you're excited."

"Yes, yes, I am. But—"

"No more buts. Think about it. Make up your own mind, then act. I will do what I can to support you. If you wish to come and stay with me in London or Bicton, then I would be very happy to welcome you."

Mary threw her arms around her, hugging her tightly. "Thank you. I was feeling so hopeless before you came to Carlsbad."

"Then I'm very glad I came. I like you. I knew I would."

"Ah, but do you like me enough to give me a peppermint?"

Aunt Louisa chortled. "I don't like anyone that much. Now, I didn't want to tell you until we had this conversation, but I'm leaving in the morning. I have business to attend to that won't wait any longer. No tears now, this isn't goodbye—at least I hope it is not." She creaked to her feet, and picked up a green bottle from a side table, with two small glasses. "Karlsbader Becherbitter, which is supposed to be for stomach ailments. Some secret recipe of herbs and spices, is what they say. Firewater is what it is, with a fancy name."

She poured them both a full glass. "Good health," she said, throwing back the entire contents.

Mary took a sip. It burned the back of her throat and made her cough. "It's horrible."

Lady Rolle poured herself another, and tipped it down her throat. "I have discovered it gets more palatable, the more you have. Right," she said, smacking her lips and sitting back down, "I think I'm ready now. The art of pleasure. Are you all ears?"

Mary picked up her glass and swallowed the contents in one gulp. Then she nodded. "Fire away."

CHAPTER TWENTY-SEVEN

London Calling

Montagu House, Whitehall, London, June 1876

THE TOWN COACH EMBLAZONED WITH the Buccleuch coat of arms turned in to the courtyard and came to a halt at the entrance of Montagu House. A footman hurried from the porte-cochère to open the door and fold down the step, allowing Charlotte to descend. Building the house had been Walter's idea, but as with so many of the projects he started, it had fallen largely to her to manage and complete. Walter had wanted his new town house to be in the French Renaissance style, imagining a smaller version of the Palace of Versailles, and that is what Charlotte had delivered. She had never liked it. The location, in the heart of Whitehall, was unsuitable for a family residence. Though the new embankment and the associated improvements to the water supply had lessened the stench of the Thames, which wafted in through the windows on the garden frontage, at low tide in the summer the smell could still be overpowering. Despite the high-pitched roof with its turrets and tall chimney stacks, the façade was bland and far too uniform.

Inside, her aesthetic taste had been given free rein. Entering the salon, Charlotte shuddered. Her preference back in the sixties had been

for elaborate decorative friezes enriched with cartouches, gilt cornicing, and ceiling panels painted in dubious taste with highly coloured,
amorous scenes. What had possessed her to have an arcade built along
the walls of this room? It was so cluttered, too. Painted screens and lac-
quered cabinets jostled for position, family portraits crowded the walls,
and on every surface sat an urn or a vase or a bust. She passed through
the salon into the drawing room. She had either run out of ideas or
come to her senses when this room had been decorated, for the cornicing and the walls were in muted tones. The furniture was arranged in
comfortable rather than formal groupings. Family photographs in silver
frames were clustered on the mantelpiece.

Discarding her hat and gloves, she wandered restlessly into the ballroom. The three crystal chandeliers were protected with muslin. Muted
sunlight glinted in through the long windows that looked out onto the
terrace, dancing off the mirrors. The highly polished wooden floor was
covered in matting. On the dais, the grand piano was swathed in
Holland cloth. One of the doors leading out to the terrace lay open.
Mary was leaning on the low balustrade, gazing out at the bustling river.

Charlotte went outside to join her daughter, touching her arm
lightly in greeting. "I was just thinking to myself how strange you must
be finding it to be back in London after all this time."

"I was trying to recall my coming-out ball. Almost six years ago,
can you believe? It was as if the memory was of another person entirely."

"I was thinking something similar," Charlotte said ruefully. "How
could I have had such appalling taste? The salon is so dated, too."

"You've concentrated all your creative energy on the gardens at
Drumlanrig."

"And what was left was spent on more practical matters. Bunk-
houses, cottages, gas lighting. I could hire myself out as a clerk of works,
if ever I lacked occupation."

"But you don't?"

Charlotte smiled. "I certainly don't. My meeting with Sister Mary Magdalen, or Frances Taylor as I still think of her, went extremely well. I've been helping her to raise money for the Poor Servants of the Mother of God since it was founded, but I've never got my hands dirty before, as your sister Margaret would say."

"What will you be doing?"

"Frances—Sister Mary—is rather sceptical. She made every effort to put me off, painted a dreadful and very graphic picture of smells and dirt and vice that I would have considered a gross exaggeration, had I not spoken to Margaret last month." Charlotte grimaced. "I am ashamed to say, I appropriated some of your sister's experiences in Edinburgh for my own. Is it wrong to lie to a nun, do you think?"

"It would be wrong if you found yourself unable to make good on your promises."

"I am to be given a trial at one of the parochial schools, helping to teach the littlest ones two days a week."

"Oh, you will be perfect," Mary said, smiling. "You were quite right to lie."

"Do you think so? I don't mean the lie, I mean do you think I can do it? You girls had a governess, the boys all went to school. I have no experience at all of teaching. What if I can't get any of them to pay attention to me? If I fail at this first hurdle . . ."

"Mama, listen to yourself."

"You're right," Charlotte said, grimacing. "I had no idea I had become so negative in my thinking until Louisa took me to task. This is what I want to do. It's more than I hoped and a great deal more than I have a right to expect. Sister Mary thinks I'll be wasting precious time that could be devoted to raising more funds, but frankly, Mary, I could do that in my sleep. It will do me good to do something practical, not simply raise money so that other people can do something useful with it."

Mary clapped her hands. "Bravo. Are you limited to teaching them reading and writing? What about gardening?"

"Now that's a thought—a little garden in the school grounds. Or we could use boxes, if there isn't enough space. What a wonderful idea, to teach the little ones the pleasure of growing flowers."

"Or vegetables," Mary suggested. "That might be even more welcome."

"There's no reason why we can't do both." Charlotte's face fell. "Now that I'm in town, the duke will be expecting me to attend functions and parties with him. And Her Majesty, once she discovers I am in London— Oh dear, I can already feel my precious time being stolen from me."

"You made a promise to Sister Mary, Mama. You're going to have to find a way to say no to others."

"Even if they are my husband and my queen?"

"Would either of them have any qualms telling you they had more important matters to attend to?"

"You are quite right. I shall have to stand firm. I am so looking forward to teaching the little ones, as much for my own sake as theirs." Charlotte turned aside to hide the tears which smarted in her eyes and which seemed to come so easily these days. "I missed so much of my own children growing up," she said awkwardly. "Francis was taken from me, but I handed all of you over to other people to raise, to a greater or lesser degree. It is how things are done in our world." She dabbed at her eyes with her handkerchief. Beside her, Mary was very still, her eyes firmly fixed on the river, but she was listening intently. "I've been doing a great deal of thinking about this since Carlsbad," she continued. "I cannot undo my past neglect of you but I want to apologize for it. I don't ask for forgiveness, but I would like us to start on a new footing. I don't know if that is possible. We've spent more than a year in each other's company and managed to remain almost as distant as ever."

"Enduring," Mary said. "We've been enduring each other's company."

Charlotte laughed wryly. "You're right. I have been so—so embroiled in my concern for my health!"

"But you are much better now, Mama. You've lost weight and regained your bounce!"

"I have never bounced in my life! For goodness sake, call it my joie de vivre."

Mary smiled wickedly. "I'd rather like to see you bounce, but as you wish. The new diet your bowel doctor prescribed has given you back your joie de vivre."

"Mary, I wish—please, I beg of you do not refer to Dr. MacLeish as a bowel doctor. He is a specialist in matters of digestion."

Mary hesitated, then leaned over to embrace her. Charlotte closed her eyes, leaning her cheek against her daughter's for a moment, conscious of her own papery skin, her slightness compared to Mary's height. Time was running away so quickly from her. She banished the thought. Mary had already released her. She had never been one of those mothers who hugged their children. Why was that? It didn't matter, another pointless regret, but she was going to remedy it. Granny B was going to hug her grandchildren, and Duchess Charlotte, as she would be known in the classroom, was going to hug her charges, no matter how smelly, dirty, and lice ridden they might prove to be.

"I've ordered the town coach for you," she said to Mary. "You'd better hurry and change."

CHAPTER TWENTY-EIGHT

Take a Chance on Me

TRE DECIDED TO WALK TO Mayfair from his office in Adelphi Terrace on the Embankment, hoping to mull over a problem, but the day was muggy and the streets crowded. Errand boys and footmen hurried past him, bearing notes and parcels. Newspaper vendors crying out the day's headlines fought to be heard over the clamour of hawkers offering ink and paper, pens and wipes, boot laces and buttons, matches, candles, and lamp wicks. Women with their mothers and their friends and their maids strolled along, stopping to look in shop windows, to greet each other, and to gossip. Carriages containing fashionable ladies blocked the streets, pulling up to let their passengers alight, or to allow them to exchange pleasantries with the passengers in an adjacent carriage. Omnibuses fought for the right of passage with vehicles, horses, drays, and carts. Everything conspired to slow him down or get in his way. It took him forty-five minutes instead of his usual thirty to reach his aunt Louisa's house in Upper Grosvenor Street where he had been commanded to take tea.

Tre disliked being late, and consequently arrived in a foul mood, but once inside the house, the air of quiet elegance of the Georgian interior with its white cornicing, pale-yellow walls, and lack of clutter had its usual calming effect. He handed over his hat and gloves to the footman, smoothed back his hair, reminding himself again that he must visit the barber, and made his way up to the drawing room on the first floor.

Half-way up the stairs, he came to a sudden halt. That scent, he would know it anywhere. Citrus. Bergamot. Vanilla. Bouquet Opoponax it was called, made by Piesse and Lubin. He knew because he'd searched New Bond Street for it once, then felt extremely foolish afterwards. It didn't necessarily mean that Mary was here. The last he had heard from his aunt was that she was in Carlsbad with the duchess. Another lady of his aunt's acquaintance could be wearing the same scent, though he had never detected it here previously. Or Mary may have called earlier in the day. Though she might be here right now, in the drawing room.

He couldn't stand on the stairs for the rest of the day. He'd carried the memory of those Yorkshire days around in his head for far too long. If Mary was here, it would serve to dispel any lingering trace of whatever the hell he felt for her, he told himself as he climbed the rest of the stairs, ignoring the pounding of his heart.

The door to the drawing room lay ajar. He peered in. She was standing by the window with her back to him. A tall, elegant woman dressed in a sea-green silk gown with a froth of lace and ruffles drawing attention to the curvaceous lines of her body. A matching confection of lace and silk was perched on her hair, the rich brown colour showing traces of auburn and chestnut in the sunlight that filtered through the voile curtains. There was no sign of his aunt. Tre closed the door behind him, and Mary turned. Her big grey eyes widened, her generous mouth curved into an "oh" of astonishment then into a slow smile that took the breath out of him.

"Tre," she said softly. "Judging from your expression, you were no more expecting me than I was you. I sense your aunt's hand in this. I hope it's a pleasant surprise?"

He collected himself and strode towards her. "Very pleasant. I had no idea you were in London."

"We arrived—Mama and I, that is—three days ago. We met your aunt in Carlsbad in March."

"She mentioned the fact. You look different. Well. Very well, in fact. You have a glow."

Mary smiled. "All those water cures must have agreed with me."

"Very droll."

"No, it's true. Didn't your aunt Louisa tell you that we learned to appreciate some of the baths? In moderation, mind you."

Aunt Louisa! Was she teasing him? He'd forgotten that way she had of quirking her brow, that smile that was only just a smile. "My aunt said next to nothing of her trip, only that she had met you and the duchess, and took a great liking to you both."

"Not enough to give me a peppermint, however."

Tre smiled at her flippancy, relieved at this sign that she wasn't as composed as she appeared to be. "I wonder where she is?"

"My guess is that she's not going to join us. The benevolent despot has clearly decided you and I need to talk. Best get it over with," Mary added, in his aunt's plummy tones, "no point in flim-flam, life is too short."

Tre laughed, then frowned. "Best get what over with?"

Her smiled faded. "Whether you are still willing to, as you so memorably put it, 'explore the possibility of a future together.'"

It took him a moment to understand her meaning. His first instinct was to shout yes, and sweep her into his arms. In this last year, he'd had to work so damned hard to forget her, and now here she was, looking quite bewitchingly attractive, offering him a second chance. Or the possibility of a second chance. He turned away, needing time to compose himself. "I'd best go and confirm that my aunt is not joining us."

"YOU WERE RIGHT," TRE SAID, returning to the drawing room bearing a tray with the tea-pot and silver kettle. "I intercepted Aunt Louisa's butler. She has gone out and is not expected back before dinner. What made you so certain?"

Mary indicated the tea things that were already laid out. "Only two cups." She sat down, watching while Tre set about making the tea, with what was obviously practised ease. "She knew that I wished to speak privately with you. It was why I came to London."

Tre continued to concentrate on the tea, spooning it from the burr walnut caddy. In Yorkshire, that day in the water garden, it must have taken a great deal of courage to speak from the heart as he did. That hadn't occurred to her at the time. All she'd wanted to do was flee, just as he had a few moments ago. "Tre, if it's too late, then I'd rather you told me now."

"Milk or lemon? You used to prefer milk, but—"

"Tre!" Mary drew a shaky breath. "I've been thinking about this conversation, rehearsing it, for weeks now, but I appreciate it's come as a bolt from the blue."

He softened marginally. "Just as my suggestion must have seemed to you last year."

"It did, and it scared me—you were right about that. I was frightened then, and I'm still frightened. I'm terrified that I've missed my chance with you. I'm terrified that even if I haven't, I might still discover that ship has sailed. Oh dear, that sounds awful. You're not a boat and it's me that's all at sea. Sorry." Her hands were shaking. She took a sip of tea. "Before I make a complete fool of myself, will you at least tell me if I'm wasting my time, and yours?"

She waited, her heart in her mouth. Tre stared down at his cup, then set it, tea untouched, back on the tray. "Why should I hear you out? What has changed?"

Mary breathed out. "I have."

"How, precisely?" he asked, uncompromisingly.

He wasn't going to make it easy for her. Why should he? "I have decided to follow your aunt Louisa's advice to stop hiding away and to grasp my life with both hands. When we met her in Carlsbad, Mama was playing the invalid and I her nursemaid, which is precisely what you predicted would happen."

"It seemed fairly obvious to me. It's what you do when you're faced with difficult decisions: you hide away, play safe, find a different way to make yourself useful. I forced you into a corner while you were already reconsidering your ability to continue with your amateur sleuthing activities. Though Sir George was extremely grateful for what you achieved, you believed you had failed."

"You know me a great deal better than I did myself at the time," Mary said, considerably taken aback. "I'm not trying to excuse myself, I did run away and I was effectively hiding by becoming my mother's nursemaid, but in my defence I had very few other options open to me. I don't have any money of my own; I'm wholly reliant on my father for my bed and board; and if I hadn't served a purpose playing Princess Beatrice to Mama's Queen Victoria, the duke would in all likelihood have turned his mind to finding me a husband."

"And marriage," Tre said dryly, "as you've made clear to me from the outset of our acquaintance, is something you'd go to any lengths to avoid."

"I don't want a marriage like Mama's or Victoria's. I don't want to be forced into the mould my mother was cast in," Mary said, recalling the words she had spoken to the duchess more than a year ago. Her heart was thumping, now she was coming to the crux of what she wanted to say. "That doesn't mean that I am determined to remain unmarried for the rest of my life, however."

Tre's brows shot up. "That is a radical turnaround."

Mary took a sip of her tea. It had gone cold. She set the cup down, wrinkling her nose. "I've spent hours and hours rehearsing what I want to say to you, and it all seemed so clear in my head, but actually saying it is much more difficult."

"Take your time. I'm all ears."

He wasn't running away. Not yet. He was still listening. *Spit it out*, she could hear Aunt Louisa commanding her. "I missed you terribly," Mary said, heart racing. "I can't imagine ever feeling for any other man what I feel for you. I can't imagine any other man understanding me as you do. I would like to find a way to share my life with you, if that's possible, but I don't want you to be all I have in my life. There, that's what I came to London to say to you."

"Good God! Is that a proposal?"

"I suppose it is, though not the kind you mean. I am proposing that we decide once and for all whether or not we are suited."

"Isn't that what I proposed, back in Yorkshire? As I recall, one of your objections was the possibility of your father interfering and removing any element of choice."

"It's still a risk, but one that I will deal with if necessary, though I hope it won't be, if we are discreet. I don't want to be courted, to go to parties and dances and make polite conversation. I would like us to talk properly, to discuss what kind of marriage we would like."

"What *kind* of marriage! Are there different types?"

"I think so." She wanted to flee. She wanted the ground to open up and swallow her. But she didn't want to have to go through this again. "After more than forty years of marriage, my mother is only just beginning to ask herself the same questions I've been posing to myself. She has dedicated her life to my father's wishes, taking over the projects he has no time to finish, deputizing for him, raising his children for him. She has done her duty, has been the perfect wife, and has been taken entirely for granted by the duke and all her children, myself included. I don't want that, Tre."

"Then what do you want?"

"A marriage more akin to what your aunt had, and what my sister Margaret now has." Mary frowned. "I don't mean exactly the same, but in the sense of a—a sort of tailored arrangement with their husbands. I want us to decide what will suit us both. I want us to share our lives, not inhabit separate spheres. I want a marriage where I feel I have an equal say, that I'm truly one half of a whole, and not just a small portion."

"None of that sounds particularly radical," Tre said, looking baffled.

"But it is! I obviously haven't made my point properly. Tell me, what do you want from marriage?"

"The obvious things. A wife I love and respect. A family in the future, if I'm fortunate."

"Yes, but what does that mean, Tre? You assume that your wife would simply become part of your life, that nothing much for you would change, while I would be—I would be subsumed by your life, I'd be the one who had to bend myself into a different shape. I wouldn't be Mary anymore, I'd be Colonel Trefusis's wife. Do you see?"

"You don't think that being a wife, in the future possibly a mother, is enough?"

Abjectly, Mary shook her head. "I know that's a shocking thing to say, but it's true."

To her surprise, Tre reached for her hand. "Why should it be any more shocking for a woman to say that than a man? Unless one is marrying the queen, we don't ask husbands to make pleasing their wives their entire reason for existing. You want to be useful, to make a differ-ence, don't you?"

Mary heaved a sigh of relief, nodding.

"In this at least, you are entirely consistent," Tre said, smiling gen-tly. "I understand that; I always have done, for I'm the same myself. How do you propose to do that?"

"That is something I'm still working out," Mary said, grimacing. "I know what I'm good at and what I enjoy doing. I know that the peo-ple I'd most like to help are women like Henny, who have even fewer choices in life than I do. That's what I'd really like to do, Tre, to give them choices, opportunities."

"Charity work, do you mean?"

"I am not the Lady Bountiful type, and I'm like you in that I prefer not to be in the limelight. There are charities such as the one my mother is involved in where there may be opportunities—but as I said, my ideas need to be thought through."

Tre got up again to look out of the window, his hands dug deep into his pockets. "I don't know what to say to you."

"I'm not expecting an answer from you right now."

"You've been very honest with me. It can't have been easy."

"No, but I knew that the suggestion would have to come from me. I have felt so dreadful about leaving you like that in Yorkshire. I want you to know that my going was nothing whatsoever to do with your condition. You do believe me, don't you?"

"It hasn't gone away, Mary. I have it back under control, but it hasn't gone completely."

"I don't care."

"But I do. I don't want to be a source of pity."

"Nor do I, which is why you have to promise me that if we discover that our ideas don't tally, that they never will, then you will say so. If you are not certain, absolutely certain that you wish to marry me, then you must not feel obliged, even if we are the cause of speculation. I know you, you're so honourable and loyal, so it's important that you promise."

"Pot and kettle, Mary?"

"Yes, but I will find the courage to speak my mind if I have to. I won't consign both of us to an unhappy marriage because I was too cowardly to say no."

"Very well then, I promise. What else?"

"There's nothing else for now. Once you've thought about it . . ."

"I've thought." Tre held out his hand and when she took it, pulled her out of her seat. "Here is to a fresh start. I really have missed you."

"Am I asking too much of you?"

"You're asking even more of yourself," Tre said, sliding his arms around her.

She wrapped her arms around his neck. It was only the first step, but it felt like the right one. "We'll have each other to rely on," she said, and kissed him.

CHAPTER TWENTY-NINE

Cliveden

Cliveden, Buckinghamshire, Two Weeks Later

C LIVEDEN HAD ORIGINALLY BEEN BUILT as a hunting lodge by the
Duke of Buckingham, eminent rake, wit, and politician in the
court of Charles II. The house had twice been burned down and re-
built. The current reincarnation was designed by Charles Barry for the
Duke and Duchess of Sutherland, a startlingly beautiful Italianate villa
with three stories, flanked by two single-storey pavilion wings with
curved colonnades to the front. The rear of the house was perched on
a long terrace with magnificent views down the parterres, which reminded Mary of Drumlanrig, and beyond to the sweep of the River
Thames in the valley below.

The Duke and Duchess of Buccleuch had been regular visitors to
Cliveden along with Queen Victoria in the Sutherlands' time, but Mary
had never been to Cliveden. The current owner, the Duke of Westminster, was married to the Duchess of Sutherland's daughter. Whilst
Mary's father very much admired his fellow duke's wide-ranging philanthropic endeavours, he could not admire his politics, for Westminster was a Whig.

It was Constance, Duchess of Westminster, who had invited Mary for the weekend, though it was Tre's idea to engineer the invitation: "In the spirit of being creative about how we find ways to legitimately spend time together." As a result, Mary had come to Cliveden armed with a plea for funding to expand the garden at the school where her mother had begun teaching. The Duchess of Westminster had been enthusiastic at first, but when she learned that the Poor Servants of the Mother of God school was a Catholic one, her eagerness waned. She would consider it at length, she had said, meaning that she would take her time to inform Mary that she didn't wish to be involved. Since Mama had already secured funding from Aunt Louisa, it hardly mattered.

Mary and her maid, Clara, arrived in the early afternoon in her mother's coach. The duchess had decided, much to Mary's relief, that since she was almost twenty-five, she no longer needed a chaperone. She had been given a room on the ground floor of the west wing which opened out onto the garden. Tre was not due to arrive until later, so she decided to explore the grounds.

It was a beautiful summer's day, and the Cliveden gardens were alive with colour. Bees hummed contentedly; doves cooed in the dovecot; and across the other side of the garden, the clock in the tower chimed the hour. Mary made her way round the house to the long terrace, then descended one of the stone staircases to the parterres with their triangular beds laid out in blocks of white and purple blooms. Her mother would immediately have set about calculating how many plants it took to fill each, though these days, the duchess was more concerned with how many radishes or carrots or cabbages could be grown in the considerably smaller beds which had become the school garden. Mama was now working at the school three days a week, and proving a resounding success with the other teachers and the children. Mary, in search of inspiration, had accompanied her twice, but all she had discovered was what she already suspected: little children simply didn't interest her. She didn't find their antics amusing, she did not enjoy the constant mopping and drying and wiping that they seemed to require, nor their endless repetitive questions. She was not destined to be a teacher.

The school was popular; the children who attended it were poor and often dirty, but they came from decent households, respectable, hard-working families, with a full complement of churchgoing parents. The one aspect of it that had caught Mary's attention was the children who were not permitted to attend. Not those excluded on the grounds of religion but because of their lack of respectability. Children born out of wedlock, whose mothers were known to frequent gin palaces or whose occupation was deemed to be improper. What happened to those children of actresses, singers, flower sellers, thieves, and streetwalkers? And the children with no parents who could be seen, if one chose to look, lurking in doorways, digging in the mud of the river at low tide, scavenging in the docks along the Embankment? Where did they come from? What became of them? Where did they sleep?

She had asked one of the Sisters at her mother's charity and was told the children came from workhouses and orphanages and factories. They lived on the streets and slept there, too, or in cheap lodging-houses if they had managed to scrounge the means to pay for a bed. They lived with criminals and inevitably they became criminals. Corruption bred corruption was the belief. There were too many other, deserving cases to worry about the undeserving. They would need to fend for themselves.

Mary reached the end of the parterres where a strange domed folly had been erected. The paths shelved steeply down to the river from here. The view was spectacular, with the keep of Windsor Castle just visible in the distance. The river flowed peacefully in soft curves; the banks were thick with greenery.

"Well, well, fancy meeting you here."

She whirled around. "Tre! I wasn't expecting you until later."

"I caught an earlier train."

"How did you know where to find me?"

"By the process of expert deduction. It's a beautiful day. These par-terres look very much like the gardens at Drumlanrig. Oh, and one of the gardeners told me he saw you heading this way. How many hours of our acquaintance do you think we've spent in gardens?"

"Goodness, I don't know. The majority of them. Do you want to go back to the house?"

Tre shook his head. Checking over his shoulder, he caught her in his arms and edged them around the side of the little grotto out of sight. "We have gone to a great deal of trouble to engineer our presence here together. What I want to do is kiss you."

"That is what is known as serendipity," Mary said, lifting her face to his. "Because I want to kiss you, too."

It was an unsatisfactory kiss. The domed building hid them from the house, but they could easily be seen from the river. "Cliveden has a history of intrigue and scandal," Tre said, reluctantly letting Mary go, "but I don't wish us to add to it."

They took the path down to the river, where the view was delightful enough to distract Mary, or for her to pretend to be distracted. The ferry was tied up on the opposite bank, awaiting the arrival of more visitors to the house. They passed the ferryman's cottage and contin-ued past another in the Tudor style with half-timbered gables, which looked to be empty. Farther on, another larger cottage was undergoing renovation works of some sort.

"I thought this was Spring Cottage but it can't be," Tre said.

270 SARAH FERGUSON, DUCHESS OF YORK

"That's where Queen Victoria liked to take tea when she visited. I remember my mother mentioning it." Mary pushed the door. "Shall we take a look?"

The leaded windows were covered in fine white dust from the newly plastered walls. There was a faint smell of whitewash and timber shavings. "We shouldn't be in here," Tre said.

"It's empty."

"Which is why we shouldn't be here."

"In the last two weeks," Mary said, "we've gone for several walks, and taken tea with your aunt twice, and though she wasn't there one of the times—it's almost as if you don't want to be alone with me."

"The problem is I want to be alone with you almost too much."

"But you think it's wrong?"

"I don't know what I think, is the honest truth."

"Did you and Sibilla make love?"

"That was different, we were betrothed. I don't want to talk about Sibilla. We're talking about you and me."

Mary ran her finger through the layer of dust on the mantelpiece. "If you feel it's wrong, I don't want you to kiss me."

"It doesn't feel wrong. That's part of the problem." He pulled her back into his arms, kissing her deeply. She kissed him back, running her fingers through his hair, knocking his hat to the floor. Her skin was hot from the sun. They staggered backwards, still kissing, until he encountered a wall. She murmured his name. He smoothed his hand over her waist, upwards to the curve of her breast, frustrated by her layers of clothing, aroused all the same by the way she shuddered in response. He shifted, wanting to hide the effect she was having on him as she slid her hands under his coat. He cupped the swell of her breast. Too many clothes.

Tre swore, dragging his mouth away. "That," he said raggedly, "is why we should not be here. I will not risk losing control and foisting a child on you when you haven't even decided whether you want to be a wife, let alone a mother."

"There are ways to avoid such an eventuality, Tre. Aunt Louisa told me—"

"You have discussed this with my aunt!"

"Not this. Not us. Only in theory. She was very helpful! She says that a great many men and women would be much happier in matters of the bedroom if they had been well briefed before they entered it!"

"Good God! I don't know what she told you and I'm not sure I want to, but whatever she has said, let me assure you, there is no such thing as risk-free lovemaking. I wish there were, as I mentioned in Yorkshire. It would have prevented a great deal of heartache and trouble in the army. We are playing with fire and I don't want you to get burned."

"You're right." Looking quite crushed, Mary set about straightening her dress. "To place ourselves in a position where the decision was made for us would be unbearable."

"A little self-control shouldn't be too much for you to expect of me." Tre grimaced inwardly. It felt like far too much to ask of himself right now. He picked up his hat. "I don't suppose there's any point in my suggesting we take a more conventional approach to courting?"

"I don't want to be courted."

Despite himself, he laughed. "No, you want to be useful. Oh, don't look like that, I'm teasing you."

"If I wasn't so completely out of practice, I might join a circus as a tightrope walker after all."

"Night after night, walking across the same piece of rope. Think how tedious that would become. Besides, you'd be obliged to perform in front of an audience, a different one every night. That wouldn't suit you at all."

She sighed. "You know me so well. Perhaps you can find me an occupation that combines all my odd talents."

Tre checked his watch. "I'll think about it. Right now, we'd better get back. They'll be serving tea, and there's a fellow guest I think you'll be keen to meet."

MARY WOKE WITH A START. Daylight streamed in through a narrow gap in the curtains. The clock on the table by the bed informed her it was after nine. She never slept this late. Her head was groggy. Dinner had been a very long and elaborate affair and she had been so delighted to be seated next to Captain Beckman that she had drunk far more wine than usual. Pulling on her wrap, she rang the bell for Clara. Captain Beckman had been extremely elusive when she tried to find out what he had been doing since they last met at Drumlanrig. This and that. Army matters, nothing that would interest you. Yes, he'd been abroad, here and there. He believed she had been to Carlsbad and had met the infamous Lady Rolle? He had heard that Mary's sister Margaret had returned from New York and was now married. Captain Beckman knew a great deal about Mary, and she still knew next to nothing about him. Why was he here?

She must ask Tre. Mary groaned, clutching her head. She had thought herself so sophisticated and worldly, when in reality she had been a naive fool. It was one thing to relish the illicit thrill of being in his arms, to lose herself in kissing him until she thought she might melt, but to go so far as to make love, if there was even the slightest chance of her conceiving a child! She shuddered, feeling quite sick. The shame and the scandal would be beyond anything that Margaret had caused, but worse still was the horror of the other consequences. What would happen to the baby? What would happen to her? Tre would feel obliged to offer marriage. She'd feel obliged to accept, because if she did not, her child wouldn't have a name, and though she was extremely ambivalent about other people's children, her own child—and Tre's—would be an entirely different proposition.

"My lady!" Clara burst through the door bearing a tea tray. "My lady, you'll never believe what has happened."

"The queen has unexpectedly arrived for breakfast dressed as a sailor?" Mary poured herself a cup, adding a splash of milk, and took a much-needed sip.

"There's been a burglary."

Mary coughed. "A what?"

"There's a secret safe in the Duchess of Westminster's private sitting room. Well, it was supposed to be a secret, but it's not now. Someone broke in, in the middle of the night. Everything in it is gone."

CHAPTER THIRTY

Two Are Better Than One

WHEN MARY ARRIVED IN THE breakfast room, the talk, in hushed tones, was all of the robbery. The safe which had been broken into was hidden behind the painting of the Duchess of Sutherland, their hostess's mother, that hung over the mantelpiece in her sitting room. Mary listened, saying little and drinking several cups of coffee very slowly, but neither Tre nor Captain Beckman had appeared by the time the last of the other guests left the breakfast table.

She assumed the party would break up early now. At a loss, Mary wandered into the drawing room, but it was empty. She ought to speak to the Duchess of Westminster, but the poor woman was presumably still closeted with the police. The drawing room opened onto the terrace. It was a beautiful soft summer morning. Mary leaned on the balustrade, trying to decide what to do. Where on earth was Tre? There was no sign of Captain Beckman either. Presumably they were together somewhere in the house, discussing intelligence business.

"Mary, there you are."

"At last! Where have you been? Goodness, Tre, you look dreadful. Is your head—"

"My head is perfectly well. What about yours?"

"I don't know how I came to drink so much wine. Captain Beckman—where is he?"

"Gone. I thought it best to get him back to London. You should go, too."

"I've already told Clara to pack. What's wrong?" A horrible suspicion took hold of her. "You're fretting about our conversation yesterday, aren't you?"

"What?"

"What you said yesterday in that little cottage. I've been thinking about it. You're right. We cannot risk any—any consequences. However, the very fact that I want so desperately to make love to you must give you some indication about the depth of my feelings."

"It does and I'm greatly reassured by that," Tre said, smoothing his brow with his fingers, "but I have more pressing matters on my mind right at the moment."

"The theft? Was much taken?"

"Fortunately, the most valuable of the duchess's jewellery is kept at the bank, but the thieves got a few expensive pieces."

"Is that all?"

"About five hundred pounds in notes, and a few items that some of the guests had left for safekeeping." Tre leaned on the parapet, gazing out at the parterres. "It's damnable."

He rarely swore aloud. He had nicked himself shaving, a tiny scratch in the cleft of his chin. His necktie was askew, too. For Tre, he was positively dishevelled. "You're reacting as if the valuables are yours. It is a dreadful state of affairs, but the Westminsters are one of the wealthiest families in the land. Five hundred pounds is a huge amount of money to some, but to them—"

"I don't give a fig about the money."

"Do the police think there's a chance they can recover the jewellery?"

Tre shrugged impatiently. "There's always a chance, but it's most likely already in the hands of a fence in London. The stones will be gouged out, the gold melted down. That's not my concern."

"Then what is your concern? Don't try and fob me off. Was something of yours stolen?"

"Not as such. You should tell your maid to pack."

"I already have, and I've already told you that I have. What is going on, Tre? Don't tell me it's nothing."

"I wish it were."

"Then tell me. I'd like to help. I would love to help in fact, and you know you can trust me implicitly."

"This is my problem, I can't embroil you."

"I see." Despite the sun, Mary shivered. "So this is how it would be, if we were married, is it? You wouldn't be able to involve me in the thing that takes up the majority of your time. The best part of your life, according to Aunt Louisa."

"I don't have time for anything else," Tre snapped. "I've told her that."

"Then how on earth did you ever imagine you'd find time for a wife? Oh no, silly me, you won't have time. She'd have to take what little you can spare when you come home in the evening. A walk in the park on a Sunday if she's lucky."

"Mary, for God's sake!"

"Tre, for God's sake!" She glared at him, furious. "This is why we've not made any progress at all. A few teas together, a few walks. You only brought me here to Cliveden because you had business with Captain

Beckman. I am not going to be the kind of wife that sits around waiting for her husband to share some of his precious time, and I'm not going to be the kind of wife who has no part of her husband's life either! I thought you knew me better than that. I thought I'd made it clear, that you agreed with me, that what we both wanted was to share our lives, yet when the first opportunity presents itself, you shut me out. Well thank goodness we've discovered our mistake before it's too late."

"Mary!" Tre hissed, looking anxiously around. "This is not the time."

"Exactly my point! I'm trying to help you, the way you helped me in Yorkshire and Drumlanrig. Two heads and all that! Talk things through, that was another thing I recall you recommending. I suppose it's all very well when it's trivial domestic matters, but when it comes to matters of state . . ."

"For the love of God, shut up! Look, I'm sorry, I shouldn't have spoken to you like that, but—"

"But this really is a matter of state?"

"Yes."

Leave it. Tre's message was clear, but Mary was torn. She could walk away right now and let him get on with his business, but she would be walking away forever. In her anger, she had uncovered some home truths that couldn't be buried. Did he understand that? The urge to try to explain it to him once more was strong, but she forced herself to remain silent, watching his profile while he stared out at the gardens again. He was an extremely intelligent man—he could work it out for himself. Unless he was choosing not to hear? She couldn't bear to fail. If Tre couldn't understand her, there was no chance any other man would. Oh God, she didn't want to lose him; but it would be a slow, painful death to change her terms in order to keep him.

At last, he turned to face her again. "Come on, we can't talk here."

TRE LED THE WAY. PASSING along the driveway at the front of the house, where an imposing statue of the Duke of Sutherland surveyed the estate which had once been his, they continued down Queen Anne's Walk and headed for the Blenheim Pavilion. It had been built by the then owner of Cliveden, the Earl of Orkney, to commemorate the Battle of Blenheim, in which he had been second in command to the Duke of Marlborough. How many of the men who had died in the battle had been given a decent grave, let alone a pavilion? Tre wondered. What the original purpose had been, he had no idea. There was no door, and most likely these days it simply provided shelter from the rain. And from prying eyes, which was why he had chosen it. The thick walls precluded anyone from overhearing what he was about to say. Provided they did not stand in the doorway, no-one would see them either.

Mary did not even pretend an interest in the building. Her hands were curled into fists. She was furious with him. Did he deserve it? No question but he did, though she hadn't been so clear in her wishes until this morning. She was very clear now. It broke every rule to confide even the smallest detail of his department's function. There were no half measures, no shades of grey, the rules were black and white. Did any of the other men confide in their wives or their lovers or their friends? If they did, they chose their confidantes well. Tre had never had a confidante. He had thrived—well, not exactly thrived, but he'd survived—in isolation.

He had already made his choice. He had already decided he wanted things to change. He wanted Mary. If those were her terms! He caught her eye and smiled wryly. "Two is better than one," he said. "A problem shared is a problem halved. It's not that I wanted to exclude you."

"Strictly speaking, you're not allowed to discuss this with me, though, are you?"

"Rules are made to be bent, on occasion. And this is one such."

"Yes, but only if you want to, not because I've forced your hand."

"I want to." He took her hand, unfurling the fist and kissing her fingertips before letting her go. "I just didn't know it." Tre took a deep breath. "So, let me tell you what I know."

Mary was right: talking to her, recounting and summarizing forced him to arrange his thoughts into a more logical sequence. Start at the beginning, he thought, with the papers.

"You remember what I told you about the importance of Russian intelligence? We have an excellent man there, Frederick Wellesley. Like me, he is a lieutenant colonel in the army, though he is in the Coldstream Guards. Her Majesty had him appointed as military attaché to Moscow and Saint Petersburg, through the offices of her cousin. That was back in seventy-two, when you and I met at Drumlanrig. When he returned to England in seventy-three to get married, I signed him up for the Intelligence Branch. He's a bit of a scoundrel frankly, with dubious morals. He has a particular penchant for actresses."

Tre smiled. "His methods are even more dubious. He borrows documents for just long enough to copy them or photograph them. He reads people's letters. He plies them with drink to elicit information. I don't know for certain if he's stooped to blackmail, but I wouldn't be surprised. However, thanks to Wellesley, we've had some invaluable intelligence from what is pretty much an empire that operates behind closed doors."

"Not a very gentlemanly gentleman then?" Mary asked, clearly fascinated.

"No, he's very unpopular with some of the establishment. Too much of a maverick. They'd be happy for an excuse to get rid of him."

"But he's one of your men, so you'll watch his back. Have I that correct?"

"It's not strictly part of my remit."

"That's not what I asked. If I were you, I'd see that as a large un-written part of my job."

"You're right. Which is why I've sent Beckman to Paris."

"Not London?"

"Beckman was our mode of transport, so to speak, for Wellesley's latest bulletin. What I can tell you is that the papers in Beckman's pos-session contain some politically explosive information. So much so that they were to be delivered in person by me to the person at the very top."

"Your commanding officer?" Mary's eyes widened when he said nothing. "You mean Her—Mrs. Brown?" she whispered.

Tre couldn't help looking over his shoulder as he spoke, though he knew it was a ridiculous thing to do. "She is the unofficial recipient of much of our intelligence."

"Oh my! Oh my goodness. And Beckman had put them in the safe? Oh, Tre!"

"The poor chap was devastated, and blames himself. That's why I packed him off to Paris, not London as I told you. I can't risk him doing something rash to try to recover the situation. This happened on my watch—it's up to me to resolve it. The Duke of Westminster assured me that only he and his wife knew the safe's location and that he never disclosed it to his guests."

"Oh, come, surely he can't have been so naive. How many servants are there at Cliveden?"

"There's around thirty permanent staff. More when the Westmin-sters are in residence obviously, and they are in the habit of employing agency staff when they have a full house."

"Tre, you know as well as I do that servants know everything that goes on in a house."

"It was one of the first things I asked—not Westminster, but his butler. It was an open secret apparently. What was much less known, though, was the mechanism for moving the painting to reveal the safe. The butler denied all knowledge, and I believe him, but one member of staff did know. The police reckon she made it her business to know. A parlourmaid who was taken on three months ago, and has now mysteriously disappeared."

"A parlourmaid picked the lock on a safe? Isn't that a specialist job?"

"Very. This was a very complex safe, too. Westminster called Scotland Yard. They say this case has all the hallmarks of a criminal gang they've been investigating for some time. They send in a woman or a girl to work in a house, using false papers and references. They give her plenty of time to settle in and do her digging, find out where the valuables are located. On the chosen night, she makes sure the relevant doors and windows are left open, acts as lookout, the safe-cracker gets in, and she flees with him—except I gather that in this gang, the safe-cracker is also a her."

"A female gang? How fascinating."

"With a formidable female called Queenie Divers in charge. Scotland Yard know them as the Brazen Hussies. Ruthless, is how they described them."

"They'd have to be, wouldn't you think, even more so than if they were men? And clever, too. It's not easy to pass yourself off as a servant if you haven't done the job. I wonder if they recruit women who used to be servants? That would make sense. Women who are sick of being in service—maybe they want to marry. Or maybe, Tre, they have been sacked."

"For thieving, you mean?"

"Or for being too pretty. Or too accommodating. Or not accommodating enough. Those women still have to make a living somehow. Some of them will have children to look after."

"Are you defending them? We're talking about a cut-throat gang of hardened criminals."

"Female criminals, who might have no option— Sorry, sorry, sorry. I'm straying far from the point."

"It wouldn't be you otherwise. I've not forgotten Henny."

"No, and you know I haven't, either. So Scotland Yard think that the Brazen Hussies have stolen your papers unintentionally? It was just a horrible coincidence that the burglary occurred when the papers were in the safe?"

Tre paced over to the opposite alcove, propping his shoulders against the wall so that he could see through the window. "That's what I'm assuming, but just in case it was the work of Russian spies, I'll need to find an excuse to get Wellesley out of Saint Petersburg as a matter of urgency, as a precaution, for a few weeks at least. His life will be in danger if these documents are traced back to him. Obviously I couldn't tell Scotland Yard what the papers were; they think they are routine army orders. I've made it clear I don't want them to expend any effort looking for them. We don't want to alert anyone to the fact that they might be valuable."

"Would it be obvious to one of the Hussies that they are valuable?"

Tre smiled—he couldn't help it—at Mary's adoption of the gang. "It's unlikely, but possible. Some of the papers bear the Golden Eagle, the tsar's seal and crest. The woman who runs the gang must be sharp-witted, but whether she can read or write, whether she'll even recognize the Cyrillic script some of it is written in, I don't know."

"But it's a risk you can't take, can you? If this woman does understand that what she has in her possession is worth its weight in gold, she could— Actually I've no idea—what could she do?"

"It really depends on whether or not she understands what she's got and what stakes she's willing to play for. Is it possible that she'd try somehow to sell them back to us? Who would she contact? It's more likely that she'd work out the papers are Russian, and contact their man in London; and if the Russians get their hands on those papers, it would be obvious they'd originated from Wellesley. Our entire operation in Saint Petersburg and Moscow would be compromised, and Wellesley's position would be untenable. It would almost be preferable, if indeed the Brazen Hussies do have the papers, to discover that they had no idea of the value and had destroyed them."

Tre hesitated, but if he was going to trust Mary—and more important if she was going to trust him—he had to be as honest with her as possible. "There's another reason I sent Beckman to Paris. He smokes opium, if you recall? I've never viewed it as a risk. He assures me he has it strictly under control; but there are always those keen to stir up trouble. Our work, our methods, they don't sit well with some, as you know; and though Beckman is a good, sound officer, those same people never forget that he's come up through the ranks."

"You mean they would be happy to see him fail?"

"I won't give them the ammunition."

"And he's your man, too, like Wellesley. You've worked so hard to set up the Intelligence Branch, and to make it a success. *And* you are the person who briefs Mrs. Brown, too. You are an extremely valuable asset, but there will be some who grudge your success, who may even want you to fail, given your history." Mary crossed over to join him. "I know you don't like to mention your condition, but there are some who won't forget, will they? They were happy to see you buried away out of sight with their map-makers, but now that you're important enough to be hobnobbing with Mrs. Brown they will see your condition as a risk."

Much moved, Tre wrapped his arms around her. This was what he wanted; this was what only Mary could give him. She understood him, and she didn't ignore his flaws and weaknesses. He released her, feeling considerably more positive than he had an hour ago.

"So"—she smiled up at him—"what are we going to do about all of this?"

"We?"

"I want to help. It's not only Captain Beckman and the scoundrel spy Wellesley who are in danger of being discredited, it's you, if you don't recover the papers."

"You have helped, just by listening."

"I want to do something tangible. Tell me your plans."

"I have to find out who carried out this robbery. Scotland Yard didn't fill me with confidence. They've tried in the past to infiltrate the Brazen Hussies, but they've never managed it."

"Infiltrate?"

Mary's eyes lit up and Tre's heart sank. "At a very low level. Find someone who can befriend one of the foot soldiers, keep their ear to the ground, do a bit of digging, that's all."

"I could do that," Mary said, as he had already guessed she would.

"No."

"Do you have anyone else in mind?"

"You know perfectly well we don't recruit women."

"Let me see. What would be the qualities you would require if you did recruit someone for this job? She'd have to be an excellent actress and mimic. She'd have to be observant. Someone who can extract information without arousing suspicion. What else? Someone who can make herself invisible, that's always useful. And someone with a creative mind, who doesn't think the way other people do."

"Stop it, Mary. There is absolutely no way—"

"You don't have anyone else, Tre. And you must admit I'm perfect for the role. Please."

"You'd have to pose undercover as this person for a week, perhaps longer. You can't simply disappear. Your mother . . ."

"I'll think of something."

"Mary, it's far too risky."

"In what way? If all I'm to do is befriend some underling, then there's no chance I'll come into contact with any of the dangerous members of the gang. They won't even know I exist. If she finds out I'm not who I pretend to be, then I'll simply stop being that person. What have you got to lose?"

"No! If anything happened to you, I'd never forgive myself."

"Please, won't you at least consider it? Your career, two of your men, and the safety of our nation depends on this, yet you won't consider letting me dress up as a—a mistreated servant down on her luck, for example, for a few days. If the shoe were on the other foot, you'd want to help me, wouldn't you?"

He stopped himself just in time from pointing out that was a very different situation. It wasn't, not in Mary's eyes. He couldn't bear to lose her again. She was too precious to him. He was even beginning to understand what it was she wanted from him, from both of them, and to want it, too. Was this a step in the right direction? He had been raised to believe that women needed protecting. If he rejected her offer, might she view it as him being overprotective? Might he lose her if he didn't let her help?

"Let me think about it," he said.

"That's what people say when they are preparing to say no."

"Then let's take this one step at a time. Show me this mistreated servant. I don't mean simply put on a costume. Let me see her, speak to her, let her tell me her tragic history. Then, if I'm convinced, we'll take it from there."

Mary nodded, biting her lip. "You're right, it's not simply a question of putting on a grubby dress and dirtying my face."

"Exactly," Tre said. "You'll need to immerse yourself in the role."

"How will I do that?"

Tre grinned. "I reckon I have just the man to help you. But we can't divulge the real reason to him. The fewer people to know anything about this the better."

CHAPTER THIRTY-ONE

Acting Up

London, One Week Later

Lewis Strange Wingfield was the youngest son of Lady Londonderry. He was slightly built and only in his mid-thirties, but his hair had receded to reveal a high, smooth forehead, for which he compensated by growing what hair nature had left him long, waving down over his ears. His jaw-line was as smooth as his pate; his features were delicate, with the exception of his nose, which was on the large side and made his mouth look too small. He had an infectious smile, a sharp tongue, and a wicked sense of humour, and he had been delighted to assist Mary.

"I was at a loose end, having just published my novel, *Slippery Ground*—have you read it yet? No, I shall get you a copy and inscribe it to you. You'll love it. Now, tell me who it is you wish to become?"

Become, not *portray*, she noted, deciding that this augured well. Lewis had been an actor and an artist, a writer and a critic, and had more recently worked as a surgeon and war correspondent for the *Times* in Paris during the Franco-Prussian War, which was when he had first come to the attention of the nascent Intelligence Branch. What Tre had described to Mary as Lewis's chameleon qualities had proved extremely useful on several occasions when an insider was required to gather specific information; though his butterfly tendencies, which meant he very quickly grew bored once he had mastered whatever it was that currently occupied him, made him unsuited to a more permanent role as one of Tre's men. He was, however, utterly trustworthy and a merciless critic, both of which qualities made him a perfect mentor, in Tre's opinion, for Mary.

She had heard of Lewis originally from Margaret, who had been befriended by him nine years ago in Ireland, when she was living at Powerscourt, the home of Lewis's elder brother Mervyn, 7th Viscount Powerscourt. She learned of some of his more colourful exploits from the man himself as she rehearsed her new role in the parlour of his London home. Lewis couldn't resist acting, even when offstage. He had posed as an attendant in an asylum and a guard in a prison. "Workhouses and lodging-houses, I've slept in them all," he had informed Mary, when she confided the role she was to play. "I have countless friends in low places. You could not have chosen a better teacher."

She had been inclined to think he exaggerated his prowess, but he very quickly proved her wrong. He had an eye for detail that covered every aspect of her new persona, from the way she dressed her hair to the way she walked, the words she used, her accent, and her clothes. Lewis's own most successful creation was Ned Smith, "the cabman's friend," he said, winking at her. "Ned was such a good-natured chap, always ready with help and advice. I was so well liked, my dear Mary, that I could have commanded a free ride from any one of hundreds of cabmen. Needless to say, I overpaid and overtipped. Now, let me see you walk again. I'm looking for a saucy sashay and not a waddle."

Unfortunately Lewis had no photographs of Ned, nor of any of his other offstage characters, but Mary was permitted to look through his stage albums, showing him in parts as diverse as a simpering Georgian buck, Mr. Primrose, in *Popping the Question*; a scheming Rizzio in *Mary, Queen of Scots*; and a down on his luck John Grumley in *Domestic Economy*.

"And though I say it myself," Lewis commented, studying a photograph from the Haymarket production of *Othello*, "my Roderigo stole the show from Ira Aldridge and Walter Montgomery, who played Othello and Iago. I had a great deal more grit. Read the poem again if you please, Mary. And this time, add a little snarl."

It took a week of intensive coaching before he pronounced her ready, despite a grudging acknowledgement on the first day that she had "a half-decent ear, thankfully."

He was determinedly uninterested in why Lady Mary Montagu Douglas Scott wished to become Mary Hughes. When she told him, the first day they met, that it was for a wager, he had raised his finely drawn brows and blown a raspberry through his pursed mouth. "The art of dissembling," he said, "is to convince yourself that what you are saying is true. You should simply have told me to mind my own business, which I am very happy to do. I make a point of asking as few questions as possible when it comes to the occasional commissions Colonel Trefusis throws my way. I have no interest in the whys and the wherefores, only in testing myself and having a little fun at the same time. I must say, though, I was most intrigued when he mentioned your name. How is dear Margaret—is she enjoying married life?"

"She is very happy, expecting her first child toward the end of the year."

Lewis shuddered. "I am not at all convinced that children are necessary to one's happiness. In fact, I suspect that the reverse is much more likely."

"But you are married, are you not?" Mary asked curiously, for he was what Lady Rolle would euphemistically have referred to as a "sensitive chap."

"Cecilia and I have been married for eight years, most of which we have spent apart, which is why I can say, hand on heart, that we are very happy."

"If you didn't wish to spend time with each other, and you have no desire for children, why on earth did you marry?"

"So forthright!" Lewis clapped his hands together. "Now, I can see that you and Margaret are indeed sisters. To return to your question, it suited us, for different reasons. I will not go into the detail, for frankly it is no-one's business but my own and Cecilia's, but it allows me to be the man I am and my wife to be the woman she is. Now, that is quite enough about me. A sentence I rarely utter, by the way. Your so-called wager is set for tonight. This friend who will witness our performance—am I permitted to know their identity?"

"I think you'll find he's a familiar face," Mary teased.

"He?" Lewis rolled his eyes. "To the best of my knowledge we share only one male acquaintance. Is the colonel testing one or both of us? No, don't answer that. Let us go over your life history one more time. Mary Hughes, if you please, enter stage left."

Mary adjusted her position on the chair, slumping her shoulders, tilting her chin, stretching one leg out in front of her. "Mary Hughes, aged twenty-five. Father was a gamekeeper on a big estate on the outskirts of Edinburgh."

"Yes, we were right to stick with the Scottish accent. While I am a master of slum slang, it would be beyond even me to teach you enough to pass as a genuine Cockney in a week. Unless you are unfortunate enough to meet a fellow Scot, very few this far south can tell the difference between a Highlander and a Sassenach. Pray continue."

Her alter ego had been fortunate enough to be taken on as a scullery maid in the big house, where she had worked hard and eventually become a chambermaid. Sadly, poor, deluded, and by that time orphaned Mary had then fallen in love with her mistress's cousin, who had seduced her with promises of marriage. She hoped Henny would forgive her for borrowing her story, but it always sounded more convincing if it was rooted in the truth. Thanks to a visit with Margaret to the Cowgate in Edinburgh last year, she could give a chilling, accurate account of the tenements where the fictional Mary Hughes had given birth to her child, too early for the bairn to live. Destitute and heartbroken, she had used her last coin to travel to London in the hope of a fresh start, only to discover that her lack of references opened no respectable doors.

"Excellent," Lewis said. "I am such a marvellous teacher, don't you think? It's those little details which are so important, remember, the little touches of colour. Are you nervous? If you're not, then there's something wrong. Nerves sharpen the wits, remind one that one is on show, in the limelight as they say."

"Rest assured, Lewis, I'm nervous."

"Where does the duchess, your mother, think that you have been this last week? Is she aware that you and I have become acquainted?"

"Oh yes, she knows. I thought it best to tell her, since she and your mother are such good friends, though she has no idea we've spent quite so much time in each other's company." Mama assumed that Mary spent most of her time with Aunt Louisa, and was too engrossed in her own concerns to enquire, thus saving Mary the need to prevaricate. Or dissemble, as Lewis put it, something she was becoming rather adept at. Was this a positive attribute? For the time being, certainly.

Lewis stood up, holding out his arm. "Come on, then, Mary," he said in a broad Cockney accent. "Let's get our togs on, and go out and have some fun."

THE OXFORD MUSIC HALL LAY in the heart of Westminster, less than a mile from his offices in Whitehall, but as Tre stood across the road from the theatre, watching out for Mary and Wingfield to arrive, he felt completely out of place. He was not a theatre-goer, he didn't enjoy opera, but even if he had, he suspected he was in for an incomparable experience. He had assumed he'd have no difficulty in recognizing them, but as the time approached for the performance to begin and the crowds pushing through the theatre doors slowed to a trickle, he realized he had missed them, unless Mary had had cold feet, which he somehow doubted. Part of him wished she had. Though in theory, the steps they had agreed on made perfect sense and were his best hope of infiltrating the women's gang, in practice he was struggling to accept it was a risk worth taking. If anything happened to Mary . . .

He caught himself. Focus on the job in hand. He had agreed only to let her prove herself, nothing more. There was still time for her to fail. But he couldn't afford for her to fail! Tre cursed himself under his breath. Focus!

Though the Oxford may indeed have once been a respectable theatre for family entertainment, those days were long gone. Tre's fears of standing out as a single gentlemen dissipated as he pushed his way into the hall. The noise assaulted him first, a cacophony of voices all shouting, calling out to one another, warming up to join in with the choruses. The balconies were crammed with people, mostly men, some respectably clad, as he was, in plain black or grey, others in cheaper versions of the same attire, still others in their working clothes and boots. The few women stood out like brightly coloured birds-of-paradise, their hair adorned with flimsy confections of feathers, lace, and net. The smell was the next thing he noticed: spilt beer, stale sweat, cheap perfume, and cheap spirits overlaid with various snacks, meat pies and jellied eels, which were being voraciously devoured.

Where the devil were they? He turned his attention to the benches set out in neat rows running back from the stage, but could see no trace of Mary or Wingfield. Under the balcony there was a lounge area with tables. Three or four people at each, again mostly men, though there were slightly more women. The audience here was even more raucous, fortified by a constantly replenished supply of strong drink.

"There's room over there, duckie." A barmaid passing with a tray of glasses filled with the amber-coloured poison that they doubtless called brandy indicated a table with only two occupants on the far side.

Tre muttered his thanks, pushing his way through the chairs, casting about in increasing desperation for a sight of Mary.

"Room for a wee one to join us, sir."

He halted in his tracks. The woman who had called to him waved, smiled roguishly, then sat down again. He began to push his way through to her. He recognized Wingfield first, in the cheery Cockney persona that he'd seen before. And beside him, Mary. It was undoubtedly Mary. The same abundant hair piled high on her head, but with several long curls falling artfully over her breast She was dressed in a plain black gown, the type of cheap material that turned rusty brown in places from too many washes. It had long sleeves and a high neckline, covering more of her than a respectable evening gown, yet respectable was the last word he would have used to describe her appearance. As he took his seat opposite the pair of them, she winked at him.

"We'll have a wee drink with you, won't we, Lewis?"

"That would be most gracious." Wingfield appeared to be glassy-eyed and affected not to recognize Tre.

Belatedly understanding what was expected of him, Tre summoned a waitress.

As soon as their drinks were delivered, Mary tilted her glass and took a deep draught, emptying it and setting it down, before picking up Wingfield's glass. "You're already steaming drunk," she said, when he looked as if he might protest.

"You'll be drunk yourself, if you take much more of that," Tre couldn't help but say.

"You think?" Mary tipped the glass back and emptied it.

"Ladies and gentlemen!" a voice boomed from the stage. "For your delight and delectation, may I introduce to you a young lady, fresh from finishing school! An innocent young miss, who will sing you a cautionary tale called 'Miss Muffet.' I give you Harriet Vernon."

Catcalls and whistles greeted the scantily clad woman. Across the table, Mary let out a loud belch and covered her mouth. "Beg pardon. Better out than in."

Struggling not to laugh, Tre sat back to watch the entertainment. Although his companions were putting on an excellent show of their own.

CHAPTER THIRTY-TWO

Slumdog Mary

THE DAY WAS SULTRY AND the tide was low, so the windows of the drawing room in Montagu House remained firmly closed against the stench from the murky Thames. The duchess was at her school, Mary's father was at Boughton, and Tre was anxiously pacing the floor in front of her.

"What's up? Your arse is making buttons, as my auld da used to say," she said, in her best Mary Hughes accent.

His smile was perfunctory. "Your performance was extremely impressive, though I'm still not entirely convinced that the altercation with the man selling the meat pies was entirely necessary."

"It wasn't, but I was having fun."

Tre sat down beside her. "Mary, if you befriend this young woman we've identified, it won't be fun, it will be deadly serious."

"You've found someone with links to the gang! Why didn't you say?"

"Because I'm having second thoughts, that's why. Pouring drink down your arm, singing bawdy songs in a music hall, it's all a long way from living in a lodging-house and pretending to be friendless and penniless."

"Mary Hughes isn't really a saucy piece," Mary said. "That was her letting her hair down because Lewis was paying. She's much more subdued and desperate. I can show you if you like."

"I just don't think I can let you do it, Mary. It's not that I doubt your ability, I simply can't risk it. What if something goes wrong?"

"What could go wrong? All I'm doing is befriending—what's her name?"

"Tilly."

His voice was toneless. His skin had a greyish tinge. No point in asking him if he had been having trouble sleeping: the answer was written on his face. She moved to a seat beside him and took his hand. "I assume that there's no word at all of the papers?"

"Nothing. I keep telling myself that no news is good news, but that's not necessarily true in this case."

"How much longer dare you wait before you have to report this to your superiors?"

"I don't know—maybe two weeks at most." His fingers tightened on hers, then he let her go. "I'll have to confess soon. It's not Beckman's fault—I can keep his name out of it. Doing the handover at Cliveden was my idea, not his. I thought a private weekend party in the country with hand-picked guests would be perfect and low risk. Ironic, isn't it?"

"But the robbery wasn't your fault," Mary exclaimed indignantly. "It was almost certainly a complete coincidence."

"*Almost certainly!* We can't be sure and the War Office won't care."

"You're thinking that you might lose your job, aren't you?" Mary asked, eyeing him with concern. "And if you lose your job, then you'll decide you're not a fit husband for me, and nothing I say or do will persuade you otherwise."

He tried to smile, but failed. "You know me too well. I've finally found my niche, something I'm good at, that I love doing, and that is worthwhile. If I didn't have that, I don't know what I would do."

"I could have said the very same words about myself, so I can't possibly say that I don't understand. And I wouldn't be enough to compensate for that loss, would I?" Mary blinked furiously. "You can say it, Tre. After all, I said it to you."

"It's not that you wouldn't be enough. You are more than I ever dreamed of, but what could I offer you, a man with no job and no prospects—for they'll blacken my name, you can be sure of it. As you've pointed out, the Intelligence Department was largely my idea. They'll say this is exactly the sort of thing I should have known might happen, that I should have been more careful. They might even argue that I've made the country less safe, not more safe. I know these people, Mary—they can turn and twist everything. I don't even earn enough now to keep us from having to scrimp and save. Without my job, the harsh truth is that we wouldn't be able to marry because we'd have no money."

"I would have my dowry."

"If your father approved of our marriage, which he wouldn't, if I have nothing at all to contribute to it. Besides—and I'm sorry to be so conventional—I don't want us to live off your dowry. If we are to make our own kind of marriage, we will need to fund it."

"Then we must ensure that you don't lose your job, which means that we have to recover those papers before anyone discovers they are missing," Mary exclaimed. "Our nation's security depends upon it, and much more important from my point of view, so do I. I'm determined not to lose you."

"I didn't know you'd decided you definitely wanted to keep me."

Her eyes met his. How long had it been since she had questioned herself? Since Cliveden, her only aim had been to be by his side, to assist him, to prove her worth. Was that love? She reached over to smooth her hand over his cheek. It was rough with stubble. He looked so very tired and world-weary. "I do want to have you in my life. Very much."

"Oh, Mary, dearest, darling Mary." He pulled her into his arms, kissing her deeply. "I couldn't bear to lose you now."

"Then let me help you," she said urgently. "We're in this together, Tre. It's not only your future that hangs in the balance, it's mine, too. Isn't that something worth fighting for?"

"Yes! But not at any price."

"If you had someone else lined up to befriend Tilly, you'd do it in an instant, wouldn't you?"

"Yes, but I don't have someone else."

"You have me. I can take lodgings tomorrow. Lewis will help me find a place that's safe. I won't actually stay there, of course."

"Don't rush me into this. Let me think."

"We don't have time to think anymore—we need to act."

"I can't let you act alone. It's too much to ask of you."

"Once and for all, Tre, I want to do it! I can do it. There is no-one, save yourself, not even Her Majesty, who has more of a vested interest in this than I do."

She waited with bated breath, Tre's internal battle writ clearly on his face and in the anxious way he paced across the room and back. "If I could arrange to have someone watch over you, I would feel a lot happier."

"Lewis?"

"Good heavens, no. I need a steady man to shadow you, someone who can be relied upon not to draw attention to himself and who is not likely to get bored and miss something important. All of which Lewis would do. I'll find someone suitable—leave it with me. How would you explain your absences from home?"

"I'll think of something—leave it with me," Mary said, earning herself a fleeting smile. "Oh, Tre, we can do this, I'm sure we can."

"Don't get too carried away. Tilly is a very junior member of the gang. She might know nothing of value at all."

"But she might know something, and if I can befriend her—"

"That has to be the beginning and the end of your involvement," Tre said firmly. "Do you understand me, Mary? I cannot emphasize enough how dangerous these women are. Under no circumstances are you to do anything other than fish for information as subtly as you can." He pulled her to her feet. "Nothing more. You're working for me now and that's a direct order."

"Loud and clear, Colonel Trefusis."

"This isn't a jest."

"I know," Mary said, immediately contrite. "It's our future we're fighting for and I am not likely to forget that, or the trust you are placing in me."

"I don't doubt your ability, my darling."

"Mary, I— Oh! Colonel Trefusis. I didn't know you were here."

"I was just taking my leave, Your Grace."

"Mama! Colonel Trefusis was here to—to tell me—"

"Oh, Mary, please don't bother trying to make something up. I came to tell you that we are to return to Dalkeith as soon as possible. Her Majesty is to unveil Prince Albert's memorial in Edinburgh next month, and there will be a reception at Holyrood Palace afterwards which we have no alternative but to attend."

"Oh no! I can't possibly come with you. I have—"

"You may stay with Louisa; I am sure she won't mind. To be frank, Mary, I would rather travel alone with your father. I have some plans I wish to discuss with him for another school garden. I shall have his full attention on the journey north. Now, if you'll excuse me, I have a great deal to do. Good day, Colonel Trefusis, I'm sure you can see your-self out."

"My aunt leaves for Bicton for the summer imminently," Tre said as the door closed. "Your mother obviously doesn't know that."

"No, she doesn't." Mary beamed. "Now all I have to do is make sure she doesn't find out."

Whitechapel, London, One Week Later

The deception as to her whereabouts had been remarkably easy to pull off, with Mary bidding a fond farewell to Aunt Louisa the day before her mother left for Scotland, and to her mother on the following day. Tre intercepted the note that the duchess had written to thank Louisa for looking after her daughter, and the coach, which he had arranged purportedly to take her from Montagu House to Lady Rolle's town house, instead took her to Bloomsbury. Here, Tre had arranged her accommodation, a sitting room and bedchamber in a house run by a stern but, Tre assured her, extremely respectable couple who would look after her needs and bring her meals.

In these rooms, every morning, Lady Mary Montagu Douglas Scott transformed herself into Mary Hughes, donning her shabby black gown and boots. Every morning, as she tied the ribbons of her old-fashioned hat, the brim big enough to shade most of her face, and draped her woollen shawl around her shoulders, butterflies fluttered in her stom-ach. *Nerves sharpen the wits, remind one that one is on show,* Lewis's voice in her head reminded her every morning as she stepped outside and into the rickety old hackney with the weather-beaten driver. Inside Bert, the man Tre had assigned to protect her, would be waiting in his unmemorable drab, dusty clothes. The cab stopped in a different place each day. Mary Hughes would alight, then it would drive off round a corner to the end of a street, and at some point, Mary never knew when, Bert would also alight.

"Don't look for me," he had said to her the first day. "Don't look, but trust me, I'll be there in the background, watching." She had looked, the first day—she couldn't help herself—but she had not once spotted him.

The room that Lewis had found for Mary Hughes was in a small terraced house. Downstairs, the front room was a makeshift shop that sold an odd selection of buttons, pins, string, cotton, pens and wipers, mops and buckets, and brushes of all sorts. There was a parlour behind it for the use of the lodgers, and a room which served as the kitchen, whose sparse contents consisted of a fire, a gridiron, and a toasting fork. There was a shed out back, referred to as the scullery, where water could be pumped on the days when water was available. The privy was also outside, for the exclusive use of the lodgers, a facility that was in this district of London still extremely unusual, Lewis had informed her, while at the same time recommending, quite unnecessarily, that she make every effort to avoid using it.

The four rooms in the house were rented out by the month rather than the day, which Mary had discovered was one of the factors which defined it as a respectable abode. Two married couples had a room each on the second floor, and she had one of the two rooms in the attic, the other being let to a lawyer's clerk. There were no pleasantries exchanged between the residents, save a mumbled "good day" if they passed each other on the stairs. Though the parlour and the kitchen were shared, it was bad form to enter either if it was in use. One did not ask questions, Mary had discovered very quickly. In a house where the walls were so thin, where every word could be heard if it was spoken above a whisper, privacy was closely guarded.

She spent very little time in her room, but dressed in her shabby clothes and carrying a basket, she spent a good deal of eye-opening time

in the streets of Whitechapel and Cheapside, venturing as far as Hol-
burn, paying careful heed to Lewis's strictures not to go any farther east.
In the daytime, dressed as she was, she could pass unnoticed, just another
unremarkable denizen. She relished her role, not only because she was
finally taking action, she was finally doing something that would help
Tre, but for the thrill of playing the role itself. She began to understand
Lewis's penchant for passing himself off as someone else, the quiet satisfaction of going completely unnoticed, of being someone she was not.
Every day was like the walk out onto the parapet at Drumlanrig, only
each time Mary Hughes ventured forth, she had a purpose. The situation
was both terrifying and exciting in equal measure, but it was never, ever
boring. If her mother ever discovered the deception, she would be devastated and furious, but Mary was determined no-one would ever know.
Unlike Lewis, the very last thing she ever wished to do was brag or boast.
It was enough for her to succeed, and she was grimly determined that
she would.

There was so much to learn about life in Whitechapel. Everything
had a price, and every vendor made sure that their price was heard.
Hawkers on the street corners, costermongers, and market stall holders
all called out their wares. Bonnets for fourpence, a peach or a handful
of parsley for a penny, a quire of paper for tuppence—the streets rang
out with the calls. Mary had no notion of what might be considered
cheap and what was expensive. She had a few coins in the purse she
kept tucked safely away, but she didn't know what they could buy her,
or what they might mean to her fellow lodgers. Roaming the streets
alone, realizing every day how vast was her ignorance, she set about
remedying it.

Sadly, and frustratingly, she had made agonizingly slow progress
with Tilly. Their first "chance" meeting on her first day in Whitechapel
was in the pie shop where Tilly worked serving tables. Having discov-

ered which market Tilly frequented, Mary managed to "bump into" her the next day, and struck up a conversation. They agreed to meet the next day to shop together, and they had done so now every morning, but while the friendship was blossoming, Tilly had confided little of use to Mary.

She had not seen Tre since she had moved into the Bloomsbury house, but she was horribly conscious of the time ticking away. The longer he waited before informing his superior at Intelligence, the hotter the water he would be in. She wanted to save him, but either Tilly was simply too low in the ranks of the Brazen Hussies to know anything, or she was too well-trained to give anything away. After a week of to-ing and froing, Mary was getting desperate and frightened that sometime soon someone would discover that Lady Mary was not where she should be.

"What is it?" Tilly asked, when Mary tapped on the door of the pie shop, which was still closed. "Why aren't you at work?"

"I walked out. Can I come in for a chinwag? I'll help you in the kitchen."

"Come in, then. I'm on my own for a bit. You can help me peel the potatoes. What happened?"

"What do you think happened?" Mary said, folding up her shawl and rolling up her sleeves, saying a silent thank you for the hours she had spent in the kitchen at Drumlanrig helping Cook.

"He tried it on again, your boss?"

"Told me if I wasn't a bit more friendly, he'd be getting someone else in to do for him. I asked him what his wife would make of him wanting me to be more friendly, and that's when he got nasty."

"They always do," Tilly said, her lip curling. "You did the right thing, Mary. Nobody needs to put up with that for a few coppers a week."

"Yes, but what am I going to do now?" Mary didn't pretend to cry.

Tears were of no use in Tilly's world, a pointless extravagance and waste of energy. "That's the third time it's happened since I came to London. Three times in six months! I thought I'd left that type of behaviour behind in Auld Reekie. Sorry, that's what we call Edinburgh. Do you think they can tell, Tilly, when they look at me?"

"What, that you let one man have his way once, so you're game for more from any man!" Tilly exclaimed scornfully. "It's not your fault, if that's what you're thinking."

"Maybe I should have, just this once. You know, kept him happy, kept my job."

"Don't go down that road. Once you give in to them, they expect it. He'd have you a few times, then he'd get bored. You know how easy it is for them to find someone else like you, desperate for the work."

"I am desperate. Is there any chance of being taken on here?"

"No, Mary, no chance. I'm sorry. It shouldn't be so bleeding hard to make an honest living, should it?"

"I don't know what to do," Mary said, allowing some of her real feelings to show. "Talking of making an honest living, I don't suppose there's any work I could do for—you know . . ."

"Hush. I don't know, Mary. Queenie's very particular."

Queenie. Tilly had not let slip a name before. "I'd do anything," Mary said. She knew she was disobeying Tre's express instructions but it was too good an opportunity to pass up. Anyway, nothing might come of it. "I could act as lookout, as you do. I'm good with a gun."

"A gun! How would the likes of you know how to shoot a gun? Come off it, Mary, I know you're desperate but if I take you to meet Queenie, and you tell her you can shoot, she'll want you to prove it."

"I can," Mary said eagerly, sensing a breakthrough at last. "My da was a gamekeeper. I was his only child, he didn't have any sons, so he taught me to shoot, a pistol first, then a rifle as soon as I was old enough to hold one. Used to take me with him when they were culling the deer on the estate. Even after they took me on at the big house, before he died, I'd help out. You have to be an excellent marksman to be allowed to take part. A clean head shot is needed to prevent the animals suffering. It's been a while, but I've got a good eye, so if Queenie wants to put me to the test, I'm ready."

CHAPTER THIRTY-THREE

When Mary Met Queenie

Limehouse, London, August 1876

TILLY SECURED A BLINDFOLD AROUND Mary's eyes as soon as she stepped into the hackney. Where was Bert? Would he be able to follow her? For the first time since she had assumed the identity of Mary Hughes, venturing into completely unknown territory, she was more terrified than excited, and unable to see a thing. She should have told Tre. But Tre would have forbidden her, and this was their best chance, perhaps their only chance, of success.

The carriage set off without needing direction. It smelled of sweat and onions and beer. She had been out in London at night many times, going to balls, the theatre, the opera, but always in the company of her mother or Annie, her sister-in-law, safe in one of the Buccleuch carriages, driven by her father's coachman. Alone with Tilly, Mary was aware of the clatter of the carriage on the cobble-stones, the thunder of other traffic. The constant calls of the street vendors were every bit as raucous as during the day, though what they sold was different—hot pies, late edition newspapers, a tot of something to keep out the cold, even though it was August—and her black dress was clinging to her, damp with the heat.

No-one knew where she was or who she was with. She could disappear from the face of the earth tonight, her body dumped into the Thames at the turn of the tide, and no-one would know what had become of her. She had leapt at the opportunity Tilly offered this morning, but she'd had all day to question the wisdom of her rash decision. Her story had fooled Tilly, but it wouldn't stand up to close scrutiny. She had duped Tilly, but Tilly was a very small cog, a minion in a notorious and dangerous gang. Even if she was accepted, how on earth would she go about discovering whether the Brazen Hussies had stolen Tre's papers? She might be on a wild goose chase.

Her stomach lurched. Tre had not expressly forbidden her to meet Queenie, but he'd been very clear about the boundaries of her engagement with Tilly.

Under no circumstances are you to do anything other than fish for information as subtly as you can. Nothing more.

She could argue that fishing for information as subtly as she could was what she was doing tonight, but she knew it wouldn't wash with him. She was his agent in the field, and she was disobeying his express orders. He had placed her here, he was responsible for her. If anything happened to her, he would take the blame. Oh dear God, if something happened to her, instead of saving Tre's career, she would have ruined it. Though it was in danger of being destroyed anyway, if he had to confess to the loss of the papers. She had the chance to act, to influence the outcome: she had to take it, she simply had to.

Besides, Mary thought, as the cab slowed and made a sharp turn, it was too late to change her mind now. Concentrate. Focus. The sick feeling in her stomach was a positive sign. Stop thinking about what might go wrong. Think only about what she had to do. Who she was. Why she was here. Mary Hughes. Out of work. Desperate. Willing to do anything to prove herself.

The cab door was flung open. "You all right about this?" Tilly asked.

"Bit late in the day if I'm not," Mary said, clinging to her arm as she stepped down.

A dog growled. "Quiet, Boysie," Tilly said. "You should know me by now. He's Queenie's bulldog," she whispered. "Watch now, there's a step."

Mary could smell beer and brandy. Sawdust. A low murmur of voices as they passed one room. A tavern, she surmised. A door opened and Tilly pushed her through, wishing her good luck.

"You can take off the blindfold now."

Mary did so, her hands shaking. Nerves were good. Mary Hughes would be nervous, but Mary had better get them under control. Blinking, her eyes adjusting to the light, she found herself in a small, cramped room dimly lit by candles. Directly in front of her was an enormously fat woman, her bosom spilling out of a black silk dress that was straining at the seams to contain her and which had surrendered to the pressure on her left shoulder. Queenie Divers had a shock of carrot-red hair and a pair of fierce black eyebrows, none of which could possibly be as nature had intended. Her face was criss-crossed with small scars, presumably inflicted with a knife. She was flanked by five women, all of whom looked both hostile and suspicious in equal measure.

"Well then, speak up, Mary Hughes. What do you want from me?"

"Work, of course," Mary said, meeting Queenie's gaze full on. "I wouldn't come all this way just for a glass of beer or a wee dram now, would I?"

There was a sharp intake of breath from one of the women, but Queenie gave a crack of laughter. "If you're going to take a drop of anything from this place, stick to the brandy."

"I don't touch the stuff, not any of it. Goes in one way, out the other. I've got better things to spend my money on, when I've got any."

Queenie's brows rose. "I don't mind confidence but cockiness is another matter. You're a lippy one and no mistake."

But it was working. The pale blue eyes fixed on her were interested. "Look," Mary said, "I know there's no point me giving you a hard luck story. Every one of us here has one, right? So my telling you that I'm desperate, or that I'm hard done by, or that some man has done me wrong, that's not exactly news, is it?"

"Go on."

"Tilly will have filled you in on my story, so there's no point in me telling it again."

"Oh, I reckon we'd like to hear it, from the horse's mouth, so to speak, dearie," Queenie said. "Wouldn't we, girls?"

"Fair enough." Mary recounted her manufactured history, trying to vary it a little from what she had told Tilly, anxious not to sound too well rehearsed. Details make the difference, she recalled Lewis saying. "Them tenements in the Canongate, the stairs are so steep, it knocks the breath out of you to get to the first storey, and all I could afford was the fifth. Had to sit down on the stairs, as I got closer to my time. And the stench from the middens out in the back court coming through the broken window. Knock you sick, they would. Course the landlord wouldn't dream to put his hand in his pocket to fix anything."

"No different down here, love," one of the women said. "I've got a place on Farringdon Street, and we've one privy for six houses. One! All that work they made such a fuss about, to fix the stink, but we've not seen any of the benefits."

"Nor likely to either," one of the other women said. "Water's only switched on three hours a day where we are."

"Ladies!" Queenie said sharply. "Let the lass finish."

Sensing that she had already done enough, Mary glossed over much of her finely crafted history. "So I came to London looking for a fresh start," she ended. "But I just can't make an honest living. I'm sick of scraping by, and I'm sick of being used. So here I am, ready to try making a dishonest living." She let her gaze sweep boldly over Queenie's coterie. "Any of that ring any bells?"

Queenie laughed, spreading her arms wide. "Mary Hughes, you could be talking about any one of us. Ain't that true, ladies?" She waited for the murmur of assent, before turning back to Mary, her expression hardening. "Tilly says you can shoot. I find that hard to believe."

"Tilly didn't lie. Do you want me to prove it?"

Queenie's eyes narrowed. "You're a bold piece. Rose, give her your revolver."

The thick-set woman to Queenie's left bridled. "With all due respect, I don't think that's wise."

Queenie raised her hand imperiously. "Rose is my bodyguard. I expect she's worried you might be a paid killer come to assassinate me, Mary Hughes. I admire your dedication, Rose, but in this case I think the risk is minimal, don't you?" she said, nodding at Mary. "I mean look at her—she looks like she wouldn't hurt a fly."

"Point taken." Rose handed Mary her weapon, which had been concealed in a pocket of her dress. "You sure you know what you're about? This isn't a toy, and it's fully loaded."

"Beaumont-Adams," Mary said. "Safe, reliable. So," she said, keeping the gun aimed at the floor, "what's the target?"

"That candle over there on the far table," Queenie said. "Snuff it out."

Mary slowly took aim. Her hand was steady. She cocked the pistol.

"When you're ready, dearie," Queenie snapped. "In my world you wouldn't have the luxury of taking your time."

Mary lowered the pistol, walked over to the candle, and blew it out. She turned around, curtsying, to howls of derision. "What? I did as you asked, didn't I?"

"You did," Queenie admitted grudgingly, "I'll give you that. I like initiative, within reason. Now give Rose her gun back."

"In a minute." From the other side of the room, Mary levelled the gun at a candle holder on the wall to Queenie's right.

The other woman sat perfectly still, a smile playing on her mouth. "Go on, then, I dare you. But just remember, if your aim is off and you hit me, you're dead meat."

Mary adjusted her aim and squeezed the trigger. The pistol's retort echoed around the stunned silence in the room. The top half inch of the wick had been neatly shot off. The bullet had buried itself in the wall behind.

"An impressive party trick." Queenie remained remarkably composed. "What else can you do?"

Mary shrugged. "Whatever it takes. I've got a head for heights. I can think on my feet."

"I don't suppose you can see in the dark?"

"I'm not a cat."

Queenie snorted. "Two out of three ain't bad. Tilly! Stop hiding in the corner. I reckon your friend deserves a chance. Take her with you tomorrow. A test," she said, turning back to Mary. "And if you pass, then we'll see. A word of warning, though. I know I look like a kindly aunt—no laughing at the back now—and I do look after my girls. But if you ever cross me, you'll wish you had never been born. Right, the rest of you, the show's over. You two, make yourselves scarce, we've got important business to discuss."

The door closed behind them. Heart thudding, scarcely able to believe what had just happened, Mary paused for a moment. Kneeling down in the narrow corridor, she pressed her ear to the door, but the thick wood muffled all sound from the other room.

"What you playing at?" Tilly stood over her, hands on hips.

"Just tying up me bootlace," Mary said, getting up.

"You're a deep one. That trick you played, it could have backfired. Just as well Queenie took a shine to you."

"Did she? How do you know?"

"Because you're still alive. Do you think Rose only packs one pistol? Come on, let's get out of here."

CHAPTER THIRTY-FOUR

The Spy Who Loves Me

IN QUEENIE'S HACKNEY, ON THE way back from her encounter, Mary accepted that she was utterly out of her depth. The cab deposited her at her lodgings in Whitechapel, and as soon as it took off again with Tilly, Bert appeared from the shadows. He was coldly furious, grabbing her by the arm and marching her off to where her own cab was waiting, but once inside he was visibly shaken.

"I thought you were a goner," he said, mopping his brow. "Never in my three years working with the colonel have I lost track of someone I was looking after, and the colonel was most specific with regards to you: I wasn't to let you out of my sight. When I saw you disappearing off with that Tilly, I swear I nearly ran after you and blew my own cover as well as yours. I'm going to have to tell the colonel, you do understand that?"

"I'm so sorry," Mary said. Now that she was safe, she was shaking. "I should have told you, I see that now, but I was afraid you would try to stop me."

"I don't know where you went, but I can guess and you are dam— beg pardon. You're right. I would have stopped you, for it's what the colonel would have expected me to do. But it's done now, and you came to no harm, did you?"

"I'm fine, but I need to speak to the colonel urgently, Bert. I'll explain that I duped you, that it wasn't your fault that I gave you the slip. I'm sure he'll understand. I'd hate for you to get into trouble."

"If I was you, it was my own skin I'd be worried about. The colonel isn't one of those that shouts and screams; he's the quiet sort, but he won't tolerate disobedience. He says that's what costs lives."

"I'm safe, though, and I think it was worth it, Bert."

"I don't want to hear. I don't need to know." The carriage had drawn up at Bloomsbury, and Bert jumped down to help her out. The door to the house was already ajar. Mary marvelled as she did every time she returned, that she was expected, but she had ceased to question Bert, who remained tight-lipped on this and every other subject. He had spoken more on this journey than he had in their entire time together, which proved how upset the man was.

"I'm so sorry," Mary said. "Will you tell the colonel I must speak to him urgently? I'll try my best to make sure he understands you are not to blame."

SHE WAS DIRECTED TO CALL at Upper Grosvenor Street first thing the next morning. Tre had left his usual rooms to stay there while Aunt Louisa was in Devon, for she didn't like to leave the house empty. He was waiting in the drawing room.

"Mary!" He held her at arm's length. "Bert said you were safe, but until I saw you . . ."

"I'm perfectly unharmed, I promise."

He dropped his hold immediately, his expression hardening. "Then will you kindly explain to me what you thought you were doing yesterday?"

Mary's knees began to shake. "It wasn't Bert's fault, Tre. I didn't give him a chance to follow me."

"I'm not interested in Bert at the moment." He was standing over at the window, his back to the light and his face in shadow. "Where did you go?"

Haltingly, she explained, trying to stick to the facts, trying to keep her voice steady. Tre listened tight-lipped without interrupting, his expression giving nothing of his thoughts or feelings away. "I was making no progress with Tilly," Mary concluded, "and I am horribly aware that time is not on our side. I realized as soon as I left Queenie that I must speak to you, without any need for Bert to prompt me. It wasn't his fault."

"So you have already said. You disobeyed my express orders. I've been to hell and back just imagining what might have happened to you."

She dug her nails into her palms. "I took a huge risk that I know I shouldn't have taken, and I disobeyed your orders and I betrayed your trust in me. I am truly sorry."

Tre let out a deep sigh. "You're safe. That's the most important thing. To be honest, if it was anyone other than you, I'd commend your initiative. If our situations had been reversed, I'd have done exactly as you did." He sat down heavily on the seat opposite her. "You're right about Tilly. Either she knows nothing, or she's going to take too long to crack. And, as you pointed out, time is not on our side. What's more, there's some news I haven't told you. We've received information that the Russians are trying to negotiate a deal to buy some papers. They can only be ours."

"So they haven't been destroyed?"

"It seems not," Tre said, "which means the stakes have just gone up. We have to recover them before the Russians get their hands on them."

"Do you think it's Queenie who has them?"

"It's highly likely. So, as it turns out, your rash act last night might work to our advantage."

"If I can prove myself to Queenie, if Mary Hughes can become one of the Brazen Hussies, there's a real chance of a breakthrough," Mary exclaimed. "I know you'll think this an odd thing to say, but under other circumstances, I could admire Queenie Divers, and I think she took to me—or rather, to Mary Hughes."

"For heaven's sake, she's a career criminal."

"She's carved a niche for herself in an underworld that's otherwise completely dominated by men. That's impressive."

"You'll be telling me next that she treats her associates like her children."

Mary was obliged to laugh. "No, though she does give women like Tilly a leg up. The streets of London are awash with them, Tre, women on their own whom nobody gives a fig about, and who no-one would miss if they disappeared. That's what Queenie Divers plays on. She gives the unwanted and unloved an opportunity no-one else will: the chance to belong. She's shaped the world in her image, not as convention dictates. I think that's what I admire about her."

"Isn't that what we are trying to do?"

"I suppose it is. Do you think that we'll succeed?"

Tre frowned, gazing down at his hands. "I want to, more than anything."

There, Mary thought, there it was. The simple truth. "So do I," she said, "more than anything. We have a chance to make it happen. Working together to secure our future. We can't *not* take this opportunity we have been presented with. It's all we have."

"I wish I could say otherwise," he agreed grimly, "but you're right. We have no other leads; you're our best and only chance, though it goes against every instinct to place you in harm's way."

"This can't be a unique situation. You must have tried and tested methods of protecting your men."

"You're not one of my men. You're the woman I love."

She hadn't realized how much she'd longed to hear those words from him, but hearing them now left her speechless. Tre loved her. Tre *loved* her.

"I love you, Mary," he repeated, misreading her silence. "This may not be the time or the place, but I'm tired of waiting to say what I know in my heart."

"I don't want to wait, either. I love you, darling Tre, so very much."

They were in each other's arms in an instant, and for a moment that was all that mattered. His lips on hers. Frantic kisses, frantic assurances, her arms around his neck, and the kisses becoming deeper. Until reality intervened.

"What are we to do now?" Mary asked, as much of herself as of him.

"The traditional way forward would be for me to go on bended knee and ask you to marry me, but since there remains a strong possibility I'll have no means of keeping a roof over our head because I've been drummed out of the service, then I'll refrain from doing so."

"Then what we need to do is sit down and try to work out a plan to ensure that doesn't come to pass."

"That would require us to get those cursed papers back."

"Then I must go back to Whitechapel. It's our best chance, Tre."

"I know," he conceded grimly. "If you can prove yourself with Queenie, get yourself on the inside, it's our best and only hope of confirming that she is the prospective seller. But it will be under my conditions, my rules. I am deadly serious, Mary. This is a very different situation from your simply befriending Tilly. The risks . . ." He winced. "I will manage the risks to the best of my ability, but you have to trust in my experience. My priority will be to keep you safe at all times. Securing the papers comes second. You must obey every order you have from me or Bert to the letter. Do you understand?"

"I do, and I promise, I'll obey you both to the letter." Mary smiled. "You're letting Bert keep his job."

"He's the best I have, and he knows that he won't get another chance. I can trust him."

"You can trust me, too, Tre. I won't let you down."

He pulled her into his arms again. "There's no question of that. From now on, for the rest of our lives, we're in this together, yes?"

"Yes." Mary twined her arms around his neck. "Yes, yes, yes," she said, punctuating each word with a kiss. "Oh, Tre, yes."

CHAPTER THIRTY-FIVE

A Fair Exchange Is No Robbery

Limehouse, London, August 1876

T HE NEXT NIGHT, MARY HUGHES took part in Queenie's initiation test along with Tilly. Mary had no idea what measures Tre had taken to ensure her safety, but as she took her place as lookout on the roof above the jewellers in New Bond Street, she was confident that the measures were in place. The two men in evening clothes loitering on the corner, pretending to be drunk, rather poorly in her opinion, gave her pause. Were they Tre's men? No, they were too obvious and he had assured her that she would have no idea they were there. The men were watching the shop intently. Acting on a hunch, she decided that the jewellers had in all probability employed plainclothes detectives to keep the premises under surveillance and quickly passed on the word. The robbery was called off at the last second.

Queenie was delighted by Mary Hughes's quick thinking and powers of observation when it transpired that the shop was indeed under observation. It was no small relief to Mary, and her conscience, that she hadn't been party to a crime and in fact had prevented one. In addition she had gained kudos with the Brazen Hussies. All in all a successful night's work. Tre would be proud of her!

In the days which followed Mary was ferried back and forward by Queenie's cab driver between the tavern at Limehouse and her lodgings in Whitechapel where she had been forced to take up full-time residence, Tre having deemed it too risky for her to travel back to Bloomsbury to sleep. She knew a watcher under Bert's control followed her at all times, and she knew that if her watcher deemed the situation too risky she would be swiftly removed. She could pass vital information on if absolutely necessary by means of a note in a hiding place in the privy out in the back court of her lodgings. On no account was she to attempt to contact Tre, or his men, directly.

Those were the rules. She stuck to them rigidly. She had never felt so alive and so full of purpose, or so terrified of making a mistake. This was her performance of a lifetime. Tre loved her. She loved him. This knowledge was what kept her nerves in check; and knowing that Tre felt every bit as strongly as she, and that he would do everything he could to protect her, was what raised her spirits when they flagged.

Queenie had strict codes of behaviour. Her tried and tested methods meant a hierarchy was in place that everyone in her tightly knit coterie understood. An existing member put you forward. If Queenie thought you could be of value, she tried you out. If you passed her test, then you were accepted on probation, and it was up to you to prove your loyalty and to take any opportunity that arose to make yourself useful. Five women, those present when Mary first met Queenie, formed her inner circle, the women who planned the various operations and who shared in the profits. There were others like Tilly, who preferred to keep a veneer of respectability. They were called upon when needed and paid well for their services. Then there were others. Women who needed a helping hand, who were grateful that Queenie had given them a hand up. They were well worth investing a few shillings in, their loyalty bought and paid for. Mary Hughes was one of those. In need of a job, worth keeping an eye on, with potential. Queenie paid her to clean the back room in the tavern she used as an office, to serve food and drink, to run errands.

Tre had been confident from his own intelligence sources that some sort of deal was imminent, but it was four long, testing days before Mary finally had the breakthrough she had been desperate for. She had collected the morning tea tray from the kitchen, with two plates of sandwiches consisting of cold tripe and piccalilli for Queenie, bloater paste for Rose, and was about to deliver it when a single word stopped her in her tracks.

"Cliveden."

The door to the back room was ajar, but she knew better than to try to eavesdrop. Queenie had ears like a bat, and if Mary was caught snooping, she would be lucky if she lived to tell the tale. She pushed the door open with her hip and walked in. Rose and Queenie were alone, sitting at the table with a sheaf of papers between them. "Here we are, ladies, tea's up." Heart pounding, Mary set out the tea things. Rose quickly turned the papers over, but not before Mary had glimpsed a bundle of photographs and letters, one of which bore the crest of what she was fairly certain was a golden eagle. Another had a gold seal.

"Did I hear you mention Cliveden?" she asked, pouring Queenie's tea and adding the two lumps of sugar she liked. "Big house near Maidenhead, right?"

"What do you know about it?" Rose snatched her plate of sandwiches. Rose had never forgiven Mary for the episode with the revolver.

"Worked there, didn't I, for a weekend," Mary replied, thinking on her feet. "There was some big party and they needed extra hands." In such cases, it was more likely that local staff would have been employed, but she took a chance on Queenie being unaware of domestic arrangements in big houses. She was about to add that there had been a robbery when she recalled that one of Queenie's girls had been on the staff. "Weekend after a burglary it was. One of the regular staff mysteriously disappeared at the same time, leading them to believe she must have been part of the gang. What do you reckon to that?"

"I reckon," Rose said, "that we're not in the least bit interested."

"No? You won't be interested in the fact that they was having a new safe fitted either, then?"

"Where?" Queenie asked.

"We don't need to know that," Rose hissed. "Same place done over in the space of a few weeks? That would be asking for trouble."

Queenie's eyebrows waggled. "When everyone would be thinking same as you, Rose, that lightning never strikes twice? Their guard would be down. You see, that's why I'm in charge here, and you're not. Low risk, it would be, if you know where that new safe is. Go on then, Mary Hughes. Where is it?"

Where? "There's a bedroom in the west wing on the ground floor," Mary said, fervently hoping that the Duke of Westminster and she were not of like minds. "It's got one of those big fancy curtains that cover the wall behind the bed. They put it in there."

"Interesting," Queenie said. "You're a smart girl, Mary Hughes. No need for me to tell you to keep that bit of information to yourself, is there?"

"I know what side my bread's buttered, Queenie. Always happy to be of service."

"You can go now," Rose said.

Ignoring her, Mary risked addressing Queenie directly. "Look, I'll be straight with you. It's not that I'm not grateful for you letting me do the fetching and carrying here, but anyone can do that sort of thing. I've got more to offer."

"Such as?"

"Whatever it takes," Mary said, continuing to meet Queenie's eyes. "I passed the first test you set me. Why not set me another? I'll get it done, no questions asked, if you make it worth my while."

"You've got a bloody nerve!" Rose exclaimed.

Queenie cackled. "She has at that."

"All I'm asking for is an opportunity," Mary said, resisting the urge to throw herself at Queenie's feet and beg for a very specific opportunity she knew must be coming up. Why else would Queenie and Rose be examining the papers? But she'd already said enough. She picked up the empty tray and turned away. "If anything comes up, bear me in mind, that's all I'm asking. One volunteer is worth a hundred conscripts, as the saying goes."

She sallied out of the room, letting her breath go as she closed the door behind her. She had baited the hook, but would Queenie bite? Mary's future happiness depended upon it.

London Docks, One Day Later

It was an oppressive night: the moon obscured by low cloud, the air damp and thick with London's fog and the stench of the Thames. The mud and slime and silt of the great river had been simmering all summer into a thick oleaginous broth. Queenie's trusty hackney came to a halt in the shadow of a looming block of warehouses at Wapping. A few steps away from where they stood, the workhouse had closed its doors for the night. It was eerily quiet at this hour as they made their way to the dockside, Queenie, Rose, and Mary Hughes. The hoists creaked. In the basin, three lighters were tied up, bobbing gently in the water. The dark shapes of some old-fashioned sailing ships could be seen farther downriver. The steamships were unloaded at the Royal Victoria Dock. A stack of ropes smelled of tar and bilge water. Mary shivered.

"I hope you're not getting cold feet," Rose hissed. "It's all very well putting yourself forward, but you have to deliver. You better not let us down, do you hear?"

"I heard you the first time, and the second," Mary said.

"All you have to do is keep a calm head."

"I don't know what you're making such a fuss about. It's just a packet of papers."

"Some toff is paying me a lot of money for those papers, dearie, so you better take bloody good care of them. Don't go dropping them in the river."

"As if I would!" Mary's knees were trembling so much, she was worried about their being able to carry her as far as the end of the pier. "I told you, you can trust me, Queenie. Give them here." She held out her hand, with a huge effort of will preventing it from shaking.

Queenie hesitated for a painful, nerve-stretching moment before handing over the package. "Now shut up, the pair of you," she hissed, "and listen. He's going to be on the other side of the pier at the end of the jetty. The Old Stairs are just there, where they used to chain the criminals up, let them drown nice and slow. We have a good view from here."

"He's here," Rose whispered as a tall, cloaked figure stepped out from the gloom about fifty yards away.

"How do we know it's him?" Mary asked.

"Who else would it be, waiting there at this time of night? You ready?"

Mary's heart began to hammer so hard she could feel it in her ears. Her palms were damp; a trickle of perspiration ran down her back.

"Right, Mary Hughes," Queenie said brusquely. "You know what to do. Remember to take the bag from him first, before you give him the package, and then come back here straight away. Got it?"

"Got it." Mary Hughes was expendable, another faceless woman who no-one would miss or care about if she were swallowed up by the river. She would never see Queenie again. Queenie was using her; yet absurdly Mary felt as if she was betraying her.

"Get on with it," Rose hissed.

Goodbye, Queenie, Mary said to herself. *Good luck.*

She made her way slowly and steadily to the end of the pier. The footbridge was very narrow. The Thames, brown and oily beneath, looked lethal. *Don't look down.* Crossing the parapet at Drumlanrig, she had said those words to herself. She had used the same words when she and Tre had been teasing Mr. Glover in the room where Cromwell was buried. *Don't look down,* she recalled saying in a hushed voice, imagining another Mary walking out on the parapet of the Tower of London, keeping her eyes up, lest she plunge to her death in the cold, stinking, roiling river. "Don't look down," she whispered softly. She could do this. A few more steps, that was all it would take, and it would be over. Courage and faith were what she needed now.

She stepped onto the bridge. Courage and faith. The Thames gurgled and slapped against the stone beneath, the tide turning. *I won't let you down.* She summoned up the memory of those words from the last time she had spoken to Tre. *I won't let you down,* she said to herself. Courage and faith.

She reached the other side. The cloaked figure waiting for her put out his hand and gestured to her to give him the package. Mary shook her head. "No," she said, more loudly than necessary. *Good girl!* she imagined Queenie whispering to Rose. "You first," Mary said.

The figure shrugged and handed over the bag. Mary gave him the package, following her instructions to the letter. Every second seemed to last an hour. The air was thick as treacle. She turned slowly, and her head was enveloped in a thick blanket. She cried out in protest, just loud enough. He pulled her into a tight grip. She cried out again, and as her feet left the ground, one more time, the sound of a woman who had already given up hope. "Queenie," Mary cried.

She was bundled off. Across the bridge, she imagined Rose and Queenie watching, helpless in a different way. *We've been had*, Rose would say, wanting to come after them. But Queenie wouldn't let her. *What would we do, call the police? No, we'll mark it down to experience, stick to robbing innocent people.*

Would Queenie care about Mary Hughes? No, she knew too much. Chances were she'd quietly disappear into the Thames. *Shame, Queenie might say, I liked her. She had promise, that one.*

The man holding her came to a halt and let her slide down to the ground. He pulled off the blanket and in the darkness smiled at her. Courage and faith, and here was her reward. "Tre!" Mary threw her arms around him.

"I wasn't going to trust the recovery of a precious package to one of my men, now was I?" Tre replied. "Two precious packages actually. You didn't have to struggle quite so hard—you kicked my shins twice."

"I had to make it convincing for our audience."

CHAPTER THIRTY-SIX

Nothing Compares to You

IN THE CARRIAGE, MARY BEGAN to shake uncontrollably. Tre wrapped her in his arms, stroking her hair. "You're safe now, my darling, you're safe now."

"You came for me," she said, burying her face in his shoulder, revelling in the comfort of his familiar bulk.

"Did you doubt me?"

"Never. Faith and courage," she said, "but I had no way of knowing it would be you. I assumed you would use Bert or one of your other men."

"I wanted to be the one there waiting for you. Watching you walk over that bridge was the longest few seconds of my life."

"Me, too. I kept thinking, what if Queenie discovers she's been duped? What if she comes after me?"

"That was one of the eventualities I had covered."

"What—you mean you had men on the docks, waiting to—"

"Don't think about it. It's over. You're safe. That's all that matters."

"Hardly all. The papers, are they all there?"

Tre reluctantly let her go and opened the package, flicking through the contents. "I can't see well enough, but I think so. I'll get these into the safe at the office, then tomorrow I'll go through them properly, decide who needs to see what, and arrange a meeting with Mrs. Brown. I'm taking you back to Aunt Louisa's house for the night. Tomorrow, when you've rested, we'll talk."

That sounded ominous. Mary hadn't considered what would happen beyond the events on the bridge, but Tre was right: their future was very far from defined. "What will the servants think, my turning up out of the blue like this?"

"I've given them a few days holiday. Bert will be around if you need anything." He folded the papers carefully back up into the package.

His hands, Mary noticed, were shaking. Only now did she consider how terrifying the ordeal must have been for him. She had her orders— she had only to follow them—but the entire operation had been Tre's responsibility, under his command. "When did you get the note I left Bert telling you that the handover would be tonight?"

"We had that within half an hour of your leaving it last night. We were watching your lodgings as usual, and my man always made a point of checking the—er, lavatory."

She had thought herself beyond embarrassment, but she had been wrong. Mary decided for once not to ask for more detail. "Queenie wouldn't tell me the exact time, and I didn't want to arouse her suspicions by pressing her on it."

"I was here from nightfall. We had the tavern watched. I got word when your little entourage left, so I had a few moments' warning. We knew from our own sources that Queenie was offering the papers to the Russians, but getting their attaché, the one who was supposed to buy the papers, out of the picture was more of a challenge. I had to concoct a diplomatic crisis. Very senior official. Highly paid courtesan. End of the week, likely, before it's untangled. Couldn't exactly say he had some urgent espionage to do."

He was talking through his pain. She recognized that staccato tone of voice, though she had not heard it for a long time, and it sent a chill down her spine. "Won't he be suspicious?" Mary asked.

Tre shrugged again, shifting his head on the cushions of the carriage. "Very, but what can he do? He can't even be sure the papers Queenie was offering for sale were genuine. No, he'll assume that Queenie lost her nerve. Or that someone else outbid him."

"And Queenie?"

"She'll guess she's been duped. Odds are she'll think the Russians double-crossed her and disposed of Mary Hughes, because she knows too much. If the Russians do go back to Queenie to reschedule the exchange . . ."

"Queenie is savvy and will want to protect herself," Mary said. "My guess is she'd tell them she handed the papers over at the agreed time in good faith, which is true. It's not her problem that the Russians let somebody queer the pitch, is how she'd see it."

"I agree. And the Russians have no idea, of course, who—er, queered their pitch," Tre said, taking her hand again. "Our country is in your debt."

His fingers were icy cold. "I didn't do it for my country. I did it for us."

"Us." Tre shifted on the seat, rolling his shoulders back. "It's happening," he said.

"I know. You know I love you, Tre? You do know that, don't you? I love you, and this is part of you."

His hand tightened on hers. "Yes." The carriage came to a halt. "We're here." He opened the door and got out.

Was it enough? Or did he still believe, despite everything she had always told him, that he was too damaged? She didn't want to get out of the carriage, not if that was what he was going to tell her. She thought foolishly that if she remained in her seat, he couldn't say it. Surely they hadn't put themselves through all this for nothing? Courage, Mary told herself, and faith. The days of running away were over. She descended from the carriage and turned to face him.

"I'll be back when I've ridden this out," Tre said to her, kissing her cheek. "Trust me, I won't let you down."

The door to the town house was opened by Bert. Tre watched her as she entered the hall, waited until the door was closed behind her. She heard the carriage wheels clatter on the cobble-stones. He would be back. That's all that mattered. He would be back.

"I'm to tell you the water's hot," Bert said, "and that there's food in the kitchen, and the blue bedchamber, which is the first on the right on the second floor, has been prepared for you. I'll be here if you need me."

"Thank you, Bert," Mary said. "For everything."

"It's been a pleasure, miss. A real pleasure."

MARY TOOK A LONG, LUXURIOUS bath in Aunt Louisa's very grand, modern bathroom, washing away the grime and the stench of White-chapel with a fresh cake of Pear's soap. Never again, she vowed, would she take hot water and clean clothes for granted. The clothes she had left in Bloomsbury were waiting for her in the blue bedchamber along with her dressing case. She donned a nightgown and wrap, brushed the tangles from her damp hair, and smoothed a thin layer of her favourite cold cream on her face and neck. A dab of Bouquet Opoponax on her wrist rid her of the last, lingering traces of Mary Hughes. Another dab, behind her ears, and Mary felt considerably better. More like herself, in every sense.

The bed had been made up with fresh linen, but she was wide

awake. Despite eating next to nothing all day, she wasn't in the least bit hungry. She went downstairs to the drawing room and perched on the window seat. Tre would be taking the papers back to his office, putting them in the safe. Then he would go back to his own rooms. Would he sleep? Would he take something for his headache? *Trust me. I won't let you down.*

She didn't doubt him. He loved her. She loved him. Tomorrow, they would discuss their future together. Smiling softly, Mary finally let herself believe that they would have a future together. Wrapping her arms around herself, she nestled down on the window seat. She would close her eyes for a moment, and if she felt sleepy, she would take herself off to her bed.

SHE WOKE TO FIND TRE smiling down at her. She had been dreaming of him. He reached for her, pulling her from the window seat. Outside, dawn was breaking. "You came back," Mary said. "I knew you would. I love you so much."

"I love you, too."

He had shaved and changed. The furrow between his brow had eased. She smoothed her hand over his cheek. "It's gone."

He sat down beside her, clasping her hands between his. "For now. Today—no, yesterday, waiting for your message, I thought my head might explode. It was bad. I got dizzy. I struggled to focus, but I fought through it. I was determined that it would be me waiting for you. I didn't conquer it—I can't do that—but I got through it. There was no way in hell I was going to let you down. I'm sorry I had to leave you here alone for a few hours."

"You needed to make sure the papers were safe, and I had Bert for company."

"I've sent him home now. It wasn't only the papers. I wanted to think.

Not about us, but about me," Tre added hurriedly. "I might be wrong, but I believe what brings it on—my condition—is when I feel helpless. Out of control. It's the only thing that links all the previous attacks. Making all the arrangements to protect you, forcing myself to think of all the many possible outcomes, all the things that could go wrong and how to mitigate them, that's what prevented me from succumbing."

"And you succeeded."

"I've never wanted anything so much as to have you back, safe and sound. To be able to sit here with you, knowing that we have a future to look forward to, even if we don't know what it will be."

A lump formed in her throat. "I was thinking almost exactly that, too. I love you. That's not all that matters, but it's enough to build on, isn't it?"

"More than enough."

Tre pulled her into his arms again and kissed her. She kissed him back without restraint, letting her kisses speak for her. "I have missed you so much."

"I missed you, too. So much."

Their kisses deepened. He stroked her back, ran his fingers through her hair. She could feel the heat of his hands through the thin layers of her nightclothes. His hand brushed her breast and her nipple hardened at his touch.

"Mary," he murmured through more kisses, circling her nipple with his thumb, pulling her more urgently close, "I want . . ."

"Yes," she said, frustrated by his clothes, tugging at his coat, "yes."

"Are you sure?"

His eyes were dark with desire. Her body was lit up, restless, urgent. "Completely."

He pulled her to her feet and picked her up holding her high against his chest. Laughing, she wrapped her arms around him. "I can walk."

Tre smiled wickedly at her. "I'm not letting you out of my arms."

The prospect thrilled her. When he set her down in the blue bed-chamber, it was only to pull her close again, to kiss her slowly, his hands stroking her back, his breath a sharp inhale as he cupped her bottom.

She had tried to imagine making love, but her imagination had fallen far short of the sensations Tre was arousing in her, of the driving need she felt to touch him, to kiss him ever more deeply, to feel his skin pressed against hers. The clothes which had always proved such a barrier in her imagination were shed easily. His coat and waistcoat were quickly discarded, allowing her to tug his shirt free from his trousers, to feel the heat of his skin beneath, the ripple of his muscles contracting as she touched him, the breadth of his shoulders, the ridge of his spine, the dip of his belly, the rough hair that covered his chest.

He untied her wrap, burrowing his face into her neck. "You smell so delightful." Kisses were scattered over her collarbone, and then he turned her around, lifting her hair to kiss her nape. "And here, too, de-lightful but different."

His hands cupped her breasts through the sheer cambric of her gown, making her shudder. She turned around, pressing herself close, and for once he made no attempt to distance himself. Her excitement became a tension, coiling tighter inside her as he lay her gently on the bed, quickly discarding the rest of his clothes. She watched, fascinated, enthralled, seeing her own desire reflected in his face as he lay down be-side her. Ignorance warred with desire for a moment, until he touched her again intimately, making her cry out in surprise and delight. She surrendered to instinct, touching him, kissing him, pressing herself against him with abandon. As he pushed inside her, at last she under-stood what it meant to make love. Not rapport, not simple pleasure, but this slow climb together, this twisting, tightening tension inside, and that wild sensation of falling, falling, falling, entwined, as one.

Sated, blissful, their legs tangled, Mary lay with her cheek on Tre's chest. She could smell his soap, but it was mingled with the citrus from her perfume, and something else. Lovemaking. The scent of Mary and Tre.

"I love you," he said, smoothing his hand over her wild tumble of hair.

Mary wriggled closer. "I love you, too." Belatedly, she realized that he had, despite their frenzied passion, taken the precautions which his aunt Louisa had explained to her. "We're playing with fire," she said, smiling up at him.

"We are, and I fear it's addictive."

"Oh yes, it is. There's only one solution before we get burned." She smiled at him in a way that she had only just learned he liked very much. "I think we had better get married."

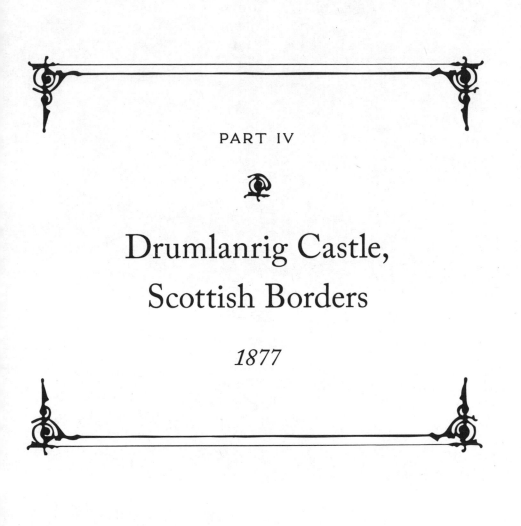

PART IV

Drumlanrig Castle, Scottish Borders

1877

CHAPTER THIRTY-SEVEN

Equal but Different

Drumlanrig Castle, Scottish Borders, Saturday, 25 August 1877

IT WAS A BEAUTIFUL DAY, the sun beaming down without a cloud
in the sky, so Charlotte had tea served in the rose garden. The trestle tables were laid with cream damask, and her favourite tea service,
painted with forget-me-nots, had been laid out in readiness. Victoria
had insisted on overseeing the food and making the tea. Charlotte's eldest daughter clearly thought her mother was an aging invalid, and took
on as many of her domestic duties as possible when she visited. In the
past, Charlotte would have found it difficult to relinquish control. Even
five years ago—goodness, was it five years?—when Mary had taken over
that infamous shooting party, she had been reluctant to let go.

"If the girl is determined to sacrifice herself on the altar of duty, do
not stand in her way," Louisa had remarked this morning, when Victoria had appeared in the dining room, wishing to help agree the place
settings for dinner. "Learn to let others take the strain, Charlotte,"
Louisa had added, "especially if they are willing volunteers."

It was a thankless task, for though there was no shooting party this
year, their annual ceilidh was going ahead as usual tonight, with twenty

guests invited to dine with the family party beforehand. The duke was most particular about which of his children, their spouses, and their many offspring he would tolerate at his end of the table. Anyone with less than perfect manners was prohibited. Any male under the age of fourteen was banned, as was any female under the age of sixteen. This resolved some, though very far from all, of the issues arising when a total of twenty-two grandchildren were gathered at Drumlanrig.

"Why must so many male members of your family include Walter in their name?" Louisa had asked, scattering place cards randomly around the table as if she were dealing a hand of bridge, much to Victoria's horror. "It is most confusing and downright inconvenient at times like these. There are any number of perfectly good names for parents to choose from. Now your daughter Margaret has added to the muddle by naming her firstborn Donald Walter."

"And my youngest daughter has married your nephew, yet another Walter," Charlotte had pointed out, taking Louisa's arm and escorting her from the dining room with an apologetic glance at Victoria.

"Dear Trefusis and Mary." Louisa had beamed, offering the duchess a peppermint. "My favourite nephew, married to my dearest friend's daughter. That is a match that fills my heart with real joy. Which reminds me, I must ask Mary if my wedding gift to her was well-received."

"What on earth do you mean?" Charlotte asked but, seeing her friend's face, immediately regretted doing so.

"Red silk undergarments trimmed with black lace." Louisa winked. "On second thought, perhaps I had better not enquire."

She and Louisa had spent a very pleasant hour after that, walking in the woodlands and discussing their next planned trip together, to the spa at Baden-Baden where they would enjoy the mountain air and the food and sample some of the latest treatments, though they would not, Louisa insisted, take the waters. Her dear friend had then gone in

search of Davy Thomson, determined to prise from him his secret recipe for the concoction he fed to the pineapples. Wandering away from
the tea-tables to inspect her precious roses, Charlotte smiled to herself.
There was no doubt of the outcome. Louisa was redoubtable.

Charlotte began to prune some of the roses, using the little secateurs
she always carried with her. In many respects her life was the same as
it always had been, filled with her own various projects and with the
projects Walter delegated to her, with her gardening, and spending
time with her friends. Her life hadn't changed, but she had. Louisa
had taught her the value of cherishing her own time, and of spending it
wisely. Such a cliché, that little phrase, though it was surprisingly difficult not to allow other people to drain her of every spare moment, to
take arbitrary possession of her days. Her mother would call it selfish,
but Charlotte didn't wish to follow in her mother's footsteps any more
than her own daughters wished to follow in hers. If only Walter understood this better—but there was no point in her wasting time trying to
change the duke. He was as immutable as one of the garden statues.

As she bent over to cut a dead head from one of her favourite damask roses, breathing in the heady scent, a high-pitched yap announced
the arrival of Pug. Charlotte smiled as the rotund dog waddled up,
snuffling his wet nose into her hand.

"That dog has escaped from the stables again! He's a persistent little
chap, isn't he?"

"Walter!" Charlotte stood up, wiping her hand clean with her handkerchief. "I've actually grown rather fond of him."

Her husband eyed the animal dubiously, but uncharacteristically
made no comment. Instead, he surprised her further by offering his arm.
"Shall we take a stroll before tea? Your roses are looking marvellous."

"The weather has been most conducive this year."

"I've just had a chat with Trefusis. I've a great deal of admiration for the man. He's the steady, quiet, reliable sort. I must say, I was rather surprised when he offered for Mary, but they are very similar in nature, don't you think? No fuss and bother, won't give us any worries." The duke patted her hand. "Between what I've settled on them and Lady Rolle's generosity, they'll be very comfortable."

Steady. Quiet. Reliable. Her husband had as little understanding of Mary as he had of Margaret, but Charlotte saw no merit in disillusioning him. She had guessed that matters between Mary and Trefusis had progressed significantly last August, when she had returned to Montagu House from Scotland. It was Louisa, of course, who had discovered that Mary had duped the pair of them, but Charlotte had needed no encouragement to bide her time and wait until they were ready to speak. She had been rewarded at Christmas when Mary confided their intentions, and Trefusis had at the same time confided in his aunt.

Walter cleared his throat, bringing her back to the present. "I confess, Charlotte, that there was a time when I would have received Trefusis's application for Mary's hand with some trepidation."

"Really? But haven't you just said that you think it's a good match?"

"It is; indeed I think they are well-suited. No, my concern was not for Mary's welfare but yours. I would not have wished to deprive you of a companion."

"Ah."

"I am aware that in recent years I have been very much preoccupied with my own concerns. It was a solace to me to know that Mary was keeping you company. Of late, however, you have been—revitalized." Walter coloured. "An odd term to use, you might think."

"No, I'm flattered."

"You have always been so resourceful. A rock," her husband continued gruffly. "I fear I have not appreciated you as I ought. I could not have asked for a better wife."

"Thank you," Charlotte said, nonplussed.

"You know I have always felt the weight of obligation that befits my station in life. There are so many calls on my time, and I do not like to scrimp on any cause which I take on. It is a relief to me, to see you happy. One less thing to worry about, eh?"

"Indeed," Charlotte said wryly. Walter was a good man, who had always felt the burden of duty. He had been a loyal and faithful husband. None of that had changed, but they had reached a new accommodation, it seemed. She was fortunate. She kissed him on the cheek and patted his shoulder. "Now, let us go and take tea with our family."

"FIVE YEARS AGO ALMOST TO the day, I first set eyes on you walking the parapet," Tre said. "It is five years since we sat together in the Heather House the next morning."

"And now here we are, married a month and a day, in the pinery where five years ago, I thought I'd never see you again." Mary wrapped her arms around her husband. "Do you think we should have made our minds up earlier that we were meant for each other?"

"Neither of us was ready for marriage, were we? What matters is making every day count now."

"You say the loveliest things, darling husband." Mary kissed him briefly on the mouth, then let him go. "I was so very young and naive. I was like this pineapple—I needed time to mature. I no longer feel the need to walk around with one of these on my head and you, my darling Tre, no longer feel the need to pretend that you're perfectly fine when you are not."

Her husband smiled crookedly. "There are some who would prefer I did."

"But there are others who are very, very relieved that you have spoken out," Mary said, slipping her arms around his waist. "That letter you published in the *Pall Mall Gazette* about your condition has received a great deal of public support."

"There have been a number of people who have replied implying I'm a coward. I don't regret it, though."

"Oh, I know that. For the few individuals who have replied to you, saying they, too, suffered similar symptoms, think how many there must be out there who will have been relieved to know they are not alone, even if they have not put it in writing. Did my father say anything about it when you saw him this morning?"

"Not a word."

Mary wrinkled her nose. "Actually, I'm not surprised. If he sympathizes, his stiff upper lip will prevent him saying so, and if he doesn't, he'll feign ignorance. What did he want to talk to you about?"

"Money. He's making a very generous settlement on us."

"Why? What are his conditions?"

"None. I promise, Mary, none at all. He doesn't want us to be forced to live beyond our means."

"We already have sufficient from Aunt Louisa for our needs. We don't need a huge town house and a country estate and a carriage and four and all those things other people consider essential to a genteel life. Did you tell him that, Tre? Of course you did, I'm sorry."

"There are no strings, I promise you, Mary, I wouldn't have accepted if there were. We don't need it now, but we don't know what the future might bring. Thanks to your father and my aunt, money won't be one of our worries."

"Should I thank him, then?"

"In this instance, I felt safe enough to speak for both of us."

"Darling, sensible Tre, have I told you that I love you?"

"You can never tell me often enough."

"I love you. You make me so very happy."

"I'll tell you something that will make you even happier. I've had word from Beckman—delivered through your father, actually—of an opportunity that might prove to be an excellent trial case to test out a female agent, or Secret Sister, to use your own euphemism. We'll need someone to play an opium addict."

"Tre!"

"One step at a time, remember? You and I know that women should have a role to play in gathering intelligence—you are the proof of that. Unfortunately, that's something we have to keep between us."

"And Bert," Mary said, smiling fondly. "Is Captain Beckman still in Paris?"

"No, Marseilles. You do understand, Mary, that we're going to have to take this whole initiative very slowly? Even if we succeed with one case, we won't be given carte blanche to start recruiting women."

"One tiny little step at a time, I do remember, Tre."

"But it's definitely worth looking into. It will mean cutting short our honeymoon and returning to London. I know you were looking forward to the Lakes, but . . ."

"We can visit the Lakes anytime. I wonder if Tilly would be a good fit for Captain Beckman's opium addict? I'm sure she'd be happy to give up working in the pie shop."

"Mary, we can't go recruiting associates of the Brazen Hussies. If Queenie Divers found out that you're still alive . . ." Tre broke off, grinning. "Very droll."

"I suppose we had better go back and change for dinner. Will you dance a strip the willow with me later, for old times' sake?"

"And carry you off to the terrace? I'll be delighted, for it will allow me to remedy something I've long regretted," Tre said.

"What's that?"

"That I didn't kiss you that first night."

He was smiling at her in a way that made her pulse race. "Remedy it now," Mary said, twining her arms around his neck

"With pleasure."

It took them several attempts to finally break apart. "Exactly how long do we have before dinner?" Tre asked, his voice ragged.

"I have perfected the art of changing my dress very quickly. Long enough, if we hurry back . . ."

Tre grabbed her hand. "Then stop talking, and let's go."

A Most Intriguing Lady has a cast of both real-life historical figures and those entirely of our own invention. We have set the story, as far as possible, against a backdrop of authentic historical events and locations. All Mary's relationships with other characters, both real and imagined, spring entirely from our imagination, as does the story we have created for her in this book. However, we have wherever possible incorporated the facts we know about her and the other real-life characters, and tried to be true to the historical context in which the story is set.

Lady Mary Montagu Douglas Scott

Our heroine was the third daughter and youngest child of Walter, the 5th Duke of Buccleuch, and his wife, Charlotte, who were the Duchess of York's great-great-great-grandparents. Mary is even more of a mystery than her sister Margaret (the heroine of our first novel, *Her Heart for a Compass*). We know when she was born (6 August 1851), and that her health was not considered to be particularly robust. We know she married Colonel Walter Trefusis, who was thirteen years older than she, on 24 July 1877, shortly before her twenty-sixth birthday. And that is it! We have so far been unable to unearth a photograph of Mary, but there is a photograph of her five daughters in the Royal Collection.

There were "lady detectives" in Mary's time. Women were employed in undercover work at the Great Exhibition of 1851, and by 1855 female detectives were employed by the Eastern Counties Railway. Whilst women were not on the staff records of the Metropolitan Police until 1883, there were press allusions to them carrying out detective work for the Met by 1870; and by the end of the decade, female detectives offered their services in newspaper advertisements. Undercover female detectives could pass unnoticed where a male equivalent would be instantly spotted. They could extract information from other women much more easily and take full advantage of their female intuition. Exactly like our heroine!

Colonel Walter Trefusis

Tre was a distant relation of Mary's—his grandmother Harriet was Mary's great-aunt—and he was also a cousin of Mary's eldest sister Victoria's husband, Schomberg, 9th Marquess of Lothian. Tre was the third son and fifth child of Charles Rodolph Trefusis, 19th Baron Clinton, and Lady Elizabeth Kerr. In February 1855, aged seventeen, he passed out of Sandhurst and commissioned as a lieutenant into the 1st Battalion Scots Fusilier Guards (later the Scots Guards). That same year he joined his regiment in the Crimea for the siege of Sevastopol.

The real Trefusis was described as "a shy and somewhat nervous man. Popular amongst both his brother officers and his men." The "condition" we attributed to Tre would now be recognized as PTSD, but it was not acknowledged in the Victorian period; and as recently as World War I, when shell shock was finally recognized, it was often labelled cowardice. It is unlikely in the extreme that Tre would have published a letter in the *Pall Mall Gazette* about his condition, though slightly later than our period, when the controversial editor W. T. Stead took over, the newspaper was infamous for adopting controversial causes, such as the plight of child prostitutes. Tre's "coming out" about his condition is our tribute to the courage and integrity it took for the Duchess of York's father, Major Ronald Ferguson, to talk openly about his prostate cancer.

Tre's role in the Intelligence Branch is our invention. The Department of Topography and Statistics was formed in the immediate aftermath of the Crimean War in order to try to rectify some of the glaring gaps in military knowledge that the conflict had laid bare. In 1873, following the Cardwell Reforms of the army—which, amongst other things, banned flogging and the purchase of army commissions, making all promotions merit based—the Intelligence Branch of the War Office was established in Adelphi Terrace. There were only seven men on the original staff, led by General Patrick MacDougall. In the twentieth century, the Intelligence Branch became MI6. As far as we know, the Duke of Buccleuch had nothing to do with intelligence, though his influence with Queen Victoria and within the government made it credible that he would be an advocate for Tre for the purpose of our story. Queen Victoria had her own informal network of "spies," utilizing her various offspring, relatives, and friends scattered across the courts of Europe, and was often better informed than her own government. Were there female spies in Tre's time in the Intelligence Branch? That's a secret!

Charlotte, Duchess of Buccleuch

In real life, the duke and duchess were known to be something of a power couple, and they did not abandon their youngest daughter at Drumlanrig. The duke was very supportive of his wife's many projects, talents, and personal interests. Charlotte was a very hands-on duchess, who played a key role in the design and build of Montagu House. Like her husband, she was also a great philanthropist. Amongst the many causes she supported was the Poor Servants of the Mother of God, though, to the best of our knowledge, she didn't actually teach in their schools.

Charlotte was the youngest daughter of Thomas Thynne, 2nd Marquess of Bath, and the Honourable Isabella Elizabeth Byng. The tale of her eldest brother, Thomas, marrying a toll-keeper's daughter is a family legend. Thomas Thynne, Viscount Weymouth, deeply in debt and with disreputable friends, was shunned by his father for his profligacy. Weymouth created a scandal by eloping to Paris and marrying Harriet Matilda Robbins, rumoured to be a toll-keeper's daughter. They then moved to Italy, where he waited to claim his inheritance. Although the Marchioness of Bath visited her son and his wife, the Marquess of Bath refused to see them and tried, unsuccessfully, to disinherit his son. Weymouth died childless, nine weeks before his father's death.

In Charlotte's time, around one-third of children died before their fifth birthday, but though it was sadly common to lose a child, in her circle it was not a subject which was discussed. Her son Francis died of measles when he was two years old. When we wrote *Her Heart for a Compass*, we were under the impression that she had seven children and not eight, and were surprised and saddened when our researcher discovered Francis through Crispin Powell, the current Duke of Buccleuch's archivist. The Duchess of York's mother lost a daughter, Sophie, as an infant, a sad secret that the duchess only discovered later in life, and her grandmother Marian also lost a son, another childhood fatality that it was not the done thing to discuss at the time. Charlotte also lost two grandchildren: Victoria's son Schomberg, aged twelve months in 1870, and Henry's son James, aged two years in 1874. It is thanks to Charles Cameron, the only living grandchild of Lady Margaret and a distant cousin of the Duchess of York, that we know Charlotte was called Granny B by her grandchildren

Louisa, Lady Rolle

Lady Rolle was twenty-six when she married the sixty-six-year-old Lord John Rolle. Lord and Lady Rolle lived most of the year at Bicton House (now an agricultural college) in Devon. Tragically their only child died in infancy. We were unable to discover their daughter's name, so we took inspiration from Lady Rolle's middle name—Barbara. After Lord Rolle died, Lady Rolle continued with her numerous philanthropic works and her passion for gardening. Like Charlotte, Lady Rolle admired Le Nôtre's work at Versailles and she developed one of the most important gardens in the country at Bicton Park, importing plants, tree, and shrubs from all over the world. Indomitable and imperious, larger than life, Lady Rolle is believed to have been the inspiration for Thackeray's Lady Kew. She spent a great deal of her wealth on philanthropic causes, and was the first woman governor of Bridewell and Bethlem Royal Hospitals.

In London Lady Rolle rented 18, Upper Grosvenor Street. Trefusis was Lady Rolle's favourite nephew. She facilitated his marriage to Lady Mary by making a considerable settlement on them.

Lt. Col. the Hon Frederick Wellesley

Wellesley (1844–1931) is one of those historical characters we came across in our research who was simply begging to be written into our story. Wellesley was the James Bond of his time, who used his position as British military attaché in the Russian Court to gather information, by fair means and foul. A classic Victorian scoundrel, he was famous for his extravagance and scandalous affairs. In the six years between 1871 and 1877, when his cover was blown, he produced some of the best intelligence ever obtained from the closed world of tsarist Moscow.

Lewis Strange Wingfield

Lewis made an appearance in *Her Heart for a Compass*, and we loved him so much that we wanted to create another cameo role for him. The third and youngest son of the 6th Viscount and Lady Elizabeth, Lewis was variously a traveller, actor, critic, playwright, theatrical costume designer, novelist, and painter (his work was exhibited at the Royal Academy) with a penchant for role-playing, spending nights in workhouses and pauper lodgings, becoming an attendant in a madhouse and a prison. He travelled to Paris as a war correspondent during the Franco-Prussian War (1870–1871) where he trained as a surgeon. Though rumoured to be gay, he did marry in 1868, though he had no children. As an actor and theatrical costume designer, he was a master of disguise. Who knows, he may even have been a spy.

The Forty Thieves

Although Queenie Divers and her gang of female criminals are fictitious, there was a notorious all-female crime syndicate called the Forty Thieves (later the Forty Elephants) operating in London, first mentioned by the press in 1873. By 1880 it was headed by queen thief Mary Carr (1862–1924), operating from the Elephant and Castle area of London. The Forty Thieves originally specialized in "hoisting," or shoplifting. They were allied to the powerful Elephant and Castle Mob (male) and also had links with criminals in the United States and Europe. Queenie herself is based on the American "Queen of Fences" Fredericka Man-delbaum (1827–1894). A female Fagin, she took children off the streets and schooled them first as pickpockets, then progressing to professional thieves, burglars, safe-crackers, and confidence tricksters.

Drumlanrig Castle

The Pink Palace has been a location in many film and television produc-tions, including *Outlander*. In the 1870s the grounds were renowned, not just for the beauty and scope of the formal gardens but also for the kitchen gardens just under a mile away at Tibbers, which was equipped with extensive heated glasshouses. Trainee gardeners and horticultur-alists from across the UK would seek apprenticeships under head gar-dener David Thomson, who published several books on the subject. A number of his trainees went on to become head gardeners of notable gardens all around the world. The gardens at Drumlanrig have changed a little since Charlotte's time but are still extremely beautiful, and both of the Summer Houses, which Mary and Tre visited, are still there. The castle and the grounds are open to the public, though sadly the pioneering kitchen gardens and glasshouses at Tibbers no longer exist.

We are indebted to Crispin Powell, the Buccleuch archivist, for his generous time in helping to sketch the outlines of Charlotte, Duchess of Buccleuch, and providing so much fascinating information on the kitchen gardens at Tibbers and the castle of Drumlanrig itself.

Newburgh Priory

Newburgh Priory, with its breath-taking views towards the White Horse of Kilburn, is still the home of the Wombwell family today, and the house and gardens are open to the public. The Long Gallery was gutted by fire in 1939, and the ivy-clad ruins are now a tearoom. The water gardens at Newburgh Priory may well have been established after the time of our story, but we thought them far too romantic a setting to ignore.

Sir George Wombwell joined the 17th Lancers in 1852 as a cornet (junior officer). He was indeed posted to the Crimea when he was twenty-two years old and was one of just a few survivors of the Charge of the Light Brigade. He was at Lord Cardigan's side during the charge when his horse was shot from under him and he was captured by the Russians. Cardigan did shout, "Catch a horse, you young fool, and come with us!" Wombwell retired from the army in 1855 and went on to marry Lady Julia Child-Villiers (granddaughter of Sir Robert Peel) and to have three daughters and two sons. In 1889 Sir George decided it was time to restore the Cursed Room. Soon after work began, his eldest son was killed in India, and in 1901 his second son also died in active service during the Boer War. The room has remained untouched ever since.

Unfortunately, due to the pandemic, we were unable to visit Newburgh Priory, so have guessed at the location of the Cursed Room and of the attic where Cromwell's vault is located. Oliver Cromwell died of natural causes and was buried in Westminster Abbey. After the restoration of Charles II, Cromwell's body was exhumed and taken to Tyburn, where it was hanged and decapitated on the twelfth anniversary of Charles I's execution. The head was then displayed on a spike above Westminster Hall for fifteen years; when it eventually came down in a storm it was offered for private sale. It had several owners before being reinterred at Sidney Sussex College in Cambridge in 1960. Cromwell's headless corpse was dumped at dusk in an unmarked pit beneath the gallows. Several places around the country claim to be its resting place. However, his daughter's home, Newburgh Priory, has a strong claim and family legend says that Countess Fauconberg paid a bribe to have the body restored to her. Cromwell's vault in the attic has never been opened, not even when Edward VII, then Prince of Wales, asked to have his curiosity satisfied.

Carlsbad

Letters and records in the Buccleuch family archives show that Charlotte was often preoccupied with her health and the health of her family, especially Mary's. Charlotte, accompanied by various family members, made regular visits to spa towns in Great Britain and Europe to take the waters. We know that she visited Carlsbad, now known as Karlovy Vary in the Czech Republic, at least once, and she would have been one of many wealthy and influential Europeans who flocked to the spot for their health, well-being, and social life. Despite her fears for her health Charlotte actually lived to nearly eighty-four, dying of "congestion of the liver" in 1895.

In 1870s Carlsbad, the neighbouring Czech and Saxon Hall hotels competed for the elite clientele visiting the spa. In 1890, under the ownership of the Pupp family, the two hotels merged, creating the prestigious Grandhotel Pupp that is still running today. The Hans Heiling Guest House, where Lady Mary and Lady Rolle have lunch on their visit to the Svatoš Rocks, still exists and has since been renamed the Jan Svatoš Restaurant, reclaiming the original Czech legend from the German legend of Hans Heiling that it became confused with.

Cliveden

Originally built by the Duke of Buckingham in 1666, Cliveden is most famous for belonging to the Astors and for the wild parties which took place there in the 1960s, which hit the headlines as a result of the notorious Profumo Affair. Cliveden has burnt down twice, the last time shortly after the Duke of Sutherland bought it in 1849. Queen Victoria saw the flames from Windsor Castle down the river Thames and sent fire engines to help. She was a frequent visitor and would sometimes travel there by boat to take tea with her friend and Mistress of the Robes, Harriet, Duchess of Sutherland, in Spring Cottage.

Lord Astor bought Cliveden in 1893 and did much to enhance its beauty, including installing the Fountain of Love, which replaced the statue of the Duke of Sutherland which stood in the same position in Mary's time. The grounds are owned by the National Trust and open to the public. The house is now a luxury hotel.

The above gives you just a taste of the historical research embedded in our book. Even more had to be reluctantly left out. We have endeavoured to be as accurate as possible in all respects, but this is a work of fiction, and there are times when we have taken a little artistic license. All oversights or errors are entirely our own.

Sarah and Marguerite

Sarah Ferguson, The Duchess of York, is an author, philanthropist, and public speaker. Her international charity, Sarah's Trust, is dedicated to being a voice and ambassador for largely forgotten women, children, families, and communities around the world. Her previous books include two personal memoirs and a large number of acclaimed children's stories which have sold all over the world. She has an extremely popular YouTube series, Storytime with Fergie and Friends, where she reads children's books including some of her own stories.

The Duchess is passionate about history and bringing the "invisible women" from the past to life—in films such as *The Young Victoria*, which she co-produced; in her nonfiction publications; and more recently in the *Sunday Times* bestseller *Her Heart for a Compass*, her first adult fiction book and her first collaboration with Marguerite Kaye. She shares her love of historical romances on her social channels through her Historical Book Club, which she hosts in conjunction with her UK publisher, Mills & Boon.

She is the mother of two daughters, Princesses Beatrice and Eugenie of York, and is delighted to have recently become a grandmother twice over. *A Most Intriguing Lady* is her second collaboration with Marguerite Kaye.

sarahstrust.com

sarahferguson15   sarahferguson15   SarahtheDuchess

Marguerite Kaye has written almost sixty historical romances for Mills & Boon, set in a variety of historical eras, and like her co-author, the Duchess of York, she is passionate about bringing history to life. Her character-driven and deeply emotional stories feature strong women fighting for independence and love on their own terms, and have been successfully published in over twenty countries worldwide.

Marguerite lives in Argyll on the west coast of her native Scotland. When not writing, she loves to garden. She is a keen seamstress, and designs and sews all her own dresses.

margueritekaye.com

Marguerite_kaye   margueritekaye   margueritekayepage